Chosen Family

Madeleine Gray

First published in Australia in 2025 by Summit Books Australia
First published in Great Britain in 2026 by Weidenfeld & Nicolson,
an imprint of The Orion Publishing Group Ltd
Carmelite House, 50 Victoria Embankment
London EC4Y 0DZ

An Hachette UK Company

The authorised representative in the EEA is Hachette Ireland,
8 Castlecourt Centre, Dublin 15, D15 XTP3, Ireland
(email: info@hbgi.ie)

1 3 5 7 9 10 8 6 4 2

Copyright © Madeleine Gray 2025

The moral right of Madeleine Gray to be identified as
the author of this work has been asserted in accordance
with the Copyright, Designs and Patents Act of 1988.

All rights reserved. No part of this publication may be
reproduced, stored in a retrieval system, or transmitted
in any form or by any means, electronic, mechanical,
photocopying, recording, or otherwise, without the
prior permission of both the copyright owner and the
above publisher of this book.

All the characters in this book are fictitious, and any resemblance
to actual persons, living or dead, is purely coincidental.

A CIP catalogue record for this book is
available from the British Library.

ISBN (Hardback) 978 1 3996 3695 7
ISBN (Export Trade Paperback) 978 1 3996 3696 4
ISBN (Ebook) 978 1 3996 3698 8
ISBN (Audio) 978 1 3996 3699 5

Printed and bound in Great Britain by Clays Ltd, Elcograf S.p.A.

www.weidenfeldandnicolson.co.uk
www.orionbooks.co.uk

Praise for *Chosen Family*

'I laughed, I cried, I fell in love with *Chosen Family*. Beautiful, devastating, hilarious and full of life' Jessica Stanley

'*Chosen Family* felt like being welcomed into a world full of in-jokes, drama, comfort, chaos and love – I was completely in its thrall until the very last page. Madeleine Gray has written something very special: an epic story of female intimacy that is gripping, poignant, extremely funny and bracingly true' Lisa Owens

'Hilarious and devastating. I was caught in the Medusa's gaze of *Chosen Family*. This book is everything to me' Siang Lu

'Madeleine Gray writes so acutely about the mess of desire and the human condition' Nigella Lawson

'*Chosen Family* really hits in that truly satisfying way of all fiction which takes high school seriously and tracks the development of characters as a continuum. A passionate ode to friendship, it is sharp and hilarious, brave and utopian, sexy but not too serious about it. Most of all it felt deeply real, and true, and lived-in, and I still feel like I'm part of its world' Niamh Campbell

'*Chosen Family* is all kinds of gorgeousness. The dialogue is razor-sharp and the novel is filled with brilliant, complicated characters, love, sex and laughter, along with a portrait of adolescence so accurate it almost broke my heart. I loved it. A worthy successor to *Green Dot*' Jennie Godfrey

'I loved *Chosen Family*'s capacious heart, and the vivacious kick of its language. Gray's generosity to her characters doesn't preclude a tough, comic astringency when it comes to revealing the foibles and posturing of her characters. Yet the mocking is never cruel: this is a novel that has a lot to say about the nature of love and of friendship. And just as importantly, a lot to say about the nature of desire and friendship. I started reading and couldn't stop till I reached the final page. It is joyously good'   Christos Tsiolkas

'This novel is an X-ray of the savage and terrified minds of teenage girls. Even once we're moving through adulthood, do those snarling younger selves stay trapped inside somewhere? *Chosen Family* is about two people reaching for love despite being burned by the world and each other. Gray is pulling all the strings: funny, devastating, shocking, heartbreaking'   Bri Lee

'In *Chosen Family*, Madeleine Gray skilfully picks apart the ties that bind us, the ones that break and the ones that can be sewn back together. Told with Gray's inimitable wit and verve, this is a story of queer love betrayal forgiveness sex family and above all friendship, in all its gory glory. *Chosen Family* has it all'   Dominic Amerena

'I inhaled this book, holding my breath at passages that felt ripped straight from my high school diary in 2007 . . . Madeleine Gray makes real the humiliation and exhilaration of teenage girlhood, and the ways it shapes the women, partners and parents we become'   Lucinda Price

Praise for *Green Dot*

'A sparkling debut – laugh out loud funny and achingly sad . . . Makes us consider that age-old question: why do something even though we know we shouldn't? Madeleine Gray is a dazzling writer – a huge talent' Gillian Anderson

'I couldn't love this book more. A brilliant evocation of heartbreak, which is painful and whoopingly witty at the same time . . . What a writer' Nigella Lawson

'Brilliant. Riveting. Sharp. Funny. Dark. I want to give *Green Dot* all the adjectives but will content myself with saying it is one of the best books you will read all year' Elizabeth Day

'I wolfed *Green Dot* down over two nights. An incredibly funny book about a woman having an affair that's a really bad idea. Every sentence sparkles' Caitlin Moran

'If you liked *Fleabag* you will love *Green Dot*' Pandora Sykes

'This book! What a gutting, funny, smart, smart, smart book it is, one that I absolutely inhaled while almost constantly emotionally bracing myself. Madeleine Gray is a hilarious, humane, and highly perceptive writer' Claire Lombardo

'Madeleine Gray takes a scalpel to millennial malaise, office romance and infidelity, and the result is a brainy, gutsy, nervy – and hilarious – wonder of a novel' Meg Howrey

'The intensity of Annie Ernaux's *Simple Passion* written with the lightness of *Bridget Jones's Diary* and the irreverence of *Fleabag*'
Sunday Times

'So droll, bawdy, sexy, hilarious and good fun, everything you read thereafter seems dull in comparison'
i Paper

'An acutely witty debut . . . *Green Dot*'s potency lies in its narrator's distinctive voice, ruthless self-scrutiny and droll observations on the absurdities of young adult life . . . Although ironic and flippant, *Green Dot* avoids nihilism, and is ultimately about the search for meaning through love'
Guardian

'Gray skillfully blends a rom-com-like breeziness with incisive, nuanced commentary on societal expectations, modern disconnection, responsibility in relationships and selfhood'
New York Times

'Impressive . . . As the story unfolds, what begins as a laugh-out-loud observation of office politics, slowly gives way to a deeply poignant and, at times, heartbreakingly detailed journey of messy self-discovery. The layered characterisation that will have you riveted'
Daily Mirror

'Gray nails the angst of being young. You'll tear through the pages'
Heat Magazine

Chosen Family

Madeleine Gray is a writer and critic from Sydney. Her first book, *Green Dot*, was published in 2024 and became an instant international sensation. It was shortlisted for Debut of the Year at the British Book Awards 2025 and awarded the 2025 Russell Prize for Humour Writing award. Television rights have been optioned by Drama Republic.

*My story has a moral—
I have a missing friend*
—Emily Dickinson

September 2023

Dear Nell,

I never thought we'd go this long without speaking. Every day it shocks me that I don't know where you live, if your freckles have faded or multiplied, if you're happy.

Sometimes I think I see you on the street. The street where you grew up is not on my way home, but I find myself driving along it all the time, like muscle memory except I couldn't drive when I used to visit you there.

I remember your parents' house so clearly. Clean lines, no clutter, items whose heaviness hinted at their expense. A menacing painting of a girl sitting by a lake next to a small column of marble in the kitchen. Your mum told me the artist's name and I hadn't heard of them before, but I pretended I had, and then I got their gender wrong. Your mum said something that made it clear she'd noticed my mistake, that she knew I knew nothing. You laughed at your mum and not at me, and I didn't understand why but I was grateful.

You made fun of your parents to me a lot. I thought your parents were glamorous, but you mocked their expensive taste. I didn't know one could do that. I didn't know a child could be more adult than the adults, until I met you.

In year seven, I was trying to impress the teachers. Nothing gave me greater pleasure than providing an answer that received acclaim from a middle-aged woman. I did my homework diligently. I used rulers to draw margins in my notebooks.

In year seven, you were trying to impress Patti Smith. You told me that you couldn't fall asleep without your headphones in. This seemed so chic to me.

Your bedroom was a messy wonderland. You saved pocket money to buy Bob Dylan EPs on eBay. You had a framed poster of Courtney Love above your knickers drawer. You knew all the lyrics to 'Subterranean Homesick Blues'. I tried to learn them to meet you at your level, but I never got past the first verse. Johnny remains in the basement.

One afternoon, early in our friendship, I wanted to ride bikes in the park near your place, and you were perplexed but you agreed. We had to borrow them from the kids next door because your family didn't own any. It quickly became apparent that you did not know how to ride a bike, that your parents hadn't taught you. So I did.

Nell, you loved it. I hadn't seen you smile like that before: wide, gleeful, like a child. Although we were the same age, you always seemed older, smarter, but on that bike you were a kid, just like me. Your laugh, eyes bright, alive, limbs flailing in abandon as inertia looped us round and round each other on the concrete basketball court.

And you never forgot it. Or maybe it's me who didn't. To this day I get our memories confused. Do I remember what you were thinking, or do I remember what I imagined you were thinking, and how different are those things?

You were a beast and I was a badger. At twelve, you already wanted to be able to abandon your own head, while I was just getting a hold of mine. I didn't belong in the world we were in then, but I felt I would belong somewhere in the world one day – I just had to find the right place, a place I could rightfully inherit. I felt quite sure about this. Whereas you – I don't know if you ever dared let yourself daydream that one day you might be at ease. I can't imagine what that must have been like for you. I envied you, but you envied me, I think. I became the person who gave you access to the joys of the mundane world.

And then I took them from you.

But you took them from me first.

I want to tell you, all the time, about stupid things I overhear on trains. I want to make eye contact with you across the dinner table and find recognition. I want for you to know our daughter, and for her to know you. She's like you; she's sharp and smarter than me. She asks about you. She asks where you went, and why. I don't know what to tell her. How much should a child really know about her mothers? And how can I be sure that I'd be telling her the truth? I don't know if I'll ever send this to you – I don't know where you live – or if you're even alive. But writing to you helps. I've always written to you. Every story I've ever written has been a letter to you. You know that. I hope that wherever you are, you're happy, and I hope you're not alone. I miss you and I'm sorry. I'm so very, very sorry.

Love, always,
Eve

[Letter not sent]

Part One

2024

Eve sits at her round kitchen table. She's drinking a cup of peppermint tea and she is pairing a seven-year-old girl's socks. The seven-year-old girl is her child. Eve is thirty. Eve had not imagined that this would be her life. Eve had thought Nell would be here helping her pair them. That was what they had planned.

Eve can hear Lake making a mess in their bedroom. (Yes, Eve and Nell named their daughter Lake, after the only lesbian in Mary McCarthy's *The Group*. They thought it would be funny, and it is, but with Nell gone it is now a humour tinged with sadness.)

At present, Lake loves Eve, she adores her. Eve does not understand what she did to deserve this love. She sees other parents with children who scream at them, call them lying cunts, tell them they hate them – and these other parents have provided whole houses for their children; these parents have stable jobs and can afford holidays; these parents aren't late to pick up their children from after-school care. Lake thinks Eve is smart, and Lake thinks Eve's job as a freelance copyeditor is good, and Lake thinks that their one-bedroom apartment is spacious. Eve dreads the day Lake realises that these things are not true and then hates her. Eve also dreads the day when Lake will ask more questions about Nell and then Eve will have to answer them.

There are two odd socks left. Eve contemplates them, then looks up to the bin next to the kitchen counter. She makes a decision.

As Lake enters the kitchen, she sees her mother throwing her socks in the bin. Eve freezes.

'Mum?' says Lake. 'Mum, why are you chucking out my socks?'

Eve swallows. 'Because they're neoliberal socks, darling, I just found out.'

Lake nods. Her mother has explained to her that neoliberalism is bad.

'How do you know the other socks aren't neoliberal?' Lake asks.

Eve considers this, then responds confidently. 'The other socks told me they voted for Bernie in 2020.'

Lake nods again, accepting but not understanding this justification. Her mother says things like this all the time.

'Okay, can we make a cake now? I've finished my homework and you promised we could after I was done.'

'That I did. Get the Betty Crocker mix out of the pantry, would you? We're going to bake the fuck out of this cake.'

Lake's mother is not like other mothers.

2006

Nell Argall sits at her desk, waiting for class to start. She is pale, embarrassingly so. She has frizzy, mousy brown hair, big brown eyes and gangly limbs. It's only week two of term one but she's already lost most of her pens and today she's using a red pencil she found on the floor near the year seven lockers.

Nell is twelve years old. She does not enjoy being twelve years old. Adults around her are always telling her that she's too smart for her age. Nell often finds it difficult not to tell these adults that they are too old to be so stupid.

Nell has been at school for seven years. This year is her eighth. After this year, she'll still have five more to go. The time seems interminable, just stretches and stretches of boredom into the horizon. She does not know how she is going to get through it.

Nell's mother, Ondine, rarely takes an interest in her life. Ondine enjoys performing maternal care in front of strangers but she does not enjoy actually giving it to her children. Over the summer, Nell sat on a stool next to her mother while Ondine got a haircut and colour. The hairdresser asked Nell if she was looking forward to high school. Nell said no. Ondine interjected, telling the hairdresser how Nell is shy but that this year was a chance to start afresh — a whole new stage! Nell would be able to recreate herself, begin again from scratch. The hairdresser agreed, and recounted her own daughter's experience of high school, and the hairdresser and Ondine talked as if they both cared equally about their children.

Nell wanted to interrupt them and ask if Ondine knew her favourite colour, or if she knew whether Nell had got her period yet or was a vegetarian. Nell knew that Ondine did not know the answers. Ondine knows nothing real about her children, their interiorities do not interest her. But what would exposing Ondine even achieve? Ondine would get icy and Nell would suffer for her wrath at home.

It is Ondine who wants Nell to change. Ondine wants a daughter who looks the part. She wants a mini-me. She wants proof of her own superior genes. Ondine does not understand that Nell has no intention of changing herself, that she does not want to start afresh. Nell knows who she is, and who she is does not fit in, which is fine. Nell came to terms with this long ago. All Nell wants is for high school to be over, and to no longer live with her mother, her father and her irritating younger sister Chelsea. Nell wants to live on her own, smoke cigarettes and make weird art. She wants to only eat Tic Tacs, drink Coca-Cola and drop out of life.

To Nell's left sits Georgia Smith, one of the more annoying girls in her year. Georgia Smith still wets the bed, and everyone knows that this is not because she is traumatised but because she is lazy – Georgia just can't be bothered getting up to go to the toilet at night, and she knows her nanny will just remake the bed for her. Georgia and Nell went to junior school together, too, so Nell has had plenty of time to dissect Georgia's faults. At a sleepover in year six, Georgia said that she was assaulted as a child and that's why her boobs were so small. None of the girls had boobs at this point, but this didn't stop the immediate rush of sympathy. When Nell didn't join in the other girls said she was mean for not caring about Georgia. Now, in high school, Georgia is a popular group hanger-oner. They tolerate her because she is rich, but they all bitch about her behind her back. Nell thinks Georgia is pathetic because she is a sheep. Georgia thinks Nell is pathetic because she is a freak.

To Nell's right sits Minnie Parker. Minnie Parker wears her blonde hair in a tight, high pony, and she is always swishing her hair around like a horse's tail. Even though Minnie Parker has facial attributes and physical tics that would suggest she is a horse girl, she is actually a runner. She can run very, very fast. Minnie spends her lunchtimes running around the school oval and drinking Gatorade with the PE teachers. Nell does not actively like Minnie, but she also does not actively hate her. Nell respects people who choose a thing and then do it all the time. At least Minnie doesn't fawn over the populars, like Georgia Smith does. Minnie has barely ever considered Nell's existence.

Nell does not have friends. In early primary school she had a few, but it's different now. She and Georgia Smith even used to be friendly. Nell would make Georgia pretend to be a vampire, sucking Nell's arm, and under Nell's direction, the girls would take turns cursing God. Then the shift occurred. Georgia and the other girls went from childhood to girlhood, and developed consciousnesses that were better able to cognise what was normal and what was not. They realised Nell was *not*. They realised the games Nell made them play were actually *weird*, that Nell herself was *actually weird*, and that distance was necessary to save themselves from the possibility of infection.

Now they're in high school, and friendship is about allegiances, about social structures. Nell does not offer anything the other girls want; indeed, what she does offer would only diminish their social standing. So Nell has accepted that hers will likely be a friendless existence. She's trained herself not to be actively rude to idiots anymore, but she just can't be bothered engaging in the tedious chat required to secure a spot in a high school friendship group. She does not care for boys, or make-up, or competing to see who can eat the least, and as these three areas of concern are essentially the triumvirate of tweenage girl social climbing, she has silently extracted herself from the race. At lunchtime Nell reads books alone in the library, or in the band room that no one uses because a cat pissed in it once and it's never smelt clean since. She draws in her notebooks, scrawls and scrawls of feeling. Sometimes she presses her pens so hard they tear the paper.

Nell's parents are rarely at home but they buy her whatever books she wants. That is, they've given her their credit card details so she can buy herself whatever books she wants. Nell is only twelve, but already she is enamoured with post-punk. She learnt about it on Tumblr. Nirvana, the Libertines, she is obsessed with Pete Doherty. His music inspires nonsensical, lyrical diary entries, all suffused with an intense melancholia that might seem melodramatic to a reader but to Nell feels very real. She buys used art books off eBay and at night she reads and re-reads them, rips out pages and blu-tacks them to her ceiling. Her favourite novel is *The Secret History* and she sees it as more of a guidebook for living than a cautionary tale.

Nell's little sister, Chelsea, is nine. Chelsea is very pretty and not very bright, and therefore Chelsea is extremely popular among her peers. Chelsea has not yet learnt that her association with her sister will not play well at school, but that time will come. Nell's parents don't really pay much attention to Chelsea, either, but when they do they like her. Chelsea is slender, inoffensive, and asks very little of anyone.

On weeknights Nell orders takeaway dinners for herself and Chelsea. They are allowed to order steak from the bistro up the road, where a sirloin costs fifty dollars, or sushi, but nothing fried. Occasionally Ondine is home from work early enough to eat with her daughters, but always with her laptop open on the dining table. The most face time the girls get with their father, James, is on Saturday mornings, when he can be found doing the crossword in the kitchen before he leaves for golf. He tests them on their general knowledge, and scowls when they get answers wrong. On Sundays he works from the office.

Ondine and James work as consultants at competing firms. Nell does not know precisely what it is that they consult on, but she knows that they are very senior in their respective workplaces because they have both told her this on separate occasions. Whenever she meets any of their colleagues – usually when someone is dropping over documents to the house on weeknights after hours – she is instructed to be very proud to have such high-achieving parents. Nell verbally assents whenever this instruction is issued.

The bell rings – class starts. Mrs Chalmer tells everyone to open their copies of *Romeo and Juliet* to page twel—

A knock on the classroom door interrupts Mrs Chalmer's directive. It's Mrs Day, the principal's secretary. Behind her is a girl. This girl has short brown hair, like a boy's, and is wearing a brand-new uniform. The fabric is different from everyone else's; shinier, more flammable-looking.

'So sorry to interrupt, Mrs Chalmer, but I have with me here our newest student – Eve Bowman. It took a little longer than expected to sort out Eve's paperwork, but all's well that ends well!'

The girls sit at their desks perplexed, abuzz. Students rarely join the school during term time.

Mrs Day turns to Eve.

'Eve, this is Mrs Chalmer, who'll be your English teacher. Mrs Chalmer will see to it that you're caught up in no time.'

'There's a desk free over there, just in front of Nell,' Mrs Chalmer says, pointing. 'Have a seat, Eve, and welcome.'

Eve's face is red, Nell observes; she is probably embarrassed to be so visible in a room full of girls her age. Eve likely knows that the girls will be judging everything she does, will be whispering to each other about her for the rest of class.

Eve nods at Mrs Chalmer, makes her way to the empty desk and sits.

Nell stares at Eve's back. Eve has sweat patches under her arms and another near the base of her spine. Nell has never seen a girl her age with such short hair before. Maybe she has cancer, and that's why she's started so late in the term? Or perhaps she's a Hare Krishna? Regardless, this girl definitely won't be accepted by the populars; Nell can intuit this much already.

'Have you read *Romeo and Juliet*, Eve?' asks Mrs Chalmer from the front of class.

Eve's head goes up, meeting her teacher's eye without fear. She does not speak like Nell imagined she would. Nell presumed this girl would be timid, her voice a whisper. That she'd know to play it understated until her social status can be properly determined at lunchtime or on the playground. But Eve's voice is deep and loud and certain.

'Sure have, lots of times, but I'm happy to read it again. Every time there's a chance the ending will be different, right?'

Mrs Chalmers laughs as if unsure of the joke, or if it is one.

'Quite so, quite so! Well, let's get to it, shall we? Georgia S, can you read from the top of page twelve?'

The girls nod at Eve's back and roll their eyes at each other. Who is this upstart, this arse-kisser? What a loser, so keen, so brash.

And as Georgia Smith starts to mangle a rhyming couplet, Nell begins to toy with a fragile concept in her mind. She holds on to it, allows it a little air, a little space to grow. Nell is wondering whether, for the first time in her life, the universe has brought her a proper friend.

*

At lunchtime, the playground is awash with girls in tartan. To the untrained eye the scene might appear to be pure chaos. Apples dumped in bins, Nutella snacks traded for Go-Gurts, a tiff breaking out in the canteen line when a year eight dares cut in front of a year ten. But on closer inspection, one can observe that the trajectories are cyclical, the movements choreographed. These girls have been formulating and safeguarding this complex ecosystem for years, and when one year twelve class graduates, the year elevens dash in to claim their spot at the top, to ensure order, to pass on received wisdom. The year sevens pick it up by osmosis, the way that each year is divided into groups and sub-groups – girls linked by common good looks; girls linked by wealth; girls linked by their blandness, by their race, by their obsessions, by their weight.

Eve is taking it all in. This is not her first rodeo; she's moved schools several times, mostly when her mother gets a new boyfriend, or wants to get rid of one. Eve has never had a father, her life is the result of a regretful one-night stand. Eve's mother is called Emerald, and she's more like a flaky older sister than a mum. Emerald has cool tops but forgets to buy milk. Emerald grew up wealthy and she talks about this a lot, how her life used to be different. Eve and Emerald live in an inner-city suburb a half an hour's drive from the sprawling riches of this school, and Emerald resents this. When she dropped Eve off at school this morning, Emerald told her to act wisely today, because this school was richer than the ones she was used to, and she could make some important connections here, connections that might help her later in life. Eve doubts this will be the case. That is, she doesn't doubt there will be pupils here who have politicians and businessmen for parents, but she also knows that she has short hair and is a bit chubby, and these attributes will not play to her advantage in a school like this. Like Nell, Eve is twelve. Like Nell, Eve already understands too much about people to see the world through her mother's scheming, hopeful eyes.

A new school is always daunting at first, because it's like a big stretch of unknown, so much to learn, and everyone else has the advantage. Eve is someone who wants to make people laugh, but each new school has its own language, its own vocabulary, and it is better to bide her time, learn what is deemed funny here and what is thought to be going too far, what is considered gauche. She's already signalled to her classmates that she's not going for queen bee – the Shakespeare concession was to make this clear. She's going for mid-tier acceptance. Who knows how long she'll stay at this school anyway.

A girl named Brenda Schneider, whose locker is next to Eve's, has asked Eve to join her group for lunch. Eve is thankful, even though she predicts that Brenda's group will sit at the bottom of the year hierarchy. Brenda has braces and pimples and has so far mentioned the periodic table three times, making sure that Eve knows argon is her favourite element because it sounds like Aragorn and has Eve read *Lord of the Rings*? Eve prophesies that she will have to find a way to politely dump Brenda's group just as soon as she can, but she also knows that sitting with a bad group is better than sitting with no group at all.

They sit on the netball court, concrete steaming in the sun. The girls are cross-legged in a circle, unpeeling the cling wrap from their sandwiches and Vegemite crackers, deciding on what to say to impress each other. This group does not have physical ease. Few girls do at this age, but this cluster is particularly awkward. Around half of them have started shaving their legs, and Eve observes the light hair lines that wrap around the tops of their knees. Eve does not shave her legs; she does not see the point, and she resents the presumption that girls should have to rid themselves of what grows naturally. She does not voice this opinion.

A blushing redhead pipes up, says the line she's been rehearsing. 'So, why'd you join two weeks into school, Eve? Are you, like, running from the police?'

Eve ponders how to respond. Wit will be wasted on this group. Wit is wasted on most people. But Eve also needs allies.

'Yeah, a hit-and-run.'

'Seriously?' The redhead is incredulous, impressed.

'Yeah. And I shot a man just to watch him die.'

The redhead is confused now; she senses she might be being played. 'You so didn't . . . right?'

Eve relents. 'Ha ha, no, of course not. Mum just got a new job in Sydney and so, here I am.' Eve shrugs, then explains further. 'I didn't start term at my old school on the Central Coast 'cause Mum was interviewing in the city, so I'm already behind in every class.' She rolls her eyes, affecting what? Coolness? Solidarity? She doesn't know. Sometimes she just says things.

Brenda senses an opportunity to indoctrinate a fellow nerd. 'Aw, no worries! We all do study group at lunchtime on Tuesdays and Wednesdays and after school most days. It's really fun. We do, like, science experiments and maths quizzes and there are prizes – you'll love it!'

Eve hypothesises that she will not love it, but she doesn't want to be rude. 'Oh, yeah, that sounds great – thanks, Brenda.'

Brenda looks pleased. *Poor thing*, thinks Eve.

A gaggle of long-legged blondes strut by on their way to somewhere worthy of them. They all have high ponies and long socks. Eve doesn't know this yet, but the bigger one at the back is Georgia Smith. Georgia Smith smirks at Brenda's group. 'Shouldn't you guys be at study club?' she asks on her way past.

Brenda doesn't get that she is being mocked; she smiles and shakes her head. 'Nah, it's only on Tuesdays and Wednesdays!'

Eve cringes internally. She needs to detach herself from this group, pronto.

She gathers her cling wrap and places it in her lunchbox next to her uneaten mandarin, flicks some crumbs off her lap.

'Hey, guys? I just remembered the front desk woman said I should go to the uniform shop at lunch to get a swimming costume before sixth period sport. Can you point me in the right direction?'

'Sure!' exclaims the nameless redhead. 'I can show you where it is!'

Eve flinches. 'Oh no, don't worry about it, honestly, I have to get some other stuff too. It'll be super boring. It's just near the staffroom, right? I feel like I saw it before.'

The redhead crumples.

'Yeah, it's opposite the staffroom. You can't miss it. See ya later!'

The girl who says this is Amy Zhao. Amy is aware that Eve has been scoping out the other groups sitting by them on the netball court. Amy saw Eve looking admiringly at the populars. Amy knows that her group is not cool, and that Eve has worked it out. Amy can't be bothered befriending someone who's just looking for a better option. She's been burnt before, and she too is just waiting for high school to end. Amy and Eve would actually be really good friends if they ever talked to each other properly, but for the next six years, they won't.

*

At 2.15 pm, the school's pool changing room is vibrating with the high-pitched screams of the girls, the smell of chlorine and the texture of wet band-aids on soaked concrete. It's easy to see which of the girls have already learnt to hate their bodies and which are still happily ensconced in the unblushing shamelessness of being twelve years old. Georgia Smith, for example, is uncomfortable in her body, but as she is on the fringes of the popular group, she must feign nonchalance. Part of being popular is projecting body confidence and making other people feel bad. Nevertheless, the fact that she's clearly sucking in her stomach betrays her anxiety. Alex Robbins is skinny, blonde and hot, for a twelve year old. As such, she parades her near-naked body around the changing room, in no particular rush to cover up. Minnie Parker, the athlete, is not exactly popular, but she is fit and therefore slim, and this counts for a lot. She sees her body as a tool and changes into her suit accordingly, with dexterity and purpose.

Nervously trying to get into her new bathing suit without displaying her burgeoning pubic hair to the mob of pre-teen girls, Eve is firmly on the ashamed team. In reality, her build is average, but she is sure she is fat. She also has very short hair, which she personally likes – it feels cleaner this way – but she understands that others construe this as evidence of her being a freak. Even the hairdresser at Just Cuts was visibly taken aback when Eve requested the chop.

Eve takes off her uniform and places it in on the wooden bench that skirts the periphery of the changing room. She evades eye contact with the others as she slides her one-piece up over her undies, and then awkwardly pulls her undies off one leg at a time under her swimmers. She tries to avoid the inevitable camel toe that accompanies this move but fails. When her undies are off she quickly rearranges her costume, and then glances around to make sure no one has observed her prudishness. Thankfully, nobody is looking at her. She has gotten through the first trial of PE.

Except that she has not. Because sitting at the back of the changing room, already in her swimmers because she's been wearing them under her uniform all day, is Nell. And Nell has been watching.

Mrs Cline, the PE teacher, orders the girls to each line up behind one of the diving boards. This is where the body comparisons can truly flourish: they are like models on a go-see, except they are also the judges. They waddle towards their respective boards, side-eyeing one another. It is cold, the wind like a whip. Their nipples poke through their costumes; they hate this. Girls chatter to each other in clusters, but Eve stands apart. She does not yet have any inside jokes to revel in – nothing that could be whispered up the line to squeals of delight. She places her hands in front of her legs, trying to hide her nascent pubic hair from the madding crowd. She has noticed that none of the other girls seem to have any. Is she simply further developed, or are they all waxing already? Eve's mum wouldn't let her wax, said pubic hair was natural and beautiful. Eve is now considering whether it would be natural and beautiful to commit matricide.

Once again, Nell is noticing all of this. She is noticing the awkward angle at which Eve has placed her arms. She has seen the wisps of brown curl tufting out, brushing Eve's inner thighs. Part of her wants to protect Eve from what she knows is going to happen. Another part of her wants to see how Eve will respond when it does.

Alex Robbins, with her tanned, lithe limbs and sun-kissed hair, is standing in front of Eve in the line. Next to her, in an adjacent line, is Georgia Smith. Alex is telling Georgia about a boy she frenched last Friday, a friend of her family who is 'so fucking hot'. Apparently he asked if he could finger Alex in the backyard after dinner, but Alex is explaining that she would like to save that experience for when it's definitely love. Georgia is stammering something in reply about that being 'so true'. Georgia is trying not to blush as she does this: if she pretends to be cool about sex talk, then maybe she will become so. As is so often the case with Georgia, she now overreaches. She says she is considering giving a gobby to the boy who lives next door to her. Alex is repelled by this crassness – fingering is one thing, but a gobby? 'You need to respect yourself more,' says Alex.

Georgia is humbled. She will get it right next time, she will. She looks at the ground. Her eyes spy Eve's feet, and then scroll up. Up, up, up – they notice Eve's leg hair, her burgeoning cellulite, and then they land on the money shot: Eve's pubic hair. This is Georgia's chance to redeem herself in Alex's eyes. This is how she will claw back her own dignity: she will take it from Eve.

'Nice bush, new girl.'

Eve tries to avoid Georgia's eyes. This cannot be happening. If she ignores it, then it might not be real.

But Georgia will not have this. Georgia will command Alex's attention. She steps closer to Eve. So close, they're almost touching.

'I *said*, nice bush, new girl.'

There is something almost sublime about the cruelty of pre-teen girls; the absolute acid of it. Eve would be having an out-of-body experience, if not for the fact that she is so inescapably, so inextricably, in her own body.

Everyone is watching now, everyone is invested. How will the new girl react? She's already proven herself to be brash in English class, but this time it's not her brain that's being spotlit, it's her appearance, and even the cleverest girls usually crumble when forced into this unfortunate starring role. Nell is trying not to express her intense interest as she stands at the back of the line, intensely interested.

Eve is scarlet. One part of her wants to run and hide, but the other cannot contain the red-hot coil of anger, the defensiveness that comes with shame.

'Thank you so much,' says Eve, the tremble in her voice almost imperceptible.

Georgia's eyes squint; a collective breath is drawn.

Eve continues. 'And thanks for taking the time to really stare at my vagina. I'm flattered, but not interested.'

In the silence that follows, you could hear a tampon drop. It is difficult to read the expression on Georgia Smith's face, simply because she herself is unsure how to respond. She could not have predicted this retort; the audacity of it. Alex Robbins' jaw has dropped, but she is not helping her so-called friend. She too is waiting to see what will happen next.

Georgia's self-protective impulse finally kicks in. With the nuance that only Georgia Smith could achieve, she snarls, 'Oh my god, you fucking *lesbian*!'

Eve has now clocked Nell observing her from the back of the line. She has noticed Nell's small but not vindictive smirk. Eve looks to Nell, then rolls her eyes in Georgia's direction, as if to say to Nell, *Go on – watch this. I want you to watch me.*

Eve directs her gaze back to Georgia. *'Au contraire, mon amie.* It seems you are the one who'd like to munch my carpet.' Eve smiles sweetly.

Georgia's face crumples. She intuits that she's been gravely insulted, she understands there's been an accusation of lesbianism, but she cannot fathom how the power shifted. She cannot work out how she has ended up on the losing side here. She looks to Alex. Alex snorts laughter, turns away from Georgia. No one else is laughing – they are too afraid of Georgia's wrath.

'What's going on here, girls?'

The oblivious PE teacher, who had been watching the girls already in the pool, has finally noticed that something is up.

'Nothing, miss,' the girls recite in unison. The teachers mustn't be made aware, they cannot know: a war has started here today.

After the lesson, back in the changing room, Eve is a pariah. Those who may have been quietly interested in courting her friendship earlier in the day are no longer so.

Nell comes to stand next to Eve.

'I'm Nell,' she whispers. 'And that was fucking amazing.'

Something else the teachers do not know: an allegiance has been forged here today.

2024

Eve's mother died eight years ago, when Eve was twenty-two. Emerald was never one for doing traditionally motherly things, such as sticking around. Emerald always said it was more important for Eve to see an independent woman than it was for her to see her mother volunteering at the tuckshop. Eve thought this was rich, considering Emerald was almost never without a boyfriend, and every boyfriend she ever had was both wealthy and terrible.

When Eve was a child she swore to herself that she would not be like Emerald, if she ever had children. Where Emerald was selfish, Eve would be generosity personified. Where Emerald was vain and often compared her figure to Eve's, Eve would make sure her child knew they were perfect at any size. Where Emerald baulked at engaging with Eve's school life, Eve would go to every parent–teacher night, every concert. Where Emerald pranced from man to man, presenting Eve with father figure after father figure, Eve would provide her child with stability, with two committed parents who would always be there.

Except that now – now Eve's doing it on her own. Nell is gone. And though she does not forgive her mother for her human failings, her maternal failings make more sense. School concerts *are* boring.

Talking to other mothers about nutritional lunches at pick-up time *does* make her want to die. Eve has not had a moment to herself that is not full of worry about either money or her child for two years. Eve loves Lake more than anything else in the world, but she is also exhausted.

Eve's postpartum months were almost doable, compared to now, because raising Lake was a group effort back then. Nell and she taking turns getting up to feed; Marcus dropping by early in the mornings, bringing croissants and baby drag outfits for Lake. Tae was around more then too, before he fully ghosted. Chelsea visited from Melbourne when she could, she always brought pink wine. And yes, Eve barely slept, and yes, it is possible that she is now applying a rosé tint to her maternal glasses, but nevertheless: it used to be *fun*. Lake's early years were a surreal but kind of ecstatic blur. Bringing Lake to gay bars, placing her in the lap of whichever dyke or bear offered to hold her first, dancing solo and then reclaiming the baby, bringing her onto the dancefloor, seeing her smile and laugh with all the men in make-up; knowing that the community they were raising Lake in was one that would always protect her. And then – snap. It was over. That world still existed, of course, but Eve couldn't feel at home in it anymore. She'd hurt one of their own. She excused herself from the frivolity. Eve doesn't deserve frivolity, and besides, she doesn't have time for it now.

And she knows that this weariness slips into her parenting. She knows that she speaks to Lake like she is an adult, and that this probably isn't fair. Last year, when Lake was six, she asked Eve if all adults were thirty. They were in the car, driving Lake to school. Without even looking back to Lake in her car seat to give her a reassuring smile, Eve responded, 'No, you become an adult when you're eighteen, and you stay an adult until you die.' Lake, in her little uniform, her brown hair in pigtails, just nodded. When Eve picked Lake up from school that afternoon, the after-school care staff asked if she could refrain from talking to her daughter about death so much: Lake had been expounding the trap of mortality that afternoon and some of the other children were very upset.

Now that Lake is seven, and in year two, her peers know what death is, theoretically at least, so she can't spoil it for them anymore. Still, at Lake's recent parent–teacher night, Lake's teacher asked Eve if she worked in politics. When Eve probed the origins of this question, the teacher told her that Lake had developed a habit of blaming all classroom mishaps on 'the man'.

'For example, if the pencil sharpener stops working, Lake will say, "That's the man having his way again," and though I think of myself as a feminist, I'm not sure that's a healthy attitude for a seven-year-old to have, don't you agree?'

Eve had to stop herself from laughing at this anecdote – god, her child is funny – but it has made her reflect on what kind of language is appropriate for a child. That being said, Lake's not an idiot, so why treat her like one?

It's 3 pm, so Eve is about to walk down the road to pick Lake up from school. Most days Lake must stay in after-school care until six, but today Eve has finished copyediting the manuscript she's been working on. She's sent it off to the publisher, and there's no use starting another project this late in the day. The book she's been dealing with is a lesbian murder mystery set in the Hudson Valley. Her publisher, Xia, assigned it to her with the note, *Sounds right up your alley ;)* Eve responded, *Which one? Murder or dykes?* and Xia pinged right back: *The Hudson Valley, duh.*

Eve works well with Xia: Xia trusts her enough not to micromanage, and knows her well enough not to send anything written by a man. Xia's company pays terribly, but not significantly less than any other publisher, and this job suits Eve. Every manuscript is a puzzle, something to be rearranged into sleeker shape. Eve always starts with tenses. It is amazing how many authors slip between past, present and future without thought, and though Eve agrees that the experience of time is not linear, she also understands that readers get frustrated when there is no grammatical consistency. She then moves on to form – it's not really her job but she can't help it – suggesting splicing chapters, shuffling sections until the tension is just right. Then it's plot inconsistencies, spelling: all the things she used not to care about when she tried to write herself. The manuscripts she edits are not her stories, but she does feel a sense of ownership over them. Every page has her fingerprint, and this is something like having power. Further, it is mutually beneficial, this co-writing, and it is consensual. There is no risk of being blamed for trying to own what is not hers. No, no, she will not be accused of that again.

2007

The girls are thirteen, and they are very aware of this. Banished are the childish games they once enjoyed. The handball court is nothing to them now. No, no, Brenda Schneider, don't even glance at it! The others will only mock you.

They are sitting in Design and Technology class. They are learning about the Bauhaus movement by constructing primary-coloured clocks. There are pots of red, yellow and blue paint everywhere, and sawdust accretes under nails and feet. Nell and Eve sit next to each other, like they do in every lesson. They roll their eyes at one another, they giggle in silence until their laughter cannot help but break the squeaky tension of enforced quiet.

Eve picks up a pair of scissors and jabs a blade through the wrist of her school cardigan. She turns the blade until a hole is formed in the fabric, and then she slips her thumb through the hole, so the whole sleeve becomes a large, fingerless glove.

Eve looks to Nell and languidly twiddles her naked thumb. With humour in her eyes and a deep, almost seductive voice, she asks Nell: 'Is *this* Bauhaus?'

Nell begins to laugh but then decides to play it straight. In a tone similar to Eve's she replies, 'It's form meets function, darling – sumptuous.'

They smirk at each other, each thinking how special the other is, each thinking that the other girl is the smartest in the room.

Unobserved by the pair, their teacher has been listening to their conversation, and she is smiling to herself. She remembers having a friendship like this in her youth. She remembers the absolute joy of discovering someone who finds you as funny as you find them. She hasn't felt like this in quite some time.

Eve looks up from Nell for a moment and catches her teacher's gaze, notes the soft warmth on her face – and maybe . . . fellow feeling? Eve's heart pounds, her cheeks immediately grow hot. Eve smiles then looks straight back down. She dips a paintbrush in some red and very concentratedly colours in a wooden tessera. She cannot look at her teacher again this lesson, she promises herself. This is a game she plays with herself every D & T lesson, and it is a game she always loses.

Nell and Eve's talents do not lie in making clocks; they lie in talk. They have spent practically every day side by side since that fateful PE period, except that over the summer holidays Nell's parents took her and Chelsea to France. It was the longest Nell had ever spent in her parents' presence and she is still recovering from the trauma. Everything reminds Nell of something annoying her mother did. Right now, Nell is telling Eve about her family's visit to the Pompidou Museum. Apparently Ondine took issue with having to cloak her Prada bag, which resulted in a terse conversation with the museum manager, who was forced from his office to the lobby to deal with the rude Australian woman. When Nell later dared suggest to her mother that she had acted inappropriately, Ondine replied, 'One day, Nell, you will understand that there are different rules for different people. I don't know how you don't know this yet.' Nell is telling this story to Eve to express how classist her mother is, and Eve gets this, she does, but she is also overwhelmed with jealousy at the casualness with which Nell mentions the Pompidou. She does not voice this jealousy. Instead she replies, 'My god, does your mum not know what happened to Marie Antoinette?' and this satisfies Nell. Eve only knows who Marie Antoinette is because Nell has the movie on DVD.

'And it's not as if Ondine even *likes* art,' continues Nell. 'She just sees it as cultural capital, something to buy to prove that she's *elite*. God forbid she ever talked to an actual artist, mind you – she used to tell me that any homeless people we saw were artists.'

Eve does not know what 'cultural capital' means – perhaps something to do with capital letters? – but she daren't ask. Nell cannot know that Eve is always floundering in the shallow end, unable keep up with Nell's brilliant mind. Eve nods and says, 'Yeah, totally.'

'Her real name's probably not even Ondine,' scoffs Nell. 'She probably just uses it because it sounds French. She was probably baptised with, like, some bogan name, like . . . Sheila.'

Eve laughs. Eve does not tell Nell that her grandmother was called Sheila.

In this class we also have our antagonist, Georgia Smith, as well as Alex Robbins (filing her nails), Amy Zhao (seated at the back, surreptitiously reading a book), Minnie Parker (excelling here at something practical) and Brenda Schneider (gormlessly trying to talk to Alex, it is excruciating to watch). Their teacher, she of the smile, is Ms Becker. Ms Becker is young, as teachers go, and she is attractive, which is dangerous for her. It is dangerous because she is attractive not in a pretty, non-threatening way but in an androgynous, poised, threatening way. Like Eve, she has short hair. This immediately singles her out for excess consideration in schoolyard gossip. She definitely doesn't have a boyfriend, if you catch the drift.

The girls spend many hours speculating about the romantic lives of all their teachers, because what else is there to do? With Ms Becker, no one has yet said *it*. That would be too final, too dangerous. Innuendo is one thing; it's another to declare that there is someone *like that* teaching them. It would make the space unclean, tinged with perversion. No, the girls must skate – fast up to the precipice and then back, slowly, down.

Georgia and Alex have convinced Ms Becker to let them use the classroom computer to 'research' Bauhaus. They say, in less elegant prose, that they can't possibly execute the Bauhaus aesthetic in their clock-making without first knowing more 'context'. Alex is mean but not stupid, and she has cleverly ascertained that Ms Becker will let them do pretty much anything if they say that it's for gathering *context*. Short-haired women seem to love context. Georgia sits by Alex's side like a dog waiting for a treat, as Alex controls the mouse and keyboard.

They're on the Wikipedia page for Walter Gropius and they're giggling very loudly. Their hunched bodies and faces close to the screen indicate nefarious designs. Nell and Eve ignore them – well, they try to. But Georgia and Alex keep turning to look over their shoulders, directing un-surreptitious glances to where Nell and Eve sit. Alex summons Brenda to come join them, to take a look at the screen. Honoured to be summoned, Brenda jumps at the opportunity, obsequiously kneels next to Alex as she reads what's on the Wikipedia page. Brenda's gaze is excited but confused; she is trying to fast-forward down the page to find the bit that she's supposed to laugh at. She doesn't want to keep Alex waiting for her reaction, because maybe then the moment will be gone.

Nell and Eve notice all this, and they do their best not to appear curious. Nevertheless, the whole class is becoming aware that something is happening; that there are now two registers of experience existing in the room – the class, and the secret thing.

Apparently Brenda finds the operative phrase, because she squeals. It must be something she considers shocking – her eyes are bulging and she's gone bright red – but she reels in her gut response, she must temper it. Be cool, Brenda. She must find this text amusing, must share her amusement with her new comrades. She is, for once, on the golden, popular side of bullying, and it feels good. She glances at Eve and Nell, focuses on Eve, and smiles.

'*What*, Brenda?' Eve asks. She can usually ignore Georgia and Alex, but Brenda Schneider is just so slappable.

'It's nothing! Nothing at all!' Brenda makes eye contact with Alex, tries to conjure further connection in complicity.

Nell will not get up. Nell is a bird on a tree branch; she is fast but fragile, she is chaos with wings. She is the watcher. She does not engage in things like this. Eve, however, does.

Eve gets up from her table, strides across the classroom. Ms Becker does not interject, it all happens so fast.

Eve is at the computer, she is reading over Alex's shoulder. There is a blinding reflection on the screen from a window across the room, so Eve squats awkwardly to avoid it. They are in the 'Early Life and Family' section of Walter Gropius's entry. Eve is a fast reader and has a quick eye for cruelty. She spots it almost immediately.

In 1915, Gropius married Alma Mahler (1879–1964), widow of Gustav Mahler. Before this he had been briefly engaged to Eve Bowman, but the engagement ended when Gropius discovered that Bowman was a raging dyke. Gropius and Mahler divorced in 1920.

Eve's face hardens. When you are a child, you know that the world has great capacity for mercilessness. Adults try to tell you otherwise, they try to protect you from it. Or they try to soften its reality: they say it's not *that* bad. But it is that bad, it can be that bad. And though Eve is shocked by the ferocity of the meanness she is now encountering, she is also not surprised, which is in some ways worse. She has known on some level, since infancy, that this was to be her lot. She somehow knew that one day someone would edit a Wikipedia page to say she was a dyke in the age of Bauhaus. She looks to Alex, then across to Nell, then back to Alex.

'Didn't realise you were so old, Eve,' says Alex.

'Or that you broke poor Walter's heart,' adds Georgia.

Eve can't help it: she starts to cry. She has no comeback. She looks again to Nell. Nell doesn't know what Eve has read to make her so distraught, but she can guess. She knows what the others say about her best friend.

Eve's voice breaks as she speed-walks out of the room, crying. 'I've just got to use the bathroom, miss.'

Just as Eve reaches the door, Georgia Smith finishes the kill. She says it under her breath but loud enough to be heard by the whole class: 'Dyke.'

*

Although girls have been calling her a dyke behind her back for years – ever since she got her hair cut short – Eve has never been confronted with it so blatantly before. There was the swimming pool incident on her first day, but that was different: it was more about Georgia Smith asserting power; the dyke factor was incidental, just the claim that would hurt any new girl the most. But here, now, this latest assault, it is so specific. Have the other girls seen how Eve looks at Ms Becker? And is how Eve looks at Ms Becker really evidence of lesbianism? Is Eve even gay? Just thinking it feels dangerous. And what does being gay even mean, at thirteen? Eve's barely touched herself, let alone anyone else. She's not ready to go there with anyone, she doesn't think. Why is the possible orientation of her future sexual desire something that produces such disgust, such fear in others?

Eve wishes she had someone to ask for their verdict. Emerald has two gay male friends, a couple, Dev and Chris; they used to come around for dinner back when Eve and Emerald lived in Gosford. This seemed perfectly normal at the time. Eve doesn't think she was particularly invested in them, particularly interested. They were as boring and self-interested as all her mum's friends. But did they see something in her? Is there a way for her to get in touch with them now to ask, 'Can you tell? Am I like you?'

Eve considers her face in the bathroom mirror. Is there something about it that marks her out? The mirror is mottled by flecks of foundation, so she sees herself through a Pollock-splattered Maybelline lens. Her hair is short, this much is true. It's not a fashionable cut; it's essentially a buzz cut that's growing out. Did the Just Cuts lady know, is that why she was so affronted by Eve's request? Was her dismay evidence of horror or of sympathy, knowing that Eve's unfortunate sexuality would now be emblazoned upon her scalp for all to see? But that's not why Eve did it! She just woke up one day and wanted it all off; she felt wrong with her hair in a ponytail, it felt insincere to her for some reason. She wanted to be free from the pageantry of tresses – is that gay?

Eve cannot bring herself to re-enter the classroom. Her thoughts circle manically: if she can just think this through logically, she will work it out. Has Eve ever felt attracted to a woman: that's the obvious question, isn't it? The thing is, Eve is a child. It's not just that she is literally thirteen, it's that she feels it. This rush to grow up and make out and rub bodies, she is not motivated by it. If she's felt attraction, it hasn't been for sex; sex is terrifying. She does feel warm when she looks at Ms Becker, yes. She does want Ms Becker to like her. She does want Ms Becker to think she is smart, and special. She does wonder what Ms Becker does at night. She has imagined what Ms Becker's girlfriend might look like: stylish, obviously. Probably gamine, thin. Another voice in Eve's head: *Ms Becker is an adult, though, there is no possibility that anything would ever happen there.* The voice goes on, whispering, *But would you want it to, if you were both adults?* Argh, it is impossible to tell! So much hypothesis, so much Eve cannot imagine. And the consequences – the consequences of it all. So much to lose for something so uncertain.

No. No. Eve will refute the charge. It's her only option. Nell will stand by her side, Nell will corroborate her claim.

*

The rest of the day is strained, certainly. Eve tries not to let the attention get to her, but everyone is whispering, directing glances her way, even girls from older years who wouldn't usually take an interest in juvenile year eight gossip.

This is another thing adults tell you: that no one is thinking about you as much as they are thinking about themselves. But in high school, in an all-girls high school no less, they *are* thinking about you. They are all thinking about you, because you are them; you are what they could be, if they don't perfect their role.

After crying and spiralling in the bathroom for the rest of the D & T period, Eve makes her way to the band practice room where she and Nell sit every lunchtime. There's a keyboard, and a drum kit, and two uncomfortable stools, and the walls are lined with black soundproofing foam, which Nell and Eve pick at.

Eve opens the door, tenses.

Thankfully, Nell is there. She is sitting on one of the stools, just like normal, like nothing has happened. Eve lets out a sigh of relief and goes to hug Nell, then pauses halfway, wondering if she should refrain from physical contact until she's cleared the air, pleaded her case, asserted her heterosexuality in no uncertain terms. She doesn't want Nell to think she's hitting on her.

'Sorry, you might not want to be hugged by the school dyke?' Eve says this with a smile, like it's a joke, so that Nell can frame her response however she likes, in jest or in earnest. But Eve's eyes are pleading.

Nell does not want to abandon Eve. Eve is Nell's only friend. Nell thinks Eve is wonderful. Eve doesn't question Nell's eccentric fixations, she just goes with them, happy to learn. Just last week, Eve came to school with a pencil case she'd decorated for Nell. She'd spent hours gluing diamantes onto it in the shape of a pentacle, because Nell's deep in a witch phase at present and always loses her pens. Nell hasn't tested it, but she thinks that if she asked Eve to play vampires with her, Eve wouldn't baulk. Eve isn't afraid of strangeness. More to the point, Eve is not afraid of Nell.

'Oh my god, shut up, you idiot. Get over here. Are you okay?' Nell stands up, crosses the small room to meet Eve where she stands. Nell's not one for shows of physical affection – she's usually folded in on herself like origami – but now she throws her arms around her friend and squeezes her in a tight, long hug.

Eve does not want to cry in front of Nell. It's one of the silent rules they seem to have developed – they're not like all the other girls, whining about small grievances. They are strong, they speak to each other in flippancies, they treat the playground like the joke that it is. Eve does not want Nell to know how much Georgia and Alex have hurt her. She manages to hold back her tears.

Eve pulls back from the hug, looks at Nell with resolve. She'll redirect the conversation from her feelings to hers and Nell's mutual loathing for Georgia. 'Georgia Smith is such a massive bitch,' Eve says, her accompanying laugh sounding a bit unconvincing even to her own ears.

'Um, duh?' replies Nell.

'Just, like, who would do that? What's in it for them? Why do they hate *me* so much?' Eve is aware she's slipping into self-pity territory, but she genuinely can't work it out, and Nell always sees things more clearly than her.

'I don't think they hate you,' says Nell. 'You're just an easy target.'

'Excuse me? I am *not*?'

'Hey!' Nell backtracks. 'I didn't mean you're, like, a loser or whatever. I just mean you look different from them, and you always take the bait.'

Eve rejects this with an offended huff. 'I do *not*!'

Nell smirks, raises an eyebrow, says, 'And that wasn't taking the bait?'

Eve huffs again, but this time more resigned than annoyed. 'I don't mean to! I honestly don't *try* to make a statement all the time.'

Nell laughs fondly. 'Sure you don't, Eve.'

Nell genuinely believes that Eve is incendiary on purpose. Nell thinks that Eve is brave, and brash, and bold. Nell admires this in Eve; she thinks of herself as cowardly.

But this is not how Eve sees it, and she's never explained as such to her friend. On some level, Eve knows that her brashness is a defence mechanism, it's armour. She's been to so many schools, and it is always the same. She cannot internalise the values and sense of humour the rest of her peers seem to share; she has tried and she has failed again and again. She cannot get their language right, she is always uneasy. She feels that she is playing at girlhood, and she is playing it wrong, and they can tell. So instead, she keeps her hair short, defiantly announcing her difference, thus preempting and lancing the possibility of rejection.

Eve sighs. 'Why don't they target *you*?' she asks.

'Honestly?' asks Nell.

'No, lie to me,' responds Eve sarcastically. 'Yes honestly, you drongo. Duh.'

Nell considers. 'I *honestly* think they're scared of me.'

'Scared? Of you? You're, like, the least scary person I know.'

Nell laughs. 'I'm pretty sure you're the only one who thinks that.'

'You leave food out on your windowsill for, like, stray birds. And you have the arm strength of a two-year-old.'

'They're not scared I'm going to physically hurt them. It's more . . .' Nell trails off; she doesn't know how to explain it to Eve. It's just that Nell doesn't *like* the world all that much. She understands it too well to like it. She doesn't respect her parents, she doesn't respect her classmates. And the other girls can sense this. They can sense her intensity, her . . . offness. Eve's the only one who sees just the light in her and brings it forth. Nell cannot tell Eve that before Eve came along, she didn't see much point to life, really. Nell will not burden Eve with this. Eve is a pure soul, she won't understand and she shouldn't have to. Because even though Eve's mum is flaky and a gold digger, at least she's genuine. Nell, on the other hand, has grown up in stiff silence; she feels she hasn't ever produced the tendrils necessary to connect to ordinary happiness, to warmth. Eve is her only tendril.

Nell sits back down on her stool, crosses her arms. 'Whatever, anyway, enough about me, back to business,' she says with brutal efficiency. 'What are we going to do about you? You're not gay: can't you just tell everybody that?'

You're not gay, that's what Nell has just said. Nell is responding exactly as Eve had hoped. Nell is being supportive; she is on Eve's side. So why does Eve feel like she's just been winded?

She recovers quickly, camouflages her upset. 'Well, yeah, exactly, like, I'm not. I'm not. But I can't just *tell* everybody; they won't believe me after the gossip Georgia and Alex have been spreading. How do I *prove* I'm not a lez?'

As she asks this, she already knows the answer, and she hates it. Nell looks at her expectantly.

The whole scene flashes before Eve's eyes, and surely Nell sees it too. They're like Phoebe having a premonition on *Charmed*, frozen in time as the future plays out in front of them, showing them the path they must take.

'I have to go to the Grove, don't I?' Eve winces. She wants Nell to disagree, but she knows that she won't.

''Fraid so,' Nell confirms. 'And it couldn't happen to a nicer girl.'
'Fuck. Me.'

'Hey, that's what you'll be saying to some slobbery boy called George this Saturday!'

'Stop it! You know I'm not going to, like, have *sex* with anyone. I just have to make out, right? That should do it, right? Right, Nell?'

Eve is trying not to let her abject terror show. Nell is trying not to let her terror show either. It's a game of chicken where the loser is Eve because she looks like a lesbian and she goes to an all-girls school in Sydney in 2007.

2024

Eve approaches the primary school gates like a puppy approaching a group of lions. It's not that she's terrified the other mums will eat her, it's that she's terrified they'll try to adopt her, raise her as their own. Many years have passed since her own school days, and she and Lake live in an inner-city suburb: she's not the only gay parent at this school. But she is the youngest gay parent, and she is the most attractive lesbian. Her soft butch aesthetic is cool but non-threatening to the straights. She works in publishing. Further, her co-parent mysteriously disappeared two years ago, and none of the other parents have been able to find out what happened. In short, talking to Eve is the prize that all the parents want.

Like a fool, Eve has arrived at the entrance a few minutes before the end-of-school bell has rung. Parents stand around on the footpath in clumps, comparing notes on their children's likes and dislikes. Maria Schoen and Bill Murphy, two staples of the parent-gossip-industrial complex, spot Eve. It's too late: she must engage or face seeming rude. This would not faze Eve personally, but it would adversely affect Lake's birthday party invitation odds.

'Eve! So good to see you! It's been so long! My Harry tells me Lake's been in after-school care till close every night this week – you must be working so hard, you poor thing.'

Eve smiles tightly. Maria Schoen is a stay-at-home mother. This is a role that Eve does not resent in theory, but in practice it is difficult not to punch Maria Schoen.

'Mmm, that's right, I've been on deadline. Lesbian murder mysteries don't copyedit themselves, you know!'

She pauses here for polite, titillated laughter. She knows enough to give the parents what they want.

Eve continues, 'Lake just loves it, though. They've got so many great craft activities, don't they? Our fridge is absolutely teeming with macramé magnets.'

'Oh, how lovely! My Harry never makes me anything – already taking after his father!' Maria laughs as though this is funny.

Eve snorts, but tries to make her snort sound agreeable. She continues, on a roll, 'And the sports programs! I'm sure all our children will grow up to be regular Megan Rapinoes!'

Here Eve winks at Bill. Bill is one part of a gay dad couple, but his partner Tom is much more camp than he is, so Bill is grateful any time a fellow queer person publicly includes him in gay discourse, thereby validating his identity.

Bill is delighted. 'Oh, Maria, you might not know her – Megan Rapinoe is an American former soccer player, pink hair, she's just—'

Here Maria cuts Bill off. 'I know who Megan Rapinoe is, Bill. Gay people don't *own* her.'

Eve can't help it. 'Oh, that's a common misconception actually, Maria. Every gay person in fact owns a very small percentage of Megan Rapinoe.'

Bill laughs and gives Eve a wide, thankful smile. Maria laughs politely, because she has to. She voted for gay marriage.

The tension is broken as the bell rings and children begin to pour out of the school, racing towards their parents, their carers, their grandparents. Eve does love this bit – she loves seeing how full of energy the children are, how delighted they are by the prospect of an afternoon of activities, treats, adventures. Anything can be framed as an adventure when speaking to a child. *We have to go to the laundromat – it's an adventure! We have to pick out tiles from a warehouse that's a forty-five-minute drive away – what an adventure!* And the children earnestly believe this, every time. Sure, they get bored quickly, they realise they've been duped. But the next day, they are willing to suspend disbelief all over again. They want to believe that *this* day will contain magic.

Eve remembers feeling like that with Nell, when they were children; neither of their parents provided the possibility of adventure, but they provided it for each other. It's not like Emerald, Ondine or James would invent worlds for them. Ondine and James did not believe in childish games. And Emerald was busy being disingenuously bohemian, drinking and haunting sports bars for businessmen. So Nell and Eve created their own universe. For Nell, Eve promised juvenile glee – bodysurfing at the beach, lighting fires, watching trashy films her parents would not approve of. For Eve, Nell promised access to a world of ideas otherwise completely foreign to her. Literature, grunge, cigarettes and Serge Gainsbourg.

One time, in year seven, they were asked to write down their dream occupations and then read them out to the class. Everyone else wrote things like 'lawyer', 'accountant', 'doctor'. Nell wrote 'head witch'. Eve wrote 'single dad of two'. No one else laughed, but the two of them were in hysterics. What a relief, to find the same things ridiculous when everyone else seemed to be taking them seriously.

It was like Nell spoke a different language to everyone else, and she taught it to Eve. Eve is still speaking that language, but only to herself now.

Eve returns to the present. Lake is marching up to her, a huge smile on her face, followed by Maria's Harry and Bill's Alan. Lake is weighed down by her huge backpack and by a large Tupperware container with a chocolate mud cake inside. She is carrying it reverently, cradling it like a newborn baby, or an iPad without a case. She looks like she could explode with joy. Next to her, Harry and Alan look like they want to stab Lake.

Eve is confused, and then she remembers. Ah, today was cake raffle day.

Every week, it's the same. All the children bring a gold coin to class; that is, if their parents have remembered to give them one. One lucky parent has been rostered on to bake a cake or muffins. After lunchtime, the children sit on the floor cross-legged as their teacher makes a show of placing their names in a hat. The winner from the previous week gets to draw the name. And then, the moment of truth. One child, just one, wins the cake.

The children are then faced with a moral dilemma. They can either take the whole cake home, and it's theirs, just theirs, their precious. Or. Or they can offer to share the cake with the whole class, see it cut up into tiny little pieces, handed out to their friends and enemies alike.

The children are obviously encouraged to choose option two: this exercise is supposed to teach them that sharing is good. Some children seem to understand this. They watch as their prize is devoured by their peers. They feel benevolent, and they reap the benefits of their classmates' goodwill. These children will grow up to be social workers, politicians, mothers.

And then there are the children who think: Fuck this. It's my fucking cake.

Eve is unsurprised that she has produced a cake-keeper. She knows that, given the choice, she too would keep the cake. Bill and Maria, however, are aghast.

She must express to the other parents that she is disappointed in Lake's choice.

'Lake, my angel! What have you got there?!' Eve bends to give her child a kiss on the forehead.

'A! CAKE!' squeals Lake.

'I see that, darling!' Eve smiles, then grimaces at Maria and Bill. 'Did you win cake raffle today, sweetie?'

'I,' Lake pants, 'did!'

'And you didn't want to share it with your friends, Lakey?'

Lake looks confused by this question. She comes back down to earth. 'Obviously . . . not?' Sometimes her mother is so thick.

Eve looks apologetically at Maria and Bill and their crestfallen, resentful children.

'You know,' says, Eve in a singsong voice, 'it's actually very fun to share! And you'd be upset if someone else won and they didn't share with you, wouldn't you?'

'I wouldn't.' Lake is firm.

'You wouldn't?'

'No. You said socialism doesn't work in real life.'

Eve stifles a guffaw. This girl, she is so much like Nell. So smart; so ridiculously, ridiculously clever.

'I don't think I said that, sweetie.' Eve shrugs again at the other parents, whose mouths are open. 'I *think* I said that socialism only works if it's by the people for the people, and that rarely happens, considering the inherent greed of human nature and the structural inequalities that govern bureaucratic systems. Besides, cake raffle isn't *Animal Farm*, baby.'

Lake is not playing ball. 'I don't know, school seems like a farm to me.'

Eve cannot win this, especially not in front of Bill and Maria, who still have not recovered from having heard a seven-year-old girl incorporate socialism into a sentence.

'Okay, honey, how about we cakewalk home then, and we can talk more about this later.'

Lake acquiesces. 'Okay, whatever.' She turns to Harry and Alan. 'Bye, guys, see you tomorrow!'

Eve makes her farewells, takes Lake's hand, and the two of them trundle towards home.

Maria mutters to Bill, 'The other night Harry asked me why he couldn't see his own eyes.'

Bill responds, 'Alan shat in the park yesterday.'

2007

It is Saturday night, the evening of the Grove mission. Nell has spent the whole day at Eve's place, preparing. They have been trying on various off-the-shoulder tops from Supré and experimenting with eye make-up. Well, Eve has. Nell has just been watching, commentating, smiling slyly. Emerald has been in and out of the apartment, occasionally engaging with the girls, but too distracted by solo drinking and texts from a new man to really pay attention to the meat of their conversation. If Emerald had been listening, she would have heard that her thirteen-year-old daughter intended to go to a seaside park that night and kiss an as-yet-unknown boy. If Emerald paid more attention to the other parents at school, she would also know that the Grove is notoriously rapey, and that on Saturday nights it is mostly inhabited by year elevens and twelves from surrounding schools who do General English. All Emerald has ascertained, however, is that her daughter has a friend, which is good, and that tonight the pair of them are going to meet some other friends, which is also good. She is going to drive them to their friend's house (it's so unlikely she's over the limit, she thinks) and she'll give them money for a taxi to get home. They've been fed, they seem happy, all is well.

Eve and Nell sit in Eve's bedroom, going over the plan. Timbaland's autotuned vocals soak the room in adolescent expectation – tonight will be a night to remember.

'So,' says Eve, 'to confirm: I get a boy to kiss me by asking him if he will kiss me?'

'That's right!' replies Nell. 'Or so I've heard. In tutor group on Friday one of the year tens was saying she made out with twelve boys in one night last weekend – she and her friend were having a competition to see who could kiss the most.'

'You're joking.' Eve is shocked. 'Did she beat her friend?'

'I assume so, or else she wouldn't have been talking about it so loudly.'

'Ha!' spits Eve. Oftentimes Nell doesn't actually mean to be funny, but it's in these moments that Eve finds her the most hilarious: her deadpan way of seeing the world, her genuine contempt for the normative trappings of teenage girlhood.

Nell's wisdom is so at odds with her tiny frame, her frizzy hair. She's an oracle, a sage, brought back to life in the body of a life-size animated Victorian doll. Eve wants to hug her, lift her up and spin her around. But no one in Nell's family hugs, and consequently Nell doesn't like being touched, and besides, the girls have a game plan to finesse.

'Okay, so the plan is, we enter the Grove, we find a group of boys, and then I ask one of them to make out with me?'

What Eve doesn't say is that she is terrified, that she finds boys repulsive, that she's self-conscious about her body, and she doesn't know if it would be worse to kiss a boy or be rejected by one.

'That's it, Einstein.' Nell doesn't like the plan either, but she can't tell Eve this. Nell can't even explain to herself why she's so uncomfortable with it. It's dangerous to hang out in parks with boys, there's that. But there's something else too. A small weight in her stomach, an extra beat in her heart. She ignores it. Her job is to stop her only friend from being bullied, and news of a pash at the Grove will achieve this. In war there are casualties, in war there are sacrifices. High school is war, and everyone is conscripted.

Nell has not dressed up; she's wearing her usual jeans and a band t-shirt. This time it's the Ramones. Eve, meanwhile, wears a frou-frou skirt, a sparkly blue top, pink eye shadow and Converse. She tried putting one of Emerald's clips in her hair but didn't have enough hair for it to grip. Eve looks ridiculous, but Nell can't tell her this either. Nell is moved by how earnestly Eve is leaning in to this plan, and by how vulnerable she is making herself. Nell would never make herself this vulnerable.

Eve's been wondering something, but has been afraid to ask. Finally, she breaks. 'Do you . . .' Eve falters. 'Do *you* want to make out with a boy tonight?'

Nell scoffs. 'Um, no, thank you very much. Boys are pigs.'

*

What teenagers call the Grove is actually a patch of grass next to a small beach. It's bordered by trees on one side, and one must walk along a track from the main road to get there. During the day it's a place where families swim and have picnics. At night, it is a hive of hormones, sweat, embarrassment, endorphins, stolen vodka and Lynx deodorant.

After being dropped off by Emerald outside a nearby house that they are absolutely not going into, Eve and Nell quickly double back. They follow the main road until they reach the dirt path that leads to dreams and debauchery. It is dark, very dark, and the leaves crunch beneath their shoes.

'Are you sure this is it?' asks Eve. Eve has never been to the Grove before, but Nell's swum there during the daytime.

'Pretty sure.'

Nell strides forward, Eve following in her wake. Nell feels duty-bound to get this done, to silence Georgia Smith forever.

'Nell?' Eve calls.

Nell pauses, turns back.

'Nell, are you sure this is a good idea?'

'Have I ever let you down?' asks Nell.

And Eve concedes that no, Nell hasn't.

On they go.

They arrive at the clearing and all eyes are immediately on them, two thirteen-year-olds so obviously out of place, like toddlers in a strip club. Clumps of teenagers stand around portable speakers and eskies; Rihanna sings about an umbrella. It is cold but no one is wearing much clothing. Eve is too dressed up. The girls wear miniskirts and ugg boots. They boys wear hoodies and board shorts. The boys look at the newcomers like they are prey. The girls look at Nell and Eve like they are interlopers, which they are.

Eve is petrified. They did not think this through. Nell looks around, however, and spots Alannah McRay, a year twelve from her tutor group, standing with a group of boys not far from them. Alannah generally tolerates Nell at school because Nell redoes her maths homework for her each morning. Nell becomes brave, waves at Alannah, strides towards her, dragging Eve along. Now the other groups see the newbies know someone here, they are less suspicious.

'Hey, Alannah! Good to see you! Do you know Eve?'

Alannah is dumbstruck. One cannot just come to the Grove without an invite, especially when one is an unpopular year eight. The gall of these youths! And yet, Alannah is not a total bitch.

She understands what it's like to want to be older than you are. She's seventeen, but she was once young.

Alannah smiles at Nell. 'It's Nell, right? Nell, this is Toby, and this is Blake, and this is Damo. Guys, this is Eve, I guess.'

The boys wolf-whistle and laugh. 'Didn't know you were mates with grommets, Lanz.'

'Ha ha.' Alannah puts her hands on her hips, smirks at the boys. 'Like you can talk, Blake. Didn't I see you in the bushes with a year nine from Holy Cross last weekend?'

Blake is chastened. He stutters, 'Yeah, but she was really mature for her age.'

Toby, the shortest of the boys, clarifies: 'You mean she had huge tits!'

Eve giggles at this, trying to ingratiate herself into the conversation. Nell stands silently, hating everything about this encounter but determined to make it work, for Eve.

'Blake, right?' Eve makes eye contact with the tallest of the boys, struggles to think of something cool to say. She lands on, 'I like your t-shirt.' Blake is wearing a plain blue t-shirt.

Blake sniggers, as do Damo, Toby and Alannah. 'Yeah, and I like your buzz cut, commando.'

Eve is hurt, but determined not to show it. She will prove she is no prudish child.

'Thanks,' she says. 'I like to keep all my hair shaved.'

The boys do a double take. So does Nell. Who knew that Eve had such crassness at the ready?

Having failed with Blake, Eve directs her advances elsewhere. 'So, Toby – do you want to show me round?'

Toby almost spits out the beer he's just swallowed. Eve is not hot but she's openly gagging for it; he'd be an idiot to let this opportunity slip. His mates might make fun of him later, but he reckons it'll be worth it.

'Um, yeah, sure. C'mon. I'll show you a secret spot.'

Toby sniggers at his friends as he leads Eve away.

Nell can't believe this is happening; but it's what they wanted, isn't it? This is why they are here.

And so, only minutes later, Eve finds herself pushed up against a tree, bark digging into her back, hot garlic breath on her face and neck, a tongue deep in her mouth, a sixteen-year-old boner against her crotch, a cold hand under her top, mechanically pinching and unpinching her right breast, which is an AA cup.

If she squints over Toby's shoulder, she can see where Nell and the others stand on the sand, suavely pretending this isn't happening. If she closes her eyes and concentrates, she can hear the waves beneath Toby's panting. She wills herself to feel pleasure, but pleasure does not come.

Toby is making moaning sounds. He's saying, 'You like that, don't you? You like that, you little slut.' He's seen porn; he knows how to turn a girl on.

Eve responds flatly, quietly, 'Yeah, I like that.'

Toby's hand is reaching down now, under her skirt, his cold fingers pressing into her undies, he's about to claw his way in –

'Wait, how about I do you?' This offer comes out of Eve's mouth before she's had a chance to consider what it entails. She can't have this boy's hand on her private parts, she can't have his knobbly fingers inside of her, it's too much, she can't do it. She thought she could, but she can't. A trade is all she can think of to make him stop, to prevent him from causing a scene.

It is for this reason that Eve now finds herself giving her first hand job.

Eve is thirteen years old, on a beach at night, and her best friend stands metres away.

Eve is gripping a penis for the first time, and it is sticky and disgusting and she wants to throw up.

Toby is oblivious, lost in his own pleasure, thrilled by this stroke of luck. He is whimpering; she is crying silently. She is pulling up and down, it is pure guesswork what she is doing, but it seems to be working. Let it be over.

Suddenly, Toby's body jerks forward and he makes an animal noise. The thing she has been holding in her hand is now soft, small, a flesh-coloured sea anemone. There is gelatinous slime between her fingers, running down her wrist. There is a splotch of it on her skirt. Enough. Enough now.

Toby checks back into reality, notices Eve staring at her hand. 'Oh, hey, here.' Toby chivalrously offers Eve the bottom of his shirt, so she can wipe her wrist on it. She does this and says, 'Thanks.' She brushes the goop off her skirt as best she can. She is sticky, everything is sticky and wet. Eve has nothing to say to Toby, and he has nothing to say to her.

'Um, should we go back to the others?' Eve asks. Her mascara has run and her voice is shaky, but Toby does not notice this.

'Yeah, alright.'

So they walk back across the sand to Blake, and Damo, to Alannah, to Nell, to all the other clusters of teens who know exactly what just happened against that tree.

'Oi, Toby, wanna beer?' yells Blake.

'Yeah, mate, cheers.' Toby takes his place in the circle and proceeds to turn his back on Eve, ignoring her, relegating her to the past.

Alannah sidles up to Eve and whispers in her ear, 'Are you okay, sweetheart?'

Eve is moved by this kindness, though it changes nothing. 'Yeah, I'm fine. Just think I want to go now.' Eve will not cry.

'Yeah, cool . . . Look, your mate's just over there. See you at school, okay?' Alannah gives Eve's shoulder a squeeze then she goes back to the boys.

Eve looks to where Alannah pointed. Nell is sitting on the sand by herself a few metres away. Nell is looking at Eve, as always.

There is so much that Nell wants to say, so much she feels but doesn't know how to express. Nell didn't know it would hurt this much. She wants to say sorry. She wishes she could take back the plan. Instead, she gets up, wipes the sand off her bum, walks over to Eve.

'Was it every bit as romantic as you'd hoped?' Nell asks.

'Even more so,' replies Eve.

They may never say what they mean to each other.

2024

Lake is finally asleep. Lake's bed is in Eve's bedroom, but Eve has divided the space in two with a bookshelf, so Lake is tricked into thinking she has her own room. This trick is growing old the more classmates' houses Lake visits, the more she sees that other children have rooms of their very own with walls around them.

It's 9 pm on a Tuesday. Lake's bedtime routine consists of dinner, then bath time, then half an hour's screen time, then reading time, then lights out. She's usually out within minutes. This was not always the case. Eve remembers when Lake was two, back when Nell was still with them. Every night when she got into bed, Lake would insist that both her mothers sit on the floor next to her and gently pat her little body to the same rhythm until she fell asleep. This could take hours. So, so many hours spent on the floor, counting pats in groups of tens, wrists strained, backs bent at bad angles, lulling this baby of theirs into the dream world. Nell and Eve would bring a bottle of wine with them and take turns swigging it as they patted. If Lake was asleep before the bottle was empty, they counted it as a successful night.

Child-raising is not always thankless. There are moments when Lake looks at Eve with such love that Eve is overcome with the luck of it all. But at times like this – when Eve has achieved the day's tasks, when she's successfully kept a human being alive for twenty-four hours, and there is no one here to commiserate with, no one to say, 'We did it' – that Eve wonders, *Is this all there is? Why did I choose this?* And then she gets to self-pitying, then she pulls out the tequila, then she drinks herself to slumber remembering Nell, remembering all the grand plans they had. Remembering what she did.

2008

Nell and Eve have reached year nine. After that evening in the Grove the year before, word of Eve's heterosexual depravity spread like a cold sore at a school dance. Now Georgia and Alex tease Eve for being a slut, but this is better than being teased for being a lesbian. There is at least grudging respect for sluts.

Nell and Eve have never spoken seriously about what happened that night. They've mentioned it in jokes; Eve often refers to her 'husband' Toby, who's away at war. Nell has even made up a ditty about Toby; she sings it in an American accent to make Eve laugh.

Eve wakes up in a sweat sometimes, having dreamt of Toby's dick in her hand, having remembered the feeling of ooze, the dual sensation of having accomplished something and also hating what one has accomplished.

Emerald, of course, has no idea that Eve is dealing with this. Nell has some idea, but she does not want to pry. She does not want to make it more real by talking about it. Plus, there's the guilt. And besides, they are fourteen now. They are practically adults.

This year they have been joined in their isolation by a new friend. Her name is Naomi Mandel and she is hilarious. She came to their band room one day at lunchtime and asked if she could hang out with them, and since then they've been an inseparable trio. Nell and Eve had never paid any attention to Naomi before; she had spent two and a half years hanging out with the band geeks. According to Naomi, this was not her fault – her mum had made friends with some of the other band parents at the beginning of year seven and then the machine was in motion, Naomi had no agency in choosing her group. This year, Naomi decided that the time had come to take control of her own life: over the summer she read a book she found in her mum's study called *Franny and Zooey* and it was all about phonies and religion and *suicide*, and she decided she couldn't hang out with the band geeks anymore. She realised she needed to be friends with people who thought about more important things than clarinets and recitals, and Nell seemed to her like someone who would understand. *And* Eve, of course. Naomi said 'and Eve' only when Eve gave her a death stare.

But Eve loves Naomi, really. Eve loves having Naomi in their group. Naomi is a great addition. Eve doesn't even mind when Nell and Naomi make jokes that she doesn't get. Eve enjoys that sleepovers now involve three of them, not two, and often Naomi shares Nell's bed and Eve sleeps on the mattress on the floor. This is fine.

Naomi's parents work in the music industry, so Naomi is extremely mature. She's been to *gigs* and she knows what a rider is. She also knows a lot of words, and Nell knows them too.

Nell's parents are reluctantly polite to Naomi's parents, whereas they barely speak to Emerald when she drops Eve off or picks her up. To Ondine, Emerald epitomises the gauche. Her caftans, her loose lips, her clear desire to be accepted into a world where she does not belong. And while Naomi's parents are in entertainment and therefore vulgar by association, at least they have money, at least they eat at the right restaurants – and at least they aren't demonstrative. To Ondine, the worst thing a person can be is visibly earnest.

'Nuclear families are just so heteronormative,' Naomi declares one lunchtime in the band room. She directs this statement to Nell, as usual.

'Absolutely,' agrees Nell. 'So bourgeois.'

Nell looks to Eve, to include her in the conversation. 'Don't you think, Eve?'

Eve does not know if this is what she thinks. Eve doesn't know what 'bourgeois' and 'heteronormative' mean. She does know 'nuclear family', so she's not entirely lost. But she doesn't want to make the mistake of pretending to know more than she does, revealing her foolishness. Naomi has tricked her with things like this before. Like the other day, Naomi asked Eve if her favourite Radiohead song was 'Tree Top High' or 'Asparagus Lane.' Eve said 'Tree Top High' and then Naomi burst out laughing, because apparently neither of those were Radiohead songs, and Eve was a phoney.

Nell senses Eve's trepidation and offers her an in. 'It's like you were saying the other day, Eve. Like how people judge you for having a single mum and that's so bullshit, because, like, I have a mum and a dad and they *both* suck.'

'Oh, well, yeah,' Eve begins with growing confidence. 'It's like, we're all told that we have to marry a man and have his babies and then we'll be complete.'

'That's, like, the motto of this school, yeah,' agrees Naomi.

Buoyed, Eve continues with her thesis. 'But aren't loving someone romantically and having a baby two very different things? I don't get why you have to be in a relationship to have a baby. If you want to have a baby, have a baby.'

'I'm listening,' says Naomi.

Eve is on a roll now. 'Okay, so: you marry someone because you love them, right? Or at least, ideally, that's why you marry them. And you want to have sex with them. And sex is complicated and so is marriage and people leave each other and get divorced and then where is the kid left in all of it? Wouldn't it be better to, like, have a baby with your friend? That way, the parents don't split up. And they can have sex with whoever they want, and it doesn't hurt the kid and they don't hurt each other.'

'We've got a modern-day Simone de Beauvoir over here, people,' says Naomi.

Eve does not know who Simone de Beauvoir is, so she stays silent.

Thankfully, Nell interjects. 'I actually think you're on to something there. Like, my parents have no business having children together, a colossal fail on their part. I'd much prefer to be parented by two best friends who consciously wanted me to be their child.'

Naomi's back in. 'But you're saying that friends should have babies together, Eve. So I'm assuming you're meaning two women. Isn't that a bit . . . gay?'

Eve starts, then tries to make it look like a twitch, like this isn't the main question in life she dreads. 'Oh my god, no, not at all!' Eve blushes, terrified she's given Naomi the wrong impression. 'It's actually, like, the least gay idea. These two women would just be friends, that's the whole point. There is no sex involved; they're just best friends and committed parents to their kid.'

'Okay, but like, how do they get pregnant then?'

Naomi makes a fair point.

'Well' – Eve hasn't thought this far ahead, so she's freestyling now – 'they could just get some sperm from a donor, or a male friend. Or I guess one of them could just sleep with a random man, steal his sperm and not tell him.'

'So, like, lie? And deprive the kid of their biological dad?'

'I'm not saying I've worked out all the kinks, Naomi. I'm just saying, I think the idea makes sense. And what has having a dad ever done for you?'

Naomi's disposition switches in an instant; she is defensive now, and angry. 'Um, my dad is awesome, thank you very much. It's not my fault that your dad left. Not all dads leave.'

Naomi actually crosses her arms, like a cheerleader who's been wronged.

'Okay, that was a bit harsh, Naomi, come on,' Nell chides.

But Eve is chastened. Naomi's right: her dad, whoever he is, is likely a deadbeat. She shouldn't project so much. She has overstepped, and she needs to keep on Naomi's good side. If Nell were forced to pick between Eve and Naomi right now, Eve is not sure she'd be the first choice, which is a terrifying truth to realise in this moment. She has no other option: she will repent.

'I'm sorry, Naomi, you're right. Your dad seems great. My bad, okay? Sorry.'

Naomi is not mollified, but she cannot make more of this than she has, at least not now, if the group dynamic is to continue. 'Yeah, sure, whatever,' she replies.

*

This weekend, the trio are having a sleepover at Nell's house. Ondine and James are out, and Chelsea is in her bedroom practising dance moves. She has by now learnt that her sister is a loser at school, so she tries to keep her distance. Sometimes, however, when there is no one else around, Chelsea and Nell do watch TV together and bitch about their parents – they alone know the particular insanity that is James and Ondine, and this bonds them, even though neither of them would ever admit this to the other.

Eve and Naomi are going through Ondine's closet as Nell sits on her parents' bed, laughing at her friends' fashion show. Ondine collects Hermès scarves, so currently Naomi is wearing one as a boob tube, while Eve has crafted a kind of halter dress.

'You know she has, like, so many of these, she probably wouldn't even notice if a few went missing,' observes Naomi.

Eve's suspicion is piqued.

'She absolutely wouldn't,' Nell concedes. 'You know, the other day she came home wearing her Burberry trench, but she was also holding an identical Burberry trench in her arms, and I said, "Mum, why do you have two of the same coat?"'

'Oh god, I see where this is going,' says Eve. Ondine's excess is no longer new to her, and though Eve remains jealous of Nell's family's money, she knows enough to continue to pretend to find it gross.

'And she goes, "Well, sweetie, an incompetent waiter spilt tea on my coat at lunch, and I wasn't exactly going to swan around the city in a stained mess, so I had my assistant dash out and buy another. And obviously I got the waiter fired, I mean, working class ineptitude is so often rewarded in this country . . . Why, do you want the stained one? It's useless to me now anyway." And she just gave me a five-thousand-dollar coat that had, like, barely a mark on it, because the waiter spilt a drop of *tea* on it, which is actually *water*?! Like, I spot-cleaned it myself in the sink and it's totally fine now. What is her *deal*?'

'Didn't you say she and your dad both grew up poor, though? It's probably, like, a new money thing.' Naomi is always offering wisdom like this, explanations that Eve could not conceive of herself. Whenever Emerald has an expensive new thing, she boasts about it at length every time she wears it.

'I mean, she grew up lower middle class, at worst,' counters Nell. 'Her dad was a country GP, for Christ's sake. It's not like she was born in a barn. And Dad's parents were both academics. So not, like, rolling in it, but fine. And now they're both so gross with money, like having lots of it makes them better than other people. But they're both *terrible* people. And they have no friends, like having friends makes people weak, or something. Whenever Ondine hears me saying "love you" on the phone to either of you, she gets angry and says that declarations like that cheapen real emotions. And James just sits there, like, nodding insipidly.'

Eve is thinking about Emerald still, about how Emerald always talks about growing up rich then her parents losing it all. How she wants that wealth for Eve, how their lives would be so much better if they were returned to their natural station, which is high. It's one of the great injustices of her life, says Emerald, that she is now forced to work, forced to date rich arseholes, when really she should *be* the rich arsehole.

Naomi has a glint in her eyes. 'I have an idea,' she says. 'You have an eBay account, right, Nell?'

'Obviously,' responds Nell cautiously.

'Well, why don't we sell a few of Ondine's scarves, and the coat, to earn some seed money for our little business venture? You have a digital camera – we could upload pics in no time.'

Eve dislikes this plan; it seems needlessly dishonest, when Nell's parents would just give her whatever money she asked for anyway. But more than this, she feels the sting of exclusion.

'Um, what business venture?' she asks.

'Oh, nothing for you to worry about, sweet Evie.' Naomi smirks.

'What is she talking about, Nell?' Eve looks to Nell, thoroughly confused, and crestfallen to be out of the loop. She knows that Naomi and Nell have conversations without her; she's not stupid. She knows that they have secret MSN chats. But for Naomi to bring it up so blatantly, it's a lot. Eve knows she is being goaded but she doesn't know why. Why does Naomi always do this, make her look so stupid in front of Nell? And when was it that her friendship with Nell shifted so much? It's like Naomi's been chipping away, chipping away, and Eve has been lying to herself, telling herself that Nell will always be her best friend, but is Naomi Nell's best friend now? What did Eve do wrong?

Nell is conflicted. She loves Eve, she does. She doesn't ever want to hurt her. But Eve is still a bit of a child, whereas she and Naomi, they have adult plans. Naomi's been diagnosed with ADHD and she's introduced Nell to the manic pleasures of Ritalin. It makes Nell feel like her brain is on fire in the best possible way. It makes her feel like she could be part of the world Pete Doherty lives in, not just trapped here in this rich suburban stupor.

Naomi's suggested that if they want access to other kinds of drugs, they need to sell the Ritalin and go from there. Nell doesn't want to be responsible for corrupting Eve. Sweet Eve. Sweet Eve who is so smart, smarter than Nell even, but who sees the world so guilelessly sometimes. The only way to protect Eve is to keep her out of it, even if it hurts her. Nell will not be responsible for something like what happened to Eve at the Grove happening again.

Nell smiles at Eve. 'Oh, Naomi's just joking, Evie, don't worry.'

Eve flinches at this – Nell has never called her Evie before. Evie is Naomi's condescending creation.

'But I agree with Naomi,' continues Nell. 'Let's sell Ondine's stuff – she deserves it. And then we can use the money to buy concert tickets or whatever. Weren't you saying you wanted a digital camera like mine, Eve? Let's get you one.'

Eve suspects that she is being lied to, but she cannot prove it. She also dislikes this plan, it makes her feel icky. But she doesn't want to spoil the fun – or, worse, seem like a wimp. Naomi would have a field day with that, and the sleepover is just beginning.

'Yeah, okay,' Eve acquiesces. 'Let's do it.'

'Yesss, Eve, I knew you had it in you!' exclaims Naomi, like a proud parent.

And so they create an eBay store called 'BitchCloset'. Its opening stock consists of five Hermès scarves, a Burberry coat and a very large diamond ring. 'Ondine said it was garish,' says Nell with a shrug.

2024

Marcus has told Eve to get on the apps. They are sitting at Eve's kitchen table, drinking a bottle of pinot, and Lake is asleep. Eve remembers a time when she drank with friends at places that were not this kitchen table. They would go to bars, to gigs, to house parties, to *restaurants*. Eve would call the waiter *garçon*, her friends would laugh at her, Nell would always make sure she got home safe.

But Eve very rarely has this pleasure anymore. She is raising Lake on a single, small income, and babysitters' fees are extortionate. Why is it that Eve should have to pay a fifteen-year-old an hourly wage that is the same as her own? And to do what? Watch TV on the couch while Lake is peacefully asleep in her room? *The system is flawed*, thinks Eve. If Nell were here, Eve would say this out loud, and Nell would say, 'Write that down! God, you're an original thinker.'

Eve swallows another swish of acrid red, and turns to her friend.

'And why, why should I get on the apps, dear Marcus? Why subject myself to something so harrowing?'

'Um, because you could find *love*?' replies Marcus. 'Or is that a foreign concept to you?' he asks.

Eve's cool breaks for a second. She says, coldly, under her breath, 'You know very well that it's not.'

'Hit a nerve there, okay, mea culpa, mea culpa. But it's been two years since everything with Bridget, babe; surely you're ready to test the waters, at least?'

Eve feels guilty; it's not Marcus's fault that she's like this. And he's been a good friend to her, and a great friend to Lake, through everything. She'll go along with him, just for now.

'Alright, stallion, let's say I got on the horse. Which app is even the hip one these days? And don't tell me to get on Grindr to challenge gender constructs. I've seen the men you fuck from there, and I have no intention of being come on in a public park.' Eve pauses, then adds, 'Again.'

Marcus looks at Eve quizzically.

'A story for another time,' says Eve.

'Okay, mystery woman,' says Marcus. 'And I'll have you know that last week I went to the theatre with a very nice man from Grindr called Arjun. We saw an experimental play about AIDS and afterwards we had dinner at a nice little bistro and discussed . . . culture and such.'

'Uh-huh. I think you're omitting the part where you gave him a wristie in the stalls, Marcus. You texted me about it, like, ten minutes after the fact, remember?'

'That was for our fallen brothers!' exclaims Marcus.

Eve smirks. 'Yes, I'm sure Harvey Milk would be pleased to know he died for that.'

Marcus gets a devious twinkle in his eye. 'Milk for Milk?' he offers.

Eve can't help but snort laughter at this one. 'Jesus Christ,' she says.

'Yes! Exactly! There's another spunk who died too soon!' cries Marcus. He's getting jazzed up now. 'Jizz for Jez, I say!' He claps at this one, in awe of his own genius.

Eve rolls her eyes. 'Did you just call Jesus "Jez"?'

'I'm sure that's what his mother would have called him,' says Marcus demurely.

Eve slaps her hand on the table. 'Enough!' she cries. 'We're getting distracted from the task at hand.' Eve picks up her phone. 'You didn't answer my question. What app is cool now for queer women of a certain age?'

Marcus scoffs. 'Eve, you are thirty – I hardly think that places you in sad old dyke territory.'

Eve grimaces, but Marcus continues. 'You're hot, babe! And I'm saying this not just as your friend, but as someone who sees the way every stallholder at Marrickville market stares at your arse on Sundays.'

'I do have a good arse,' Eve concedes.

'So, it's all about Hinge, baby girl. Or Bumble. Or Feeld, if you're feeling kinky.'

'I'm *feeling* like a gay single mother of one who already regrets agreeing to this hypothetical,' replies Eve flatly.

'Bumble it is,' says Marcus.

He opens the app on Eve's phone and signs her up. He makes a profile for her, and as they are picking display photographs, he suggests keeping her daughter out of it.

'Because women with children are terrifying?' asks Eve.

'Because no one wants to look at a child when they're considering fucking someone,' responds Marcus.

Eve laughs. 'Have you ever met a lesbian, Marcus? I think the rules might be different for U-Haul queers than they are for libidinous gay men.'

Marcus raises his hand in mock surrender. 'You do you, Evie-pie. But don't blame me when no one wants to munch a carpet that's excreted a live human.'

'You are disgusting, Marcus.'

'Thank you,' says Marcus. 'I'll add that to my bio.'

As they scroll through the contenders, Eve gets that wrong feeling in her stomach, the one she's had since she first discovered that some things feel icky. This futch in the Alpha 60 deserves better than Eve. That eco-queer with the gardening tools deserves better too. Eve is not a good person. Eve should not have done what she did. Eve is doomed to live with it, alone. Well, alone with Lake.

'Come on, honey,' Marcus says gently, having perceived the direction of Eve's thoughts. 'It was not all you. You could not have known how she'd react. You deserve love – or at least sex.'

Eve sighs. She could have known how Nell would react. She thinks perhaps she always knew. But she did it anyway, and that's the problem. Why did she do it? She knew the story, of course; she knew her version, anyway. But it was not her story to share.

Marcus risks the suggestion, though Eve always shoots him down. 'Have you tried to contact her recently? Maybe if you got in touch with Chelsea, she might—'

Eve cuts him off. 'Nell made it perfectly clear she doesn't want anything to do with us. She's changed her phone number, she doesn't have socials, she's erased herself. Maybe literally.'

Marcus's eyes soften. 'You don't really mean that,' he says.

Eve swallows. 'No, of course I don't.' She might, though.

2008

The girls are in English class. Eve doesn't know how it's happened, but Naomi now sits next to Nell, and Eve's place is at a desk behind them, next to Brenda fucking Schneider, of all people. One day three weeks ago, not long after the BitchCloset night, Eve was late to class as she'd been in the bathroom attempting to clean a spot of period blood off her uniform, and when she arrived, Naomi was in her seat. Now, Naomi sits at this desk every class, as if it was always hers. Eve is brimming with resentment, but she hasn't said a word. It would be childish – and, worse, so *obvious* – if Eve were to make a thing of it. And besides, what Eve really wants, what she's really waiting for, is for Nell to say something, to correct the injustice. But Nell has said nothing. Now Eve must bear the brutal indignity of seeing her best friend whispering with another, not knowing what they are talking about.

They're studying *Frankenstein* now, which means that the words 'hubris' and 'epistolary' have become part of the year nine vernacular. They are rarely used correctly.

Their English teacher, Miss Gibbs, is doing her best to maintain the class's interest in this verbose morality tale, though even she, an English nerd, concedes privately that it's a bit overwritten.

'And what,' asks Miss Gibbs grandly, 'might we say is Frankenstein's intention in making his creation?'

Georgia Smith raises her hand.

'Yes, Georgia, go on.'

'I think Frankenstein's problem is that he's not hot. Like, everyone hates him because he's an uggo, so obviously he goes crazy.' Here Georgia Smith looks directly at Eve. 'It really *sucks* to be an uggo.'

If teachers were allowed to slap students, Miss Gibbs' right hand would be red raw. But child protection laws exist, so Miss Gibbs must continue with grace.

'A fascinating take on the intersection of biological aesthetics and mental health there, Miss Smith. Nuanced stuff.'

Georgia smirks, believing she is genuinely being complimented.

'But, class, may I remind you for the thousandth time that Frankenstein is *not* the name of the monster.' Every year. Every fucking year it's the same.

Eve raises her hand. Miss Gibbs is grateful.

'Yes, Miss Bowman?'

'I think Frankenstein makes the creature because he's on a power trip.' Here Eve stares back at Georgia. 'And he doesn't think through the implications of his experiment, because he's totally wrapped up in his own ego, and that's why eventually he gets murdered.'

Georgia scoffs, but again, she is not getting any of this. Nell turns around and gives Eve a quick smile, and Eve's heart speeds up. *See?* she wants to say to Nell. *See, I'm like you. Why don't you remember that you love me? What changed?*

Miss Gibbs is energised now, excited that someone has said something resembling sense.

'That's a solid hypothesis, Eve, well done. And what do you think Frankenstein could have done differently? What would thinking through the implications of his experiment entail?'

'Um . . .' Eve ponders this. 'Well, I guess, like, if you're going to make a child, you should probably, like, look after it when it arrives?'

Miss Gibbs laughs. 'Yes, I think that would be a good start.' She looks around the room.

'Anyone else?'

Naomi raises her hand.

She glances at Nell slyly before she directs her gaze to Miss Gibbs and speaks. Eve watches this interaction and wants to scream. *She* used to be the one sitting there. *She* used to share those glances.

'I think Eve's right – not committing to parenthood is obviously where Frankenstein screws up. But what was he supposed to do? The monster was gross and terrifying and, like, didn't seem very bright. Maybe Frank should have stuck around, but he had a life too, and who wants to spend their whole life caring for a little freak child?'

Eve can sense what Naomi is implying here, but Nell isn't coming to her rescue. Is Nell not reading the subtext, or is she enjoying it? Or is it Eve who is reading too much into it? Maybe Naomi isn't having a dig at her.

Eve responds, 'But I think the thing is, *Naomi*, that the monster would not have become a monster if he'd been treated with care by the person who made him? Like, he is obvi inherently good, that's Shelley's point – he's super nice to that random peasant family, he teaches himself to read, write and speak . . . he's smart. Like, he just needed Frankenstein to be, like, "Hey, buddy, you're unfortunately ugly by today's beauty standards, but that's chill, you have other things to offer," right?'

Miss Gibbs is about to speak, but Naomi interjects. 'No, I get that, for sure, but the world was never going to accept a creature made out of dead body parts; like, that's just facts, even if he was nice or whatever. Frankenstein made a mistake, but why should two lives be ruined? He probs should have just killed the monster when he saw what he made, but considering that option quickly disappeared, cut and run, I say.'

'Classy,' mutters Eve.

'Mmm,' murmurs Miss Gibbs, trying to keep the peace. 'I see the point you're making there, Naomi, though I'm not sure it's exactly the directive we're supposed to take from the novel.'

Naomi shrugs defiantly, and the class goes on.

Brenda Schneider whispers to Eve, 'I thought Nell was your best friend, Eve. Why aren't you sitting together anymore? Did you guys have a lovers' quarrel or something?'

Brenda Schneider has recently weaselled her way into the popular group, and subsequently has become more confident in her cruelty. As she sits right on the outer, her barbs come quickly and often – she deploys them like arrows off a castle wall. She has risen, and now no one else must.

'Um, we *are* best friends, Brenda. Not that it's any of your business. Nell just doesn't have any other classes with Naomi this year, so I suggested they sit together in English. It's no big deal.' Eve is aware of the weakness of her justification, and knows Brenda can sense it too, which kills her.

'Uh-huh,' replies Brenda. 'You keep telling yourself that.'

And Eve will keep telling herself that, she must. She cannot face what it would mean to lose Nell's friendship. Nell is her whole world. Eve will be funnier. Eve will make herself indispensable. Eve will be the life of the party. Eve will not let Naomi steal her friend.

*

That Saturday evening, they have another sleepover, this time at Naomi's house. Naomi's place has a pool, there are limitless snacks in the fridge, and the girls are encouraged to just take whatever they want, when they want, which is bizarre and exciting for Eve; Emerald never has anything in the fridge, and she requires Eve to ask permission before she consumes anything. Naomi's mum is nice, her name is Claire. She's a tour manager for a famous indie singer, and she's always harried but she seems kind. She brings the girls merch from gigs.

Sometimes Eve thinks Claire notices when Naomi is being short with her, and she wills her to have a word with her daughter, tell her to stop being such a cunt. Of course, such a conversation would be impossible to have. Eve has learnt from television that mothers are supposed to root for their children first; enlisting Claire would be a losing game. Eve feels both seen and on edge when Claire is around; Claire knows things, thinks Eve.

The girls are getting in the pool. Naomi's body is lean and tanned, and her bikini is fluoro pink. She bought it from a stall at Bondi markets, and says the guy who sold it to her was flirting with her. Eve looks on enviously. She wishes she could look like that, wishes her thighs didn't touch, wishes her stomach was flat, wishes market guys flirted with her. Naomi cannonballs into the pool and barely makes a splash.

'Come on, Nell!' shouts Naomi. 'Stop being a little bitch and get in here!'

Nell stands on the first of the pool steps and enters the water slowly. Nell is uncoordinated, she knows this about herself, so she takes her time. Plus, she's just taken a Ritalin, so she's a bit jerky, her limbs not quite in her control. Her costume is a black one-piece. She's pale and skinny and freckly, but she doesn't think too much about her body: she lives a life of the mind. And right now her mind is racing.

Eve stands at the side of the pool – she herself is wearing a one-piece and a t-shirt over the top – and watches Nell. Nell's eyes are so lovely, they glisten from the reflection of the pool. Does Nell know how lovely her eyes are? And Nell's boobs have grown since they last went swimming; they're almost spilling out of her costume. The water is chilly, and her nipples are hard through the neoprene fabric. Eve finds that she can't take her eyes off Nell's chest. It's like she's become an ogling teenage boy, one that she hates. When Nell finally starts breaststroking across the pool, her boobs bob ahead of her, water streaming down her cleavage with each semicircle her hands make. When did Nell become a woman? And why does Eve still have the body of a chubby child?

Eve feels warm at her groin, she feels the pulse of her blood in *that part* of her body. The hairs on her arms are alert, her own nipples harden. It's the same feeling she experiences when she sees Ms Becker in the hallway at school, but she's not felt it with Nell before, not like this, so directly. It feels good and so, so bad at the same time. It feels unthinkable, like lusting after your own sister, if you had one. Thank god Nell isn't looking up at her; thank god Nell isn't seeing Eve's reaction.

Nell's eyes dart up to Eve, she is about to say something, so Eve hurriedly looks away from her.

'Get in here, Eve, stop being a cute little chicken!' yells Nell.

Eve is not looking at Nell; Eve is looking anywhere else. Eve's cheeks have turned scarlet, her arms are folded over her own tiny breasts. In their journey away from Nell, Eve's eyes catch Naomi's. And, in Naomi's knowing expression, it is obvious: Naomi has seen everything. And she wants Eve to know that she knows.

'Yeah, get in here, Eve,' deadpans Naomi. 'It's girls gone wild.'

'I – I'm coming!' Eve stammers. She belly-flops into the pool and makes a gigantic splash. It is not a graceful move, but it is what is required to steer attention away from her throbbing want. *Please don't let Nell see it.*

As the girls now wade around in the water, Eve is careful not to look at Nell again. They play Marco Polo at Eve's suggestion, even though they're fourteen and probably too old for this. When it is Naomi's turn to close her eyes, Eve allows herself to make eye contact with Nell. Nell smiles at Eve, a brilliant, earnest smile. This particular smile of Nell's is Eve's favourite – it means she's truly in the moment, and is usually offered when they're doing something childish and simple and silly. It's how Nell smiles when she's singing a made-up song about bogans and mullets, lost in the hilarity of language. Or when she makes a pun about Ivan Milat in class, knowing that only Eve will get the joke. Eve grins back.

Nell mouths to Eve, 'You go that way,' and she gestures to the shallow end of the pool.

Eve does as commanded. Naomi is still counting. Nell propels herself down under the water and there's a splash and then Eve can't see Nell, she's lost her. Naomi's counting has come to an end, she's swimming blindly around the pool with her arms raised in front of her, a zombie on a mission.

And then Eve feels a tickle at her foot, then her lower leg. She almost squeals but she holds it in. She looks down to see Nell swimming around her legs, mischievous under the water. Eve shakes her head, laughing silently, and uses her legs to trap Nell beneath her. Nell bucks and jerks, and finally gets free, popping up beside Eve, spluttering. Her coughs turn into laughs, and the pair of them cannot stay silent, they are stuck in a laughing fit. Every time they try to stop laughing, the laughs only get louder, more obnoxious. It's like trying not to giggle during a church service, it's like holding back a gasp of delight when a teacher falls over.

Naomi, of course, hears the racket. She changes direction and in a few strokes she has found them, her eyes open as she touches flesh.

She looks pissed. 'Um, the aim of the game is *not* to be found, you two?'

Eve is thrilled. It's her and Nell together again, a duo, as they should be! She can't help but rub it in.

'Sorry, Naomi! *This one* doesn't seem to understand the rules.' She tousles Nell's hair affectionately, and what she is really saying is: *Mine, she is mine.*

Naomi recognises the provocation. Nell, yet again, doesn't seem to notice the battle that is raging in front of her.

'I have an idea,' announces Naomi. 'How about we play a different game?'

'Sure,' replies Eve, catching her breath. 'What kind of game?'

Naomi's voice is assertive. 'Let's play kiss chicken.'

Eve freezes.

'Ha ha ha, for god's sake, Nome, we're not in primary school,' chides Nell.

'Indeed we are not, but it'll be fun! Look, I'll go first with you, Nell.'

Nell rolls her eyes but does not object. She stands firm, puts her hands on her hips, and puckers her lips in Naomi's direction.

Naomi looks at Eve with a devilish smirk, then moves towards Nell. Slowly, slowly, Naomi gets closer. Her eyes are on Nell's eyes; she doesn't look like she's going to back down. She places her hands on Nell's shoulders, she leans in . . . in . . . so close now.

Eve thinks she is going to die. It's like being strapped to a chair and forced to witness a murder. She can't stop it, she can't say anything, she must watch.

And then, just a nanosecond before contact, Naomi breaks away, splashes Nell in the face, bursts out laughing, and so does Nell. The two of them are in hysterics. 'Jesus, Naomi, that was close!' screams Nell. 'I actually thought you were going to do it for a second there!'

Eve joins in the laughter a beat too late. She is relieved and angry and hurt, and she doesn't know which vectors these emotions are going in, just that they are all very intense and that she cannot let her face or body language express them. She must show that she is in on the fun, that she too thinks the idea of kissing her friends is hilarious.

Naomi stops laughing, clears her throat, looks at Eve. 'Okay, quick sticks, next round. Nell, you kiss Eve.'

And does Nell falter for a second? Does her expression reveal a twinge of something else? If it does, it's gone before Eve can decode it, and now Nell is coming towards her, and Naomi is watching with glee, and Eve cannot think of a worse or better situation than this in the whole entire world. It is ecstasy and it is terror.

Naomi wants to see desire on Eve's face, Eve knows it. Naomi wants to trick Eve into showing Nell what she feels. And yet, as Nell's soft lips come closer, as Nell's eyes are on Eve's eyes, as Nell's hands wrap around Eve's back, maybe it would be worth it. Maybe Nell does want to kiss Eve, maybe this feeling is mutual, maybe it's going to happen, right here, in Naomi's pool. Eve leans in, opens herself up for the kiss. Her eyes are full of love for Nell; how could they not be? Eve wants this, and she's willing to show it. Who cares what Naomi thinks about it, if Nell wants her too?

Nell's eyes widen now, because for the first time she sees the full extent of Eve's want. She is scared but she isn't sure of what.

So as Eve puckers her lips and closes her eyes, Nell unwraps her arms from Eve's back, crouches a little and uses the floor of the pool as a springboard, and propels herself up and away from Eve. As Nell's jump disturbs the water's surface, Eve feels a cascade of splashes and opens her eyes. There is shrieking, there is movement.

It's like coming to after sleep, like your eyes adjusting to a new kind of light. It's hard for Eve to comprehend what is happening, to take herself out of the state she was just in and to place herself here, in this alternative universe, where the worst has happened.

Naomi is bent over herself laughing, but what's worse – what is so much worse – is that Nell is also laughing. They are laughing together.

Eve wants to cry. She can feel the tears welling. Instead, she summons all her strength, and she starts laughing too. Nell is not meeting her eyes, but Naomi is. And Naomi's eyes are saying, *I see you, lesbian.*

*

Later that night, the three girls sit on Naomi's bed and watch a box set of *The O.C.* Naomi has a television in her room, which is exhilarating for Nell and Eve for different reasons. Nell's parents do not allow her to have a TV in her room because they do not believe in popular culture. Emerald does not allow a TV in Eve's room because she says they are too poor. The show is a good distraction, as it allows the girls to sit in their thoughts, to consider how the afternoon's events have affected each of them personally. Because while they have ostensibly moved on from the almost-kiss moment, each girl knows something new now, and the room is charged with it.

Eve knows that she wants to kiss Nell, and that she has wanted this for a long time. Nell realises that Eve wants more from her than she thinks she can give. Naomi has long suspected, but now she knows for sure – Eve is in love with Nell, and this will be Eve's Achilles heel, and Naomi will leverage this.

On screen, Seth is being forced to choose between a blonde with a pixie cut and a brunette dressed up as Wonder Woman.

Nell sits in the middle of the bed, with Naomi and Eve on either side of her. Eve is acutely aware of her leg touching Nell's, of her fingers only inches from Nell's palm. Nell is watching the show. Naomi is watching Eve watch Nell.

'I don't get why Seth would go for Anna, considering she's basically a female version of him and Summer is clearly hotter,' says Naomi.

Eve knows she is being baited, but she cannot not respond, for this would seem even more suspicious than commenting. Truthfully, Eve doesn't understand why either of these women would be interested in Seth, when he's such a wet mop, and his stomach is, like, concave. But liking Seth has become a personality trait for her – in avowing her adoration for Seth, Eve is part of the conversation of girlhood.

'They're both hot, come on!' says Eve. 'And Summer treats Seth like trash, so I get Anna's appeal. What do you reckon, Nell?'

Nell considers it. She says, 'I don't know. I think Seth should probably just focus on his art.'

Naomi and Eve both laugh at this, the tension broken slightly.

*

That night, Eve sleeps on a mattress on the floor next to the bed, while Naomi and Nell share Naomi's bed. The pair of them whisper to each other, and Eve can only make out sporadic words. Something about pills, something about the Grove. Eve is being excluded, again, but from what she cannot fathom. And she won't ask, because after this afternoon, she must ensure more than ever that she does not come across as overeager. Nell giggles quietly at something Naomi says, and Eve feels rage climb inside her mouth and slide down into her stomach. She holds it in, she stays still.

Eventually, Nell and Naomi are silent. They have fallen asleep.

Eve lies quietly and attempts to calm her mind. But pink. But soft. Her memory keeps replaying Nell's lips in the pool. Nell was so close, so close to her, before it all went wrong. If Naomi wasn't there, would Nell have kissed her? It really did seem for a second like maybe she wanted to.

Eve feels that heat again, she feels the bodily yearning she experienced in the water. She closes her eyes, and she gives in.

God, it feels like relief.

For the first time, she allows herself to imagine what it might be like. Not just a kiss, but all of it. Nell's lips on her own, Nell's tongue in her mouth, Nell's breasts against hers, warm, soft, hot. Her breath on Nell's wetness, Nell's smell on her hands. Nell hers forever, in every way.

And now, she can't resist it. Eve does the unthinkable. With Nell just feet away, Eve cautiously lowers her hand under her knickers, trying not to make a noise. She looks to Nell's resting body, sees her steady breathing, and – gently at first – Eve touches herself. She caresses her pubic hair, and imagines it is Nell's hand doing the touching. Her index finger strokes the wet sliver she now finds, it moves up and down, slowly, slowly, and this feels like sunshine.

A feeling takes hold, like a mouth about to speak, like a cup soon to overflow. Faster, faster, she rubs, hard and fervent and desperate. Eve is no longer in control of her own hand; it is Nell who is doing it, Nell is doing this to her. It is building, this sensation, it is taking over everything. And just when Eve does not think she can stand it anymore, suddenly she can. She has taken the jump, she is weightless. Her hips are bucking, every nerve ending is electric, and Eve understands now what bodies are made for. She gasps, and covers her mouth with her other hand. Her hips fall. All is released. Her body becomes matter once more, and the feeling recedes, white waves dissolving into sand. Eve removes her hand, which is slick now. She looks again to Nell, and immediately feels sick. How could she have done this, how could she have violated Nell like this? She is disgusting. She is perverted.

She wants more.

2024

A person being gone can feel like a lot of things to the person who is left.

For Eve, Nell's absence feels like all her favourite books have had their pages scrubbed, and where there were once stories, and joy, and hope, there is now blank paper between the covers, and only the title pages are left to remind her that once they contained magic. Once, there was meaning, and that meaning was shared.

Now Eve sits at her laptop, on which she is supposed to be editing a queer body horror parable, and instead she thinks about how Nell used to describe painting. In the early hours of the morning, when neither of them could sleep and Lake was finally down, they used to speak in their own code. Metaphors that no one else would understand fell freely from their mouths, two minds coalesced. For Nell, painting was thinking. Nell said that when she was painting, her mind became like a sea, and the waves were rough and the surface opaque, and it was her task to sense what was beneath – to feel the temperature, the rhythm, the beat, and finally, when she knew she had the right spot, to plunge down and find what was waiting for her, something that had always existed but that couldn't be grasped till now. Nell said that her favourite moment in painting was when she could feel the temperature change in her head, when she knew that the hiding thing was about to be revealed.

When Nell had told her that, Eve felt sure, once again, that Nell was the only person who could ever properly understand her brain. Because for Eve, that feeling came with writing, and it wasn't a sea so much as a dense, dense web, and the alchemy happened only rarely, only when Eve had totally familiarised herself with every strand, with the tension of every cross-hair, and suddenly a pattern emerged, and the centre of the web became clear, and she understood that each thread was woven with a specific purpose, and now she alone could see the web for what it really was. And when Eve explained that to Nell, Nell nodded quietly, and she said, 'Yes, exactly.'

2008

Oh, how time does not fly, for some. For Eve Bowman, every term of year nine is a decade, every year of school an eternity, the holidays stretch on forever, even lunchtime seems to be stuck in a temporal loop. Because on the Monday following the weekend's sleepover, a curious thing occurs. The thing is this. Eve's best friend, Nell Argall, stops being friends with her.

There is no outright fight, no skirmish, no ponytail pulled – not at first. These are teenage girls: everything is subtext. It's not subtle subtext, but it is literally unsaid. What happens is that when Eve spies Nell in the hallway on the way to English, Eve smiles, a big bright smile, and Nell does not return it; instead she grimaces. And when Eve asks how Nell's Sunday was, Nell gives a noncommittal response and doesn't reciprocate the question. And when they get to class, Nell sits next to Naomi, and neither of them turn around to make eye contact with Eve for the duration of the lesson. And later that day, when lunchtime comes, Eve goes to their band room as usual, and neither Nell nor Naomi is there. And after school, when Eve corners Nell at her locker and asks if everything is alright, Nell says it is – but everything about her demeanour says it isn't. Then Naomi swings by with her backpack and tells Nell they are going to be late, and the pair of them walk off without a goodbye, and Eve is just standing there, not knowing what has happened. And the next day, the same thing occurs. And the next. High school is like this sometimes. One's place can be snatched away in an instant.

For the rest of the week, Eve does not give up. This is surely a strange aberration, a miscommunication, a tear in the fabric of the universe that will soon be explained and repaired. She continues to make overtures, to suggest group hangs, to IM the girls after school. She is needy, she is desperate, she can see the pity and revulsion in both Nell's and Naomi's eyes as they come up with ways to deflect her. Their responses are clipped, the plans are left to hang in the air, the IMs are unread.

From Monday through Friday, Eve does not allow herself to cry, or even to consider another confrontation. Assuredly things will just go back to normal. She continues getting the bus to school, attending classes, sitting by herself in the band room at lunch, coming home. Emerald can sense that something is up, but she is not really attuned enough to Eve's emotional rhythms to guess at the gravity of the situation.

By adulthood, we have hopefully learnt that open communication is a necessary life skill, crucial to maintaining relationships and ensuring we get what we need. But at fourteen, we do not know this. Or, perhaps, we do know it, but we just don't want to face the ramifications this forthrightness might entail. What if we find out something we wish we hadn't? Better just to stew in it.

On Friday afternoon, Eve lies on her bed alone and hypothesises about the cause of her exile. It was the sleepover – the sleepover, obviously. She went too far at the sleepover. But which moment was the breaking point, what unforgivable faux pas had she committed?

The others were asleep when Eve had her moment of weakness in bed, it cannot be that; the prospect is too awful to consider. Nell could not have known what Eve was doing beneath the covers, what she was thinking about. But oh god, what if she did? Eve dry-heaves. No, no, that can't be it.

She looks to the posters on the wall next to her bed – pages of magazines ripped out with rulers, blu-tacked over the years in various fervours. They're male teen heart-throbs, all of them, in various poses, in various band tees. Adam Brody, Heath Ledger, Ed Westwick. Eve feels nothing for these men, except maybe jealousy, but they act as her totems of normalcy. She's been trying so hard for so long.

What if it was just the almost-kiss that scared Nell, and Naomi has convinced her that Eve is a sick freak? If so, it's fixable. Eve still has Nell's ear, surely. She can call her, she can explain, make Naomi look like a troublemaker, a liar. It was a game; they were just playing a game!

Energised by this idea, Eve pulls her phone from her pocket. Within seconds she has dialled Nell's number and the phone is ringing. It is all happening so fast, Eve doesn't even know what she is going to say when—

'Hello?' Nell has answered. She's picked up.

'Nell! Hi!' What now? 'Look, I just wanted to call because I . . . I've been pretty confused at school this week?'

Nell isn't saying anything.

Eve continues. 'And I don't know if I did something to upset you, but if I did, I'm sorry, and I want to know what it is so I don't do it again?' Eve's voice breaks; she is close to crying.

Nell sighs. 'Oh, Eve. Don't cry.' Nell's voice is gentle. This is promising.

'So, are we okay?' Eve says this so softly, with so much hope, and something shifts in Nell. She finds this weak version of Eve gross. She does not want to be involved in any part of it.

'Look, Eve, it's just that Naomi and I had a talk after the sleepover, and we both feel that you've become a bit . . . fake.'

Eve almost laughs, this is so far from any answer she was expecting. 'Fake?'

'Fake,' confirms Nell, without emotion.

'What do you even mean?' asks Eve.

'I mean that you're always laughing when Naomi laughs, even when you don't get it, and you go along with our ideas when it's clear that you don't want to, and you're always trying to impress the populars, which honestly is pretty fucked up considering they're such bitches to you.'

Eve has never heard Nell speak like this before. Eve is actually crying now, the silent heaves that precede the howls. Why is Nell saying this, why is she doing this? Eve isn't fake. What even is 'fake'? Being fake is something that teenagers would argue about on an American high school show – but this is Nell. Nell is smart, and Australian.

'I' – Eve gulps – 'I don't understand.'

Nell continues, her voice cold. 'And you say you love Seth, but you don't, Eve, you just don't. And I don't get why you won't just admit that. It's pathetic. And it's sad.' She pauses. 'I feel sad for you.'

'W-what?' Eve manages. 'I – I do like Seth.'

'I think,' Nell starts, then she rephrases. 'Well, Naomi and I both think that you should take some time to work on yourself.'

Eve is silent; she does not know what she can say to this.

'Anyway, I have to go, so – bye.' Nell hangs up.

Eve is in shock. So it was about the almost-kiss? Nell felt it, Nell knew? Nell knows? But the way Nell phrased it, Eve had no chance to defend herself. The character assassination of it, the indictment of Eve's very personality. Every fear Eve has ever had about how she is perceived, voiced to her in such extremes, by the person she loves the most.

The howls begin, and they do not stop.

Up until now, Eve has always used crying as a tactical release – a tunnel to get from bad feeling to good feeling. As a child, when something happened that was upsetting, or if she was caught in a lie and shamed, Eve would go to her bedroom, lie on her stomach, and heave. And as she heaved, the pain would lessen, like she was a balloon that was deflating with each sob, willing herself into flatness, into a dimension that could not be popped. When she finished crying, the pain would be gone, dispersed into the air.

Today, for the first time, Eve's crying trick does not work. She cries for hours and hours, she wails like an animal. She thinks of every time she has laughed with Nell, thinks of all the dreams she has had for the two of them, and then she thinks of Nell laughing at her, thinks of Nell finding her repulsive, thinks of Naomi telling Nell she did the right thing. For a minute, the tears stop. But the pain – the pain is still there.

There are some types of pain that crying will expunge. This is not one of them.

*

A few suburbs away, lying on her own bed in her own soup of tears, Nell is learning the exact same thing.

2010

By this point, aged sixteen, Eve should feel used to her isolation. School is something to get through, and she will, she will, but Christ it's hard. She's in year eleven, she can almost see the end. There are two girls in her year, Lila and Grace, who stand at about her level of popularity – i.e. they have none – and some lunchtimes, Eve sits with them. They are genuinely sweet girls, but so, so boring. Nevertheless, Eve is thankful – were it not for them she would spend literally every minute alone. She tries to make herself find them funny. She asks them about their cousins, their recitals. She tries to be kind. But they cannot compare with what Eve has lost.

Eve overhears other girls talking about parties, sleepovers, crushes: Eve does not experience any of these things. She is a teenager, but she is shut off from teenage life. Nell's abandonment has stunted Eve's growth – she's stuck in limbo, with books and television shows as her only real friends. She learns about love triangles from *Dawson's Creek*. She learns what drugs feel like from *On the Road*. Her understanding of so much is theoretical, and she thirsts for this not to be the case, but she has no way to break the fourth wall of her life. She simply must wait.

Nell and Naomi are part of the popular crowd now, because the popular crowd like drugs, and Nell and Naomi sell these. Eve is not aware of this reason for the alliance, because no one popular ever talks to her, so she is perplexed that Nell is part of this group. Nell and Naomi hang out at the Grove, Eve's seen photos on Facebook. Eve cannot fathom what Nell would enjoy about this. Nell hates these people, their values, their crudeness. Eve imagines Nell sitting on the beach and judging everyone, having no one to relate her criticisms to. And the boys – Eve doesn't want to think about how the boys in that circle must treat Nell. They wouldn't know what to make of her. And Naomi – Naomi is now buddy-buddy with none other than Georgia Smith. It could not hurt more than it does.

Eve has no access to Nell's life; it is so weird. Like, earlier this term Nell was absent from school for a few weeks, and when she came back she seemed even paler than usual, and all Eve wanted to do was give her a hug, take her to the beach and force her to bodysurf; eat a mountain of grapes and read poems aloud in a melodramatic drawl; remind her that there was silly joy to be had, and that they could have it together. But when Eve tried to say something to Nell in the locker hallway, Nell changed direction. Whenever Nell so much as notices Eve looking in her direction, she turns away. Eve should be used to it now, but it's a kick to the ankle every time.

In English they've been doing creative writing projects, and this has been a release for Eve. In writing she can tell Nell all the things she cannot tell her in real life. There is a decadence to her self-torture that provides some kind of feeling, even if it is a bad feeling. There's a writing competition all the girls have been forced to enter, and Eve is feeling quietly confident about her story's chances. Because she does not have friends, she reads. She reads everything.

She now knows all the words Nell and Naomi used to mock her for not knowing. She's first in English now, whereas Nell barely contributes to class. Nell's always in the Art rooms these days, working on God knows what. Nell no longer laughs, no longer acts like the girl Eve used to know.

Eve's story is about teenage depression, so she has to win, right? Their English teacher this year is Miss Kelly. Miss Kelly is Irish, with the classic red hair and rosy cheeks, and she is kind to Eve, so naturally Eve loves her.

Eve's even told Emerald about the competition, this is how little she has in her life to share. Emerald tells Eve to 'get out and have fun!' but has no understanding of how futile this request is. Eve's place in her year's ecosystem has been cemented, and now there is no getting out of it. She is the loner, the weirdo. Because she is perceived this way by others, everything she says is construed as strange, even if it is totally inane. It's like how once you've been committed to an insane asylum, it is almost impossible to get out: every protestation that you are not crazy seems to prove your insanity, your denial. Eve is the year loser, so even if she utters a phrase as innocuous as, 'Yeah, sounds good,' she is met with derision. It is a horrendous but nevertheless state-mandated situation.

Another weekend spent home alone – well, with Emerald, as it happens, because her date cancelled – and Eve sits on the couch watching *Downton Abbey*. Emerald pops her head into the lounge room from time to time, mostly when the evil butler is onscreen, as she thinks he is 'devilishly handsome'.

The home phone rings, and Eve gets up from the couch to answer it.

A woman with an Irish accent says, 'Hello, is this the Bowman residence?'

Eve is perplexed by this official-sounding salutation. It is 8 pm on a Saturday night. Who is this, and why does their voice sound strangely familiar but also a bit off?

'Yes, it is, this is Eve. Whom may I ask is calling?' Eve is always very polite on the phone.

'Oh, Eve! It's Miss Kelly, from school! How are you?!'

It is truly bizarre that a teacher would be calling a student on a weekend evening, and Eve half-considers this, but she is also just so thrilled by this attention from her favourite teacher. What on earth could she possibly want?

Eve thinks she hears a noise in the background on Miss Kelly's end, but she ignores it. She wonders where Miss Kelly is right now, what she's wearing, if she has a glass of wine in her hand.

'I'm g-good, Miss Kelly, thank you. How – how are you?'

'Oh, just marking papers, it never ends, you know. But Eve . . .'

'Yes?' Eve can hear the desperation in her own voice. She tries again, concertedly calmly, 'I mean, yes?'

'I'm calling because I've just got some wonderful news from the William Ashby Foundation.'

'Oh my god.' Eve swallows in excitement.

'Oh my god indeed! Your story won the competition, Eve!'

Eve's grin invades her whole face. She's in shock. She hasn't had good news in such a very long time, she's almost forgotten what it's like to receive it.

'I'm just so proud of you,' Miss Kelly continues. 'There'll be an announcement at assembly next week, and of course I'll see you in class on Monday, but I just thought you'd want to know. I would, if it were me!'

'Um, wow. Thank you so much, Miss Kelly. This is so huge. And thank you so much for calling, that's so nice of you.'

'It's not every day your favourite student wins a writing competition. I got in to teaching for moments like this. Now, it's Saturday night, I'm sure you have better things to do than talk to your English teacher, so go celebrate! Well done, Eve – well done.'

Favourite student? Prize-winning story? It's too much for Eve to take in.

'Well, thank you again, Miss Kelly. Thank you. Okay, goodnight.'

'Goodnight, Eve.'

And can Eve hear a faint giggle from the other end? Does something feel off to her? Maybe it does, but who cares, she's riding high.

When she puts down the phone, Emerald emerges from the other room.

'Who was that on the phone?' she asks.

And Eve does not like sharing her emotions with her mother, but this is objectively a good thing, and she has no one else to tell.

'Well' – Eve can't conceal how pleased she is with herself – 'you know that story competition I was telling you about?'

'The one through your school?'

'That's the one. Well, my teacher just called to let me know I won it. Like, the whole competition. Which is, like, students from schools all over the state.'

Emerald breaks into a genuine smile. She hasn't seen her daughter happy in years. 'Oh, Evie, that's so wonderful! I'm so proud of you. Come here, you.' And Emerald motions for her daughter to hug her, which is something she never offers, and Eve does so, she allows herself to be held in her mother's arms, and it feels safe and it feels good.

*

The next Monday at school, Eve's back is straighter, her stride more confident. She might not have friends, but it's now been confirmed that she has *talent*. She's envisioning the bright future that surely lies ahead for her now – university, and poetry slams, and book deals, and prizes, and glamour, and community. All of this will come to her.

Period two is English, and Eve arrives a little late, as she's been to the bathroom to reapply lip balm, to be ready for her moment with Miss Kelly. All the other girls are already seated, Nell and Naomi and Georgia and Alex all in the back row, smirking as usual. Eve pays them no heed.

Miss Kelly sits at her own desk at the front of class. Her head is down, she's looking at some paperwork.

'Um, Miss Kelly?' Eve says.

'Hmm?' Miss Kelly does not look up.

'It's me – Eve.' Eve smiles hopefully, with promise.

Miss Kelly meets Eve's gaze. 'So it is, Eve. Hello. Are you going to take a seat?'

Eve doesn't move. She's waiting for her recognition, but it does seem to be taking a beat.

'I just wanted to say thank you, miss.'

Miss Kelly gives her a quizzical look.

'For letting me know about the writing competition?' Eve prompts.

'I'm so sorry, Eve, but I'm not sure what you're referring to. Do you mean the William Ashby Prize?'

'Um, yes?' Eve falters.

'Oh, well, you're quite welcome. It's a great opportunity for you girls. Now, would you mind taking your seat, please? We've got a lot to cover today.'

Eve stares at her teacher, confused. 'Oh, ye—' Eve's response is cut off by the sounds now coming from the back of the classroom. Georgia, Alex and Naomi are in fits of giggles, staring at Eve. Nell is looking at Eve too, not laughing, but not confused, clearly in on the joke.

It all becomes terribly obvious.

Nell looks at Eve with pity. Eve looks at Nell with realisation, and with the kind of profound hurt that makes one's eyes large and round and swimming. Eve's heart is breaking anew, which she didn't know to be possible. How can a broken heart shatter?

Not only has Nell forsaken her, but she has publicly betrayed her. Nell has offered Eve up to be used for sport. Eve will never forget this moment, the intensity of the kick. They must have all laughed so much. They must have thought they were so clever. And the but of the joke is *but why?* Why does Nell hate her this much?

Eve takes her seat and sits through the lesson in silence. Her body is shuddering from the sobs she is holding in.

When class ends, she goes to her usual bathroom. The tears fall, but Eve feels strangely empty. She looks at herself in the mirror, sees the pathetic person reflected back at her.

This will not do. It's so sad. Her whole life is so fucking sad.

She will wait out the rest of high school as a ghost. She will read, she will learn, she will watch. She will not give any more energy to this place, to Nell. She will bide her time until she enters a place where she can be appreciated for who she is. She will become worldly, she will memorise every reference. Soon enough, she will find her people.

In a few years, Nell will not recognise the person Eve has become.

Part Two

2012

On her first day of uni, Eve sits alone in her intro to Language, Texts and Time. She wears a Christine Baranski t-shirt and jeans. Her hair is still short, although hopefully better cut than in previous years. She's done the week's reading, and she believes she has a basic understanding of the origins of the Western grammatical metalanguage. She owns a MacBook – this seems key. Over the summer she even trained herself to enjoy coffee. One must start with long blacks and work backwards from there. Artfully placed next to her laptop is a roughed-up copy of *The Color Purple*. Eve knows queer symbols now, she's learnt them from a website called Autostraddle. Her people will find her and come, she is sure of it. They must.

All around her, students start to file into the auditorium. The space is grey, with tiered seating, but the students are dressed in streaming colours, filing down the stairs like ants carrying a Pride flag. Some of them are already in groups, laughing, clutching coffees. How on earth can they all know each other so soon? It is literally the first day of class.

The lecturer stands at the front of the room, and behind him is a giant screen, on which *A book must be the axe for the frozen sea inside us – Franz Kafka* is projected. The lecturer looks like he has some kind of secret wisdom that only he can impart. He plays with his tie as he watches the people whose lives he is about to revolutionise take their seats. Eve resents his smugness, but she wants his knowledge nonetheless. She wants all of it. She refuses to ever be caught out in conversation again. Over the summer she read Woolf, Eliot, Morrison, hooks, Lorde. A very good-looking bookseller recommended the Woolf, and so each week Eve came back for more. As such, Eve's literary knowledge has at this stage been almost entirely curated by a twenty-four-year-old lesbian she has a crush on. Eve does not know it yet, but she is already engaged in queer feminist praxis.

The lecturer begins his spiel. 'What *is* language,' he asks rhetorically, 'when we really consider it? Is it sound, is it marks on a page? Is language the words themselves or the meaning they make? Can these two things ever be separated?' He pauses, as if daring someone to be stupid enough to answer. Thankfully, no one falls for it. Eve imagines if this were early high school – how Georgia Smith would have said something dumb, and she and Nell would have rolled their eyes at each other. Eve's gotten pretty good at not wondering how every moment in her life would be different if Nell were there, but this context is triggering. It's the first day of school all over again. It's the queue at the diving blocks, it's the changing room before. It's working out where to sit at lunchtime, except every class is like lunchtime. No. No, Eve will not let history repeat herself. No one knows her here. She can be anyone she likes.

'Here in Language, Texts and Time, we will take a journey together. We will sail through semiotics, grammar, Middle English, world Englishes, and hopefully, by the end of this semester, we'll all understand that the exhortation to "say what you mean" is never quite as simple as it might first appear. My name is Dr Thomas Reynolds. Now, let's get to it, shall we?'

Despite now being one of the few people with an empty seat on either side of them, Eve does feel that by sitting in this room she is becoming part of something larger than herself. While she understands that she should probably find the grandiosity of Dr Reynolds' speech embarrassing, she can't help but admire the man. Here is someone who has dedicated his whole life to thinking about words. Given that words have been her only companion for some years, Eve sees much value in Dr Reynolds' vocation, and she very much wants him to like her. Some things do not change.

Dr Reynolds begins to speak of someone called Charles F. Hockett, and Eve struggles to type quickly enough to catch everything he says. How is she to know which bits will be important and which she can afford to miss?

Some others like Eve are ferociously typing, clacking at high speeds that betray their competitiveness. A girl in front of Eve is in the middle of an eBay bidding war for a blue Leica. She keeps upping her bid by fifty cents.

Dr Reynolds is having everyone in the lecture hall raise their left hand. It's something about taxonomic structuralism, Eve has gathered. Signs mean different things dependent on their relation to . . . other stuff. Apparently, context is everything. But Eve already knows this – she had short-haired Ms Becker for Design and Technology, after all. It seems that both lesbian high school teachers and university English professors like context. Eve imagines what Nell would say in response to this observation. Probably something like, 'That Venn diagram is a circle, Eve.' Eve smirks, then tries to concentrate again.

She becomes distracted, however, by some chatter in the row behind her. She cannot risk turning around to see the faces of the people speaking – that would read as far too keen. So she listens.

'Lol, did you even look at the syllabus?' a male voice asks.

'That's your job, honey,' a higher male voice replies. 'I'm just here for the easy pass. But because I'm a curious man, an elf of sorts, a kind of . . . raconteur . . . why do you ask?'

'Okay, so we're supposed to be learning about, like, the history of English or whatever, right?'

'I've gathered that that's the idea, yes.'

'But, like, there are no women writers on this syllabus. There's one week on feminism in, like, week eight, and of the three academics listed there, only *one* of them is a woman. Sketchy, no?'

'Bottoms and tops we all hate cops, I guess,' replies the higher voice.

'Tae, as much as you're structurally correct, in this instance that's a non sequitur, and you know it.'

'Is it, though?' Tae asks philosophically.

'Yes,' replies lower-pitch.

Eve's feelings are conflicted. On one level, she is amazed and excited that someone in this class has actually read the syllabus more than a week ahead (she was the only one to do this in year twelve), and she is impressed that these men have views about feminism. But on another level, she's kicking herself – because she read the syllabus, and she didn't think twice about there being no women on it. She simply accepted this as reality and assumed that whoever made the syllabus knew better than her. Now, hearing these young men critique the institution, she feels ashamed. She needs to become more critical, and she needs to become more confident. The lesbian in the bookshop would be so disappointed in her.

She must befriend these gays.

When the lecture is over, Eve decides to shoot her shot. Quickly, quickly, all the students begin to file out. Eve turns around in her seat, tries to make eye contact with one of the men, but they are gone already. How did they achieve this? The passageways between the chairs in the auditorium are all clogged, but there is no sign of them. Are they magic?

Eve is yet to learn that gay walking speed is different to straight walking speed. For today, at least, she has been thwarted in her attempt to make friends.

*

When Eve gets home it is 4.30 pm and Emerald is in the kitchen drinking chardonnay out of a tumbler.

'Want some?' she asks.

Eve debates the pros and cons of drinking with her mother this early in the day. Emerald now generally exists in a chardonnay haze, but it's only when the spirits come out after a bad date that her drinking becomes particularly annoying. When this happens, Emerald tends to come and lie in Eve's bed and cry to her about her bad romantic luck, asking Eve to stroke her like a baby. As a result, Eve has avoided alcohol – not that she's had much opportunity to avoid it, but still.

But today, Eve thinks, *Why not?* She's a university student now. She's an adult. And she has no other plans tonight.

'Sure. Thanks, Mum.'

Emerald reaches into the cupboard for another tumbler. She fills it almost to the top and passes it to Eve.

Taking the glass, Eve asks her mother, 'What are we celebrating, then?'

'Your first day of university, of course!' replies Emerald.

Eve hadn't realised that her mother even knew today was her first day of uni, and she is strangely touched, even though she suspects her initiation into tertiary education is not the real reason her mother is drinking.

'Cheers to taxonomical structuralism!' cries Eve.

'To *what*?' asks Emerald.

'I honestly have no idea,' admits Eve.

The two women stand at the kitchen bench, observing each other. Emerald does not comprehend her daughter, but it would not be true to say she does not love her. She's raised Eve for eighteen years, she's sent her to a good school, she wants her to be happy. But Eve never tells her anything. And she's always felt trepidatious with Eve, she's always felt intimidated. Like, even when Eve was a baby, Emerald felt like her daughter knew exactly who she was.

In high school, Eve once overheard a group of girls talking to each other about the first time they realised that their parents existed apart from them. It took some time to grasp what the girls were getting at. It seemed that these girls' understandings of their parents were so caught up in having their own needs met that it took them years to understand that their parents were still active in the world even when their children weren't present. It was like the girls had to develop object permanence, but for their parents. This was funny to Eve, because for her it felt kind of like the opposite. Eve was always surprised when her mother *was* around. Emerald always acted like she had a real life, and Eve was getting in the way of it. Eve was the pretend part of Emerald's life. Eve was the ball when it went under the couch.

But here they are, drinking wine together, each deciding that they'll give conversation a go.

'So,' Emerald begins, 'how was it? Did you meet any cuties? Were your classes interesting?'

Eve takes a big gulp. 'Um, no "cuties" to speak of, but yes, the classes were interesting.' She corrects herself, 'Well, the *class* was interesting. I only had one today, my timetable's all spread ou—'

'Oh, gosh, I remember *my* first week of uni,' Emerald interrupts. 'I met a boy called Josh Taylor in Intro to Psych and we just hit it off, it was such a time. He and his friends had a share house on King Street, and I don't think I slept in my own bed for a month. My parents were livid! But god, it was worth it.'

Emerald zones out, her mind returning to times gone by. She re-emerges and makes eye contact with her daughter. 'Promise me, Eve,' she says seriously, 'that if someone offers you a tequila shot, you'll always find some lime first.'

'Um, okay?' says Eve.

Emerald nods to herself. 'Boys notice that kind of thing. A girl who doesn't ask for lime is a girl who doesn't value herself.'

'Right.'

'And friends!' Emerald exclaims. 'Did you make any friends?!'

This is so like Emerald, Eve thinks. 'Um, no, not yet, but it's only the first day. I think I'll have better luck in tutes, the lectures are just so bi—'

'God, the first day of uni! That was when I met Binny, and Theresa, and Char. You know, they're my friends for life, Eve. My friends *for life*. I don't know what I'd do without them. They have been there through *all of it*.' Emerald has finished her glass and now she's pouring another. 'We were all late for the first lecture, so one after another we snuck into the back row, and then Binny – of course, I didn't know she was Binny yet – Binny held up a pack of fags and the four of us just sidled right back out of that lecture hall and into the sun, and we smoked and talked about boys, and oh, it was just divine.' She takes another large sip. 'You've got to find your – what do the young people call it now? – you've got to find your *people*, Eve. You won't survive without them.'

'Mmm,' Eve exhales.

Emerald is in full-on diatribe mode now. 'These past few years you've been so . . . so *antisocial*, Eve. I don't know where you get it from; I was certainly never like that. You used to have such good friends. I remember you girls having sleepovers, and getting ready for parties, it was so sweet . . . And you had that one very good friend, didn't you? I liked her. What was her name again?'

Eve swallows. This is why she does not talk to her mother. 'Nell, Mum – her name was Nell.'

'Well, why don't you give her a call?' asks Emerald. 'She was bright, I'm sure she's at uni too. Do you know which one she's at? You girls should have a drink.'

'Yeah, for sure, I'll look her up,' says Eve. Eve is not on speaking terms with anyone from school. Eve thinks it's likely that Nell is at her university, but she's made a very conscious effort not to cyberstalk her. And besides, Nell always rejected social media.

'Whatever happened between you two?' asks Emerald, which is funny in a dark kind of way, because she has never asked Eve this before – particularly, for example, when it fucking happened.

What Eve wouldn't give to be able to tell her mother the truth – that she was in love, and she thought Nell was too, but actually Nell was disgusted by her and cut her off instead. That for years she has been friendless because accusations of queerness in a girls high school are akin to accusations of paedophilia or murder.

She's seen other girls with their mothers. They talk and giggle and make fun of each other. They share. But her mother is not that kind of mother. Theirs is not that kind of relationship. Besides, Emerald doesn't really want to know. If she did, she would have asked Eve at literally any point over the past several years why she was always alone.

'Um, just drifted apart, I guess,' answers Eve.

'That's a shame,' murmurs Emerald.

Emerald swallows what's left in her glass, rinses it under the tap, places it on the drying rack and turns to Eve. 'Well, I've got to go now, sweetheart,' she says. 'It's been lovely chatting.'

It's so sudden, Emerald's departure. She always does this. At the very moment when Eve is thinking that maybe, just maybe, they're finally getting through to each other, Emerald will leave. It's like she has an internal alarm clock that can sense opportunities for maternal intimacy. *Ding ding ding!* Not today.

And so Emerald swans off into the night, leaving Eve alone in their apartment, which is fine, because Eve is an adult now. But she does not feel like an adult. This year, she will change this. Tomorrow, she will change this.

2024

It's been said that the rise in queer body horror fiction speaks to readers' hunger for representations of the material liminality of queer experience – the sense of being directed by one's desires, the fear of being perceived by others as monstrous, the blissful sense of agency attained when one embraces their own so-called monstrosity. Eve is aware of the discourse, and she is, obviously, contributing to it as she copyedits this manuscript. She laughs at these kinds of books, at their self-seriousness, but even so, the themes do get to her.

Eve has felt shame about her desires, of course she has. In her adolescent years shame was presented to her as her cross to bear, and she bore it for far too long. In the years since high school she has been training herself to repatriate the shame, to return it to those who bequeathed it to her. And mostly, now, she has gotten good at this.

Eve is no longer disgusted by herself simply because she is gay. Eve likes her body, its sturdiness. She likes her hair, she likes the way her shoulders look in a tank top. She likes her lips, soft and supple and always slightly parted. She likes women, and she is at peace with this.

Eve is now disgusted with herself not because she is gay but because she fears she is a cruel person, and she does not know how to make it right. She tries to persuade herself that these two things – her sexuality and her cruelty – are not necessarily linked, yet something whispers to her that they are. Eve could never say this out loud, as it would be deemed problematic and bad PR for the queer community, but she fears that cruelty grew from her shame and made a home in her, and when she got rid of the shame, the cruelty stayed latched to her insides. Maybe Eve is cruel for the same reason that gay men are so often bitches? But she does feel regret, every day, so doesn't this make her different from them?

As she's been contemplating this, she's read the same paragraph twice without processing it. She rolls her shoulders, cracks her wrist bones and attempts to focus. She's on chapter three and already the author has switched between American and Australian spellings of 'odour' several times.

The protagonist in this manuscript keeps turning into a medusa jellyfish whenever she swims. There are a lot of entangled metaphors about the stony gaze of the butch jellyfish, and while Eve knows that this is not what the author is going for, she keeps thinking it's like Leslie Feinberg meets *H2O: Just Add Water.*

She and Nell used to be obsessed with Medusa. After classes and work they'd sit around and pretend they were a lot smarter than they were. Eve remembers afternoons spent lying on Nell's bed with printouts of Cixous, of Arendt. Conversations are always coming back to her, memories she thinks have disappeared are always crawling through the cracks.

She slogs on, page after page, looking for small faults. When she finds them, she gets a little dopamine rush. It's quaint, it's silly, maybe, to derive self-worth from spotting typos, but Eve has always felt best about herself when presented with proof that she is able to see things that other people are not. Having this skill in life, however, has turned out to be dangerous for Eve. She has misused her power. So now she directs her energies to the page, to other people's words, to the places where her perception can't hurt the ones she loves.

Eve hears movement and chatter outside her front door, which now opens, and her daughter bowls in. Her neighbour Leah has a child in Lake's year, and today Leah has picked up both girls from school, a blessing.

Lake drops her schoolbag next to the entrance; it's almost bigger than she is.

Leah yells from the hallway, 'All good in there, Eve? I got the girls ice creams on the way home, I hope you don't mind.'

Eve yells, 'Hello! Of course not, thank you so much! Have a lovely arvo!'

The front door closes.

'Now' – Eve turns to Lake – 'let me look at you.'

And Lake is perfect. Eve has so many regrets, but Lake is not one of them. Look at that face, those eyes, that gorgeous wispy hair!

'Mum,' Lake whines, 'why do you always stare at me like that?'

'Because I love you, sweetheart, you know that! Now, come here and give me a cuddle.'

Lake walks to her mother and climbs onto her lap. She's not yet learnt to be reticent about this. Eve strokes Lake's hair, kisses her scalp.

'What did you learn at school today, munchkin?'

Lake considers the question. 'Well, I got to hold Nibbles during free time. Did you know guinea pigs only have four toes on each front paw?'

'I did not know that sweetheart, how cute!' Nibbles is the class guinea pig and Eve does not find him cute, he makes her uncomfortable, his twitchiness is unnerving. But who is she to deprive her child of such innocent joy?

'And what else, sweetheart? What else went on today?' She changes the subject from the little rat-freak.

'We had to do paintings,' Lake says.

'Oh yeah?' asks Eve. 'And what did my little genius paint?'

'I painted the Twin Towers falling.'

Eve almost chokes. How do kids know about 9/11, and why are they always so obsessed with it? A sudden, vivid memory of Nell in a bowling alley emerges. 'Oh, my darling. Why on earth did you paint that? How did you even know about it? That was a long time ago now, and nothing like that will ever, ever happen to you. You know that right?'

Lake nods serenely. 'Of course I know that, Mum.'

'Okay. So . . . why, sweetie?'

'Well, whenever anyone paints anything sad or violent Mr Haight freaks out and lets them sit in the contemplation corner with a Freddo for the rest of the lesson.'

Eve knows that this is an opportunity for serious parenting, but she can't help it, she laughs.

'Honey, how long have you been painting atrocities in order to get Freddos?' she asks.

Eve shrugs. 'I don't know – a while? Last week I painted Christ on the cross and pretended to cry. I got two Freddos for that.'

'Lake Bowman,' says Eve, 'I am very proud that you came out of my vagina.'

2012

It is Eve's second day at university. After googling how to look even gayer, she's Sharpied *sisters not cis-ters* onto her t-shirt.

The tutorial for Language, Texts and Time is in an old demountable building next to a sandstone one. When she enters the classroom, she's one of the last to arrive. Chairs and desks line the perimeter of the room, like society girls waiting nervously to be asked to dance at a ball. The tutor, a PhD candidate called Gee with blue hair and a Sleater-Kinney t-shirt, sits at the far end of the room, secretly bemoaning the tedium they will be forced to endure over the next term. Their fellow PhD mate Jez was assigned Queer Australasian Literature, and their other friend Mel got Tilda Swinton and Flat Aesthetics, but no, not Gee – they have to teach a bunch of seventeen- and eighteen-year-olds what grammar is. Life is not fair.

Gee does enjoy watching what they all choose to wear, though. It's pretty cute to observe all these mini-adults trying to pick the styles that will work for them, trying to signal to the world how they want to be known. It wasn't so long ago that Gee was like them, they think nostalgically. Dr Reynolds passes the classroom and sticks his head in the door to smile at Gee. They give him a thumbs up, and he walks on, thinking to himself how young Gee is, and trying to count how many hair colours he's seen them try. He misses that urge to experiment; he remembers how he too used to have different versions of himself to offer up, and now he just has this one.

Eve, meanwhile, is so caught up in sitting down without knocking anything over that it takes her a second to clock the two gay boys sitting at the desks opposite her. Their voices are familiar; she is almost certain they are the mysterious feminist queers who sat behind her in yesterday's lecture.

She will be unapologetic and queer and social. She makes eye contact with one of the gays, the beefier one, and gives him a cheeky eyebrow raise. Miraculously, he winks back at her.

Gee opens the class with icebreakers, because this is university policy and also because it is thoughtless work that thankfully takes up a good twenty minutes of the lesson. They direct the students to pair up with the person seated to their right and discuss their lives and loves for five minutes, and then to go around in a circle and use one word to describe the person they've been talking to.

Eve finds this prospect terrifying. She knows what would happen if this game were to be played back at school. No matter what she said, Eve would be described as either a dyke or a freak, the feeling being that the two characterisations were synonymous.

But this is not school. No one knows Eve here. She can be anyone.

She turns to her seatmate, a country girl called Beth who is new to Sydney and is living in one of the residential colleges. Beth is wearing tracksuit pants and boots, and seems scared out of her mind. She's pretty, but in an untampered kind of way. Those college boys will crush her.

Beth and Eve introduce themselves and begin to swap life stories. Eve edits hers, obviously. According to her version, Eve grew up in the city and loves social justice, beer and Courtney Love. This is not technically untrue – she would prefer justice to injustice, Nell taught her enough about Love to demonstrate an obsession, and Eve has tasted beer before and she didn't vomit. As she meets Beth's encouraging smile, Eve begins to speak more vivaciously. She tells Beth about the books she's been reading over the summer, and pretends she came to them herself rather than being totally compelled by the hot bookseller. Beth is impressed, Eve can see it on her face. This is a very new reaction for Eve.

Beth is from Dubbo, and arrived in Sydney the week before last. She's finding university life completely overwhelming, and the girls in her college all seem to know each other from private schools in Sydney but she doesn't really know anyone here. Her parents are both farmers, and she misses her horse. Her favourite musician is Justin Bieber. She has never heard of any of the books Eve has mentioned, but they sound really interesting, she says.

When the five minutes is up and the students go around the room and describe each other, Eve is taken aback. Everyone chooses complimentary adjectives. No one is using this as an opportunity to assert their power over the rest. Even the guy whose face looks like a crater moon has been described as 'friendly'. People are using words like 'kind' or 'smart' or 'funny'. It's a revelation. When it's Eve's turn to describe Beth, she says Beth is 'genuine'. Beth seems thrilled with this. Now Beth goes on to bestow her adjective upon Eve. She chooses 'cool'.

Eve tries not to show it, but she is ecstatic. Her chest feels warm, her cheeks glow. Finding herself in the spotlight in a positive way is a thrill. A line comes rushing out of Eve's mouth, and she directs it to the class at large: 'Look, that's very kind, and I'm flattered, but none of you have seen me lose at Monopoly . . . not so cool then, I'm afraid.' She smirks, but kindly, to show she's speaking in self-deprecating jest. And then another miraculous thing happens: the class laughs with her, including the gay boys.

One of them, the taller one, whose name has now been established as Tae, says, 'You should see Marcus when he lands on a dark blue that someone else owns, the light literally leaves his eyes.'

Marcus punches Tae playfully. 'Aw, shut up, man. You're the one always totally pissed off if someone nabs the thimble token before you.'

'Hey, my pinkie is delicate!' exclaims Tae.

Gee is laughing too, but soon directs the next students to say their words, and the icebreaker goes on. Eve feels, for the first time in ages, that maybe she could be happy here. Maybe she could be a person here. Maybe these boys would actually want to be her friends.

Icebreaker over and they're talking about structuralism again, which is something that Eve has barely got her head around. It's about signs and symbols, yes? But all the readings they've been assigned speak in such abstract terms, Eve is unsure what they're on about. Eve's tenuous grasp of structuralism seems problematic to her because the syllabus tells her that in a few weeks she'll also be tasked with understanding post-structuralism.

Most people's tutorial strategy seems to be paraphrasing what the person before them has just said, usually with a caveat like, 'Speaking to what _____ said,' or, 'Just to expand on that . . .' Eve deftly adapts to this rhetorical style and finds that the tutorial passes quite easily this way, although she has no greater understanding of structuralism than she did forty minutes ago.

When the class ends, Marcus and Tae wait until Eve reaches them at the door.

They've been whispering to each other, and greet Eve with a smile.

Marcus begins. 'So – Eve. You should know that we don't do this a lot, so this is, like, a really huge deal.' He turns to Tae, who picks up where Marcus left off. 'We wanna invite you to have lunch with us every day for the rest of the week!'

Eve bursts out laughing. 'Did you just quote *Mean Girls* at me?'

Tae squeals and claps his hands. 'It was a test! Yay, girl, you passed!'

Marcus ushers them out the door. 'Come on, girls, we're getting a beer.'

Now, the thing Eve has dreamt about for so long comes true. She is being offered friendship by people she thinks are funny. They think she is funny too. And they're *gay*. They are gay and they know she is gay and they are all gay together! It's like a movie but it's her life!

They walk over a footbridge, and the sun is shining, and they are talking together naturally, and Eve imagines what they might look like to the people they pass. They might look like friends, she thinks. They might appear to be carefree youths in the prime of their lives. And maybe, Eve lets herself dream, maybe those things can be true.

They arrive at a dingy pub where many other students are also not studying. At the sticky bar they order a jug and three glasses – Marcus pays, like it's nothing. He tells Eve she can get the next round, which suggests that he thinks there will be another round, which is exhilarating. Eve has never been for drinks with friends before, let alone bought *rounds*. They take a seat at one of the bench tables outside. It's hot and humid in Sydney, and Eve feels blessed by the heavens.

'*So*,' says Tae, 'how long have you been licking the light fantastic?'

Eve swallows her beer quickly. 'Sorry?'

Marcus interprets. 'He means, how long have you been out for?'

'Oh,' stammers Eve, playing with her ring, 'right, of course. I've been out . . . for ages. So long. For sure.'

'Uh-huh.' Tae rolls his eyes. 'Come on, girl, tell us the truth.'

And Eve thinks that maybe she can.

She tries again. 'Well, to be honest, I wasn't out in high school, but everyone made fun of me for being gay, so for ages I was like: they're wrong. But even though they were cunts, they weren't wrong. So now I'm, like, annoyed that a pack of douchebags knew me better than I knew myself?'

'I swear the heteros can sense faggotry a mile away, which honestly seems very gay to me,' says Marcus.

'Right!' Eve exclaims. 'But in terms of being "out"? I don't know; I've never really come out to anyone. I mean, I look like this.' She gestures to herself.

'Yeah, to be honest, if broadcasting your sexuality is your aesthetic goal here, the t-shirt is probably overkill,' says Marcus.

Eve giggles. She's never had a conversation like this before, and it feels like jumping into the ocean on a hot day.

'We think I can tone down the handmade slogan tees?' she asks.

Tae scrunches his nose and presses his thumb to forefinger. 'Just a touch. Your hair is already doing most of the heavy lifting.'

'Okay, noted.' She takes another sip of her beer. It's cold and refreshing. She senses the beginning of another friendship here – with lager. 'So, how do you two know each other?' she asks.

Tae and Marcus look at each other conspiratorially. 'From Paris, baby, Paris,' says Tae.

Marcus laughs. 'And what Tae means by Paris is, we both went to the same shithole high school in the Shire.'

'Yikes,' says Eve. 'How was that?'

'Well,' says Marcus, 'we started secretly dating in year ten, and then in year eleven Tae was caught with his mouth around my dick in the disabled toilet, and after that we were outcasts. So, pretty standard narrative, I think.'

'That's awful,' Eve sympathises. 'I'm sorry that happened to you both.'

'Doesn't sound like it's much worse than what happened to you, pet,' says Marcus.

And Eve supposes that Marcus is right – it's just that she's never had anyone to commiserate about it with before.

'At least you guys got some action, I guess,' offers Eve. 'Are you still together? You're not giving couple vibes, but you're also not *not* giving couple vibes.'

'That's so sweet,' says Marcus, 'but no, we are happily platonic now.'

'Save the occasional suck,' interjects Tae.

'Yeah, save that. But, like, sue us, you know? Proximity is everything in this modern world. *Anyway*, let's go back a beat. Are you telling us that your blatant sapphism has so far acquired you *no* action?'

With other people, Eve might be embarrassed by this question. But Tae and Marcus seem so kind, so genuinely interested in her life. 'Um, I wish I could answer differently, but yeah, so far I've gotten zilch. To be honest, I don't know any other lesbians.'

Marcus and Tae burst out laughing. 'Honey?' says Tae.

'Yes?' says Eve.

'You do.'

'Is that so?' asks Eve. 'Is one of you a . . . a friend of Ellen? Is that offensive? Sorry if it is. I've actually never met a trans lesbian before.'

'Very considerate, but no,' responds Tae. 'We're both cis male gays, as boring as it comes.' He clears his throat. 'What I mean is, babe, look around you. Every second woman on this campus is queer. And we're in the *Arts faculty*. Your next three years are going to be an extended exercise in lesbian speed dating. Like, look here.' Tae directs his gaze through the window of the pub to the bartender who served them. 'That there is a lesbian, Eve, and she was totally checking you out. How did you not notice this?'

Eve blushes. She had not considered the possibility that she was being flirted with.

'How could you tell?' asks Eve.

Marcus cracks his knuckles, clears his throat, ready to deliver a teachable moment.

'Okay, so, first of all' – he raises one finger – 'she had short nails and a carabiner, so we know she's queer.'

Eve laughs but Marcus does not pause.

'Second' – another finger raised – 'she complimented your haircut. And while your hair is short, baby, it's not exactly styled. So she was signalling to you.'

Eve is flabbergasted and disbelieving. 'I really don't think she was,' she says.

Tae looks Eve up and down, like he can see into her. 'Why wouldn't she want to go out with you?'

Eve begins to speak but Tae interrupts.

'Shh! Like, I've only known you for an hour, but from what I can tell, you're cute, you're funny, you're smart: you're a catch. You've got to let go of whatever other bullshit you've been believing, trust me. We've passed through the pearly gates and we're in queer heaven. The deadshits who bullied us in high school have no hold over us now.'

Could it be that simple? Could one just decide to let go of the past? Marcus and Tae seem to have.

When the pub closes, Eve, Tae and Marcus make plans to link back up on Friday, like it's the most obvious thing in the world. As Eve walks home along the brick back lanes of Camperdown and Redfern, the soft yellow glow from the streetlamps makes everything seem poetic. It's like a key has been turned, and Eve's finally been let into the world. There's a strange sensation pulsing in her chest; it's familiar but it's not, it's giving déjà vu. Then it hits her. It reminds Eve of how she felt when Nell first introduced herself, all those years ago. Eve realises that what she is feeling is excitement. She is excited by life.

*

That Friday, the new trio meet back at the same bar, where pints are cheap and chips are salty. They continue ordering jugs and snacking on plates of hot snacks until the sun has well and truly fallen and talk has now turned to *the evening*. What to do with *the evening*? Eve likes the way Marcus and Tae frame it, as if the night ahead is a gift to be unwrapped. Eve finds that after this many beers it is quite easy to orientate one's way of thinking to this perspective. The night is still warm, and since Tuesday, Eve's decided that Sydney has a special way of embracing happy people, it's a city that opens its doors to frivolity and closes them to the morose. Eve is one of the happy people now, why shouldn't she be? She's spent years being sad and alone, and it's time to shrug it off, let that version of her fall like a jacket off the back of a chair. Let it be left at the bar like a forgotten umbrella. It will never rain again! Eve is drunk. 'Let it never rain again!' Eve exclaims. And without skipping a beat, Marcus and Tae yell this back to her, no questions asked. 'Let it never rain again!' they cry.

Tae contends that the only plausible option for *the evening* is Head Hunters, a queer bar in Newtown, just a short walk away. Eve has never been to a queer bar before but tonight seems like a good time to change that. They all have their backpacks with their laptops in them, and this poses a challenge to optimum dancefloor activity, so they decide to stop by Tae and Marcus's place first to drop off their bags.

They stagger drunkenly down King Street, Marcus and Tae dancing around in front of Eve. She begins to move her body with them, and as they pass each new shopfront, Eve is gradually shaking off her corporeal unease. She begins to adjust her body like she is not ashamed of it – an arm wave here, a pirouette there. Before this moment, she's never understood why people claim to find dancing freeing; she has for a long time found that it is the opposite of this, every desire or insecurity thrust into the spotlight in the form of a limb bending, a hip swaying. But now, with friends, she's beginning to get it for the first time since that sleepover with Nell and Naomi, when freedom was immediately followed by self-hatred. Being in a body might be fun, she is realising.

The street is a hive of activity – families eating dinner at tables on the footpath, drunk youths like Eve encountering the world as if for the first time, students from the nearby residential colleges swarming the pavement in matching t-shirts, doing scavenger hunts and grasping for inclusion. Eve smiles happily as she watches one college boy pause to throw up then catch up with his bros to a chorus of exulting cheers. This is the stuff of life.

'So where is your place, anyway?' asks Eve, and Marcus shouts back, 'Just around the corner, babe!' and Eve follows the boys joyously, honoured to be led.

They tumble into a tiny, tiny terrace off the main road. So far the living room is decorated with a couch and a pride flag, and that's it.

'So this is a share house,' muses Eve. It is wonderful. 'I hope it's not rude, but, like, how do you pay for this?'

Tae collapses onto the couch and addresses Eve. 'Well, my sweet, I don't know if you've heard of this because you went to that fancy posh school, but where we come from, to pay for stuff, you get a job.'

Eve laughs.

'That's spelt j-o-b,' adds Marcus.

'Ohhh, I've always wondered about that,' says Eve.

'Right, exactly, so! The thing with a *job*,' continues Tae, 'is you do labour—'

'Mmm, labour, I think I've heard of that?' interjects Eve. She's got this one. 'That's when a woman pushes out a baby so civilisation can continue and then she gets paid less than men for the rest of her life?'

'Ha ha, very good. Feminism. But I'm not done with my explanation – it's very rousing.'

'Let him do it, he loves this bit,' says Marcus fondly.

'Okay, okay,' says Eve. 'Please go on, Tae – I implore you.'

'So! A job is where you do labour and then someone pays you, like, twelve per cent of what that labour is worth, and then you give eighty per cent of that twelve per cent to a landlord who doesn't work, all so you can sleep somewhere that isn't the street before you get up and go to work again, and then the landlord buys a holiday house.' Tae says this all very quickly, almost all in one breath.

'Bravo!' cries Marcus. 'Karl Marx could *never!*'

Tae looks to Eve. 'I mean, I think we all know I'm just reciting what Marcus tells me, he's the reader in this house, but I think I have the charisma, no?'

'*Very* charismatic,' agrees Eve. 'But you're both also at uni full-time, right? So, like, how much is the rent on this place? Surely you must have to work a lot of hours to pay for this. How do you do that and study?'

'Ahh, the secret here, Eve' – Marcus lowers his voice slyly – 'is concrete cancer.'

'Concrete cancer?'

Marcus nods. 'That and potentially asbestos.' He explains: 'So we both work about two full days each. I'm a casual at the uni library, like, shelving and stuff, and—'

'Yeah, he's an expert in that,' says Tae.

'—Tae bartends a few nights a week and personal trains some old ladies at the gym nearby, and with those two jobs, and Youth Allowance obviously, and the fact that this house is riddled with concrete cancer and the owner doesn't want to pay to fix it and the roof is probably going to fall down and kill us in our sleep, we can pretty much cover the rent.'

'That sounds like a great deal,' says Eve.

'It is!' squeals Tae.

'But here's the thing,' adds Marcus, softly, seriously. 'In this house there exists a third bedroom.'

'Is that so?' Eve raises an eyebrow.

'And that third bedroom – despite being tiny and, yes, probably plagued with the building blocks of incurable illness – is as yet unrented.'

'You don't say,' murmurs Eve.

The boys gather close now, sitting either side of Eve on the couch like two angels on her shoulders – or two devils, she isn't sure which yet, but she doesn't care.

'If there were someone that we thought was suitable . . .' says Marcus.

'Someone who could add to the ambiance of the household . . .' says Tae.

'Someone that neither of us would be tempted to fuck, but who would still want to party with us . . .' says Marcus. 'Well, that would be a very enticing prospect.'

'The rent would go down for all of us, of course, but the tenant of the third bedroom would pay even less, because it's essentially a storage closet,' adds Tae.

'So, what do you think of that?' Marcus asks. 'Hypothetically, of course.'

Eve has been taking this all in like a factory worker being told they've won the lottery, though she's been trying not to express just how very keen she is. How can one's life go from nothing to everything over the course of one day?

'Hypothetically,' ventures Eve, 'I would say that sounds like a beneficial set-up for all involved. But – again, hypothetically – what if the potential third party . . . had no job?'

Marcus guffaws, and pats Eve's head like she's an adorable child. 'Well then I reckon she'd have to get one, babe.'

'Uh-huh, of course. Of course.' Eve nods. 'And would you give her some time to work that out?' she asks.

Marcus looks to Tae, who inclines his head.

'We would, yes,' says Marcus.

Tae leans even closer to Eve and stage-whispers in her ear, 'We're talking about you for the room!'

Eve chuckles. 'Yeah, I got that, darling, thank you.' She scruffs up Tae's hair affectionately. He's not the brains of the operation but by goodness he is sweet.

'Alright, enough business!' exclaims Marcus as he rises from the couch. 'We're going to do a shot and then we're gonna get the fuck out of here.'

Marcus lines up three Bunnings promotional mugs on the kitchen bench and pours a generous slug of Sierra into each. They down their drinks, and then they are off, back into the night, for it is only just beginning.

2024

It's Mother's Day morning and Lake is begging Eve for ten dollars to spend at the Mother's Day fete at her school. The P and C has harangued guilty parents into donating gifts for the children to purchase for their mothers – scented candles, tea towels, mugs filled with cheap chocolates and wrapped in cellophane. It's an ingenious process by which mothers are essentially forced to buy their own terrible presents, but the kids love it. Eve remembers how she used to try to buy her own mother presents with her meagre pocket money, and how Emerald would nod politely and then never look at the gift again. Eve used to feel so worthless when this happened, and she does not want Lake to have that same experience. Lake is adamant that five dollars will not enable her to purchase the premium goods, and this is the source of their conflict today. So much of being the parent of a primary school child is battling over small amounts of cash at 8 am at the kitchen table.

'Darling, you know I'd be just as happy – happier, even – if you made me one of your gorgeous cards,' says Eve to her daughter. 'As much as I love tea towels, we have more than enough of them. Wouldn't you prefer we spent our extra five dollars on a treat after school?'

Lake looks at her mother like she is entirely missing the point. 'No, Mum! You don't understand. Five dollars will only get you a dodgy bracelet or, like, a bookmark. You are worth more than a bookmark, Mum.'

Eve laughs. 'Well, that's very sweet, Lakey. But the answer is still no.'

Lake senses an opportunity. She bats her eyelashes and says, 'Well, when we still had Nell, she used to help me make things for you, like macaroni necklaces, paintings, cool stuff. But now she's not here, and you can't help me make your own Mother's Day present, Mum – that would be stupid.'

Eve finds it very hard to say no to her daughter when Lake brings up Nell. But she will not bend, she won't.

'Ten dollars it is.'

Fuck.

2012

It's not very late but Head Hunters is half full, which, for Sydney, is good. Eve, Marcus and Tae stand at the bar and consider their drink options, surveying the territory as they do. It's mostly men – unsurprising – but there are a decent amount of women and non-binary people, too. The dancefloor is in the centre of the room, the bar to one side, and out back is a smoking area for intimate conversations and fingering. The lights sparkle and flash, glitter floats through the air like smoke, the floors are comfortingly sticky – indexical traces of drinks having been sacrificed for dance. Pop music pulsates – music with lyrics, thank goodness. Eve has only ever watched scenes like this on TV. For the second time tonight, she feels like her life is a movie, shining and full of vitality and fun – and she's not even an extra, she's a *protagonist*.

Eve is not really sure what her 'type' is. So far, she has presumed her type is 'woman'. Just the prospect of having a woman in her arms who is not ashamed to be there is still intoxicating for Eve. But standing here, seeing the range on offer, it is enough to make Eve consider that she might have more of a say in the specifics of her desire. Perhaps she can be pickier than just 'woman'? Does she want short woman, tall woman, woman with snapback, woman with nose ring, woman with the most mischievous smile? Oh – woman with the most mischievous smile. Who is *she*?

Woman with mischievous smile is talking with friends in a corner of the room, close to the smoking section. Her friends look cool; they look like they know that it was a queer, sultry summer, the summer they executed the Rosenbergs.

Woman with mischievous smile has tanned skin, long limbs, a peroxide bob, a tattoo of a . . . is that a frog? Eve's heart begins to pump with urgency, perhaps in solidarity with the frog, she doesn't know, she feels very hot all of a sudden. Woman with mischievous smile is laughing with her friends, and what would it be like if she laughed at something Eve said?

Eve looks to Marcus and Tae. She says, 'Would it be weird if I bought that girl a drink? Or is that, like, patriarchal?'

'Ooooh, which one?' asks Tae.

'That one – the one who looks like if Holly Golightly and Kristen Stewart had a baby.' Eve slides her hand behind her ear as if she is stroking her hair and as she does, she points a finger in mischievous smile girl's direction.

'Very smooth,' says Marcus.

'Oh, she's gorgeous,' whispers Tae. 'Very Chanel.'

'Sorry?' asks Eve.

'Oh, it's just what he says when something is good,' Marcus explains. 'Don't think about the class implications too much.'

'Okay, but can I buy her a drink? And if yes, which drink?'

Marcus and Tae contemplate this. They call over the bartender, who is yet another beautiful lesbian in this actual utopia. The bartender has a buzz cut and wears a singlet, so Eve already implicitly trusts anything that may come out of her mouth.

'Hey, Sabrina,' yells Marcus. 'What drink should baby dyke Eve here buy for platinum over there?!'

The music is too loud. 'What?' yells Sabrina.

'Baby! Dyke! Eve! Want! Fuck! Platinum! Which! Drink!' bellows Marcus.

'Ohhh, I see!' Like the seasoned lesbian sherpa she is, Sabrina assesses Eve's vibe. She's not clocked her before, and usually she knows everyone here. She makes a mental note. She leans in close so she can be heard. 'Um, she's been doing pints of lager all night, so I reckon that's a safe bet. You want one too, love?' She directs her question to Eve, and Eve blushes.

'Yes, please. Thank you. And two for my friends here.' Eve considers the paltry amount of funds in her savings account and then decides not to care. 'And one for yourself, too, to thank you for the advice.' Eve smiles; she feels like she could walk on water right now.

'I like this one, boys,' says Sabrina, as she pulls the taps.

The new gang cheers together, and then, buoyed up on adrenaline, animal desire and alcohol, Eve strides towards mischievous smile with two beers in hand. 'See you in a bit,' she yells to her friends over her shoulder.

It all seemed like a very good idea in Eve's mind. She'd waltz up to the girl, offer her the drink, say something suave, and then it would be on. Now, as she stands footsteps away from her intended, her confidence ebbs. How does she do this?

The beautiful girl looks up, catches Eve's gaze. She smiles.

'Hey,' she says.

'Hi,' says Eve. Then she laughs, because she doesn't know what else to do. And the beautiful girl laughs too. It's incredible. The nameless girl's friends politely and silently melt away to let this flirtation unfold unencumbered.

'I saw you looking over here,' the nameless girl says.

Eve falters, berates herself. She's already seeming too keen. How to attenuate this? 'Oh, I wasn't looking over here,' counters Eve. 'I can't look anywhere. I'm blind.' Why did Eve just say that?

'Um, my dad's blind and that's not how blind people look, just saying.'

The beautiful girl's face is unreadable. Eve wants to crawl into a recycling bin and stay there until the council transforms her into something useful, like straws.

'I'm not blind,' says Eve.

The girl's lip curls, amused. 'Neither's my dad.'

'Cool,' responds Eve. She adds hurriedly, 'Not that it's cooler to be not blind than blind. I love . . . blind people.'

'I also love blind people,' says the girl.

Eve tries and fails to suppress a grin. 'Can we start again?' she asks.

'Are you kidding? This is the perfect meet-cute. We're gonna tell our kids about this moment!'

'What will their names be?' Eve is attempting to bite her lip in a flirtatious way but she is worried that it is coming across as auto-carnivorous.

'Annabelle and Clarabelle.'

'They're beautiful,' Eve coos. 'And if we have boys?'

'We won't have boys.'

Eve thinks she is in love.

'I did bring this beer for you,' concedes Eve. 'But first, do you have a name?'

'I do,' says mischievous smile.

'And?' prompts Eve.

'It's Nell.'

Why?! Why must her name be Nell? Eve knows that she should be more evolved than to baulk at someone having the same name as her ex-best friend, but the vibe has shifted. Now all Eve can think about is her Nell. Eve sees Nell's big eyes superimposed on this woman's face. She sees Nell's freckles on this woman's spotless arms. She sees the way Nell used to grimace and roll her eyes upwards whenever she got too excited and tripped over her words, like it was her duty to provide running commentary on herself in case anyone ever thought she was taking herself seriously. She can see Nell laughing at her as she attempts to flirt.

She has two choices. She can abandon this pursuit, blame nerves, and return to Marcus and Tae. Or, she can perform a kind of transfiguration. She can continue talking with this woman, and soon, her hand can be on Nell's thigh. Her lips can be on Nell's lips. She can have what she always wanted, but with a Nell who wants it too, and with a Nell who hasn't destroyed her teenage life.

Eve says, 'That's a gorgeous name. Do you know what it means?'

Nell shifts – a bit nervous maybe, for a second? Or like she's deliberating about telling the truth or not?

'Oh, thank you. That's so nice of you. I always hated it because it rhymes with "smell" and, like, obviously that did not skip the attention of all the kids in my primary school.'

'Fuck, kids are cunts,' Eve says.

'They really are,' Nell agrees. 'But my mum says she chose it because it means "shining light", which . . . that's kind of nice, I guess?'

'That's very nice. I mean, light is literally the most beautiful thing in existence and the reason that anything grows, ever. So, I'd say you got a good one.' Here, Eve shocks herself. She reaches forward and strokes Nell's forearm. What's more, Nell doesn't back away. She moves closer.

'Do you want to have these beers outside?' asks Eve.

'Yeah, I do,' says Nell. She gestures to her friends across the room that she's going out to the smoking area.

Nell and Eve sit outside on a half-broken bench as Nell rolls cigarettes for the two of them. Nell does not have to know that Eve doesn't smoke.

They raise their glasses and they look at each other. It's the moment before the moment. If they keep talking here. If nothing goes spectacularly wrong. Soon enough there will be touch. There will be flesh pressed against flesh. Later, there might even be flesh inside flesh. Eve is salivating.

'You never told me your name, I'm just realising,' says Nell.

'It's Eve.'

'Temptress, hey?'

'Would a temptress do this?' asks Eve, as she leans forward and kisses Nell. (Yes, a temptress would do this.)

The kiss is so soft, so pillowy. It's better than Eve has imagined, and she's imagined a lot. It's slow at first, gentle, and then of course – *of course* – instinct kicks in, and Eve knows exactly what to do, how could she ever have thought that she didn't know? Eve's hand is around Nell's neck, she's grabbing the wisps of hair that curl there, she's pulling them so hard it hurts a little, but Nell likes it, she likes the definitiveness of each grasp, she's moving closer, closer. Nell's hands are around Eve's waist, she's touching her skin, she's feeling Eve's curves and the incline of her spine, and their tongues are in each other's mouths, feeling, caressing, playing a game of – what? It's kind of like dancing? Whatever it is, it's not at all like that time on the beach with Toby, with his washing-machine mouth.

It's nothing like that. This wipes that away. That awful evening has been replaced by this softness, by this tender flesh, by this shared want.

'Get a room, faggots!'

It's Marcus and Tae, who have now entered the smoking area. This is fair, because Eve and Nell are in a public area at a bar and for the past ten minutes have been making out like they're in a hotel room with a mirror on the ceiling.

Eve and Nell draw apart, cracking up, both unsure now what to do with their hands. Eve rolls her eyes at her new friends. Such cock-blockers, they are!

'We had one before you two bowled in here,' replies Eve, and Nell giggles.

'Ignore us!' says Marcus. 'We are but ghosts!'

'Oooooh,' rumbles Tae, helpfully.

Eve drops her voice, looks at Nell. She says, 'Hey, do you want to . . . you know?' She's too nervous to say the actual words.

Nell clarifies. 'Get out of here?'

Eve smiles, relieved. 'Do you . . . ?'

'My place is just around the corner,' offers Nell, reading Eve's mind.

*

It's happening. And yes, this is a random hook-up, Eve has just met this girl, they're both drunk; maybe in another timeline this encounter would exist purely as a funny anecdote. But for Eve, this moment is epoch-making. She doesn't know anything about Nell except her name, the shape of her body and the feel of her lips, and this does not matter, because what is happening now feels weirdly spiritual. Eve doesn't believe in God, but she believes that whatever is occurring right now, in this room, is evidence of magic.

Nell's body is so beautiful, so long and tanned and sure of itself, so different from Eve's own body, and Nell's already naked – how did that happen? – and she's lying back on her bed, she's gesturing to Eve to come join her, and any moment now the two of them will be entwined. Eve's skin is hot, blushed, her white arms are patched with red, as is her chest. Her body is betraying her excitement, but she doesn't mind. She wants Nell to see her want; that's all she's ever wanted. Nell's already dragged off Eve's jeans, her t-shirt, that must have happened when they were kissing, upright, only moments ago – but seconds are stretching like elastics in slow motion, in the best way. And now it's up to Eve to do the rest. She's wearing boy-short undies and a sports bra, and she somehow removes these with deft expertise, like she's undressed in front of a naked woman many times before. Her body is working with her for once, getting rid of extraneous material. Eve's arms are powerful, her thighs are coiled and ready.

And Eve pounces. Something wild, something assertive, some other part of her, comes to the fore, and she's acting on instinct, her body is making the decisions. She straddles Nell and bends down to kiss her, her hands are tracing Nell's collarbones, they're making their way to Nell's nipples, which are so hard already, so acutely aware of what's happening. She's kissing Nell with an urgency that would be embarrassing if Nell weren't kissing her right back with the same intensity. Eve is caressing Nell's breasts like she would want her own to be caressed, she's tracing the curve of their fall, she's circumnavigating Nell's areolae with the lightest touch of her index fingers, and Nell's got goosebumps. Nell is moaning, and it's a fervent sound, Eve cannot believe that these murmurs are the result of what she is doing. Eve is licking Nell's sweat, it's salty and sweet, and Nell is moaning, moaning now, close to begging, for Eve to touch her where she needs to be touched.

Eve's left forearm is on the bed next to Nell's reclining body, she is hovering just above Nell's skin, her own breasts stroking Nell's stomach, and now Eve's right hand is free to explore, to go down. Slowly, her fingertips make the journey, past Nell's belly button, over her hip bones, and then back in again, into the centre, to where it is warm, and oh, she stops there for just a moment, enough to make Nell moan in desperation again, and she smirks at Nell, who bites her lips in frustration, and then, only then, finally, Eve lets her fingers sink into the wet, slick, glorious folds she finds there.

Nell's stomach tenses; she likes this, she likes it a lot. Eve experiments, circling her fingertips around Nell's clit again, and again, and Nell raises her body to try to get Eve to push harder, but Eve won't, she won't do it, not yet. It's only when Nell murmurs, 'Please,' that Eve capitulates, and she presses down hard on the spot she knows holds all the power, and Nell yelps – a new sound, it pierces the reverie, signals a shift.

Eve looks up to Nell, gestures with her chin to Nell's clit. 'Can I?'

'Oh god, yes – please, yes,' replies Nell, who immediately spreads her legs.

Eve rearranges herself so she is kneeling between Nell's knees, and from this angle, she sees perfection. It is a spectacular sight, it is one she will never forget. Nell is not shaved and her pubic hair betrays her natural hair colour, a dark brown. Eve lowers her face, and the smell is intoxicating, it's not like anything she's ever smelt before. Eve didn't know it before, but this is the smell of sex. It smells of want and need and grace; there is grace in the earnestness of this desire.

Eve licks Nell lightly at first, and the response is a shudder. Eve lifts her face to meet Nell's eyes for a moment, and a sticky thread connects her lips to Nell's body. Nell's want is attaching itself to Eve, drawing her back in.

And back in she goes, more forcefully now, her tongue laps and burrows, and starts to make a rhythm, starts to build. Eve's aware of every vibration in Nell's body, every sound, and her tongue races to find the slips of flesh, the grooves that elicit the strongest responses. Up and down, Eve nods her head as she licks, and her mouth has become the most powerful thing on this earth. Something is happening, something has changed, Nell's body is pulsating at a different frequency now, her eyes are glazed over and her mouth is half open, spurting a series of affirmative sounds; she's grasping Eve's short hair, she's pulling for more, *more*, and that's all Eve wants to give her, but not yet. Eve feels it, the moment is so near, Nell is readying herself for release. She's about to—

Eve lifts her tongue from where she's been keeping pressure, and Nell yells, 'No!' Her cry is so sincere, so totally without pretence.

'Okay, okay!' Eve smirks and lowers her lips again. Her tongue makes contact with Nell's clit, and Nell is done for. Her hips buck upwards, her whole body tenses, she gyrates like it's all too much, like the pressure is too intense, but Eve will not relent, she burrows further as Nell rides wave after wave, and when the crashing finally subsides, Eve continues licking, playing with the mess she has created.

Finally, Eve raises her head, rests it on Nell's stomach. Nell is still shaking.

After a minute or two of contented silence, Eve asks Nell if she'd like a glass of water.

'I mean, sure, but it's my house, shouldn't I be the one to get water for you?' says Nell sleepily.

'No worries, back in a tick.'

Eve finds a towel on a chair and wraps it around herself, in case she encounters any housemates in the kitchen. She finds glasses, fills them with water from the tap, and returns to Nell, closes the bedroom door. They are both parched. As Nell sips from her glass, Eve begins to comb through the clothing on the floor, looking for her jeans and her t-shirt. She finds the jeans and begins to pull them on.

Nell clocks this, and is confused. 'Wait, are you going?' she asks.

Eve nods. 'Oh, yeah, I thought I'd better go back to the bar to check in on Marcus and Tae – I kind of just left them there, so . . .'

And why is Eve doing this? Obviously, Eve wants to stay with Nell. She wants to cuddle, she wants to be woken up in the night by Nell eating her out. She wants them to make breakfast together in the morning, and every day after that. She is a cliché, as we all are.

But Nell mustn't know this. Eve can't stay. At least, not tonight. Nell does not know that she's been standing in for another Nell, that when Eve was inside her, she was inside her oldest friend as well as the woman in front of her. Eve is processing a lot in this moment, and she can't do it here. She has now experienced giving someone bliss, and she is high on it. She needs a drink, needs to debrief with her new friends. Is she being cruel, leaving like this, so abruptly? Maybe. But she's also eighteen.

'Give me your phone?' Eve says, and Nell, still perplexed, but accepting the situation, does.

Eve punches in her number, saves herself as a contact ('Eve – Head Hunter'), and throws the phone back to Nell. Eve locates her top, her shoes, dresses herself quickly.

'Text me sometime this week, so we can continue where we left off?' Eve suggests.

'You're a strange woman, Eve,' says Nell. 'But yes, I'll text you. I might even call.'

'Call?!' Eve laughs. 'Who's the strange one now?'

'Piss off, hot stuff,' says Nell. 'I'll talk to you soon.'

And so it is that Eve leaves Nell's house and walks the few blocks back to the bar. It's late but not crazily so. The dancefloor is going off, but Eve can see Marcus and Tae talking with Sabrina the bartender out the back.

When she enters the smoking area, her new friends greet her like a hero. And she really does feel like one.

'Well, well, well,' says Marcus. 'Look what the cat dragged in.'

'No, Marcus, I think in this instance she *is* the cat,' says Tae.

Tae looks at Sabrina, and they pronounce it in unison, like it's been rehearsed, but how could it have been? *'The cat that got the cream!'*

'I can't believe you came back,' says Tae. 'Platinum looked like she wanted to eat you alive.'

'A lady never kisses and tells,' responds Eve.

'Babe, I realise we haven't known you long, but I'm pretty sure you ain't no lady,' says Tae.

Eve feels a bit guilty, because maybe it's disrespectful to Nell; it feels a bit bro-y. But also, is it actually okay? Eve's overheard girls talk about their exploits with males, and no one has ever suggested this was uncouth. Is it different when it's two women? Is there a lesbian code of honour? All she's learnt about this stuff has come from pirated episodes of *The L Word*, round tables on lesbian websites and, like, Radclyffe Hall. She decides to get another dyke's opinion.

'What do you reckon, Sabrina? Is it okay to talk about someone you've just had sex with?'

'I think you just did?' says Sabrina flatly, but then she laughs, to show that she is amused rather than angry.

'Ha ha, fuck. I guess I did, hey?'

'It's okay, darling – the first time I slept with a woman I told pretty much everyone I met for the next month. Not that I know this was your first time . . .' Sabrina pauses, looks Eve over once more, curls her lips, 'Except, it so was, wasn't it?'

Eve blushes, laughs, rolls her eyes at herself. 'It's that obvious?'

Sabrina chuckles. 'Hey, no shame, girl, like I said, I told everyone . . . Except for, like, my parents, obviously, and the teachers at my school, and anyone who might have been homophobic . . . So yeah, actually, when I think about it, I told, like, three people. And one of them outed me. Hmmm, not great odds.'

Instead of appearing sad about this, Sabrina laughs, and the boys laugh with her. Eve is quickly picking up that laughter is the shared language here. Dark, dark laughter.

'Hey, if you can't laugh, you die,' says Sabrina, confirming Eve's hypothesis. 'Anyway,' she continues, 'I think a toast is in order. No one celebrated the first time I tipped the velvet, and they fucking should have, it's the best thing ever. Tequila?'

'Tequila!' the boys sing back.

Sabrina heads inside to get the shots.

Tae gives Eve a shoulder squeeze, 'So, what the hell just happened, girl? Just confirming – you had sex for the first time and then came back to the bar to brag about it?'

Eve blushes, but she cannot deny that this is exactly what she has done.

'Tae?' says Marcus. 'I think we've created a monster.'

'Oh, shush,' responds Tae. 'We've created a queen and you know it.'

Sabrina returns to the smoking area with a bottle of tequila and three shot glasses.

'No lime?' asks Marcus.

'Would you like to pay for your own tequila, Marcus?'

Sabrina pours shots and raises a toast. 'To our new friend Eve,' she says. 'May the road rise to meet you, may the wind be forever at your back, may the pussoir shine warm upon your face.'

'Wow,' says Eve. 'That's really beautiful, thank you.'

'My Dad's Irish,' says Sabrina, as if this explains anything.

They down the shots, and the night takes another turn.

2024

Lake's school is lit up with fairy lights and banners, for it is the most important day of the year, barring the athletics carnival, the swimming carnival, Diversity Day, school photo day, parents' assembly and the Book Week parade. That's right: it's parent–teacher night once more.

Lake has been prepping Eve all week. She says that Mr Haight, her teacher, is out to get her, and that he mispronounces 'croissant' and therefore nothing he says should be taken seriously anyway. 'During dictation tests he pronounces "aich" as "haich",' warns Lake. If Lake was not Eve's daughter, she might find this kind of chat insufferable from a seven-year-old, but as Lake is the fruit of Eve's loins, her commentary is very amusing. Still, Eve tries to reprimand her. 'Lake, you shouldn't talk about your teachers like that,' she says. 'But you're the one who taught me about croissants and haich?' is Lake's rejoinder, to which Eve has no answer.

A few feet from the front gates, Lake runs into Bill, who is trying to smoke a cigarette surreptitiously, an impossible task.

'Well, well, well,' says Eve, 'if it isn't the gay dad giving the queer parents a bad name.'

Bill splutters, 'I – I just – I—'

Eve laughs. 'I'm *joking*, Bill! Don't worry about it – I usually smoke *into* Lake's face as she sleeps.'

Now Bill looks horrified and confused. Eve ignores this.

'And how is Alan going in school, do you think?' Eve asks. 'Do we have a little prodigy on our hands?' She is half facetious and half trying to be a good parent, a responsible member of the school community. 'How is he with one, and two, and such?'

Bill stammers. He never knows where he stands with Eve, but he wants them to be friends, obviously. He is aware that Eve thinks him a simpleton, even though she knows he's a fucking lawyer, but that is not enough for Eve Bowman, queen dyke. If they just talked together as normal people, he thinks, they'd have so much in common. He was outed by his brother at fourteen – he intuits some kind of similar fear in Eve. But every time he's tried to break through, she's closed up like a pair of twenty-year-old thighs in Advanced Pilates.

It's hard being a gay dad in a school full of straight couples and single mums – the straight dads are overfriendly with him, but this friendliness masks a suspicion; is he one of them, or is he more of a mum? So it makes sense, he supposes, that he craves validation from Eve. She has this air of aloofness even as she small-talks and jokes. And what *did* happen to Nell? He really liked her – Nell was the one who humanised Eve to him. He used to watch the pair of them picking up Lake from kindy, and they always looked so simpatico – Nell, the little bird, twitchy but unfailingly polite, and Eve, tall, a bit haughty, but always snorting with laughter at some whispered comment from Nell. The two of them always seemed to be in on a joke that no one else understood.

Bill titters politely. 'He's gotten the hang of "one",' he says.

'Well, good on him,' says Eve. 'I don't think maths will ever be Lake's strong point. She doesn't like it when things don't lend themselves to being stories.'

Eve gestures that she'd like Bill's cigarette, so Bill gives it to her. She takes a big, exaggerated drag, looks at her surroundings, takes in the conversation she is having – small talk about primary school maths. Is this the life she wanted?

'I've been trying to make Lake do long division,' she says, 'but she doesn't know her times tables and neither do I.' Eve pauses, takes another drag. 'Also,' she adds, 'what *is* long division?'

Bill shrugs. Usually he tries to impress Eve, but he doesn't know either. He must have once – maybe?

He decides to try authenticity again. 'Do you sometimes look at Lake and just think – how?' he asks. 'How will you one day be an independent, functioning person, when right now you need *everything* from me?'

Eve considers this. Usually she sees Bill as a kind of sweet simp, a gay wifey, but what he's asking resonates.

'I think that every day,' says Eve.

Bill looks at his phone and realises the time. The pair of them had better hurry in – there's an address by the school principal before their individual ten-minute sessions with the teacher, and while neither of them has any actual interest in hearing the principal speak, it is imperative they do not arrive too late, for fear of being judged by the likes of Maria.

2012

Eve has now been out with Marcus and Tae four nights in a row. A week ago, she'd never had a hangover. Now, she's had . . . four. She's heard the sensation described as a train running through one's head, but this doesn't quite do justice to what is happening to her right now. The pain in her head is sharp, like a blade has been pushed from the back of her skull through the front of her right eye, and now water balloons have been squeezed through the holes and they are expanding, pushing on her brain matter, threatening to drown her. The blinds in the room are closed, but the small amount of light that does creep through is excruciating. She knows she needs water but she predicts that any liquid she consumes will immediately find its way out of her body the same way it goes in. Her stomach is making noises that legitimise this projection. She's got the sweats and her body is shaking. How do people do this?

Eve is lying on a mattress in a tiny room that is not her own. Her clothes are strewn on the floor next to her, as is her backpack, and a glass of water sits next to her pillow. She doesn't remember getting home – or, rather, she doesn't remember getting here, wherever here is. She recalls shots, and more shots, and dancing, and a long conversation with Sabrina in the smoking area, and then another area, maybe a stock room, she thinks with Sabrina too? Where were Marcus and Tae? Did she embarrass herself? She can't recall doing so but it's the not knowing that is terrifying.

Still lying down, she musters the strength to reach for her backpack and drag it towards her. The carabiner clasp, which usually poses no trouble, now seems like an elaborate algorithm only a genius could solve. After a few minutes of trying and failing to click it open, she manages to slip her hand inside the still-closed bag and feel for its contents. Inside are her phone and wallet, thank god. She fishes her phone out and manages to type in the code. The device feels very heavy. It's on twelve per cent battery, and she has received no texts. The previous three nights she somehow made her way back to her own bed. Before now, she's never spent a night away from Emerald's place without explanation. It seems, however, that Emerald does not give a fuck, which is in some ways good and in some ways sad.

She goes on Google Maps to see where she is in the world. The blue dot tells her she is in Newtown, which must mean she is at Tae and Marcus's place. This would be the best option. The worst option would be that she somehow crawled back to Other Nell's place and passed out there in a spare bedroom – or, god, did she hook up with someone else? Is she in another random woman's house right now? But if that's the case, where is the other woman?

She must have totally blacked out. But, ah, that's right – a flash of memory – Sabrina introduced her to Long Island iced teas; she recalls the sickly-sweet taste. She fights the urge to gag.

From outside the room she hears male laughter, which is a promising sign. Slowly, cautiously, she rises from the mattress and proceeds to get her clothes on. This too is an effort of gigantean proportions. Is her t-shirt on inside out? It might be; who cares.

She exits the safe cocoon of the room into a hallway. She follows the voices, and finds herself in Marcus and Tae's lounge room, where the aforementioned gays are sitting on the couch drinking coffee and not looking like they are about to die, which is shocking.

They burst out laughing when they see her: Eve looks as bad as she feels.

Marcus gets up and pats Eve on the shoulder. 'Ohhh, honey! Are you okay? We were worried about you! When we got you to bed last night you kept going on about being stuck in the Hunger Games but the sponsors were only sending you Limonata?'

Eve laughs, and it hurts to laugh. 'Fuuuck,' says Eve. 'How are you guys not wrecked?' The boys giggle.

Tae says, 'Well, first of all, we're piss-fit, which you clearly need to work on.'

Marcus chimes in, 'And second, *we* didn't drink half a bottle of tequila and make out with Sabrina in the stock room . . . at least, I'm pretty sure we didn't.'

'Jesus Christ,' mutters Eve.

'Sab doesn't usually go for baby dykes,' Tae notes. 'I'd be proud if I were you.'

'I, like, *vaguely* remember that, I think?' says Eve. 'Fuck, I didn't, like, vom or anything, did I?'

'You did not! Excellent work, girlie! Plus, you were *networking*.'

'Excuse me?' says Eve.

Tae gawks at her, as if he cannot believe the level of Eve's amnesia. 'Ummm . . . you persuaded Sab to give you a job?'

'I *what?*'

'First shift is tonight, baby girl, six sharp. I'd change into a different outfit, if I were you, but that's just me. Plus I'm pretty sure you were saying you have a tute at midday, which is in' – Tae looks at his phone – 'twenty-seven minutes.'

'Fuck.'

'You said that already,' Tae reminds her. 'But on the bright side, your slutty debauchery last night now means that you can live with us! Yay! Employment!'

And so it happens that Eve moves out of Emerald's place and into the queer share house, and the rest of her life begins.

2024

Having stubbed out Bill's cigarette, Eve is now sitting opposite Mr Haight at his desk, feeling like she is back at school. The walls of the classroom are covered in garish posters and children's art, the lighting is fluorescent and harsh: this is an interrogation room.

'Lake is a smart girl,' her teacher says, 'but she tends to tell white lies. And when she is faced with her own libel, she gets rather defensive and, I'm sorry to say, she becomes quite rude. Is she rude at home at all?'

Right, so no small talk, then. Eve considers the question. Lake is never rude to Eve, really. What is being 'rude' anyway? She can be a tad sharp, sometimes, and she doesn't like being talked down to, but how rude can a seven-year-old be? This man needs to get out more.

'To be honest, Mr Haight, I'm surprised to hear that. Lake's not one for tantrums or curse words, and she plays well with other children. Could you give me an example of Lake's misbehaviour, so I can know what to look out for?'

Mr Haight clears his throat. 'Well, at lunchtime, for instance, Lake generally gathers a cluster of children and tells them they need to "work". She has them all collecting leaves and sticks, and when any of them express displeasure at this forced labour, Lake tells them that they are "not being very Christ-like".' Mr Haight looks very grave, and Eve is doing her very best not to laugh. 'I was on playground duty yesterday, and one of Lake's conscripted workers was crying, so I confronted Lake and asked her what had happened.'

'And what did she say?' prompts Eve, more out of amused curiosity than anything, though she is trying to feign concern.

'She said that the other children happily volunteered to collect the sticks, and that no coercion was involved, and that the child who was crying was only doing so because her cat died over the weekend. I checked – that child's family have never had a cat.' Mr Haight purses his lips. 'I must ask, Ms Bowman: is everything alright at home? Is there any reason Lake might be acting out? Or any reason she might think lying is acceptable?'

Eve contemplates how to respond to this. Is she being accused of teaching her daughter to lie? Is it being insinuated that Lake misbehaves because she is being raised by a single mother, or by a lesbian? Or is Eve projecting?

'Our home life is great, thank you. All is well. Lake is a very happy child.'

'Uh-huh,' Mr Haight responds. 'And can I ask you what you think this painting might be about?' He presents Eve with a sample of her daughter's latest work.

Eve gasps. It's a watercolour painting of a small female child with two women, but one of the women has big crosses over her eyes. Also, they are in a graveyard, next to an empty plot. It is terrifying, and it is clear to Eve that it is supposed to be a depiction of Lake, Eve and Nell, except Nell appears to be deceased. Fuck.

'As you can imagine, this painting is worrying, from my perspective. Could you shed some light on what you think Lake might be trying to express here?' Mr Haight stares Eve down.

Eve laughs anxiously. 'Ah, well, you see, the thing is . . . Lake's other mother left us a couple of years back, which I think you know. It was a hard time for us, but Lake's fine with it now, really. She's remarkably well adjusted.'

Mr Haight looks at Eve like she's an idiot.

'This painting suggests to me that she may not be as well adjusted as she lets on. Considering she painted her other mother dead, that is.'

2012

'Okay, Marcus, do you think you can scavenge some extra bevs from BWS?' asks Eve.

Marcus has moved from shelving books at the library to shelving beers at the grog shop, a change he describes as 'upward mobility'.

Eve is sitting Buddha-like on top of the kitchen table, and though she does not see herself as a queen of organisation, she is living with two eighteen-year-old gay men, so the labour of party-planning falls to her. In ten years these boys will be preparing cheese boards and mixing botanicals, but right now they are still domestically disgusting. They never clean the toilet, they leave dishes in the sink, and the money they earn through their part-time jobs predominantly goes to condoms, lube and off-brand vodka from ALDI. On the other hand, they are both funny and kind, and they have adopted Eve into their little family, for which she is eternally grateful.

Marcus is wearing a tight tank top and army pants, and he is squatting on the floor trying to get his broken iPhone charger to make love to the electricity outlet, so far with little success. He looks up to respond. 'Yeah, I reckon there's some surplus that can be appropriated. It's not like they pay me enough *not* to steal.'

'Good man, good man,' encourages Eve. 'And what about you, Tae, what are you contributing to hedonism?'

Tae is standing by the sink, washing a tomato he just found in the gutter outside the house. He's wearing a Britney t-shirt and basketball shorts which he says are ironic, though both Eve and Marcus have seen him miming hoops before.

'I'm a good Korean boy, I don't fuck with hedonism,' says Tae.

'Okay, but from the sounds of it hedonism fucked you last night,' Eve counters. 'Pretty sure no one this side of the train station could fall asleep because of what you were doing with that boy from the Rose.'

'That was my civic duty,' says Tae. 'My mother taught me to value education. And last night, I educated hard.'

'You educated so hard you earned yourself a post-doc,' Marcus teases.

Eve piles on. 'You educated so hard your middle name is eduroam.'

'I won't have you speaking about . . . Brian? . . . like this.'

Eve laughs. 'You can't remember his name, can you?'

Tae folds his arms defensively. 'It definitely *could* be Brian. But it could also be Chad.'

'Blake?'

'Brent?'

'Kyle?'

'Mike?'

Tae laughs. 'Okay, I get it, he was white. Whatever. Anyway, what was it you were asking before you decided to slut-shame me?'

Eve frowns. 'Ah, yes!' She claps. 'The party.' She addresses them formally now. 'As you both know, this Friday's party is very important.'

'Yes, ma'am.' Marcus salutes.

'Not only will this house be full of hotties for you two sleazeballs to feast upon, *but*, far more crucially, Ella from my gender studies tute is coming, and I intend to get what's Mama's.'

'Jesus, you've been living with us for, what, six months, and already this is how you're speaking?'

'Ha ha,' says Eve. 'I'm serious. Last week I saw Ella at Birdcage making out with a snapback lesbian followed by a little soft butch cutie, so we definitely know she's queer and open. Further, she specifically DM'd me asking for our address, even though it is clearly set out on the Facebook event. *And*, I must add, I need to get back on the horse, because the last girl I hooked up with refused to go down on me, even though I'd just made her come so hard she screamed, because she "isn't really gay". Do you see what I mean? Friday is crucial to my wellbeing and to the equilibrium of the house.'

'Babe, didn't that chick just leave, like, two hours ago?' asks Marcus.

'Exactly. The dry spell has already gone on too long. So' – Eve squints at Tae – 'I'll ask you again: what are you bringing to the party?'

Tae shrugs. 'Ketamine and nangs?'

Eve smiles benevolently. 'That'll do, pig. That'll do.'

*

It's Friday night, 10 pm, and the house is packed. All the queer university factions are in attendance. The Socialist Alternative queers smoke in the backyard, talking impassionedly about Rev. They are drinking longnecks and they are all ostensibly polyamorous, but the uncomfortable tension that crackles between two of the male members would suggest that the ground rules were not adequately established in at least one polycule.

Nearby stand the vegan queers. They share a substantial crossover with the Socialist Alternative crew, and a lot of this crossover involves oral sex. The backyard is the size of two portaloos, so all these people are essentially sardines in the game of life. The vegan queers have varying majors, from gender studies to environmental studies to gender studies, but they are united in a shared hatred of animal cruelty and a shared love of talking about *trauma*. People also spill out onto the street at the front of the house, where milk crates have been gathered for those who would prefer to sit bisexually. (Eve now knows that if she doesn't provide specific seating for the bisexuals, they protest that they are being erased).

Eve and the boys are inside, where they've turned the living room into a temporary dancefloor. The couch has been pushed to one side, and one of Marcus's friends' friends has brought a sound system and speakers. He's making hand motions that would imply he is mixing tracks, but really he is playing Britney's *Blackout* album on repeat. People are swaying and gyrating and trying to move their bodies in ways that show they are sexy but also unbothered. The tenants have sealed off their rooms – they learnt the hard way that bedrooms should not be accessible when all three were vomited in during one of their first house parties.

Eve is filling a cup with some of Marcus's appropriated BWS loot when she turns back to the dancefloor to see that Ella has arrived. It's been months since Eve had her first sapphic experience, and since then she's been working at Head Hunters three nights a week: she is no longer a stranger to queer mating rituals. Since that fateful night, she's slept with Other Nell twice more – and these times, she has let Nell fuck her right back. She's slept with butch dykes, non-binary queers, femmes, futches, trans lesbians . . . anyone who is not a cis male, really. Eve now believes that orgasming at the hands of another is the single best thing experienceable on this planet, very closely followed by the feeling of making another woman or enby orgasm. Eve treats sex as transactional in the best possible way – she sees her body as a tool for giving and receiving pleasure. She does not disrespect the people she sleeps with, but as a rule she doesn't sleep with the same person more than three times. Too messy, too intimate. Women want so much from one another. Eve knows this because so does she, actually.

Ella first caught Eve's eye in a tute, but since then they've been scoping each other out as they are each propelled through the veins of Sydney's various gay bars and events; from Newtown to Marrickville to Redfern, from the Bank to the Vic to the Tit, they are compeers on the road now taken. Ella's high femme energy is almost garish, and Eve loves this. Ella gives such a full character to her femininity; she's red lips, elvish long hair, corset dresses and a smile that says she's laughing with you *and* at you. From queer brunch to Sad Dyke Sundays, Eve and Ella have observed each other, occasionally partaking in banter. Tonight Eve intends to change this. Ella is here, in Eve's house, and Eve is going to seduce her.

Eve makes eye contact with Ella across the crowded room: this could not be going better. Eve nods to the drink in her hand to say, *Would you like one?* Ella smiles and nods, begins to make her way through the throng. She's wearing a high-waisted skirt and a crop top so short that her underboob is showing, and Eve is trying not to hyperventilate with excitement.

'Hey, stranger,' says Ella, as she comes to a halt in front of Eve.

'Ella! Hey!' Eve hands Ella a drink and then takes a swig of her own. 'I'm so glad you could come!'

'I'll be glad if I do come,' replies Ella, deadpan.

Eve almost chokes. Oh, okay, so it's on then. To think, just six months ago Eve would have been terrified of this interaction, and now she feels not only like she knows what's happening, but that she can direct the play right back. Can the world really be this simple, this lovely? You can desire someone, and they can desire you, and then you can have each other.

'Noted,' replies Eve, as she extends her hand to tuck a lock of her hair behind Ella's ear. 'I think we can make that happen.'

Ella is looking at Eve as if she would like to devour her.

Tae is standing a few feet away, flirting with a muscle bro from the water polo scene. Eve catches his eye and points to Ella, then to herself and then in the direction of her bedroom. 'We'll be back in a bit,' she mouths.

She takes Ella's hand – 'Shall we?' – and proceeds to guide her through the crowded living room, back down the packed corridor to her minuscule room by the front door.

As Eve enters the room, Ella steps around her, and suddenly Ella has Eve against the back of her door, and Ella's hands are everywhere, and her mouth is on Eve's mouth, and Eve is quickly transformed into her animal self again, grabbing, scratching, needing. She pushes Ella's arms up over her head and yanks off her top. Ella is not wearing a bra and Eve stalls, just for a moment, in the thrall of the majesty she gets to behold, touch, taste. Ella removes Eve's smock dress in one fell swoop, and Eve is completely naked underneath. Ella pushes Eve back onto her bed and proceeds to eat her out like she's licking the cake batter from the mixing bowl: Eve's legs splayed wide at the end of the bed, Ella's knees getting carpet burn as she kneels at her living shrine, her skirt blooming around her. It's early enough in the night that Eve is not blasted, and she's wanted this for weeks: she comes in under a minute.

Usually she likes to let her paramours play with her after they've made her orgasm, but she's promised Ella her share, and this is Eve's party – she can't disappear for too long. Like a choreographed wrestling match in which nobody gets hurt and everybody wins, Eve sits up and drags Ella onto the bed. She brusquely slides off Ella's skirt, her underwear, and Ella is wet, panting, sweaty on her back. Eve straddles Ella, leans over her face, bites her bottom lip, and feels her way down. Eve's fingers find the slick and they dive right in, and Ella bucks, confirming that yes, this is what she wants. Ella's making whimpering sounds as Eve moves in and out, in and out, intent on finding that beautiful spot where sensitivity becomes transcendence, where force applied is soaked in, building until it cannot contain the energy anymore. Eve's discovered the locus; she knows just what to do. Her fingers curl, just a little, and she gives all of herself to what she does now. Push, pull, push, pull, *push*. And it happens. Ella screams. Ella claws at Eve's back – she can't take anymore. Eve slowly removes her fingers, licks the sweetness that now coats them, kisses Ella on the lips, then straightens.

'Enough?' she asks Ella.

'For now,' says Ella.

And just like that the scene is cut. The two women separate, begin to search around the bed for their clothes.

Dressed, barely, they move to exit the room. Eve opens the door to the corridor, takes Ella's hand again, is about to guide her back to the kitchen for a drink, when she happens to look to her left. Walking up her front steps, about to enter her house, looking at Eve, dumbstruck. Her frizzy hair still untamed, but shorter now: she's as pale as ever, her eyes as wide as ever. She's small, even smaller than

Eve remembers, like the years have built her backwards. She wears a pinafore dress, her skinny, white arms and angular collarbones on show. She's not smiling, she appears terrified. But it's Nell; it's Eve's Nell. Eve's original Nell.

Nell looks to Eve's hand in Ella's. Eve keeps holding on. Seven years of wanting, of betrayal, of lust, of resentment, it all fills Eve's head in an instant. She doesn't know whether she wants to hug Nell or slap her, whether she wants to engage or hide.

Nell hasn't moved forward; she's frozen, it seems. Ella looks to Eve expectantly. What to say? How to say anything? Ella clears her throat.

Eve can walk away, or she can 'yes, and'. It's an improv class and only she has the power to animate it. That's right, this is her house. It's up to her to set the tone. She will try to quash her fear. She looks directly at Nell.

'Hi,' says Eve. 'Are you coming in?'

Nell blinks. 'Hey. Oh, um, yes?'

'Awesome,' says Eve. She drops Ella's hand, looks at her. 'Ella, this is my . . . old friend, Nell. Nell, this Ella.'

'Nice to meet you,' says Ella, and she stretches her lips in an approximation of a smile.

'You too.'

Ella can sense tension but she doesn't know its cause. If she were to guess, she'd say this Nell person must be Eve's ex? Unclear, though, as there's something else here too. The current mood is a far cry from what was going on in Eve's bedroom two minutes ago. Ella decides that whatever is happening here, she doesn't care enough to find out.

'Babe?' she says. 'I'm gonna head back inside and grab a beer. I'll see you in there, yeah?'

'Oh, yeah, sure, of course,' responds Eve.

Ella kisses Eve on the cheek and retreats into the house. Eve is left standing in front of Nell, not knowing how to behave.

'I . . . it's been a while,' says Eve. She is clenching with her whole body; she has that feeling in her stomach like when you realise you've forgotten to do something very important and now you're going to have to face the consequences.

'Yeah, it has. It's good to see you, though. Are you . . . are you well?' asks Nell, desperately patting her pockets, trying to find a cigarette. Christ, she needs a cigarette. She does her manic tight smile with the big eyes, the one she can't control when she's particularly anxious.

'Yeah, I'm very well,' says Eve. 'And you? Are you well?'

Why are they talking to each other like this?

How else are they supposed to talk?

'Yep, I'm well too,' says Nell.

'*Well*, then,' replies Eve. A little smile. A tiny breath of fresh air in the claustrophobic vent of this conversation.

Nell exhales, senses the shift. 'Well, well, well,' she offers.

'Well now,' says Eve.

'Well later, too, of course,' replies Nell.

'Well always, well forever?' says Eve reverently.

Nell nods. 'Amen.'

They both laugh: to themselves, to each other, in spite of each other, or because.

Eve had promised herself that, if she were ever to see Nell again, she'd be honest, say exactly how much Nell hurt her, ask why Nell did what she did. She'd demand answers, she wouldn't let anyone get out unscathed. She'd make Nell feel the hurt she caused. She'd ruin her fucking life.

But now, in this moment, all she feels is: *I've missed you.* She wants her friend back. She swallows her feelings, forcing them down like phlegm when there's nowhere to spit.

'Are you friends with Marcus, or Tae, or . . . ?' asks Eve.

'Oh, neither,' says Nell. 'Is this their party? I'm just here because my housemate invited me. He lent the DJ some amps, I think, so I assume they're friends?'

'Oh, right,' responds Eve. 'And yeah, it is Marcus and Tae's party, yeah.' She pauses. 'And it's my party too . . . because . . . this is my house?'

Nell's face drops. 'Oh shit, for real?' She pushes her hair behind her ear nervously. 'I'm sorry. If I'd known I . . .' Nell stops. It seems like she was going to say that if she'd known she wouldn't have come. She begins again. 'If I'd known, I would have, I don't know, texted you to ask if it was alright that I came?'

'You would have?' Eve raises an eyebrow, unconvinced.

'Yeah, I mean, of course I would have. You still have the same number?'

Eve scoffs at this, hurt rising. 'Yep, the same one since you last texted. So that was probably like, what, five years ago?' She can't help this one jab. She's trying to make it sound friendly, though, like it's all good, we're okay, don't worry about it.

Nell blushes. 'Yeah, probably about that,' she concedes. 'Look,' she says quickly, 'do you want me to go? Because I will if you want me to.'

'I don't want you to go,' says Eve, and she means it.

'You're sure?'

'As ocean laps the sand, I'm shore,' says Eve.

'I'm not going to dignify that with a laugh. That was terrible, Eve, terrible.'

'Ah well, one must live as one can.' Eve laughs. 'Come on, I'll get you a drink.' And she turns, walks confidently down the hall, trusting Nell to follow in her wake. This is Eve's territory, after all. This is her house, these are her people. Nell is the stranger here, Nell is the one who doesn't know anyone. What a strange reversal, what a curious position to be in.

The party is loud, the lounge room dense with bodies. Eve strides over to Tae, who is now in the kitchen making people do jello shots. She glances behind her to see Nell trailing her cautiously, and so she loops her elbow around Nell's arm, brings her into the inner circle. She's about to introduce Nell, then pauses, looking around at the people in her house – all clearly queer, dressed up to the nines, arses out, boobs up, tattoos, tank tops, carabiners – and she wonders: how will Nell react to this? Back in high school, the word 'gay' was an insult. But surely Nell doesn't think like that still. They're adults. Nell's not an idiot. And she's not actually a bigot; that was bourgeois shame, right, or just self-defence? It's too late now, anyway – they're here. What's Nell going to do, run from the gays?

'Tae!' Eve shouts over the music. 'This is Nell! She's an old friend of mine!'

Tae regards Nell, clocks her timidity, her blush, her outfit. She doesn't seem gay, but then again, maybe she is. He's sizing her up, trying to work out what she means to Eve, then looking at Eve, trying to gauge from her expression if this is a genuine, happy introduction or if it is laced with something else. Eve does appear to be a bit frantic, but overall she seems positive. He'll be nice to this girl, if Eve wants him to be, he decides.

'Hello, Nell, gorgeous to meet you! Love that pinafore for you – it's giving Velma realness.' Tae goes in for a hug, and Nell smiles shyly, allows herself to be held. (*This is new*, thinks Eve.)

'You too,' Nell says, unsure but polite.

'Can I get you a jello shot, a beer?'

'Oh, um—'

Eve cuts her off. 'She'll take both, and so will I.'

Nell acquiesces with a nod.

Tae rustles up the goods, then the three of them dip their tongues into gelatinous vodka and swallow.

'So, how do you know the fabulous Eve?' asks Tae.

Nell falters, then whispers, 'Uh, high school.' She looks at Eve guiltily – or is Eve imagining that? She's following Eve's lead. Eve is in control. Nell is the mouse, the plaything.

'God!' exclaims Tae. 'I would have *loved* to have known Evie in high school. Tell me, was she always the same as she is now? Just crazy and smart and ridiculous? I feel like she just would have been, like, *born* fully formed, you know what I mean?'

'Oh my god, Tae, stop it,' chides Eve.

Nell smiles at this. 'Well yeah, actually, she was always all those things. I first met her because she was talking down to a bully about pubic hair? I just thought, *I want to be friends with whoever that is.*'

Tae is cackling, and Eve is taking in this new information, this new version of the story that Nell has never told her before. She has spent so much time imagining how Nell must see her.

'That's our bb!' says Tae. 'And was she just, like, a huge nerd, too? I'm obsessed with how into books this girlie is. It's like, we get it, girl, you can read!'

Nell smiles again, like she's remembering. 'She was always the smartest, that's incontrovertible.'

Eve is caught totally off balance by the flow of this conversation. Are they just going to pretend that they were always friends? That Nell didn't cruelly reject her? And if they are, does Eve want to contribute to this game of pretend? Can the past become irrelevant if no one acknowledges it?

Eve decides that a tete-a-tete is required. She grabs two stubbies. 'I'm just gonna show Nell the majesty that is our back courtyard, and we're gonna catch up a bit. Haven't seen this one for an eternity, have I?'

'For sure!' says Tae. 'See you in a bit, babe, and' – to Nell – 'so cute to meet you, hon.'

Eve directs Nell out back. The bench in the courtyard is taken, but Eve orders that it be vacated and it is. She is the empress here, she is Mother. She takes a seat and pats the space next to her.

Nell sits. She lights a cigarette, offers one to Eve, who declines.

'So, I didn't expect to see you tonight,' says Nell. 'But it's a good surprise – for me, at least.'

'Yep, life's funny like that sometimes,' replies Eve, ignoring the second part of Nell's statement. 'So, are you at uni? Are you working? Are you still living at home?'

'Oh, okay, we're small-talking. I can do that. I'm honestly flattered that the party queen has singled me out for conversation.'

'Sorry, what?' asks Eve. She can't make out Nell's tone. Is Nell being sarcastic? Eve suddenly feels like she's fourteen years old again, sitting in the band room with Nell and Naomi, not sure if she is being made fun of or not.

'I'm being facetious, sorry,' says Nell. 'I just meant, it seems like everyone here is obsessed with you. It's nice. It makes me really happy.'

'It does?' asks Eve. 'How do you mean?'

'I just mean, like . . . argh, we don't, like, have to go into this or whatever, but you deserve . . . you've always deserved . . . to have people love you, and to have fun and be happy, and it's just good to see you getting what you deserve.' Nell is fumbling for words, her body tensed up, like whatever she is saying is physically painful for her to enunciate. Is this because she means what she is saying, or because she doesn't?

'Oh, well, thank you? I don't really know what to say to that.'

'Yeah, that's fair. I . . . I guess, this is weird, sitting here with you, saying this, but . . . I can't really say anything else to you until I say . . . I guess I want to say sorry. Sorry doesn't really cover it. But I am – sorry.'

Eve has wanted Nell to say this for such a long time, but now that she's hearing it, it's harder than she expected. Because sorry might never be enough. And because this girl next to her – Eve feels this intense pull, this need: she wants Nell in her life. Living without her best friend has been shit. She loves Marcus and Tae, she loves her new queer life, but even now, no one else gets her like Nell – well, well, well, indeed.

It feels as though, if this conversation continues in the same vein, however, they're going to get to a really intense place, and Eve might not like what she hears, or it might be too painful. Will Nell present her with some brilliant justification, some secret trauma, some reason she did what she did, and then Eve will have to temper her resentment, even though she is the one who was wronged? Eve doesn't want to hear it. And she's fearful, too, that if they go back that far, she'll say what she didn't say then, which is, 'I was in love with you and you knew that and you destroyed me.' If she says that, well then, she'll have lost her power. And she kind of likes the feeling she has right now: vindicated, and in control. Like Nell's asking for forgiveness and it's up to Eve to give it to her. Eve isn't sure what she wants to give, or give up.

Eve takes a swig of beer.

'It's okay,' she says.

Nell goes to retort, but Eve interrupts her. 'Seriously, it's okay. We were young, school was shit, I'm okay now. All's well that ends well. Don't worry about it.'

'But I want to explain. It's just, back then, everything was so . . . my family was so . . . and I was scared, and I was dealing with my own shit, and I hurt you. And once I cut you off, it just kind of felt like there was no going back, and I thought you wouldn't want me anyway if I tried. It felt like that would have been insulting to you. And then I just did worse and worse things, but even then I could still see you looking at me sometimes like you wanted to help me, like you didn't hate me, and that just made me feel more shit, even less deserving . . .' Nell is looking so much like she wants to be absolved of her sins. Her eyes are begging for Eve to understand, for Eve to understand without her having to say the words.

Eve does not want to deal with this. She's too tipsy, too hurt, too flabbergasted that she's even in this situation. 'Like I said, it's fine.'

'Okay?' says Nell. She doesn't believe Eve but she accepts that this is how Eve wants this conversation to go for now and she will respect her wishes. She will do whatever Eve wants. Nell has spent many years hating herself for what she did. The fact that Eve is even speaking to her is utopic, epic, zeitgeist-shifting. For so long now, Nell's mind has raced and raced in loops, creating a metanarrative, an Urtext for her life. Nell as betrayer, Eve as saviour. She's never let herself imagine that Eve might forgive her, but now! What grace Eve is showing – even more proof of her divinity. The votive image Nell has formed of Eve in her mind glows brighter.

'Yeah, okay,' says Eve. 'So, we'll try again. Are you at uni?'

'Uh-huh, yeah,' confirms Nell, tapping the side of her stubby. 'Yeah, I'm doing Fine Arts.'

'You are?' Eve appears pleased by this. 'You *were* always doodling on something. Do you remember those caricatures we used to do of the boys on the bus?'

'How could I forget?'

'That one guy with the totally spherical head?'

'Spherical Sam!' exclaims Nell. 'And that gross dude who always carried a cotton handkerchief? I swear I still get like, shivers when I think of him putting that mottled snot rag back into his own pocket.'

'Exactly! He clearly never washed it, either, it was just, like, accreting globs. Do you remember he offered it to you once when you sneezed?'

Nell convulses and relaxes, her body easing into this dynamic, remembering its home in the back and forth of her and Eve. 'Of course! And you said . . .'

'If she wanted to rub her face in trash, she'd make out with your dad.'

'A classic line,' says Nell.

'I appreciate that.' Eve smiles. 'So, what kind of art are you doing now? Still important portraiture, or . . . ?'

Nell squirms on the bench. She's not used to being asked questions about herself. Her housemates certainly don't talk like this, like they consider her life to be a serious thing worthy of conversation. Everything is a dark joke to them. Nell's posture is still inverted, hunched, but there's this crackle, this pull, too, she must stop herself from reaching out to touch Eve's hand.

'Yeah, not so much. At the moment it's more, like, anthropomorphic portraits of cigarettes?'

'Are you fucking with me?' asks Eve.

Nell scoff-laughs, but like she's laughing at herself. 'I wish I was, but I'm actually not, lol. I hadn't prepared anything for class one day and so on the bus I just drew, like, a Marlboro trying to water a plant, and my tutor thought it was really incisive and, like, a reference to Dali and capitalism or something, so I just went along with it.'

Eve is shuddering with silent chuckles. 'Uni really is just like that, hey?'

'It is; it really is.' Nell pauses, says more hesitantly, 'I have been working on stuff by myself, though – like, not to show the tutors or whatever, but just because I like it, it's like . . . do you know Tacita Dean?'

'No?'

'Right, so she does these, like, ginormous chalk-on-blackboard pieces, usually of mountains or clouds or other huge natural things, and they kind of look like they might crumble down on you, and you're awed but also a bit frightened when you look at them – or I am, at least – and I thought, what if I did something like that, but with faces?'

'Go on,' says Eve.

'Okay, so, imagine, like, every face you've ever loved, or hated, or that's made some mark on your psyche, people you see when you close your eyes. Well, what if they made a kind of mountain, and maybe it'll crush you, or maybe you'll climb up it, but they're always looming and, like, terrifying?' Nell looks to Eve here, to gauge if Eve is willing to follow her. Eve nods; she is. 'But if you painted them, or drew them or whatever, maybe you'd come to know them better, maybe you'd take some ownership of them – though ownership's not the right word. Maybe, if they were a mountain that you created, you could see them more for what they are rather than the mind's-eye view that haunts you behind your eyelids? Sorry, I'm probably not making any sense.'

'So, like, your own personal Mount Rushmore?' says Eve.

'Yes, Eve, like my own personal Mount Rushmore.' She punches Eve on the shoulder. 'No, bitch, not like that.'

'I'm sorry, I'm sorry, as you were,' says Eve.

'I don't know; I'm not explaining it right. I've been drawing on the walls in my room, and—'

'Whoa, are you okay? That's very *Beautiful Mind*.'

Nell tenses, like she's revealed too much perhaps, or like she didn't stop to anticipate how that would sound. *Does she not have any friends who ask her these questions?* wonders Eve. *Has no one else suggested that drawing on her walls might be a bit weird?*

'No, I'm fine! My share house is, like, haunted or whatever, and the landlord was, like, do whatever you want with it.'

'Sorry, your share house is haunted?'

'Oh, yeah, totally. Very witchy vibes. Definitely murder happened there.' Nell shrugs.

Eve bursts out laughing. She has missed Nell's insanity, although it has certainly intensified. When they were kids, Eve didn't think to question Nell's particular strangeness, she just accepted it. Now she does see that others might find it off-putting, a bit too weird. But no one else in her life says things like this. Eve loves it.

'Definitely murder happened there?' Eve repeats, as if for confirmation.

'Do you really not get murder-y vibes from places?' asks Nell. 'I get them all the time.'

'Hey, you're the artist,' says Eve, holding up her hands in surrender. 'Okay, so you're doing mountain-faces on your walls, you're going to art school . . . you're clearly no longer living with your fam?'

Nell tenses again. 'Ah, no,' she says. 'I moved out, like, literally the day that school finished.'

'I'm sorry,' Eve replies softly. 'I didn't realise it was that bad.'

Nell lights another cigarette, takes a big drag. 'No, don't be sorry. You remember my parents. When I told them I wanted to study art they told me to enjoy being a heroin addict. The only thing I feel guilty about is leaving Chelsea there.'

'Is she still a perfect little blonde angel?' asks Eve.

'Oh, absolutely. But, I don't know, she's pretty funny sometimes, actually. I feel like maybe she understands how terrible they are but she's willing to play the game, take what she can from them, use it to her advantage. I kind of admire that. I just couldn't stay; I'd get so frustrated and, like, angry whenever they said anything problematic, which was all the time. But Chelsea just kind of grits her teeth and wears the Hermès, you know?'

'I mean, I understand what you're saying,' says Eve. 'You can't choose your family, this we both know . . . but it sounds like you're forging your own path – that's very *evolved* of you.'

Nell shrugs. 'I'm not sure about that – I feel more like I'm just swimming in a mire of chaos all the time, but what's new there. Like, I want to make art, but to what end? So rich people like my parents can buy it and then I can afford a life like theirs? Seems pretty pointless to me. It all seems pretty pointless.'

It makes Eve very sad to see Nell caged by her brain like this, unable to imagine a better future. But then, she also feels naive herself for believing so ardently in one – like, she's supposed to be more grown-up than that. Hope is so uncool, but Eve has it. She certainly never imagined that she'd be sitting on a bench at her own queer house party, talking with Nell about art. That's got to be proof that the experience of doom does not preclude the possibility of future goodness.

'Here's what I think,' says Eve. 'I think you can make art without selling out. Why not just start by making it for yourself, like you were saying before? Do it for you.' She hears herself. 'Argh, everything I say to you sounds like a cliché, doesn't it?'

Nell laughs, but kindly. 'Yeah, it does, but I don't mind. When you say them I kind of believe them.'

Eve blushes, changes the subject.

'And who are you living with? Randoms, or friends, or . . .?' *Please don't say Naomi, please don't say Naomi*, Eve thinks.

'Oh, yeah.' Nell knows Eve will not receive this well. 'So . . . Naomi?'

'Uh-huh.' Eve is unsurprised, unimpressed and triggered, but she will not give Naomi the satisfaction of a reaction, even if Naomi isn't here to see her restraint. 'Anyone else?'

'Yeah, and this guy Pat, who's just, like, exactly how you would imagine an eighteen-year-old white male DJ in Sydney.'

'Sounds delightful,' says Eve.

'Mmm . . . it's not,' concedes Nell. 'And you? You're living here, obviously. And studying, I guess?'

'Yeah, exactly. Studying English lit, working at a bar a few nights a week . . . It's good, to be honest. I like my life, which is . . . odd . . . for me.'

Nell grimaces, the guilt flows through her. She doesn't verbally acknowledge it. 'And do you still see Emerald much?'

Eve hesitates. She has not seen much of her mother this year, no. Very, very occasionally, Emerald will call to check up on her, and these conversations usually last about thirty seconds. They saw a film together a few months ago about a feminist who paints men's nails, and Emerald's only takeaway was that she liked the lead actress's outfits.

'No, not much,' Eve says. 'I know she's my mother and I lived with her for my whole life up until this year, but honestly I couldn't tell you that much about her. When people hear I have a single mum they usually imagine I've lived some, like, *Gilmore Girls* fantasy, but it's like – my mum is resentful and that's her main attribute. She's not terrible, but she's just not that nice. She cares about herself more than me, which is fine, it just is what it is. But people don't like to hear a daughter say that about her mother; they get very put out.'

Nell nods emphatically. 'Right?' she says. 'As soon as you describe your parents in, like, un-glowing terms, people immediately go, "Oh, but life's too short not to make amends with your family; family's the most important thing," yada yada.'

'Exactly!' Eve exhales. 'I'm like, maybe *your* family is, and that's cool for you, but leave me out of it.'

'Leave me to my wall paintings and cigarettes!' exclaims Nell.

'Leave me to my twink housemates and my longneck!' says Eve. 'I guess, though – and this is going to sound super cheesy – but I would say that Marcus and Tae kind of feel like my family. Like, we cook meals together, we call each other out on our bullshit, we bring each other treats when we're hungover . . .'

'That sounds really nice,' says Nell.

'Yeah . . . it actually is.'

Nell thinks of what awaits her at home – cigarette smoke in all her clothes, bong water on the floors, an icetray that is never refilled, housemates she doesn't like. This is what she deserves, she thinks. Eve deserves happiness, and Nell deserves an empty icetray.

'And . . .' Nell begins, then stops.

'Yes?'

'That girl you introduced me to before . . . Ella, I think it was? . . . Is she your girlfriend, or . . .?'

Nell is attempting to make it seem like she does not care one way or the other about the answer to this question. Eve cannot access Nell's mind, so she cannot possibly know this.

Eve laughs. The lesbian in the room has been brought up, finally. It's kind of a relief. 'No,' she says, 'not my girlfriend.'

'Oh! Okay,' says Nell – relieved, maybe?

'She's just a girl I had sex with an hour ago.'

'Right, of course,' says Nell. 'Duh.' She fidgets, uncomfortable.

'And you? Any partner on the scene? A boyfriend?'

Nell smiles into her lap. 'No, no boyfriend,' she says.

'Right.'

'Right.'

There is a prolonged silence for the first time since they started talking. Eve looks around the garden. A few people have left. How did that happen? What time is it even? Eve sees through the window, however, that Ella is still here, chatting with Marcus and Tae in the lounge room.

'Okay,' says Eve brusquely. 'I better get back in there and see how Ella's doing. I think she's staying over tonight, so.'

'Yeah, okay, of course,' says Nell. 'Well, I'll probably go, then. But . . .'

'Yeah?'

'Well,' tries Nell, 'would you want to hang out again sometime soon? We could see a movie, or . . .'

Eve tries to hide her smile but can't. 'Yeah,' she says. 'I'd like that a lot.'

All things pivot, all things return, just never in the ways we expect. Some people we think of as satellites – we see them as bit parts in our lives, revolving around us, enriching our story but never quite penetrating our interiority. Some people – this is rarer – some people are our fellow travellers: they're following a path like our own, we see them at rest stops, we share a sausage roll, we compare our routes.

And then some people – usually it's only one other person, actually – some people are us, but not. Like a trick mirror warping one's reflection, turning one into two.

Nell has come back to Eve. Eve has returned to Nell. But neither is as they were. The trick mirror has reversed their roles.

Part Three

2012

It's ten o'clock on Wednesday morning, a few days after the party, and Nell is sitting on her bed, smoking a rollie and scrolling the internet. Her shared apartment is dark and mouldy, with little decoration and lots of garbage on the floor. Her bed, if one were generous enough to call it that, is a mattress sitting atop pilfered wooden pallets. Her bedroom is the lounge room; after everyone else goes to sleep, the room transforms into her private oasis. She plays music and draws and takes pills and it is dark and the darkness is hers. Nell always dreamt of moving out of her parents' house, and she's achieved it now, she's at liberty to be alone. As she told Eve, she lives with Naomi and Naomi's friend Pat. Nell grew tired of Naomi's shit years ago, but since she did what she did, she sees Naomi's company as just deserts. Nell listens to Pat's loud sounds, and takes the drugs Naomi offers. Nell's been smoking weed and taking any drug she can obtain for so long now she's not sure what her brain would be like without them. The last few years of high school were a blur.

But seeing Eve again after so long – and Eve not outright rejecting her – it's reawakened something in Nell. The seed of a feeling; a feeling that seems pure. A feeling not conjured with hallucinogens or dexies or DMT. She's been drafting texts to Eve since Friday, deleting them one after the other. Eve was probably just being polite, classic Eve. There's no way Eve could actually want to be friends with her. But what if, somehow, she does?

No one else is awake yet, which is normal. Nell's the only one going to uni so, unlike Naomi and Pat, she does leave the flat most days. She's never thought of herself as someone who has her life together – she wouldn't want that, anyway – but compared to Pat and Naomi, she is objectively killing it.

Nell doesn't really know how she achieved it, considering she did not really study at all in the final two years of school, but she's gotten into a Bachelor of Fine Arts. Her parents will not pay for her to do any course other than law or medicine, so her HECS debt silently accrues each week. It's only the second semester of her first year of uni, but already Nell owes the government $14,000, and this figure will rise every year that Nell does not settle her loan. Nell is of the belief, however, that debt is not real if you never pay it. She used to try to explain this concept to Ondine and James – the resistant agency of the vandal, the utility of a politics of sabotage for the living indebted – but she's given up. They only ever tell her that once she gets a decent wage she'll stop pretending to be a Marxist.

Nell's parents do not think she is killing it, and they have made this abundantly clear to her. She sees them and Chelsea once every two months at a 'family dinner', always at a different fancy restaurant of their choosing. The silences are hideous, and the words are worse. Nell is throwing away her privilege, she is ruining her life, and most importantly, she is making James and Ondine look bad – but this is always enunciated so cleanly, so coolly. Ondine and James would never raise their voices.

Chelsea can see her parents' point most of the time, but she secretly believes that her sister is pretty cool, in an artsy layabout kind of way. Now Nell's moved out, she and Chelsea even text occasionally, maybe a few times a week, which represents huge progress for their relationship. Their discourse mostly involves observational humour about their parents. Chelsea will text, *mum infuriated w dad because hes lost their symphony tix lol*, and Nell will respond, *is she doing the weird neck clenching thing?* and Chelsea will reply, *ahahaha yes.*

Naomi was out till 4 am last night – she woke Nell up when she arrived home and started making eggs – so it'll be hours before she ventures out into the living room. Nell's not really sure what Pat does with his time, or how he pays rent. He always says he's working on mixes, but whenever Nell goes into his room he's either gaming, masturbating or sleeping. He's usually pretty chill to live with, but when he's high he gets handsy; Nell brought it up once with Naomi, who said it's because he has ADHD and it's not his fault. Nell has heard this excuse from men before.

Nell stubs out her cigarette on the windowsill and goes to the toilet. She's shat before she observes that there is no toilet paper. Under the sink there are six empty rolls. Toilet paper is a constant source of resentment in the apartment. No one ever wants to pay for it. Pat is the worst – when Nell does buy it he hoards it in his room and takes it to the bathroom as required. Naomi promised she'd get some a few days ago, which has clearly not happened. Nell looks around for anything that could be of use. She's only wearing undies and a t-shirt so there are no pockets she can pilfer for old receipts. Arse still over the bowl, she leans forward and grabs an empty roll off the floor. She rips a cardboard curl from its tubular home. This will have to do.

Nell has class in an hour. As usual she has not done her readings but generally she can just bastardise some Foucault and the tutor will leave her alone. After class she has studio time – she spends hours in the studio painting strange figures, drawing over them with black ink in minute detail, scoring the paint with peculiar, obsessive designs over and over and over.

So is Nell happy? Well, no. She's read that the only way to save your life in a compromised world is to take it. When she's manic, she is swayed by this. When she's painting and she's on a roll and the canvas seems to become an extension of her soul, she is less persuaded. Nell thinks then that the only way to save your life in a compromised world might be to *make* it. Her mind exists on a very thin tightrope between these two viewpoints.

She chucks a few tens and some loose change into a calico bag and she's as ready as she'll ever be to exist in the world. She did have a wallet but she lost it. She's lost her house keys so many times now she just keeps a key in a gap in the brick on the outside of her building. She finds herself in strange situations all the time, because she's both disorganised and shyly polite. For example, one time she needed to use the bathroom halfway through a film at the cinema, but she exited through the wrong door and found herself trapped in the emergency stairwell. Her phone was out of battery, so she stood at the locked door and knocked very softly three times – she didn't want to inconvenience the other movie-goers. No one heard her, obviously. Eventually she got out when a maintenance person used the stairwell some hours later.

She steps out onto the busy street. She'll take her chances with the world again, even though it doesn't seem to favour her. It's another day, and there'll be one tomorrow, too. She drafts another text to Eve.

*

Exactly one week after the party, Eve receives a text from Nell, asking if she'd like to hang out. Yes, Eve would like to hang out, even though she is very much preoccupied by decoding the position she finds herself in now. What was her demeanour at the party? It's hard to recall; she was overwhelmed. She thinks she acted blasé, she's pretty sure she would have appeared chill. She's basically decided that if – when – she sees Nell again, her attitude is going to be cool, unaffected – not towards Nell, but about her lifestyle choices. She's going to make it appear that her being gay is not a big deal to her, that this is just the way her life has worked out, that she sees her sexual partners as lovely and amusing, like nothing affects her but pleasure. Like it was not something she suffered over in silence for years, like it's not the part of her that's made her. She wonders if Nell will buy this, but why shouldn't she? Nell hasn't known her properly since she was in her early teen years. Can someone who knew all of you when you were thirteen somehow jump forward and know if you're lying at eighteen?

Where does Nell want to go, what does Nell want to do? Eve asks. Eve doesn't want to be the one to suggest things; she intends to gauge from Nell's responses where they're at.

Nell pushes back. What does Eve want to do, where does Eve want to go?

Will Eve force Nell out of her comfort zone, or keep her in it? Will she signpost nostalgia, will she barrage into new territory? A French film, breakfast in a cafe, a stroll in the park? Her own house was too personal, too revealing. Besides, Nell's already been to her house. Nell's place – not yet. Eve is not at all ready to encounter Naomi.

Ten-pin bowling, Eve suggests, like they are children, or naughty teenagers. They *are* naughty teenagers. Nell, to her credit, accepts. Eve does not know that Nell will agree to anything Eve wants.

The ten-pin bowling place Eve chooses is in an entertainment park, the kind of place the two of them might have come to years ago for childhood birthday parties. It's a Saturday, and the fake cobblestone streets are being trod mostly by tired parents carting around their sugar-fuelled kids. Slushies and ice creams and soggy hot chips, these are the days of our lives. There's a cinema in the complex too, and a dodgem car rink: this is where divorced dads bring their children on the weekend.

Eve doesn't know why this is what she suggested for her and Nell's first intentional reunion – she could have chosen somewhere cool, a hip bar with fifteen-dollar cocktails, waiters who say they 'do things a little differently here', or an art exhibition where nothing makes sense and everyone working there hates you. On the bus she psychoanalyses herself. By re-friending Nell, is she regressing into her childhood self, playing at children's games? Or does she want to infuse this meeting with a sense of time having passed – Eve and Nell, two adults at a place for infants?

She's wearing an ostentatiously queer outfit – baggy cargo pants, a crop top and a carabiner. She had to borrow the pants from Tae. She climbs the stairs to the bowling alley and finds Nell already there, sitting on a bench opposite the front desk, looking anxious. Nell wears light pink overalls over a tight black skivvy, her arms look like pickup sticks. Speakers blare pop covers and children scream. The smell of dagwood dogs permeates the air.

Spotting Eve, Nell immediately stands up, like an old-fashioned man greeting a woman in a restaurant in a black-and-white film. They exchange hellos, and Nell goes in for a hug. Eve experiences a kind of déjà vu – Nell's smell is the same as it ever was, musky with a hint of Dove deodorant. Nell is skinny and small, but her grip has strength to it. She's all angles, bone and skin. Eve blushes, more in the anticipation of feeling desire than in the actual feeling of it, which she is surprised to note.

'So, are you ready to do this thing?' asks Eve.

Nell laughs self-consciously. 'Not at all, but I'll try. Do you . . . come here often?'

Now it's Eve's turn to laugh. 'Um . . . no. I actually have no idea why I picked this place? It literally just popped into my head when we were deciding about where to go. What do you think that says?'

'Arrested development?' suggests Nell.

'Um, ouch?!' replies Eve.

'But you're joking, right?' asks Nell. She looks at Eve with both confusion and knowingness.

'What do you mean?'

'Eve, your thirteenth birthday party was here.'

'Wait, seriously?' Eve is thrown. She's never had a birthday party here, has she?

'Very seriously,' says Nell. 'You don't remember? Emerald was being an absolute psycho that day. She kept complaining about how much everything cost and telling the kids to ask their parents for money to reimburse her, and she refused to pay for the birthday cake party pack, and you spent like an hour of the party in the bathroom crying. I had to go in and convince you to come back out again – you were a mess. You really don't remember?'

Images are returning – Eve red, overwhelmed, embarrassed; Emerald loud, pissed off, wearing a tight dress and heels, flirting with the dads.

Eve laughs with the shock of recognition. 'Oh my god,' she says. 'I really didn't remember until you just said that. Jesus.'

'Yeah, I kind of assumed that's why you chose the place,' says Nell.

'Honestly, you always did remember my life better than me,' Eve reflects. 'I feel like my memory has so many blank spaces in it, like I just forget things as soon as they happen – you were never like that.'

'I remembered things when they were about you,' Nell corrects her.

Eve blushes again, deflects. 'Alright, well, we're here now, traumatic backstory and all – sorry, I don't know what's up with that – so let's, like, get some shoes and buy a game?'

They both look ridiculous in the rented black-and-red bowling shoes, and this ruptures the tension somewhat. Eve's feet are massive, and Nell rightfully compares her to Sideshow Bob. Eve says Nell looks like an off-duty nurse.

They talk about meaningless things as they acclimatise to their new bowling home. Bags draped on pleather benches, they each choose a favourite ball from the machine. Nell goes for a plain black with sparkles, Eve goes for the gaudy tie-dye.

'What do you reckon that machine thingy's called?' asks Eve.

Nell considers the question with the gravity it deserves. 'Hmm . . . a ball boomerang?'

Eve laughs. 'Yes, because ten-pin bowling is famously an Aboriginal invention.'

Nell shrugs. 'I don't know, white people steal words all the time. I feel like the inventors of the mechanical bowling alley could have appropriated "boomerang" for sure.'

'But where did bowling even start?' wonders Eve. 'I'm feeling it's either, like, a Gaelic thing or just super, super American.'

'I love that you think it's Gaelic.' Nell smiles. 'Like, Boudicca was pausing on her way to pillage Londinium because she wanted to knock some pins?'

Eve stands up from the bench she's been sitting on, huffing in mock rage. 'You know what?' she says. 'I'm going to go ask the counter guy right now what this machine is called.' She storms off, wondering if Nell is looking at her bum.

Nell sits at the bench, fondling her ball, wondering how it is that she could not talk to her best friend for five years and now be ten-pin bowling with her. Nell thinks she is a petty person – she does not forgive wrongs easily – so it really doesn't make sense to her that Eve would want to hang out with her. She keeps readying herself for Eve to pause the conversation and berate her. She's waiting for the other bowling shoe to drop, so to speak.

Eve returns, clearly disappointed with whatever answer she's received.

'Is everything okay?' asks Nell.

Eve pouts. 'According to the guy at the desk, the machine is called "ten-pin ball return system".' She sits down. 'It's just such a boring name,' she laments. 'I'm upset by it, I don't know. I hate it. Like – inventors, be better.'

Nell is amused but is doing her best to camouflage her amusement and act supportive. She sits down next to Eve, pats her on the shoulder. 'Oh, Eve, I'm sorry.'

'Thank you,' Eve says. Then she bursts out laughing. 'Alright, bitch, let's go.'

The manager won't let them put the children's guard rails up, so almost all their balls find their way to the gutters rather than the pins. It doesn't matter – the activity gives them licence to speak freely, absent-mindedly, their disconnected observations somehow in harmony with the rhythm of the rolls, the return of the balls, the celebration sound of the screen when one of them manages to knock something down.

It's Eve's turn to bowl. She stands up, looks to Nell, finds her ball, begins to finger it slowly, dramatically, in and out, in and out. 'Is this sexy?' she asks.

Nell does, in fact, find this sexy. She can't help but find everything about Eve sexy. This is a problem. To distract from the pulsing in her groin, she snickers. 'Have you even thought about how many snotty fingers have been in there? Like, the amount of human gunk that has accreted in those holes?'

'Luckily, I love gunk in my holes.'

'That's disgusting, Eve,' deadpans Nell. She needs to change the subject. This is not safe territory, even in jest.

The lane next to them has been filling up with screaming children and their adults. There are balloons, there is bunting, there are parents looking like they want to die: this is a birthday party. The kids are around six or seven, if Eve had to guess, and the parents are a mixture of men and women – but mostly women. The few men stand in a huddle, drinking beer from plastic cups and avoiding eye contact with their wives, while the women deal with the children; wipe noses, clean spills, comfort the children who are crying, which is at least two of them at any one time.

'Do you think those parents are happy?' Eve asks Nell.

Nell looks at the bleary-eyed adults. She's not sure what answer Eve wants.

'I mean, happy is not the first word that comes to mind,' she says. 'Tired? Yes. Happy? Who knows? How can you tell if someone is happy, anyway?'

Eve bowls another open frame and yells in frustration. 'Can you tell I'm not happy?'

'Mmm, I'd describe you more as distraught right now,' says Nell. 'But yeah, how can you tell if someone's happy? That's a hard one.

I think it's much easier to tell if someone's *unhappy*. Whenever anyone looks, like, deliriously happy – big smile, no worries, et cetera – I tend to assume they're just stupid.'

'Ouch,' says Eve. 'Age has wearied you, Nell, made you cold to the joys of the world.'

Nell focuses on the parents again. 'This sounds like a very basic assessment, but I feel like all those parents would be happier if they, like, wanted to be here? Like, what are those dads even doing here? They all look like they've been dragged here under duress.'

'Dads always look like that, though,' says Eve. She goes on. 'Do you think all those couples just got to a certain age and, like, they'd seen every TV show, they'd tried rock-climbing, their fridge was full of pickles and they'd run out of things to talk about and they were like: what do we do now? And the logical option, because they'd seen everyone else do it, was to have kids?' she asks.

'I think that's the standard arc, yes,' confirms Nell.

Eve sighs. 'That's so shit.'

'You have such a way with words,' says Nell.

'Ha ha,' says Eve. 'But for real. Having a kid is, like, the most life-changing thing you can do. I'm not saying that in, like, "a woman's place is in the home" way, but it really does alter every single minute of your life, right? You're no longer free, you're tethered to this being you have to care for all the time, and if you don't give them enough love or stability or whatever, then they get fucked up and pass that fucked-up-ness on to their children, and that's how we wind up with, like, Justin Bieber.' Eve is getting worked up now. 'And straight people just reproduce, and reproduce, with very little thought given to whether they would actually be beneficial to the development of a new human being. Like, literally, they just raw dog and then they have a person to take care of forever and we're all pretending like that's okay? I don't think that's okay.'

Eve and Nell study the parents once more. The mothers are attempting to establish some semblance of calm and order, but a little blonde girl is yelling that Jake stole her ball and, therefore, must be responsible for 9/11. 'Jake blew up the Twin Towers!' she yells.

'Emma, darling, Jake did not blow up the Twin Towers,' chides a mother at her wits' end.

'He did! He did! I saw him do it!' yells Emma, as she stomps her feet.

'A little help here, Graham?' the mother calls to her husband, but he is engaged in masculine discourse with the other dads.

'Graham and Jeff and Bob and Luke over there do not deserve the privilege of raising children,' says Eve.

'Is it a privilege, though?' asks Nell. 'Is it not more like a punish?'

'Depends how you look at it, I guess, but I see it as the biggest privilege of all. And it annoys me when I see parents who don't give a shit, treat it like a chore,' says Eve.

Nell nods, understanding the source of Eve's anger. 'I get that, I do. It's just . . . is it possible that your bitterness isn't directed towards these parents but actually just towards your own?'

'No,' says Eve. 'I am fully self-realised and not at all navel-gazing and I am speaking purely objectively.' She pauses. 'Also, fuck Emerald.'

Nell laughs. 'You are maturity personified.'

She stands up and proceeds to bowl a perfect strike.

'That was hot,' concedes Eve.

Nell blushes and goes to the bathroom before Eve can see the effect the compliment has had on her cheeks.

When Nell returns, Eve says, 'Is it a straight thing, do you think?'

'What, genocide? Absolutely.'

Eve laughs. 'Well yes, that, obviously, but no – I meant, like, resenting parenthood.'

Nell sighs. 'Look, I don't know that I'm the best person to answer that, as I don't know any gay parents. But I would assume resenting parenthood is not limited to straight people.'

'But do you think it could be different if you decided to make it different?' Eve is clearly fixated on this.

Nell narrows her eyes. 'How do you mean?'

'Like, if you decided from the get-go to very consciously have a child, and raise that child not with a mother and a father and a mortgage, but with, like, a community, or with a friend, or in some different set-up where the roles are less established, and there's a chance that resentment won't immediately fester and turn the parents into zombies who don't even like each other anymore?' Eve takes a breath, as she's been speaking very fast. This idea, it's been playing in her head since she was a teen. She assumed she would grow out of it, but she hasn't. The last time she voiced it was to Nell. And it's only with Nell, now, that she feels the need to bring it up again. Curious.

Nell holds up her hand. 'First of all,' she says, 'I think we should acknowledge that there probably are some straight couples in the world who have children and are happy about it. I know it sounds crazy, but for argument's sake, let's just say.'

'Okay, for argument's sake, I'll allow that there might be, like, five of those couples. But generally speaking – no. Come on, think of your own parents, think of Ondine and James.' Eve wonders whether she's getting too personal now, digging in too deep so early in her and Nell's rapprochement, but it's too late now.

'I'd prefer not to think of them, to be honest,' says Nell.

'Come on, face it: do you think they should have had children? Like, I'm glad that you exist, but those are two people who probably should not have procreated, right?'

Nell's eyes widen. 'You're glad that I exist?'

Eve smiles, taken aback by the effect she seems to have on Nell, just getting used to it, the control she somehow has now.

Eve pats Nell on the shoulder. 'Yes, you numpkin. I'm glad that you exist.'

2024

Eve and Lake are at the park. The markets are on, it's a Saturday morning, and it is extremely hot. It's a sweat-dripping-from-under-your-boobs-before-you've-even-left-the-house kind of hot. Lake is wearing a cap, a pair of baseball shorts and a t-shirt with a stylised photograph of Kesha on it, and she is contentedly licking a gelato next to the playground entrance. Her favourite flavour is lemon, always has been.

Thankfully, they've now worked through Lake's phase of refusing to wear underpants. Between the ages of two and five, every morning it was a struggle, every morning there were tantrums. No matter how much Eve begged, pleaded, insisted, bargained, Lake would not put on her own undies for Eve, though she would sometimes do it for Nell. Nell and Lake had a shorthand Eve couldn't fathom.

When Nell left, Eve supposed that Lake's rage spirals would get worse, that she'd refuse to wear socks as well as underwear. But this didn't happen. It was like Lake knew, somehow, that Eve couldn't bear it. Kids are like this: they test you and they test you, they make life hell until you think you're going to break, you can't do it anymore, you're going to give up – and then they change entirely.

Lake was five when Nell left. The very next morning, she dressed herself for the first time. The next day, she did it again.

Since Lake was born, Eve's queer community rallied – they toasted to Lake at queer bingo, they knitted onesies, they brought wine and food to the house. They chipped in with babysitting, they painted Lake's baby nails. But the reality was that none of the other queers in their group had children. When the party was over, everyone else had work to go to, uni to attend. But being a parent is a twenty-four seven job: when the party was over, Lake still existed. And so Eve and Lake would go to the park.

Here at the park, Lake rules over her own kingdom. The neighbourhood kids are her followers. She has been playing with them since she was a baby, when Eve would spend each day perambulating around the greenery with Lake strapped to her chest, desperate to connect with the other mothers making the same pilgrimage. Eve has watched these children grow up. She's attended their birthday parties, she's seen them transform from personality-less crying machines into little humans with minds and wants of their own. Eve feels great affection for each of them, even for 'Mean Louis', a boy whose main priority has always been pushing over whatever or whomever is standing in front of him.

Most of the kids are accompanied by one parent, almost always a mum. The mums sit on the benches that circle the park, guarding the strollers, the snacks, the water bottles. They make vague conversation with each other, half-listening as they keep one eye on their child.

'Incredible climbing, Sophia! . . . What was that? Oh, yes, I've heard that kiddie tennis enrolments are down.'

'Leave Jaygo alone, Boris, he doesn't want to hold your spider toy! . . . Oh, I'm sorry, yes, no, yes, we've signed Jaygo up for swim school this term. Is Clarissa going too? . . . Oh, lovely, they're such good friends.'

'Henry! *Careful* on the monkey bars, you'll break a leg! . . . Huh, is that *so*? I never picked him for the cheating type, but then again, you can never tell . . . Henry! *Enough!*'

All these ways we are split, when we become mothers. We are doubled and we are halved. Eve could not have understood this before she had Lake; indeed, she's still grappling with it now. If she'd understood what it entailed, would she have done it? There's no way to know: she's in it forever.

Nell used to come to the park every Saturday with Eve and Lake. Eve and Nell used to pick Lake up from school together. Bath time was all three of them. They were a unit, a well-established troupe. Then Eve messed with the line-up.

In Nell's absence, Eve feels as though part of her is missing. And in Lake's presence, Eve also feels that she is the very stuff that makes the world; she is Lake's everything. But she does not deserve to be.

Lake finishes her gelato. Eve digs into her backpack and procures a wet wipe, sponges the sticky residue from her child's fingers and face, sends her back into the fray. Eve watches the crowd across the playground, the ebbs and flows of the market; she smiles at the flower stall woman, who does not smile back. For a second, she thinks she sees Nell's mother, Ondine. She hasn't spoken to Ondine since that awful morning two years ago: Eve calling everyone Nell knew, begging them to tell her where Nell had gone. Getting Ondine at work – the brusqueness of her response, the indignation she clearly felt at being assailed in this way. No evident concern that her daughter had seemingly disappeared without a trace, only irritation at the melodrama of the situation and the suggestion that she might be implicated in it. 'Do not call me again,' Ondine had said, and Eve hadn't.

This woman Eve now sees – crushed silks, resin bangles – it could be Ondine, or it could be any other wealthy woman in her sixties. Anger, embarrassment, rage, sadness, all these feelings evoked by the sight of a silhouette. Eve sees ghosts everywhere. She's learnt, you see, that most ghosts aren't dead. Most ghosts look just like you and just like me.

2012

It's two months into Nell and Eve's rekindled friendship, and Nell now spends more time at Eve's place than she does at her own. The vibe at Eve's place is so warm, and Tae and Marcus are so kind, and they all do such wholesome things together – wholesome things supplemented with alcohol, party drugs and weed, obviously, but still. Nell, however, has stopped taking so many substances. She has a new drug, and it's Eve. Most afternoons after classes, Nell brings a few blank canvases to the share house, and the four of them will sit around in the tiny backyard drinking cheap wine and painting each other, before one or all of them have to go to work. Only Nell's portraits are any good, of course, but the quality of the work is beside the point. It's the conversation that flows so naturally between them, it's watching Marcus absent-mindedly stroke Tae's hair, it's seeing Eve make a cup of tea for Marcus. It's the way that Nell feels here – like she's part of a group where people actually want nice things for each other. Eve, Marcus and Tae seem to genuinely believe that the present is good, and that the future will be good also. They all have dreams – Eve wants to write novels, Marcus wants to design house interiors, Tae wants to be the Anna Wintour of Australian fashion, or at least the Patsy. They're all earnestly invested in their projects, in the dynamics of the queer social water polo team they occasionally play in, in pop culture trivia night at Head Hunters. Nell is still technically the interloper, in that this is not her house, but her connection to Eve gives her special dispensation – she's an honorary household member, and she feels privileged.

Yes, there is still that one thing Nell wants that she does not dare ask for. Still the feeling in her stomach every time Eve sits next to her and their arms brush. Or when Eve changes outfits in front of Nell, parading her beautiful body, as if she is saying, *You can't have this.* Eve's tall, muscular body, which hides curves, secret softness. The glint in Eve's eyes when she tells a joke that she thinks is very funny. The way Eve looks at Nell: like Nell matters. Is it really possible that Eve does not know the effect she has on Nell – the effect she's always had?

Eve regales Tae and Marcus and Nell with tales of her hook-ups, with anecdotes about women she's fucked in the storeroom at the bar, and they all laugh, except . . . do they notice that Nell laughs less? That she must force herself to look amused? Nell's sensed that maybe Tae, of all people, has started to notice. She once caught him surreptitiously side-eyeing her as she stared at Eve's clavicle just a little too long for it to be totally platonic. He's never said anything, and considering his general lack of discretion, Nell is very grateful for this. It is the desire that cannot be voiced. Nell does not deserve Eve's love like that, no.

Nell, Eve and Marcus sit on the couch in the living room, while Tae sits on the floor, between Marcus's knees. It's a balmy Wednesday night and none of them have work. Tae's mum Hana is on the phone – she calls Tae most days, and when he's with the housemates, he puts her on speaker. Her calming, maternal voice undulates into the room from Tae's iPhone. Nell, Eve and Marcus each take it in, the sound of a mother asking about their lives and listening to the answers.

'And how about you, Marky?' Hana asks. 'You still the smartest boy in your year?'

Marcus laughs, clearly pleased. "Hana, you flatter me! But yes, yes I am!'

'That's my boy,' says Hana. 'I always tell Tae, you must keep that *baekin* around, he'll teach you how to use your brain and not just your abs.'

'Mum!' whines Tae.

'What? It's true!' says Hana with a laugh. 'And how are the ladies of the house? Eve, how are your studies? Tae said you were finding one of your subjects a bit tricky, yes?'

Tae looks at Eve, shrugs and mouths, 'Sorry.'

Eve sighs. 'Yes.'

'What is it that's so hard?' Hana asks kindly.

'It's just that – I don't know – sometimes I'm not sure if I'm smart enough to, like, fully *get* some of the theorists we're reading. I keep having to translate texts into a dummy version for myself. And everyone else seems to know what's going on.'

'I'll tell you a secret, Eve,' says Hana. 'No one understands without effort. And if you're doing the work of translation, you're almost certainly doing more than everyone else in your class. Trust me, from someone who knows – translation is knowledge. You'll be okay, sweetheart. Keep translating.'

Eve blinks back a tear. 'Thank you, Hana,' she says softly.

And Hana goes on to quiz the others about their lives, make thoughtful suggestions, give praise. At the call's end, Tae says, 'Bye, Mama!' and without thinking the other three copy him, chorusing, 'Bye, Mama!'

And Hana laughs and says, 'Bye, children!'

When the line is dead, Eve asks Tae, as she regularly does, 'How the fuck is your mum so *nice*?'

Tae shrugs. 'Beats me,' he says. But he doesn't want to dwell on the topic – Marcus inevitably gets upset, thinking of his own parents, and then so does Eve, and Nell goes quiet. Tae changes the subject. 'Let's rewatch *Gossip Girl*,' he suggests.

And soon enough the housemates are a joint in, immersed in the lives of the wealthy adolescents of Manhattan's Upper East Side.

'I never get why they show so much of the parents in this,' says Tae. 'Like, who is interested in whether Lily and Rufus get together? Why do teen shows always think we care about the old people?'

Marcus laughs. 'I'm pretty sure they're, like, forty.'

'That's what I mean,' Tae declares, taking a long drag. 'They're ancient.'

'The old people are where the drama lies,' counters Nell. 'Like, the vendettas Blair and Serena have are all comparatively fresh, they haven't had decades to fester in resentments and feuds, to feel like every interaction is picking the scab of an old wound . . . this is why *Housewives* is so compelling. It's, like, anthropology.' She looks to Eve to back her up – their old dynamic is resurfacing, the 'yes, and' of it all.

'Exactly,' says Eve. 'Lily is what Serena will become – it's a Faustian warning.' Eve has recently learnt the word 'Faustian' and now uses it incorrectly at least once a day. 'All this yearning and switching romantic partners and cheating and lying, it all just ends up with you doing the same thing on a higher economic scale later on. If you start your life seeing relationships as games, that's how they will continue to play out, and Josh Schwartz is warning us. He's like, all you win is a Prada Marfa print – is it really worth it?'

Marcus bursts out laughing. 'You think that's Josh Schwartz's message to us? I think you may have too much faith in the Schwartzer, babe. I think he's more saying, "be hot, do drugs," no?'

'You've got it all wrong,' says Nell. 'Eve's right: Josh Schwartz and Andy Cohen, these are the philosophers of our time.'

Tae looks at Nell. 'That doesn't seem very feminist of you, Nell. Shouldn't you at least say the philosopher of our time is, like, I don't know, Oprah? And besides, *you'd* never be on one of those reality shows, would you?'

'Oh, fuck no.' She snorts. 'But these women, their lives – like, they *are* late capitalism. It's the faux-feminist energy intertwined with the, like, desperation of middle-aged obscurity, the feminisation of commerce, the alienation of wealth, the clinging to interpersonal connection combined with the suspicion of intimacy . . . it's all there. My life very much does not qualify for embodying the spirit of our times,' she concludes.

Tae laughs. 'You say so many words, Nell, has anyone ever told you that?'

Nell shrugs. 'My dad wanted me to seem smarter than his colleagues' kids, so he paid me five hundred dollars to read *Ulysses* when I was like, eleven . . . He had no interest in reading it himself, of course.'

Marcus looks at Nell, observes her physical awkwardness, her fierce intelligence, her clear infatuation with Eve and her terribly concealed internalised homophobia. Maybe it's the weed making him harsh, but he says, 'I don't know, I think you'd be a pretty clear representation of a young white woman in late capitalism.'

Nell flinches. 'Excuse me?' she snaps. 'I don't even have social media.'

'Let's face it, we're all pretty archetypal *of the times*,' he says. 'Like, Nell, let's be real – you're the child of rich parents whose wealth you despise but which got you a private school education; you're a visual arts student so you'll always rely on the state to fund your life unless your parents leave you money when they die, which they probably will; you live in a shitty apartment with people you don't love, but you still crave connection so you're making a chosen family with a bunch of queers; and you're sitting around getting high, engaging in meta-commentary about what it means to exist in late capitalism.' Marcus takes a big drag and exhales, his expression briefly obscured by a big puff of smoke. 'I'd say,' he continues, 'that you *are* late capitalism.'

Nell's eyes have become slits. Eve is watching this all unfold but is also slightly removed from reality as the weed has hit and everything is taking an extra minute or so to sieve through her ears and into her brain, by which point the conversation has moved on and she has no context through which to comprehend anything.

Marcus raises his hands in surrender, responding to the scowl Nell is giving him. 'As we all are!' he yells, then giggles. 'I'm, like, the biggest cliché of all, don't get me wrong. I'm just saying, babe, that it is impossible not to exist *in* the culture and be *of* the culture. You can't think that by commentating on the present you exclude yourself from it. We *are* the moment.' Marcus considers what he just said. 'Actually, maybe *I'm* the philosopher of our time. That was deep.'

Nell stops scowling; she sees that Marcus is not trying to insult her, he's merely testing out some theories, he's trying to diagnose the contemporary, he's a stoned critical theorist. The weed messed with her for a bit there – she is trying not to smoke so much anymore, but tonight is an exception – and she truly thought she was being dragged, and in front of Eve, too. But, glancing at Eve, she intuits that Eve is not only not following the conversation, she's also been actively trying and failing to dip a Dorito into a jar of salsa for the past ten seconds. She can now see that Marcus is doing her a kindness: he's discursively initiating her into the community; he's saying that she belongs.

Nell changes tack, decides to play along. 'I don't know, I think I can exclude myself, Marcus. I'm not like other girls, you see.'

Marcus mimes vomiting.

Eve succeeds in getting some salsa on a chip, and the chip into her mouth. Elated, she can now concentrate on something she heard a little while ago. 'Wait, Marcus, did you say before that we're a family? That's so cute.'

Marcus giggles. 'Yes, Evie, we're a little family. I'm the mummy and Tae is the daddy and you are our daughter and Nell is the cousin who lives with us because her parents died in a freak gasoline accident.'

'Nawww, bub!' She turns to Nell. 'Did you hear that, Nell? We're family! I'm sorry about your parents, though.'

Nell shrugs. 'It was their time.'

Tae has stopped participating in the conversation and is now fully invested in watching Blake Lively's hairstyles change within scenes.

When it gets to 1 am, it's time to retire. The boys trundle off to their rooms, and Nell begins the arduous task of getting herself up and finding her bag and shoes. Seeing this, Eve says casually, 'You want to stay here tonight, boo? I feel like getting home right now would be challenging.'

Nell tries to hold back the huge grin that would take over her face were she not the queen of suppressed emotions.

'Okay, thanks, Evie,' she says, equally casually. She pulls a pillow up to one side of the couch. 'Do you have a spare blanket?'

Eve frowns, confused. 'Huh?'

'A blanket?' Nell prompts. 'For the couch?'

Eve purses her lips, tilts her head to one side. 'Why would the couch need a blanket?'

Must Nell really spell it out? It seems she must. 'The blanket is for me, when I sleep on the couch, so I don't get, like . . . cold?'

Comprehension dawns on Eve's face.

'Ohhhhhhh,' she breathes. 'Babe, don't worry about that; you can share my bed. We'll have a sleepover and gossip about boys.'

Can it be this simple? Is Eve asking Nell to . . . share her bed? Are they having the same conversation?

'Are you sure?' asks Nell. 'I really don't mind sleeping here.'

'Don't be silly – come on.'

And so it is that Nell finds herself stripping down in Eve's bedroom. The lights are off, but in the faint glow from the streetlights filters through the curtains and Nell can see Eve taking off first her t-shirt, then her shorts, so that she's wearing only black underpants and her breasts are on full display. Eve acts like this is not a big deal, and maybe it isn't. Nell is 99.9 per cent sure that Eve does not have seduction in mind: Eve is simply stoned. But still, there's that 0.1 per cent chance. When we desire someone, every single move they make can be interpreted as reciprocation. Every single move can also be read as evidence that they find us disgusting. Nell takes off her own shorts but keeps her t-shirt and underpants on.

'Do you have a preferred side, or . . . ?' Nell asks, unable to hide the strain in her voice.

Eve turns to face Nell, her body just there in front of Nell, in all its glory. 'Yeah, if it's alright I prefer to sleep next to the wall.'

It's like Eve is daring Nell to glance at her tits, but Nell will not fall for it, she will not. She assents coolly, maintaining eye contact with Eve. 'Yep, sure thing.'

Eve climbs into bed and scooches over to the far side, making space for Nell to slide in. Nell does so carefully, ensuring that she does not overestimate the size of the bed and the amount of space she can take up before her skin touches Eve's. She lies on her back, arms plastered to her sides, stiff like a corpse, avoiding bodily contact with Eve. Now all she has to do is stay like this for the rest of the night.

The night is long, Nell barely sleeps, so conscious is she of the limbs unspooled next to her. She contemplates every terrible thing she's ever done, how she is a bad person, how it's bizarre Eve's even trusted Nell to share her bed considering Nell is morally horrible and now also a creep.

Eve, meanwhile, seems to fall asleep almost instantly, rolling carelessly around the bed. She flails, she turns, she sighs. And then, somehow, suddenly, Eve's flesh skims Nell's, and Nell is enveloped: Eve, still asleep, wraps her leg around Nell's leg, nestles her face into Nell's neck, throws her arm over Nell's stomach; Nell is covered in Eve.

Nell is very, very awake.

Nell wants more than anything to cuddle Eve back, but she can't. What if Eve wakes up and is disgusted? What if she thinks Nell has taken advantage of her? Nell's mind is awash with terrible scenarios in which she comes across as a predator caressing an innocent sleeping woman.

Nell coughs to make sure that Eve is asleep; Eve does not even flinch.

Nell whispers, 'Eve?'

Eve does not respond; her eyes stay shut, her body remains entwined with Nell's.

Silently, silently, Nell adjusts her left arm and places her hand ever so gently on Eve's forearm. She holds her breath and takes the plunge. With her index finger, Nell traces circles on Eve's skin. She feels the warmth of Eve's body, the rise of her veins. She moves her fingers to make pictures, she senses the tiny, soft hairs on Eve's arms stiffen – goosebumps, she's given Eve goosebumps. She continues stroking Eve's skin for an hour or more, totally lost in the loveliness of it, the forbidden-ness of it.

And behind her eyelids Eve is very much awake, she has been for all of this. Eve knows exactly what she is doing, and she berates herself for her cruelty even as she gives in to the pleasure of having Nell desire her. Want, can't have; can't have, want. This has been Eve's life up until this year. Now Nell is the one who will be forced to want and not have. Eve will dangle herself, offering Nell just enough hope that she won't give up, and Nell will be suspended in the present tense of desire. Only Eve will be the one with the power to reanimate time.

2024

Eve Bowman, thirty, is on a date. She has resisted and resisted, but Marcus's pestering has become near constant, like the hum of an old fridge. To his credit, Marcus is at Eve's house right now, looking after Lake: after seeing Eve and Nell through all the early years of parenting, he is not one of those gay men who ignores the practicalities involved in having total responsibility for the life and safety of a growing human being. Yes, he's probably showing her seven-year-old YouTube videos of Trixie and Katya right now, but Lake's no stranger to unhinged women and drag queens – she and Nell essentially taught Lake how to walk on the sticky floor of Head Hunters. Lake's first word was 'cheers', after all.

The woman Eve's about to flirt with is called Mei Ling. On her profile, Mei Ling has self-identified as 'a lover, not a fighter', which is not that bad, Eve supposes; peace is better than war. She is trying to suppress the flight instinct taking hold in her right now as she sits on a bar stool and attempts to act casual. She used to be so good at this – in her late teens, her early twenties, dating was her dopamine hit; meet, assess, drink, fuck. And she knows she is not technically old, she knows that women her age date all the time, but the thought of explaining all her trauma to a new person makes her so tired. And even if it goes well – even if they click and they fall in love and they move in together and Mei Ling is good to Lake and they attend queer family meet-ups together and talk about emotional accountability over vegan hot dogs – even then there would still be the hole, there would still be the guilt, Eve would still have done what she did to Nell, and one day Lake will find out and she will hate her. This is what Eve is thinking when Mei Ling enters the bar, looking frazzled and sweaty but gorgeous, actually, disarmingly beautiful. Long, black hair, a mane; clear skin, a tight singlet, high-waisted trousers, a work satchel over one shoulder.

Mei Ling spots Eve immediately. 'Eve?' she asks warmly.

Eve smiles, something about this woman is making her show her teeth. 'Mei Ling?' she replies.

'You got me,' says Mei Ling, and in one smooth motion she is sitting on the bar stool next to Eve. The confidence with which Mei Ling makes this transition is extremely sexy; Eve has often felt the ick watching women struggle to position themselves on a high chair.

'Have you been waiting long? I'm sorry I'm late – a meeting ran over and I was racing across town trying to get here before you up and left, as would have been your right, of course.' Mei Ling says this all in one breath, then makes eye contact with Eve and exhales. Mei Ling's eyes are a golden brown and they are bordered by laugh lines, the only lines that Eve trusts.

'That's okay,' Eve says. 'Don't worry about it, honestly. I grew up with a mother who was always running late, and to be honest it wasn't the lateness that bothered me so much, it was the fact that she never acknowledged it.' Eve goes red. 'So you're already doing well – I mean, by comparison . . .' Eve trails off, watching amusement dance across Mei Ling's face, realising that her opening line to a beautiful woman on a first date has involved complaining about her mother and then comparing the date to her mother.

To her credit, Mei Ling doesn't make fun. 'I'm glad to hear it,' she says. 'I'm glad I'm not your mother, too.' She smirks. 'Shall we order drinks before I start making terrible incest puns that I'll never be able to take back?'

'Please,' says Eve.

They both order margaritas, extra salt, a promising sign.

'So, what do you do, Mei Ling?' Eve asks.

'I'm a couples therapist,' Mei Ling responds.

Eve chokes on her drink. 'You're joking, right?'

Mei Ling smiles, touches Eve's arm playfully. 'I'm sorry,' she says. 'I really am sorry! But yes, I am, in fact, a couples therapist.' She looks at Eve. 'Do you want to finish your drink and then go, or do you want to just leave right now? I won't hold it against you, I swear.'

Eve is in shock, and is laughing at herself for being in shock. 'Oh my god, *I'm* sorry!' exclaims Eve. 'Jesus, what am I? Like, "local lesbian freaks out when realising her date is a therapist"? What does that even say about me?'

Mei Ling laughs. 'Hey,' she says, 'it's honestly a better reaction than, like, downright glee, which is something I've experienced one too many times. You can practically see most lesbians salivating when I tell them, like they're already picturing how open our communication style will be, how much we'll make each other *feel seen* – I swear, that's the worst. Freaking out is better, trust me.'

'Can I ask you a question?' says Eve, taking a sip of her drink.

'Hey, see, you're already reversing the therapist–client dynamic,' Mei Ling says. 'Well done you!'

Eve smiles again. 'So, I was wondering about the "lover not a fighter" thing on your profile . . . It's just . . .' Eve is struggling to articulate her question, which is: *Are you actually a basic bitch or were you joking?* She's wondering how she'll respond if it turns out that Mei Ling wrote this unironically. Could she look past the cringe, or no?

Mei Ling sees where this is going. 'You're wondering if that was supposed to be funny or not?'

Eve laughs nervously. 'Well, yes, exactly.'

'The thing is,' Mei Ling says solemnly, 'I did have "live, love, laugh", but I got sued by Pinterest for copyright infringement, so . . .'

Eve bursts out laughing. 'Oh, thank god.'

'It's not funny, Eve,' says Mei Ling. 'I live in my car now. Big Scrapbook took everything from me.'

'I'm sorry, I'm sorry!' says Eve. She finishes her drink, looks at Mei Ling contemplatively.

'But seriously, though, why do you have that on your profile? Surely you'd attract, like, the worst people?'

'Hey' – Mei Ling grins – 'don't put yourself down like that.' She takes a sip of her margarita. 'No,' she continues, 'I guess I have it there because I feel like a lot of profiles on the apps are . . . lacking humanity? And to be honest, I actually am a lover not a fighter. I get that it sounds silly, but it's also . . . authentic to me?'

Were anyone else to say the words 'authentic to me', Eve might vomit. But this woman is clearly no fool, and the sincerity she's exhibiting here, well, it's kind of refreshing? The ironic distance she used to think was her armour – well, look where that's gotten her.

*

Three margaritas in, the date feels like having arthritic feet and finding the perfect pair of shoes. It feels like the doctor telling you that you have great liver function despite all the poison you've pumped into it over the years.

And when Eve and Mei Ling kiss at the end of the evening, and they exchange phone numbers and plan their next meeting, and the nightscape of Sydney is hazy and lush and warm, and it seems that right now a new chapter may be beginning, and Eve feels high on promise and affection and the sensation of Mei Ling's finger tracing her collarbone – when all of this is happening, where is Nell?

The next day, Mei Ling messages, and Eve does not respond. She doesn't respond the day after that either. She can't. She's not ready. She may never be ready.

2014

Two years have passed since Nell and Eve reunited – with Nell suspended in time, Eve abusing her power, Nell not understanding the rules of the game they are playing. The four friends move into a bigger share house, one with bedrooms for each of them, a luxury. Nell never really told her housemates she was moving out – she just transferred all her stuff one day and stopped paying rent. She left a note, so there's that. Naomi hasn't texted her since, but she must have noticed, because she's not asking for money, so clearly she's gotten someone else in on the lease. Naomi was a bitch, Nell always knew that, but it used to seem safer to side with the devil she knew rather than the angel she wanted. Naomi's complete lack of reaction to Nell's absence only confirms what Nell has long known: Naomi was only ever interested in Nell for what she could give her – and Nell's been unable to give Naomi anything for years now. Naomi will have replaced her without a second thought.

The new place is a terrace house about a block away from Head Hunters, where Eve still works and baits her conquests. Marcus has an unpaid internship at an interior design firm while also studying full-time and continuing to do shifts at BWS. Tae's scrapped bar work and now trains rich old ladies exclusively. He compliments them on their form and they take him out to fancy lunches post-session. He now says he cannot live life without caviar, and is mocked accordingly.

The four of them are midway through their third year of university – unless they choose to pursue further study, this will be their final year as students. The future looms threateningly in front of them, but only Nell seems to see it this way. Eve, Tae and Marcus are decidedly on *paths*; they view adulthood as a space in which to spread their wings, as it were. They seem to believe that the *future is theirs for the taking*, like they are a trio of well-adjusted human greeting cards. But Nell does not see the world like this, she never has. Nell is happy *now*, happier than she ever thought she could be, and she doesn't want it to end. Sure, she isn't with Eve *romantically*, but she gets to spend all her time with her, she gets to be Eve's confidante, she gets to stroke Eve's back when she is sleeping. Eve routinely sleeps in Nell's bed, and this is its own type of intimacy. Eve tells Nell about the stories she writes and her dalliances and her stresses and her mum, and Nell laughs with her, comforts her, looks after her. In the share house with Eve and the boys, responsibility is forestalled, friendship is watered daily, like the peace lilies that grow on their balcony because no other plant will flower with such little access to light. Nell spends her days painting, Eve spends her days writing; they are Gertrude Stein and Alice B. Toklas, but they are also Virginia Woolf and Vanessa Bell. They are Anne Lister and Ann Walker, but they are also Tegan and Sara.

Marcus and Tae are both aware of Nell's obsession but not that Eve knows about it – though Tae has his suspicions. They've never said anything about it to either of the girls, but they feel sorry for Nell, who is so obviously pining. Tae has tried to talk to Nell about crushes in the abstract, has attempted to open the door to more unguarded conversation, but she always shuts it. He's recounted his own outing, and how his family accepts his queerness while Marcus's family doesn't, which is a fun reversal of racist stereotypes but still personally devastating for Marcus. He's casually mentioned his childhood crush on Marcus, and how that was hard to navigate but how now they're in a really good place because they're honest with each other. He doesn't know how much more he can spell it out – it's like trying to coax a child into admitting wrongdoing by 'admitting' that you've done something similar. But either Nell is completely oblivious, or she's an expert in deception.

Marcus doesn't know if Nell thinks of herself as gay and in the closet or if she is simply in love with Eve regardless of gender. He'd previously diagnosed her with internalised homophobia, but over the past two years he's begun to suspect that it's something more than this: Nell just does not seem like a sexually interested person, except in relation to Eve, and this interest is sexual but it's also, like, fully covetous. Nell has never once brought a boy or a girl home. Marcus has had a few short-term relationships since he's lived with Nell, and he has seen her observe his little physical acts of intimacy with these partners with discomfort – it's not a disapproving discomfort, though; more of a shyness, perhaps. Nell often looks like she's been caught spying on something she shouldn't, even though what she's doing is perfectly normal, like drinking tea in her own lounge room.

Because Marcus and Tae are not technically sleeping together anymore, a lot of their interaction involves either competing about who can snag the hottest men or gossiping about their housemates and what the fuck is going on between them.

'Do we feel like it's possible that Eve *knows* Nell is obsessed with her?' Tae asks Marcus, the pair of them lying on Tae's bed.

Marcus scoffs. 'God, no!' he says. 'She's fully oblivious, that's the whole problem.'

Tae is not so sure. Marcus seems to have a blind spot when it comes to Eve; he can't conceive of the possibility that his friend may be a touch Machiavellian. Eve is Marcus's chosen sister – he can only see the good in her. But Tae has a sister of his own. He has a mother too. He is less emotionally dependent on the fantasy of a chosen family. 'I don't know,' counters Tae. 'I think she's oblivious and she's *not* oblivious. Like, she's definitely oblivious to Nell's moods, but I don't know if she's as oblivious to Nell's crush as she makes out.'

'What do you mean by Nell's "moods"?' asks Marcus.

'You know – her *moods*. Like when she doesn't come out of her room for days and she says she's been on a roll with her art but, like, she clearly hasn't eaten for sixty hours. And I don't think Eve even questions it. It's like she doesn't want to, maybe?'

Marcus is not sure how to respond. He hasn't questioned Nell's absences either; he too has taken her justifications at face value. Is he stupid? Marcus has always been the smart one: that is his and Tae's dynamic. What is happening here?

'Have *you* talked to Nell about this?' asks Marcus.

'Oh god, no, whenever I've tried she's, like, totally closed herself off. The only person I think she would speak to about it is Eve. But you know Nell: she'll never bring it up herself. It's like she's hoping that Eve will notice and ask – but I don't think Eve is ever going to do that.'

'Huh,' says Marcus.

'Yeah, *huh*,' echoes Tae.

Marcus is stumped. He doesn't like this information, wants to go back to when he didn't have it in his mind. So he starts jerking Tae off.

2014

Towards the end of the university year, Emerald phones Eve with a plan. Emerald rarely calls her daughter, and when she does it is usually to bitch about someone while she's driving. Emerald has come over to the house maybe twice, and both times she has gotten blackout drunk and had to stay the night on the couch. She's holding down a job as a medical secretary, and the last man she shagged was not rich; she's beginning to fear she may never sleep with a rich man again. This call, however, is different – apparently Emerald saw a photo on an acquaintance's Facebook feed taking her child out to lunch to celebrate the end of university, and Emerald had a twinge of maternal longing, or more likely guilt, and she is calling to invite Eve and her housemates to lunch on Sunday. She's booked a table at the exact same restaurant she saw the other mother dining at, and she's being weirdly interested in Eve's life.

'So how's that job you're doing – what is it, waitressing?'

'Bartending,' corrects Eve.

'That's right,' says Emerald. 'And how long have you been doing that for now?'

Eve breathes in, holds in her annoyance. 'About two and a half years, Mum.'

'Right, yes. And have you made any friends there? Any *special* friends?'

Eve shudders. 'I don't have a girlfriend at the moment, if that's what you're asking,' she says flatly.

Emerald makes a face, Eve can sense it. 'You know, you've never let me meet any of your little gal pals. My colleague's son is a gay man and he's always taking her to gay events. The other weekend they even went to . . . what was it called? Dine and Drag. Rhonda said it was thrilling; all that make-up, all that testosterone in a dress.'

'I invited you to a QueerSoc family event in first year and you told me that being in a gay university society made my being gay less interesting to you.' Eve's tone is still flat.

'Oh, I wouldn't have said that, I don't think! I just don't like how everything has to have a *society* these days, and forms, and minutes. Just have sex with who you want! That's what I've always done.'

Eve is not in the mood to educate her mother about the gay rights movement. 'You certainly have always done that,' she says instead.

'You know, I've always been a friend to the gays,' muses Emerald.
'Oh yeah?'
'Oh, absolutely. You know, I was at the first Mardi Gras.'
Eve is genuinely shocked by this. 'You *were?*'
Emerald expands. 'Well I was dating a bisexual man at the time, and he said there would be good coke there, that protests always have the best drugs. And he was right, of course, but the police did ruin the atmosphere a little. We had to run away and I was wearing the tallest heels you could imagine.'

'So you're actually telling me you were not a seventy-eighter but instead a coke fiend who fled when gay people were being bashed?'

'Mmm, and Nell, is she well?'

Eve braces herself; her mother loves to pick at scabs. 'Yeah, Nell's good. She has an art show coming up, portraits of housewives.'

'Mmm,' says Emerald. 'I never did understand why you two stopped being friends; you were thick as thieves until you weren't.'

Eve grits her teeth. 'We just drifted apart, Mum, it happens. And now we're friends again. It's as simple as that.'

'If you say so,' says Emerald, and her daughter can practically see her mother's cynical squint. 'I just think *something* must have happened. People don't just stop being friends over nothing. And you became so dour back then, do you remember?'

Eve can't help it: her mind races to recall the details she usually attempts to repress. Lunches eaten alone, classes in which she was avoided, never getting invitations to birthday parties, the curious process via which a person can go from believing they matter to questioning if they exist. The many, many years of self-hatred. The belief that *she* was the problem. And the person who did it to her.

'Anyway, I'm so looking forward to lunch on Sunday – spending time with you all keeps me young.'

Eve swallows the urge to say that from the looks of it Emerald's not spent much time with them, then. 'Yeah, well, I'll have to double-check that everyone's free, but hypothetically it sounds nice, thanks, Mum.'

Later in the day, Eve relays her mother's invitation to the group and, annoyingly, they are all free and keen to attend.

'I would love to know big Em better,' says Tae. 'She's insane – I love her.'

'You love her because she's not *your* mother,' snaps Eve.

'Two things can be true at once,' says Tae with a shrug. 'I love her *and* she's not my mother. Plus, I love my mother.'

Marcus stands at the kitchen sink washing a stack of dirty glasses and mugs he's just heaved in from his bedroom. 'I'm sorry, Eve, I really am, but I also think she's amazing,' he says. 'I realise that you're traumatised by her, and that is so valid, but my own mum doesn't speak to me at all and she definitely doesn't offer me a fancy free lunch.' He pauses, adds sassily, 'Bitches gotta eat.'

'I hate it when you do your Tae impression,' says Eve. 'It's like, we get it, you both have the same five cultural references.'

'Ohhhh, spicy!' Tae and Marcus exclaim in perfect unison, proving Eve's point.

Nell pipes up from where she's been sitting comparatively quietly on the couch. 'Look, I don't love Emerald either, Eve, she's not exactly a present maternal figure. But she's trying, you know? I say we go to lunch. What's the worst that could happen?'

*

The four housemates arrive for lunch on time. The restaurant is extremely posh: linen tablecloths; a greeter their own age who frowns at them dismissively; still water by the bottle, no tap unless you expressly ask for it, revealing your poverty. They're dressed in their adult best – Tae is even wearing a shirt that covers his midriff. Rich little children run amok outside in the kitchen garden, ripping out heirloom carrots, messing with the edible flowers, but the waiters smile sweetly at these monsters; they are free from all repercussions: they wear Zimmermann and Ralph Lauren Kids. Eve watches the children and feels sorry for all of them. When she has a child, she'll teach it manners, humility, grace. These poor sprogs, already trapped in the quagmire of privilege – they'll never know what it is to earn anything.

The four sit at their table, pretending that they belong here. One seat – Emerald's – sits empty at the head of the table, while Eve and Nell are on one side, and Marcus and Tae on the other. Nell is theoretically used to this level of fanciness; her parents have been taking her to restaurants like this since she was a child. She knows which fork to use, how much banter with the waitstaff is necessary to seem polite but not engaged enough to invite further conversation. She hates that she knows this; she resents this knowledge, like agnostic adults who've been to Catholic school and unwillingly remember all the words to mass every time they go to a wedding or funeral in a church.

The waiter asks if they'll be waiting long for their fifth guest, and Eve tries to sound both unbothered and honest when she says her mother will be here any minute. Really, she will be surprised if Emerald is less than an hour late, and even more surprised if she apologises for it.

Marcus can sense Eve's anxiety; he has been trying to calm her down all week. He clears his throat, then rests his chin on his fist, his elbow on the table, in an imitation of *The Thinker*. 'I'd just like to say that I, personally, identify more as a negroni Marxist than a champagne socialist.'

'That's really brave, Marcus,' says Eve gravely. 'Thank you for sharing.' She jumps into the shark tank to join her shark friend. 'I think *more* people should be killed in custody.'

A bit of a baulk here, but her friends are strong, they retain their poker faces.

'Amen,' says Marcus.

He looks to Tae.

Tae frowns, thinking, then smirks. 'I masturbate to videos of coalmines,' he declares.

This gets a giggle from Eve, who then manages to regain her composure as they all face Nell.

She considers. 'I think less people would be gay if we stopped calling women "actors",' she says softly.

'So *true*, honey!' cries Tae.

Marcus clicks his fingers. 'Don't I *know* it!'

Eve laughs, but her heart is not in it. She does not think that Nell gets to make this joke. She knows it was meant in jest, as were all their declarations, but Nell making gay jokes? It hurts Eve. She recalls sitting alone on her bed on Saturday nights, the years during which her every utterance was met with derisive laughter.

They lapse into silence. Emerald is now twenty minutes late.

Fuck this. Eve gestures to the waiter, and she orders four margaritas and a mezze plate. 'These drinks are on Mama,' she says.

Nell pipes up, 'Are you sure that's okay? Isn't she living on a secretary's wage right now?'

'Look,' says Eve, 'Emerald has always lived beyond her means, and today is another classic example – like, why *this* place? So I'm thinking maybe a large bill will shock her out of her denial.'

'Or she'll have to move in with us,' Marcus says under his breath.

The drinks arrive, sips are taken, and the chat is now normal, reasonable – who is sleeping with whom (everyone), how is Tae's mum's treatment going (slowly, it's been on and off for years – now it's on again), is Marcus going to do Honours (yes), will Nell attempt to get permanent gallery representation (no) – and the weird atmosphere of undeserved wealth in the restaurant is beginning to feel more palatable, enjoyable even.

'You know,' says Tae, 'the thing about rich people is that films actually do get them right – like, they do actually just sit around drinking twenty-five-dollar cocktails and eating organic parsnips all day. That's not a Hollywood bit, that's reality. It's fucking mental. You should meet some of the women I work with: they literally get up, drink some vodka, take their bordoodle for a walk, sit in a cafe for a few hours, go to lunch, and then they just stay there drinking martinis till it's their bedtime. Occasionally they'll squeeze in some art buying in the early morning or afternoon, but that's pretty much it. How does one get a life like that?'

And it's at this point that Emerald strides in. She sits down, takes a swig of Eve's drink, and answers Tae's question: 'Marriage.' Then she blows Eve a kiss. 'So good to see you, darling,' she coos. 'And you three!' she cries, turning to the others. 'So fresh-faced, so full of hope! I'm thrilled you could make it. Eve seemed to think that you might not have the time, but I told her, "Evie, darling, everyone has time for lunch." *So*, what's the gossip? Tell me everything.' She takes a breath; she has been speaking without air.

The housemates look to each other – who is going to go first? Who has something to say that will please Emerald? This is the task they have been assigned, in not so many words. Entertain her, and she'll pay the bill. Amuse her, and you can have dessert. They silently agree that Marcus has the best shot, and he is urged, by telepathy, to say something.

'Well,' he begins, 'first of all, *so* good to see you, Emerald, and thank you for inviting us to lunch.' He pauses. What to say, what to say? He could tell Emerald about his internship – older women love interior design – but it seems she's after something juicier. Sex, he decides. He'll start with sex. Older women love tales of young gay men having sex. Not his own mother, obviously, or any of the women he grew up with, but the kind of women who come to this restaurant adore it. They repeat it to their hairdressers and recount it to their friends after a few chardonnays. He can give this to Emerald; he can be her gay anecdote.

'Well,' he begins again, 'I've been seeing a clown called Charles.'

Emerald's eyes widen at this. 'A *clown?*' she asks. 'Like a real, big-red-nose clown? Is that what's sexy at the moment? I had no idea.'

Marcus smiles encouragingly. 'I'm not sure that clowning is a generally desired gay trait, but I like this clown, yes.'

Emerald is momentarily distracted by a passing waiter. 'Excuse me, darling, could we have the banquet menu and a bottle of whatever GSM you recommend?' She returns her gaze to Marcus. 'And do you do – how should I put it? – "clowny" things in the bedroom?'

Eve steps in here. 'Mum, you can't just ask Marcus about his sex life,' she chides.

'I certainly can,' counters Emerald. 'Marcus is happy to share, aren't you, Marcus?'

'Absolutely,' he says. 'Thrilled to share. "Clowny things", you ask. We do some clowning, certainly. There's a lot that red nose can be used for, you know.' He winks at Emerald. 'We've also made love in a very small car, which is typical clownery, as you know.' He pauses. 'And sometimes he puts a puppet on my dick.'

Emerald, who has just taken the last swig of Eve's drink, immediately spits it out. Tae is watching, enthralled, eager to see if this last line was too much or exactly what Emerald wanted.

She slaps her hands on the table. '*That!*' she cries. 'That is the kind of conversation I've been missing. I think we're going to have an excellent time.'

Eve cups her palms around her chin and drags her fingers down her face. She will get through this; she must.

Observing Eve's discomfort, Nell rubs Eve's leg and whispers in her ear, 'It's okay, Evie, I got you.'

Eve gives her a wry grimace. She didn't like Nell's gay joke, but they're friends again now, they're on the same side, she tries to remember this. Emerald, watching this exchange surreptitiously, forms her own conjectures but keeps them to herself.

The first course arrives: a sweet potato scallop with a green jus. The waiter places the plates down ceremonially, and Eve wonders if they should be prostrating themselves before the vegetables – would this make their server happy?

'A bit off to serve us green jus,' notes Emerald, after the server has left. 'Haven't their people suffered enough?!'

Tae is laughing into his napkin; he is enjoying all of this far too much.

'For fuck's sake,' Eve mutters. It's okay for Eve and her friends to make inappropriate jokes, but for some reason, when Emerald does it, she is enraged.

'Language, Evie,' Emerald reprimands her. 'We have guests.'

Nell grips Eve's hand under the table, trying to give her strength. Eve holds on for dear life.

'So what's going on with you, Mum?' she says, trying to change the subject. 'How's work?'

Emerald lets out a large sigh, takes a big swig of wine, swallows. 'Work is work, sweetie,' she says. 'Did I think, in my youth, that I'd be stuck behind a desk dealing with sick people and all their little neuroses? Did I think that, at my age, I'd still be struggling to make ends meet? After everything I've been through – bathing you, feeding you, dressing you, putting you through school, seeing you into university – you'd think I'd get a bit of respite, but no, on it drags.' She takes another swig, looks to Tae. 'A woman's work is never done, you know.'

'I can only imagine,' says Tae. 'It sounds harrowing.'

Emerald likes this. 'Harrowing! Yes, harrowing, exactly! Speaking of harrowing, how are your parents, Nell?'

Tae laughs aloud at this, he can't help it.

Nell has been trying to make herself smaller, to evade Emerald's notice, but no such luck. 'They're well, thank you, Emerald.' She hopes this will be enough, but of course it isn't.

'Are they thinking about retiring soon?' asks Emerald. She takes a bite of her potato scallop and frowns, as if it isn't up to her standards. 'Surely they've made enough money by now.'

Nell pauses. She's been brought up to believe that to talk explicitly about money at the lunch or dinner table is in very bad taste. Inference is fine, subtle shows of wealth are acceptable, but outright recognition of wealth disparity outside of the family is frowned upon. But she is not like her parents, she reminds herself. It is important for money to be discussed transparently, even if Emerald is not asking with socialist intent.

'Yes, they could retire, and I think they'd be better people if they did. But they don't have any friends and work is their life. I genuinely don't know how they'd spend their time if they retired.'

'Mmm . . . how sad for them. And is the little one still at school? Claire, was it?'

Emerald has ordered another bottle of wine and is now refilling everyone's glasses – having topped up her own first, of course.

Nell takes a small sip of wine and responds. 'It's Chelsea, and she's just finishing her first year at uni, actually. She's in Melbourne doing law.'

Emerald laughs. 'Couldn't wait to fly the nest, huh? How's she finding it?'

Nell thinks about this. She knows that Emerald doesn't actually care, that she's just making conversation, but over the years Nell has come to feel very protective of Chelsea – she is very sweet and surprisingly clever, and though neither Nell nor Chelsea truly understand what makes the other tick, they do actually love each other. Whenever Nell has had a bit of an episode – Eve knows nothing of this – Chelsea has been the one to answer the phone and talk her down. And when Chelsea gets a mark that isn't a high distinction, or one of the boys in her college says something cruel about women, Nell is the one who Chelsea calls.

'She's going okay, I think,' says Nell. 'She's in the college system, so she has "in-built-friends", or whatever the term is they use to advertise that, and she's doing well in her courses. I think law actually suits her – she's very focused and pedantic, and she does actually believe in justice. I think she finds the crassness of college galling – like, the parties where they dress up as doctors and nurses. But I think she likes Melbourne. And she's been seeing a boy – Charlie – who she says is genuinely nice and not a bro, and she seems very happy with him.'

Emerald laughs again. Her laughs are sounding more like scoffs the more she drinks.

'Chelsea and Charlie, hey? They sound like quite the pair.'

Nell stiffens. 'I think they're both good people,' she says.

And now comes the moment Nell has been dreading, and that Eve, Marcus and Tae have been readying themselves for too, each for different reasons.

'And what about you, Nell?' Emerald is slurring now.

'Sorry,' Nell says, 'what about me?'

'Well, is there a special someone in your life?' Her voice is heavy with insinuation. 'Someone who makes your groin go boom, boom, *boom*?' Emerald beats her own chest as she asks this. (Jesus, this is a lot, even for Emerald.) 'God, I remember the days,' she says. 'No responsibilities, no problems, just *sex*. I won't lie: I'm jealous. I'm jealous of all of you.'

Nell thinks she may have got away with not responding, as Emerald seems to have moved on to her favourite subject: her young self. The next course has been delivered: squid ink pasta with salmon roe, which seems excessively fishy. Nell takes a tiny bite.

'Nell? I asked you a question. Who are you sleeping with?'

Nell colours and looks to Eve for backup, but Eve is regarding her curiously, as if she, too, is keen to hear Nell's answer.

'Oh, no one, at the moment,' says Nell.

Tae has been drinking steadily; he doesn't realise it yet, but he is drunk. 'More like who has she *ever* slept with!' he cries.

Nell's face drops; her white skin turns red. Eve freezes in the awkwardness of it. Tae has gone too far. He regrets the words as soon as they leave his mouth, but it's done: it's the bottle of wine on the white tablecloth; it's the dog that's shat on the rug.

Emerald is oblivious to Nell's obvious discomfort. 'Oh, are you a *prude*, dear Nell? That's a damn shame. Tell me: are you interested in the boys or the girls or both? It made so much *sense* to me when Eve told me she liked the ladies – she didn't have that, you know, that *appeal* to men; never did, I could see it from when she was a child.'

Nell does not share Eve's deflective powers; she does not know how to respond to an affront as dangerous as this, and in the presence of Eve, no less.

'So, which is it, Nell, girls or boys?'

She must speak, she has to say something. 'Oh, um, I don't . . . I guess it's about the person?'

Nell has never said anything this explicit about her sexuality before. To be honest, she's not sure that what she feels could even count as a sexuality. She has known since she was a teenager that her 'sexuality' is just *Eve*, and sex isn't even the main part of it. Eve is the best person in the world. Eve is fundamentally good. Eve has forgiven Nell's treachery even though Nell doesn't deserve her forgiveness. Eve is grace. Knowing that Eve is alive makes Nell feel that she can be alive too. Nell wants nothing more than to stay by Eve's side for the rest of her life – to love her, to be what she needs. But she cannot say all this aloud.

Emerald barrels on. 'Okay, mysterious woman. I'll rephrase. Which *people* are you interested in fucking, or are you fucking?'

The blush has spread to Nell's chest, her neck, her heart is pounding, she is having a panic response. She could tell Emerald about the boys she kissed without conviction – or who forcefully kissed her, more truly – back in high school, when she'd go to parties with Naomi and Georgia and sit in the corner with her baggie of pills, the demon dealer of sweet treats. She could lie, say she has a secret boyfriend. But she's no good at lying.

And what's worse is that every person at this table has some information, some awareness, of all that is so far unsaid. Nell can sense the conversational possibilities that lie before her, and they are all bad.

Finally, Eve swoops in to save Nell. When Nell made the joke earlier, yes, Eve was annoyed, hurt. Observing Nell struggle to talk about her sexuality has felt like karmic payback. *Squirm, Nell, hate yourself. Hate yourself like you made me hate myself.* But the better part of Eve is winning now: she is not evil, and she knows that she has essentially been watching her mother make Nell live out her biggest fear.

'Nell's too busy making beautiful art to worry about romance,' Eve declares. 'She's working on a series at the moment that's actually so gorgeous it hurts.' Eve looks to Nell, smiles encouragingly. 'Isn't that right, Nell? Tell Emerald about your work.'

Marcus swings in behind Eve, effortlessly emancipating himself from the tenterhooks he's been fastened to for the past few minutes. 'Oh my god, yes, Nell, the new stuff is so fucking good. Like, I don't fully understand it, but I love it.'

Nell is sensing the path to freedom, laid out for her by her friends. Now, she must follow it carefully, avoiding obvious pitfalls.

'Well,' she says, 'it's a series of abstract portraits . . . they're mostly ink, but some watercolour too, and they're all kind of, like, close-ups, of, like, people who've been frozen by Medusa.'

Emerald drains another bottle – how many are they up to now? – and says, 'Huh. Medusa, eh? Isn't she the one so ugly that she turns people to stone?'

Nell smiles politely, easing into her comfort zone, that of esoteric postulation. 'Well, yeah, some myths say she was once beautiful and was then turned monstrous, some stories say she never lost her looks, but what's not disputed is that Poseidon raped her and, in an act of OG internalised misogyny, Minerva turned Medusa's hair into snakes and made it so that anyone Medusa made eye contact with would turn to stone.'

'Charming,' scoffs Emerald, as a giant plate of smoked duck is placed on the table before them.

'Yeah,' says Nell, 'so the thing is, most feminist scholars see Medusa's transformation as, like, an example of victim-blaming, and there's all this stuff about how victims retraumatise others too, but I'm more curious about the stone bit.'

Emerald is forking the duck directly from the share plate into her mouth. 'The stone bit?' she slurs.

Nell looks to her friends for solidarity. Tae, who has been uncharacteristically silent, offers a thumbs up.

Fortified, Nell continues. 'So, my works are kind of questioning, like, what if being turned to stone by the one you love was the ultimate lover's dream? To meet the gaze of the lover and then be forever frozen in that moment of mutual recognition? It's poetic, right, and kind of heartbreakingly hopeful?' Nell's blush has returned. It is her turn to take a big gulp of wine.

Tae raises his hand. No one in this group thinks of him as an intellectual, but he's pretty sure he's reading the subtext correctly here. 'Sorry,' he interjects, 'but, like, doesn't being turned to stone kill you? Am I crazy, or is it not super romantic to straight up murder the ones you love?'

Eve laughs. 'That's a fair point,' she says to Nell.

Nell doesn't laugh; she's taking this very seriously, even though she knows she should be affecting a more casual air. 'Yes,' she says, considering. 'I guess you are technically dead if you're made of stone. But I think it's more symbolic than that.'

She glances at Eve, hoping that Eve cannot see into her soul, and also hoping that she can.

Eve gives nothing away.

Nell goes on. 'But that's the thing, too – Medusa doesn't want to turn people to stone. She's been made this way. And that's why it's a tragedy for her, as well as for the people whose eyes she meets. But if we were to reconceptualise the whole thing, see it from another perspective, isn't there beauty in devotion, two trapped people staring at each other forever?'

She realises she's been speaking for a long time. 'Anyway,' she mumbles, 'that's kind of what I'm trying to get at in the work I'm doing at the moment. I want to draw the faces of Medusa's victims like they're not victims – like they've chosen for this to be their fate.'

Emerald experiences a moment of clarity – and empathy, even, for Nell. Emerald may be drunk, she may be a bad mother, but she is no stranger to desire, and she recognises the look that Nell is giving her daughter. Nell wants to believe that adoring Eve without possessing her is its own kind of intimacy. Emerald remembers feeling like that in her youth – wanting someone so much that proximity to them seemed beautiful, even if it hurt her. Emerald must save this girl from her daughter.

'Nell, darling, you forget one thing.' Emerald is holding her glass carelessly; wine sloshes about, some landing on the table.

'What's that?' asks Nell.

'Medusa's victims may be staring at her forever, but Medusa herself, well, I bet on my life that that woman isn't waiting around. She's on to the next one to petrify, mark my words.' Emerald nods at Nell drunkenly. 'There's nothing romantic about being stopped in your tracks while the person you love moves on freely without you. All that snake woman wants is a trophy room full of stone faces.'

Nell does not know what to say. She understands that Emerald is hinting at subtext, but she's so drunk, so garbled, it's hard to make out what it might be.

Eve, meanwhile, is aghast; she knows exactly what her mother is getting at. Emerald is saying that Eve is a Medusa. Emerald is calling Eve a callous bitch. This is so unfair, and so not true.

She hasn't frozen Nell; Nell froze her! What does Emerald know about anything? Fuck her.

Conveniently blind to the emotional fire she has lit, Emerald glances at her phone, raises her eyebrows. She looks up, addresses the table, announces, 'Anyway, darlings, I've got to be off. Duty calls and such. But it's been so lovely seeing you all, you're all just gorgeous.'

Rising unsteadily from her chair, she picks up her handbag and blows air kisses to her stunned companions. Nell, Eve, Marcus and Tae watch as Emerald walks away, leaving them with dessert yet to come – and the bill.

*

Later that day, it is night. Marcus and Tae are in Marcus's room 'watching a movie', but Eve and Nell can hear their groans from the lounge room. The lunch was not naked but the aftermath, it appears, is.

Nell and Eve are on the couch in their classic position: Nell sitting upright at one end and Eve reclining with her head in Nell's lap. Nell strokes Eve's hair as they watch music videos on Eve's laptop. Nell pauses occasionally to stick her finger into her mouth; she's been trying to do it surreptitiously, but Eve has noticed.

They watch Taylor Swift repel men in a mansion, then Nicki Minaj gyrates and stares down the camera, then, as is inevitable this year, Pharrell's 'Happy' starts playing before either one of them can skip it.

Eve mumbles something incoherent into Nell's lap, and Nell asks her to repeat it.

'I said, I'm sorry about Emerald today.'

Nell continues combing her fingers through Eve's short hair; she loves the texture of it, like a freshly shorn puppy. She exhales.

Emerald doesn't understand what Nell and Eve have. Nell refuses to be touched by it, by all her insinuations – except for the fact that she can't stop thinking about them.

'That's okay, Evie,' says Nell quietly. 'I'm sorry that she's your mum.'

Pharrell is replaced by an old t.A.T.u video, which seems portentous to Nell and maybe it would to Eve too, if she noticed it was playing, which she doesn't.

'Your parents suck too,' Eve says sympathetically.

'Yeahhh, they really do.'

Eve notices that Nell's finger is inside her mouth again. 'What's going on in your mouth, babe?' she asks. 'Are you okay? You look like me when I first had braces. Do you have, like, a cold sore?'

Nell cringes at the thought of Eve imagining a cold sore in her mouth. 'No,' she says. 'I just . . . I cut my tongue on something at lunch and I've looked in the mirror and I can't see where the cut is.'

Eve lifts her head up further, becomes upright next to Nell. 'Does it hurt?' she asks.

'Yeah.'

'Well let me see.'

And Eve gently places her fingers on Nell's chin, slowly applying pressure, coaxing her lower jaw down, opening her mouth. And Nell's desire beats through her body, the love she wants to give screams from behind her irises. Eve's fingers slip their way into Nell's mouth, they're stroking Nell's tongue, feeling for an indent, feeling for a wound. Nell's tongue is wet, as tongues tend to be. It's warm and soft and for a second Eve wonders, *Am I turned on by this?* But then just as quickly she dismisses the thought, feels betrayed by it. She's looking for an abrasion; she's a medical professional of sorts.

Nell lets out a groan. She doesn't mean to, but it happens, it undeniably happens, it's a groan of pleasure and they both hear it, and suddenly Eve is repulsed. Eve is repulsed and she is also angry. It's not fair of Nell to love her like this. What Eve wants is a best friend. Why shouldn't she be able to feel her friend's tongue without feeling guilty for leading her on? Nell is the one who is in the wrong. Nell is the one whose wants taint this. It's not Eve's fault how Nell reads things.

'I can't find anything,' Eve says gruffly, removing her fingers from Nell's mouth. She stands up and walks to her room, apparently retiring for the evening.

Nell is left alone on the couch, Eve's touch still vibrating on her tongue.

2024

'Mum, why did Nell leave?'

There, it's happened. Lake has asked Eve the question straight up, Eve can't ignore it, can't talk her way out of this one. But what if . . . she can?

They're in the craft corner of the bedroom, making bugs out of toilet rolls, and Lake asks the question so casually, the same way she'd ask if she could have a snack.

Eve freezes, her hand on a pipe cleaner. 'Oh, honey, that's a big question,' she says.

Lake doesn't falter. 'You said big questions are the ones we should ask.'

Eve frowns, hating her own wisdom. 'Yes, I did say that, didn't I?'

'Why did she leave, Mum?' Lake has put down her toilet roll, intent on getting an answer. 'You said you'd tell me everything when I was older. Now I'm older.'

'You're seven, Lake.'

'Exactly?'

Eve will start with what all the parenting books say to emphasise in a situation such as this. 'Well, Lakey, first of all, I just need you to understand that Nell didn't leave because of anything you did, okay? She loves you, and she will always be your mama.'

Lake is unblinking. 'But how can she be my mama if she's not here?'

Eve is trying very hard not to cry. She must hold it all in, for her daughter's sake. But yes, she feels the tears welling. Yes, the liquid pools and threatens to spill down her cheeks.

'Well . . . how can I explain this?' Eve blinks, trying to get her mind on track. 'You know how . . . how there are things that are real that we can't see?'

Lake does not miss a beat. 'Like the money in your credit card?'

Eve half-laughs here, despite herself. Trust that her kid would go for the most abstract iteration of the hypothetical. This is not the time to teach Lake about the falsity of credit, however. 'Yeah, kind of like that,' she says. 'Or even say' – Eve picks up a red pipe cleaner – 'you see this pipe cleaner?'

'Yeah,' says Lake suspiciously. Her mother is avoiding her question.

'So, you can touch it, feel its fuzziness, it has weight, it's undeniably *real*, right?'

'I guess?' says Lake, not convinced that whatever this metaphor is will be helpful.

'So, if I put this pipe cleaner behind the craft box' – Eve now does so – '*you* know that it's still there, right?'

'Obviously?' answers Lake.

Eve's eyes bug out, willing her daughter to make the connection so Eve can feel like she's done a good job of mothering.

Lake frowns. 'So you're saying that Nell is like the pipe cleaner?' she says, dubious.

Eve nods fervently; maybe she's nailed this? 'Exactly! Just because you can't see her, doesn't mean she's not with us, sweetie.'

Lake is still sitting on the floor, cross-legged. Now she crosses her arms to match. 'That's such crap,' she says. 'First, Nell isn't a pipe cleaner. Second, you taught me about object permanence when I was five, and it doesn't work with people who've been gone for two years.' She stares at her mother, eyes narrowed. 'Mum, why did Nell leave us? Was it something to do with Bridget?'

Fuck. Why does Lake have to be so fucking perceptive? Eve had hoped Lake might have forgotten about Bridget. She was only around for a year, after all.

Eve has to say something. She'd always told herself she'd never lie to her child, said she'd never be like Emerald, who always said she was 'working' when really she was just at a bar. But she can't tell her the truth – she just can't.

The words that now come out of Eve's mouth feel like self-induced vomit, poisonous and shameful. Nell deserves so much better than this.

'Darling,' says Eve, 'Mama Nell was very sick. She went away to get better. And that's all you need to know for now, okay, sweetie?'

Okay, and who made her sick, Eve?

2016

It's happened again: two more years have passed. It's not that every day hasn't had time in it, hasn't been comprised of waking and breakfast and running for the bus and work and lunches and drunken nights and hangovers and dreams crystallising and dreams being crushed and infatuations and sex and loss and midnight chocolate – but Nell and Eve and Tae and Marcus have somehow managed to carry on in the little bubble they made together at university. It's against the odds, you would think – how could a queer share house in which romantic tension lives so heavily not yet have crumbled or, worse, imploded?

But Marcus has finished his Honours year, won an award for his thesis on queer ecology in retail environments, and he's got a grad job with a firm he doesn't totally hate. Tae's managed to swing himself an assistant role at a fashion PR company, where he happily spends his days sending bitchy emails to other hot, under-paid people. Nell, despite her best efforts to chart her own path, has started to have some of her work shown and sold at the kind of galleries her parents shop at. Her work is good and the market likes it: she sees this as a curse. Eve is working as assistant fiction editor for an online literary magazine called *Infictus* – a full-time role that pays her a stipend of three hundred dollars per week – and she is Uber driving on the side to afford rent. They all still live in the same share house not far from Head Hunters. Nell still loves Eve. They still have not broached this.

Eve is writing her own fiction, or trying to, but everything she makes up reads as either saccharine or glib. She submitted one of her stories to *Infictus* under a pseudonym, and had to sit there in silence as her boss rejected her piece, calling it 'chick lit'. Writing about other people's work is a lot easier: she does the research, the close reading, brings in some theory texts, finds the right metaphor and then it happens, her ideas multiply and entwine, they grow across the page like vines. Choosing stories for the magazine has its own logic – pieces must be either completely flat, like Hemingway had a stroke and became even more terse, or they have to be about trauma but free of any specific context; it is imperative that the reader not understand what the fuck is happening.

Every day when Eve gets home from work she and Nell lie on her bed with a blunt while Eve regales Nell with tales of writers who refuse to accept edits, arguments over whether something is Kafkaesque.

'Today my boss said that "we have to embrace a Weilian philosophy of attentiveness", and she was talking about, like, copyedits,' Eve says. 'And I was like, I really don't think old mate Simone was thinking about semicolons when she was writing about, like, the decreation of personality, and—'

Nell finishes: 'and also *we* don't have to do anything, hunni?'

They both burst out laughing.

'Exactly!' yells Eve. 'Fucking exactly!'

Nell takes a hit and says, 'It's like that with art stuff too. Like, whenever I read manifestos from art movements or whatever, they're always so holier than thou, and so definitive, and so totally ensconced in their own ego . . . like, these artists get off on speaking for their time, speaking for others, and I get that maybe that could seem like a better alternative than getting trapped in multiplicity and partiality, but also – what makes anyone the authority on anyone else? No one can ever get inside someone else's head, like interpersonally even, so to speak so vehemently "for" a generation or a movement just seems so fucked up to me.'

'Mmm.' Eve is still sober enough to follow most of the thread Nell is weaving. 'So you think that in your paintings you only speak for yourself?'

'I mean, I try to. I think the worst thing you can do, as an artist, is try to tell someone else's story without involving them in the telling. Because you're never going to get it right.'

Eve ponders this. A lot of thoughts are swirling and a moment ago she felt very lucid and she was going to say something about cannibalistic empathy but her brain has entered a different realm now and all she can get out is nonsense. She speaks dreamily, sentences connecting like blu-tack stretched too thin. 'But don't you think that, by working in a medium that's existed for millennia, you're engaging in a conversation that's been unfurling since long before you existed? So maybe your voice isn't just yours, it's an accretion of and also a divergence from all the voices that have spoken through paint before?'

'I don't know, darling,' says Nell. She strokes Eve's hair. 'I don't think that made any sense, actually. But I love hearing you speak, regardless.'

Eve is laughing, convulsing with laughter, now. 'It didn't, did it?'

And Nell is laughing too, their stomachs are hurting from laughing, as Eve's phone rings.

With a lot of effort, she answers the call, still giggling. 'Hello?'

And it's the hospital, the voice on the other line says. It's the hospital, and her mother is dead.

*

Dead, dead, yes, people just die, and this is what Eve's mother has done. One moment they are alive, and the thoughts they have can be transmuted into action, and they can get on a train and then be somewhere else, and they can laugh and cry and feel sorrow and joy. And then, no. They can't anymore. Their heart has stopped beating and their brain has switched off and a minute ago you had a mother and now you don't.

Emerald has died of a heart attack. Her cleaner found her cold in her bed. Eve didn't even know Emerald had a cleaner. She's been taken to the morgue, and can Eve come in and identify her?

Eve is stoned; she can't identify her own hand.

'What? What is it, Eve?'

Nell's voice is urgent, hushed, and Eve hears it but she also doesn't? Her mind has ceased to work; is she dead too?

Nell has never seen this expression on Eve's face before; it's pure shock. A moment ago Eve's skin was rosy, now it is a grim white verging on bilious green. She's crying. She's not making any sound, but she is crying. There are tears dripping down her face, and the phone is still at her ear, suspended.

Eve is twenty-two years old. Her mother is dead. These truths should not exist side by side, yet here they are.

Images flash before Eve's eyes, a series of tableaus she doesn't want to see. Eve as a small child, cradled in her mother's arms, sobbing because she's just fallen over on asphalt. Emerald sitting in the audience at Eve's year three talent quest, at the end of the row, having only just arrived, but there nonetheless. Emerald tucking Eve into bed at night – it didn't happen often, but when it did Eve would try to memorise every second, play it back to herself on those more common evenings when Emerald would fall asleep on the couch before her daughter's bedtime. Eve waiting to be picked up from school, calling and calling, Emerald's phone ringing out. Emerald, a glass of wine in hand, telling Eve that the best thing she can do in life is look after herself first. Emerald stumbling, Emerald vomiting, Emerald leaving early.

Eve returns to the moment she is in, wipes her face with the back of her left hand, looks to Nell and says, 'Mum's dead, just a sec.'

Nell's jaw drops open, eyes misting over with sympathy, she moves forward to take Eve in her arms, hold her, hug her, comfort her. 'Oh, Evie, I—'

No; it will not do. Eve cuts Nell off with a raised hand. Eve will not accept this sympathy, she does not need it. Eve will go to the hospital, she will identify the body, she will come home, she will sleep, and her life will go on. Emerald is dead, so what? She was never much of a mother anyway. On many occasions she told Eve she hadn't wanted a child, even warned Eve against having one herself. This is fine, Eve is fine.

Eve responds to the nurse, or the morgue assistant, or whoever's voice is speaking to her, says she'll be there soon, ends the call.

Nell drives Eve to the morgue. Nell is also stoned, so the car crawls forward extremely slowly, or maybe that's just how it feels to Eve. Neon signs send strobes of colour into a world that Emerald is no longer in. They pass a cinema advertising films that Emerald will not watch.

They park at the hospital. Three patients are smoking outside the entrance, like an anthropomorphised Cerberus with emphysema.

The receptionist asks Eve how her day is going, which is like a far worse version of when the chemist asks how you are while you're paying for antidepressants.

In a big, bright room, Emerald is dead. The body is hers, Eve confirms it. Emerald looks smaller in death, which is something Eve has heard characters say on television, but it's true. Nell waits outside the door as Eve looks at her mother's body. The technician says it's okay if Eve wants to touch the body, but she doesn't. She cried when she got the call, but she's not crying now.

A week later, at the funeral, Eve recites a poem. She wants to read *I Could Not Tell* by Sharon Olds, but Nell convinces her not to, to choose Dickinson's *Because I Could Not Stop For Death* instead. She can't bring herself to deliver a eulogy, because a lot of what she's feeling right now, she's realised, is anger. There is anger coursing through her veins, anger sweating out of her pores. Over the past seven days, all these people have emerged from their crevices – her mum's colleagues, her mum's friends – and they've attempted to console her, they've told her that losing one's mother is the hardest thing one can bear. They've hugged her, and she can feel that they want her to cry for them.

Eve is angry because in death it's like Emerald's role has been rewritten; in death everyone is acting like Emerald was the perfect mother. Eve's role is to grieve, to be distraught. But she won't do it. Because Emerald was not the perfect mother; she was barely a mother at all. Eve feels like if she's grieving anything, it's the mother she never had rather than the person who just died. Her thoughts flicker back to that idea she used to drone on about. What if you could parent differently? What if there was a way to ensure a child would always be loved?

A lawyer reads Emerald's will to her. Eve is surprised Emerald ever had the foresight to write a will.

Eve inherits Emerald's apartment.

Eve is twenty-two, and she now has $500,000 in assets.

Part Four

2016

The months after the funeral are, unsurprisingly, surreal. Eve fucks more women in this period than in the past five years combined. Day after day, the women enter the share house, and sometimes it's up to Nell to open the front door and direct them to Eve's room. This kills Nell, but it is something she is willing to do for her friend who is in pain and refuses to admit it.

Eve goes to work, goes to bars, sometimes she even goes to parties. But she does not wash her sheets: they are yellow with sweat and other bodily fluids. Each morning Nell trades Eve's empty teacups for full ones. Eve is existing, but to what end? Nell misses Eve's smile.

Marcus and Tae attempt to keep up the level of cheer in the house, playing pop songs and regaling Eve with any gay gossip they encounter. Eve listens but she doesn't hear.

Tae's mum Hana comes over once a week with bulgogi, fried chicken, japchae. Hana's going through chemo, for fuck's sake, and still she drives halfway across Sydney every week with home-cooked food for her son's friend.

Sometimes, after depositing everything in the fridge and freezer, Hana sits with Eve in her room. She sits on the end of the bed and tells Eve that she's a beautiful girl and that everything will be okay. Tae doesn't come in the room when Eve and Hana are having these moments – he's very aware that, of the four housemates, he's the only one with a good mum. He can share.

Hana tells Eve that it's okay to grieve her mother even if she didn't always like her – that the maternal bond is the most complicated of all, that she didn't like her own mother all that much.

'How did you know how to parent Tae then, if you had no model for it yourself?' Eve asks.

'Oh, darling, you don't need a model to know how to love,' replies Hana. 'And you already know very well how to do that. Besides, you've been parenting these two gay boys for years. Remember when you first moved in? Tae called me and said you made a roster for cleaning the toilet; he was so put out. But look at him now – he never misses my appointments, he cooks, he cleans. You deserve some of the credit for that. When you do decide to parent, you'll be just fine.'

Eve smiles forlornly. 'Thanks, Hana.'

Sometimes, Hana stays to eat with them, and when this happens Eve comes out of her room and joins the others in the lounge room. Eve watches Hana with her son; it is clear she is proud of him, and he is proud of her. Eve does cry at this.

*

One day, about six months after Emerald's death, Eve calls Nell into her room. It's a Saturday and the boys are at Carriageworks, ostensibly buying kombucha and wild mushrooms, but mostly flirting with the hot guy who runs the coffee stall.

Nell enters Eve's room to find Eve sitting up in bed – still under the covers, but upright, at least.

'Come, sit,' says Eve. She pats the mattress near her.

Nell sits. 'This is ominous,' she says.

Eve laughs, which surprises Nell. Eve hasn't laughed in some time.

'It's nothing bad, I promise.'

'I feel like that's what people say before they give you the worst news ever, but okay, I'm listening.'

'Okay,' Eve begins. She scooches up a bit in the bed, so now she's pretty much sitting cross-legged. 'So. You know how Emerald left me her apartment, right?'

'Right . . .' Nell says cautiously, unsure where Eve is going with this.

'And it's just been like . . . sitting there. Well, about a month ago I . . . sold it."

'Okay?' Nell can't imagine how Eve did this without her knowing.

'Yeah, I mean, it was just . . . I didn't want to rent it out. Like, the mortgage was paid off, so it wasn't haemorrhaging money . . . but yeah. The new owners settle soon, and I'll have to go through Emerald's furniture and whatever, but honestly I don't care about it . . . anyway, that's beside the point.'

'It is?' Nell is still very confused as to where this conversation is going.

'The point *is*', says Eve, 'I have all this money. And it's like, what do I do with it? Or what do I actually *want* to do with it?'

Nell is pleased to hear that Eve has been contemplating the future; this is a good sign. 'It's great you're thinking about this, Evie,' she says. She gives her friend's shoulder a squeeze. 'So, what are you planning? Please don't say "investment property", but also I'll understand if you do.'

'Well . . .' Eve pauses. 'I want to have a baby.'

Nell gasps. She did not see this coming. 'Whoa, okay, I—'

Eve cuts Nell off. 'Sorry, what I meant to say was, I want *us* to have a baby.'

'Hold on, *what?*' Nell gapes at her, not sure if she's heard correctly. A baby? With Eve? What does that even mean? Eve's not – she not saying she wants them to be together, is she? No, surely not. But maybe? No, wait, fuck, a baby, what? Eve's grieving, she's gone temporarily insane, that must be it. She hasn't been herself since Emerald died, Nell must talk her down from the ledge, even if, yes, obviously having a baby with Eve and the two of them being together forever is literally the best thing that Nell could ever imagine. But it's crazy, it can't happen, no. They're twenty-two, for fuck's sake.

Nell is about to speak but Eve gets there first, in a rush of words. Clearly she's been rehearsing this.

'Just think about it,' says Eve. 'Really, we've been talking about this forever, right? It's like, people usually have babies because they're in long-term relationships and they're financially stable and they can't think what else to do, so they just, like, pop one out, right? It's like what we were saying at the bowling alley all those years ago – do you remember, with all those devo parents? And we even talked about it when we were kids; maybe you don't remember, but I do. This is not just some new idea I've had in the throes of grief or something, I swear.' Eve is gesticulating emphatically, like a general in a Hollywood movie trying to convince the American president to bomb Australia to save the world. 'And Emerald dying has, like, really clarified some things for me. And even having Hana over here all the time, and seeing how she is with Tae, it's just, it's made me think, I want that. I want a baby of my own, of *our* own. I want to be a mother. I want a baby to love, and to care for, and I want to be the exact opposite of what my mother was like with me, and, well – I want to do it with you, Nell. I want us to be best friends who raise a child together.'

Eve takes a breath, looks at Nell, who is silent, still in shock. 'Nell, are you okay?' She reaches out and strokes Nell's cheek.

Nell's heart pumps harder. Some might say that Eve knows exactly what she is doing in this moment.

'Yeah, no, I am . . . I'm just . . . processing.'

'Okay.'

'So,' says Nell, 'say I'm going to entertain this idea just for a second, like, totally hypothetically?'

'Fine.'

'So, hypothetically, how would it even work? Even if we *were* together – which we're not, *obviously*!' Nell waits a beat to see if Eve will interject and miraculously tell her what she wants to hear. Eve does not. 'Even if we *were*, it might have skipped your mind that we're both women? So . . . we *can't* just have a baby? Plus, we're twenty-two and we live in a share house and we have no money. When are you going to have time to write? When will I have time to make art? Do you see there are some issues here?'

Eve smiles magnanimously; she's got answers for all these questions. 'But that's what's so brilliant about having a dead mum!' she exclaims. 'I have five hundred thousand dollars! That's enough to put down a huge deposit on an apartment, and instead of what we've been paying for rent, we'll pay toward the mortgage, and we'll still have savings left over.'

'Okay, sure.' Nell does see that financially it's not so crazy. Still, she must put a stop to this. 'And what about the whole *sperm* thing, then? I hardly think any sperm bank is going to agree to inseminate a single, twenty-two-year-old literary magazine assistant editor.'

'Fuck no, they wouldn't, but that's okay, because it's *sorted*!'

Nell puts her head in her hands. 'Please don't tell me you've raw-dogged some random, Eve, I beg you. I'm pretty sure there are, like, laws against covertly stealing sperm during sex. You would not do well in jail, Eve, you wouldn't.'

Eve is hysterical with laughter. 'Ha! *Ewww!* No, Nell, gross!' She flicks her hands as if trying to get sewage off them. 'It won't be like that at all, yucky yuck yuck! No, see, the thing is I've already talked to Marcus and he's in!'

'You've *what*?'

'I've talked to Marcus! It's perfect! He doesn't want kids of his own but he has all this sperm just, like, clogging up his balls, and he loves us and we're family anyway, and he and Tae will be like uncles to the little sprog!'

'And Marcus has expressly told you that he thinks this is a good idea? He hasn't said, for instance, that it's fucking batshit?' Nell cannot *believe* Marcus, encouraging this unhinged scheme.

'Nope, he has not said that. He says that queer family is the way of the future and more people should be doing this.'

Nell grimaces. 'And what about Tae?'

'What *about* Tae?' asks Eve, like this is a silly question.

'Well, what does he think about all of this? If we're a family, then surely he gets a say?'

When Eve flagged her plan with Tae a week ago, after one of Hana's visits, he expressed extreme disapproval, but Eve is not going to tell Nell this. Tae told Eve that having a baby is a serious, life-changing act, and that you can't just decide to have one on a whim, even if you are grieving. Tae also said that it would be unfair to ask Nell to co-parent. Tae insinuated that Eve was being selfish, and that even if she thought she could manage the transition to motherhood, Nell would not be able to handle the responsibility or the dynamic. Eve did not respond to this kindly. Eve said some things she shouldn't have.

Eve goes in for the kill. 'Oh, Nellie, no. Like yes, Tae is our family, but this would be *our* baby, yours and mine. Marcus would be the donor – I'll try, like, a turkey baster scenario, and if that doesn't work I'll do IUI or IVF, courtesy of Emerald – and then you and I will live together and raise the bub and we'll be co-parents and nothing can ever go wrong because we'll never stop being best friends, you know? It's not like we're going to break up.'

Eve looks at Nell with the widest eyes, and Nell can feel her resistance melting.

Then Eve delivers the line she knows Nell won't be able to refuse. 'You'd never break up with me, would you, Nell? I love you more than anyone else in the world – you know that, right?'

Nell doesn't respond; she is thinking.

'Right?' asks Eve again.

Nell sighs. Eve has her cornered. What else is she going to say? She'll do anything to make Eve happy, of course she will.

'I love you more than anyone else in the world too, Eve.'

'Good!' cries Eve. 'And you'll never leave me?'

'I'll never leave you, Eve. You know that. What would I do without you?'

2024

'What was Nell sick from, Mum?' asks Lake. They are at the park, yet again. They are always at the park. Most of parenting is being at the park.

Lake has taken to asking about Nell most days. It's like she's scratched a half-healed mosquito bite and now it is weeping, it is pulsing, it refuses to close over.

Eve is pushing Lake on the swing. 'Well' – *push* – 'like I said, honey' – *push* – 'Nell had a kind of sickness that was very' – *push* – 'hard to diagnose' – *push*.

Why, why did Eve choose to pathologise Lake's other mother? In what world was that a healthy parenting decision? And worse than that, it was untrue. Nell wasn't sick; Nell was destroyed. By Eve. Eve didn't have to write about it, but she did, because she saw an opportunity and she took it, consequences be damned.

'Like the flu?' asks Lake. *Push.*

'Not like the flu.' *Push.*

'Like cancer?' *Push.*

'Not like cancer.' *Push.*

'Like depression?' *Hold.*

Eve grabs the swing's chains, brings Lake to a halt, walks around to the swing seat, kneels down, now at eye level with her daughter.

'How do you know about depression, sweetheart?' asks Eve. God, what has she done to this child?

Lake looks unbothered. 'You told me depression is a symptom of late capitalism,' she answers.

Eve heaves a sigh of relief, 'Ah, yet again, my dear, you are right. I did say that. But no, honey, Nell didn't have depression.' Well, she probably did, but Eve didn't want to know. 'No, Nell had a kind of . . . other malady. It was from' – what is she going to say now? – *Think of something, Eve.* Oh god, she has it. It's almost too poetic. Damn her English degree. 'It was from a medusa jellyfish sting.'

'What?!' exclaims Lake. 'You're lying, Mum.'

'Am not,' says Eve. 'She was stung, and she had to go away to get better.'

'Stung by a jellyfish?' Lake crosses her arms, distrustful.

'They're very rare, you know,' says Eve. 'Sometimes a medusa jellyfish sting can take years and years to heal.'

Lake thinks about this. 'Can people die from medusa jellyfish stings?'

The answer is yes.

Eve says no, of course not.

2016

Now Eve has strongarmed Nell into agreeing with her plan, the house has become tense, uncomfortable. Tae thinks Eve's baby-making scheme is insane, cruel even, but she won't listen to him, and Nell certainly won't. Every time he's tried to bring up the practicalities with Nell, she gets defensive, spouting the lines Eve has fed her. Marcus is vehemently on board with the idea. He keeps quoting scenes from *Priscilla, Queen of the Desert*, saying, 'If gay Hugo Weaving can do it, so can I!'

Eve starts donating old clothes to Vinnies, to 'make space for the baby.' She is manic, juiced up on imagined scenes of domestic bliss and reparative maternity. Nell is terrified, obviously, but Eve is so happy, so excited: Nell can't take these feelings from her. Besides, Nell reasons, it's hard to get pregnant. Eve will probably try a few times, fail, and then move on to grieving properly. This nesting desire is part of Eve's healing process, but it won't come to fruition.

So they go forward with the scheme.

Two months later, Eve and Nell move out into their own new place, so the hypothetical crying baby won't disturb Tae's beauty sleep – or Marcus's, for that matter. It's a one-bedroom apartment in Newtown, previously unoccupied, and now it's all theirs, thanks to Emerald. Nell suggested that a two-bedroom apartment might be more sensible, but Eve pointed out that they sleep in the same bed most nights anyway, and with the baby, well, one of them will always be up, so what was the point in having two bedrooms? It's cheaper this way, and it's sensible. Plus, Eve loves a platonic snuggle.

Sabrina from Head Hunters moves into Eve's old room in the share house, which has a nice queer synchronicity to it, Eve thinks. After all, Eve hooked up with Sab all those years ago, which brought her to her first job, which brought her to queer community, which brought her to queer motherhood. The boys are going to use Nell's room as a study, because they are both now earning salaries and can afford the extra rent. All is well with the world!

After googling 'turkey baster technique,' the girls discover that it doesn't involve an actual turkey baster. They are glad they checked this, because Eve really was planning on going to Chef's Warehouse. For intracervical insemination all you need to do is buy a syringe kit off the internet, get a dude to jizz, wait for the most fertile moment in your menstrual cycle, and then up goes the sperm. For women over twenty-five, the rate of success goes way down, but Eve is fertile as hell. She's brimming with maternal juices.

The boys come round to Nell and Eve's new flat for pizza nights, for wine, but the group dynamic has shifted. Tae routinely suggests that if they are really going to go through with this, it might be a good idea to draft a parenting plan or engage lawyers to work out parental rights for Nell. Eve laughs at this, because Tae has never suggested anything so practical in his life. She also laughs because she has no intention of involving the medical authorities – 'Big Pharma can suck my dick,' she says, even though Big Pharma would have nothing to do with what Tae is suggesting.

Even though Marcus is decidedly Team Baby, he has asked if they've considered what would happen if one of them gets a new partner. How would she or he fit into the equation? Would they be a parent to the child too, and where would they live? How will they handle expenses, how will they divide parenting duties, how will their work be affected by having a child? And on and on and on he goes, such a killjoy!

'No way I'm having some lawyer involved in this,' Eve says to Nell. 'Right?'

The two of them are sitting on their new bed. 'Like, that's the whole point of this, don't you agree? We're making new life in a way that works for us, and we're not letting non-community members make rules about how we parent.'

Nell will not disagree with Eve about any of it. She has her fears, she has her qualms, obviously – but it is joyous to by buoyed along by Eve's blind conviction. She's watching her friend come back to life. And again, the chances of Eve actually conceiving are so slim, she tells herself. When it doesn't work after a turn or two, Eve will give up, surely.

Eve lies flat, stomach down on the bed, as Nell tickles her feet.

'Hey, are you going to tell James and Ondine about this? Or Chelsea, even?' Eve asks this almost as an afterthought, but Nell has been considering it a lot. Her regular lunches with her parents have dwindled. Four strained meals ago Ondine made a comment about people who commit suicide being 'selfish,' and then proceeded to argue that if one is to suicide then the 'least they can do is keep it clean . . . so rude to make others wipe up one's splatter.' Since then, it's like a chord has snapped. Nell isn't sure that she is able to keep trying with them.

'Well, like . . . no? I think no is the right answer. I haven't talked to them in ages anyway; I don't see why it's any of their business. James and Ondine wouldn't understand, obviously. They'd just go on about how irresponsible I am, and how they always knew I'd fuck up my life.'

'And Chelsea?'

'Well, Chelsea I think I have to tell. She's more likely to get it. And she's going to be an aunty, after all. I think she'll freak out initially and then warm to the idea. And once the baby's here, what's she gonna do? Like, excommunicate me? I'm the only family member she actually likes.'

Nell speaks to Eve as if the baby is a certainty, because this is what Eve needs to hear. In her own mind, Nell is thinking through how she will support Eve when it doesn't work.

Eve nods serenely. Everything is so easy! She's going to be a mother and so is Nell! *Why do people get so worked up about pregnancy?* she wonders. It's the most natural thing in the world. And twenty-two isn't *that* young. Women used to get pregnant at twenty-two all the time.

Besides, pregnancy is good for mental health, she's decided. Since coming up with the baby idea, Eve has blossomed into vitality once more. She's energised, she's happy, she's researching baby blankets and bassinets and preschools and sleep cycles and breast pumps. She's started writing stories again, all about motherhood and queer family, and lo and behold some of them are even getting accepted into journals. People love queer family fiction; it's so sellable, it's so *now*! She slides quotes from Kristeva into creative non-fiction about monstrous maternity, and it's like she's found the golden ticket. Suddenly, editors are calling her writing 'brave' and 'necessary' rather than shallow and florid. This is it, this is her calling!

And with Nell, with dear, sweet, loyal Nell. Nell, who would do anything for her. It's perfect.

*

Four months after Eve's maternal declaration, she decides she and Nell are ready to shake the rattle and try impregnation.

The girls decide to do the insemination in what is now Marcus and Tae's share house, an homage to the family who taught them they could make their own.

The four of them plus Sabrina eat a dinner of baked vegetables and tahini, and then Marcus goes to his bedroom and gets down to the business of masturbating into a cup. Tae sits quietly, on edge. Eve has insisted that Marcus listen to 'smooth lesbian pop' as he wanks, to increase the chances of the baby being queer. A few minutes later, Marcus emerges, cup in hand, and the group (bar Tae) applaud him for his valiant efforts.

'What did you think about while you stroked, Marcus?' asks Sabrina.

'Queer futurity,' says Marcus solemnly.

'Okay, and what did you actually think about?' Sabrina asks.

Marcus doesn't even pause. 'Rupert Everett circa 1995.'

Tae is still quiet, but the rest of the gang are in a jubilant mood.

'Pass me the jizz, would you, Marcus?' asks Eve.

She takes the cup in her hands, inspects it.

'Wow, sperm really is gross, isn't it?' she observes.

'Excuse me!' cries Marcus. 'I've been told I have prime spunk on more than one occasion. Now, shouldn't you two be shoving that up Eve's vag now?'

'Correct, correct!' exclaims Eve. 'Come on, Nell, let's get this show on the road!'

In Marcus's bedroom, Eve speedily undresses. Nell does her usual trick of counting sheep in her head to try to distract from the heat she feels in her groin when she sees Eve naked. She transfers the sperm from the cup to a needle-less syringe; it reminds Nell of one of those applicator tampons nerds used back in school.

Eve lies down on her back, puts a pillow under her bum, spreads her legs. This is not how Nell pictured seeing Eve's vagina up close for the first time, but life is full of surprises. She can do this. She *will* do this.

'Inseminate me, babe!'

If Nell hadn't been with Eve all day, she might think that Eve has been doing lines, she is that energised.

'The instructions said you should listen to calm music and try to breathe slowly,' says Nell. 'Shall I put something on?'

'Fuck it!' says Eve. 'I'm as ready as I'll ever be!' She widens her legs even further.

'Alright then,' says Nell. 'Well . . . I guess I'm just going to . . . do it?'

'Atta girl!'

And so Nell kneels down at the end of Marcus's bed, places her left hand on the mattress next to Eve's stomach. She then realises this won't work; she needs more purchase on Eve's body. She readjusts her left hand, places it on the inside of Eve's right thigh. Still, it's not enough. So, finally, she hovers her left hand above Eve's labia and, ever so gently, she uses her thumb and forefinger to open Eve up.

She glances at her friend; Eve is watching Nell like she trusts her implicitly.

With her right hand, Nell brings the syringe up to Eve's vagina. Slowly, slowly, she inserts it. Up, and up, and Eve doesn't so much as whimper. 'Does it hurt?' Nell asks.

'It's fine,' Eve assures her. 'Up we go.'

Nell continues pushing, her fingers are inside Eve now, she's trying to guide the tip of the syringe as close as possible to the entrance to Eve's cervix. She's watched some YouTube videos; it can't be that hard. When she thinks she's there, she says, 'Do you think that's it?'

'Only one way to find out,' Eve responds.

So Nell goes for it. Tenderly, she depresses the plunger on the end of the syringe, and she keeps pressing until she cannot press any more. The sperm must be out by now, she thinks. She holds the syringe there, her hand still inside Eve, for about ten seconds, before she slowly withdraws it.

'Okay,' says Nell. 'It's done. You have to lie there for about fifteen minutes, okay? I'll stay with you the whole time. You're being so brave.'

At this moment, it hits Eve for the first time, the enormity of what she's doing. She blinks back tears. What the actual fuck is she on about? She loves sleeping in. She has no idea how to care for a child. But she will not back out. She will not show that she is scared. Her mother is dead, and now she is going to be a mother, and she is going to be fucking good at it.

Nell is also panicking, wishing she hadn't encouraged Eve. Like, yes, she wants to support Eve in any way she can, and the odds of this sperm taking are so low – but what if it works? Eve is grieving, she's not in her right mind. Nell should have talked her out of it. But it's too late now. They'll make this one attempt, and then Nell will counsel Eve out of trying again.

'I love you, Nellie,' whispers Eve. And she says it with such affection, such hope, such adoration, that Nell wavers. Maybe this idea is actually genius. Nell wants to be looked at this way by Eve forever.

'I love you too, Evie. Always have, always will.'

*

Two weeks later, Eve takes a pregnancy test. Nell is with her, in their new bathroom. A single line appears on the stick first; this is the control.

The urine creeps up, and the two young women hold their breaths.

A second line appears. It's not even faint.

Eve is pregnant, and on the first try, too. Eve and Nell are going to have a baby.

*

My baby. My *baby.*

Eve repeats the words to herself over and over, the intonation somehow different each time, even though there are only three syllables and thus there should really be a finite number of variations. The thing is, every time Eve says it to herself – *my baby* – it becomes loaded with every other thought and emotion she's ever had. Every time Eve thinks *my baby*, she thinks of her own body, what it has meant to her over the years, how it's going to change, how it's not going to be just hers anymore, and what does that mean for when the baby is outside of her – will her body still belong to the baby? She thinks about Emerald, and how she must have thought the same words at some point, and she wonders how Emerald felt about them; certainly differently from Eve. She thinks about Nell, and how it's actually Nell's baby too, but it's growing inside *her* body and it's *her* egg and it's *her* uterus and it's *her* expanding tits, and it's probably bad to be feeling so possessive already when the express point of this parenting situation is supposed to be about *co*-caring, parental reciprocity, mutual aid and anti-heteronormative concatenation. She's a bad lesbian mother. She's a bad lesbian mother co-parenting platonically with her female best friend. My *baby*. It's been five weeks since the pregnancy test. The baby isn't even the size of a blueberry yet. My baby.

Eve is already worried about when the baby will start replacing herself. One day the baby will be lying down, the next sitting, the next crawling, and then one day, one day she'll speak. And Eve might not remember the baby she was the day before. Eve's mind works like this, it always has – each day becomes the next and the day before is forgotten. Feelings are the through line, they braid each day together, but the idiosyncrasies of the knots are soon forgotten. Right now, the baby is a clump of cells inside Eve's insides. Tomorrow, she will be more. Eve does not imagine that the baby inside of her might be a boy. This possibility is unthinkable. She will be a girl, and Eve will love her, and so will Nell, and they will all live together and they will all be happy, and the baby will never know loneliness or pain. And where Eve's memories fade – when she forgets what the baby was like at three months, at eight years old, at twelve – Nell's will not.

*

As Eve's stomach grows, she and Nell prepare the apartment for the newborn. The internet has a lot of advice about how to prepare for a baby, and most of it costs a lot of money. Eve and Nell have some money, but they also both work in the arts – economy is key. Sabrina spreads the word at Head Hunters that there's a young pregnant queer in need of baby paraphernalia, and the community does what it does best – rallies. Suddenly, the apartment has a change table, a crib, a pram, twelve sleep suits, nappies, a variety of blankets, about nine million onesies, and enough ugly plastic toys to entertain an army of children. Where there was once space, now there is *stuff*. While Eve and Nell had planned to dedicate their bookshelf to the likes of Audre Lorde and John Berger, they now have every baby book known to woman – that is, every queer baby book known to woman. The titles are amazing – *A is for Activist*; *Heather Has Two Mummies*; *The Rainbow Serpent* (it's not technically gay but they've decided it is queer-coded); *Mommy, Mama, and Me* – and Nell and Eve spend evenings lying on the couch reading them to each other and giggling.

A few nights a week, Marcus joins them. He drinks wine while Eve resentfully drinks ginger ale and Nell stays sober in solidarity with Eve. Tae comes over far less regularly, and when he does, he's distant. Eve and Nell pretend to each other that this is not the case, because were they to unpack Tae's unease, they would also have to face the reality of his concerns, and this is not something that they want to do. Nell sympathises with Tae's position; she was critical of the plan also, but it's too late for naysaying now: there is a baby coming. Tae can either get on board or not. It pains both Eve and Nell to see a member of their family gradually detaching himself from them, but how are they to remedy this? They can't. They must go on.

'Did you know that C stands for "creative counter to corporate cultures"?' says Eve, laughing.

'I think any baby of ours is going to know that *in the womb*,' says Nell. She pats Eve's stomach, which hasn't popped, but has gotten larger, like she's eaten a really big burrito that won't ever digest. She whispers to the baby, 'Bottoms and tops we all hate cops, isn't that right, little one?'

'I think she'll be a top,' says Marcus. 'I mean, half her genes are mine and half are yours, Eve, and I don't think there's a bottom element between us . . . That being said, there's also the whole nature versus nurture thing, and she will be half-raised by Nell – and I don't know if you consider this offensive or not, Nell, but you give serious bottom energy.'

Nell tries not to blush. She still goes red every time her sexuality is discussed in front of Eve. She is trying to appear sexless, totally safe. Eve can never know how she feels, especially now.

'Not offended at all, Marcus,' she says. 'Every top needs a bottom, and every bottom needs a top.' She pauses. 'Do you think the baby can hear us?'

Eve smiles. 'Oh, absolutely. She's learning our voices and she's taking it all in. She's going to be the first baby who comes out of the womb reciting passages of *Capitalist Realism*. And she's going to be so, so loved. *So*, so loved!' She says this in a baby voice and directs it towards her stomach.

She's started speaking in a baby voice a lot, which is confronting. How did she not know there was this whole other persona inside of her, this mushy, squishy person who repeats every sentence twice with an upward inflection, like everything's a question?

At two and a half months pregnant, the hormones are filling her up. A few older queers at Head Hunters have warned her that her emotions are going to be all over the place, that irritation is normal, that nausea is likely in the first trimester but it will pass – Eve's felt none of these undesirable symptoms. She's euphoric, in fact. She's glowing. She's been craving a lot of pickles but this doesn't seem like a negative to her.

Nell gets serious for a second. She's been considering a possibility that she fears Eve has not adequately prepared herself for. 'Evie, just hypothetically, of course, but on the very off chance . . . how are you going to feel if *she* turns out to be a *he*?'

Eve pretends to gag. 'Okay, well, first of all, I can feel in my bones that this baby is a girl. But if they do turn out to be biologically male, then I guess it's on us to create the best man this world has ever seen. And if they're assigned male, then there's always the hope that they'll be trans, right? Fingers crossed.'

'Or they could be non-binary!' adds Nell.

Marcus scoffs. 'Knowing you, Evie, they'll probably be dog-binary.'

'*Que?*' says Eve.

Marcus smirks, takes a sip of his wine. 'I mean they'll use "bitch" pronouns.'

'Ouch!' cries Eve, punching Marcus on the arm.

When Marcus has left, the girls lie in bed and watch YouTube videos about birthing. In between harrowing recordings of vaginas being ruined, they've started getting targeted ads about the marriage equality plebiscite, which is set to happen the following year.

'Would you ever want to get married, Eve?' asks Nell.

Eve screws up her nose. 'Ew, fuck no. Like, obviously I support gay people being allowed to get married, but to me, the whole institution just seems so antiquated; like, why would I want to be part of that, you know?'

'Mmm.' Nell nods. 'For sure, for sure.' She is secretly pleased that Eve opposes marriage, because Nell doesn't think she could stand it if one day Eve were to marry someone else.

They fall asleep spooning, the laptop still open at the end of the bed.

*

At eighteen weeks, the anatomy scan. Nell and Eve sit in uncomfortable seats, waiting to be called in to the doctor's office. Eve's bump is bigger now, but still not so large that strangers realise she is pregnant. Last week she told her boss at the literary mag that she's expecting, and he seemed bewildered but he congratulated her. The magazine doesn't offer maternity leave but Eve will be eligible for paid parental leave from the government, which means she'll get eighteen weeks on minimum wage. As minimum wage is much higher than what she currently earns, this is a win.

'Bowman? Eve Bowman?'

The doctor is a man, which is a shame, but he's very keen to show that he is not homophobic. 'And you're the other mum, I take it?' he asks Nell as Eve lies back in the ultrasound chair.

'Yep, that's right.'

'Well, you two make a very lovely couple!' he says, and before Nell can correct him, Eve interjects: 'We're not a couple,' she says. 'We're friends who are co-parenting.'

The doctor's face shows his confusion, but he rearranges it as quickly as he can. He has been around long enough to know that any advice he gives to expecting mothers is rarely well received, let alone when there are *lesbians* involved. 'Right, well, lovely!' he says. 'Very modern!'

Nell and Eve roll their eyes at each other when the doctor's back is turned.

When he turns back around, the doctor is holding a tube of gel.

'Okay,' he says to Eve, 'now, I'm going to get you to lift your t-shirt for me, and then I'll apply this gel to your abdomen. That'll make it easier for the sound waves to transmit, and then I'm going to move this transducer' – he points to a probe-like instrument – 'over your tummy, and we should be able to see baby up there on the screen. Does that sound good?'

'It sounds amazing,' says Eve dryly. 'You ready, Nell?'

Nell is not ready, she cannot believe this is reality, but it is her job to be calm and strong. She takes Eve's hand. 'Absolutely,' she says. 'Take it away, doc.'

The doctor slides the probe over Eve's belly, up and down and all around, and suddenly, there is an image on the screen. It's blobby, it's moving, and Eve can't really make out what she is seeing.

'So,' says the doctor, 'at first glance, organs look good, placenta looks good . . . do you already know the sex of the baby?'

'Um, no?' says Eve. 'This is our first scan?'

The doctor's brow furrows. 'Ah, right, okay. Apologies – I just presumed you would have had the ten-week blood test. No matter. Well, do you want to know the sex of the baby?'

Eve speaks before she realises she is doing so: 'Yes please thank you very much,' she blurts.

The doctor studies the screen then smiles. 'Well, it seems to me that you are going to have a little baby girl.'

The sigh of relief from both Eve and Nell is audible.

'Oh my god,' says Eve.

'Oh thank god,' says Nell. She squeezes Eve's hand. 'We're going to have a girl, Evie! A little girl! You were right!'

Eve is crying happy tears, and so is Nell. Everything is perfect, everything is as it should be. A girl! A little girl of their own! Nell didn't know it was possible to love Eve more than she already does, and yet she can feel her heart doubling in size. An image of Ondine flashes into her mind. It would be nice if she could share this moment with her mother. If she could call her, tell her the wonderful news that she's going to be a grandmother. But Ondine would never accept that. Nell is alone in this – well, alone with Eve, and with the baby. So, not alone, actually. Nell will never be alone in the world again. Realising this, she cries more, with joy and relief in equal measure.

*

Wanting a baby and having a baby growing inside you are two very different things. Eve's never been much of planner – when people talk about ten-year plans, for example, Eve has always baulked. How could Eve make room for worrying about the future when the present itself is so very worrisome, and the past even more so? But having this little being kicking inside of her is shifting her relation to time. Now in the second trimester, Eve is imagining what the world will be like in ten years, in twenty. She's reading climate reports and attending environmental rallies. She's become obsessed with avoiding single-use plastics. Nell is doing her best to calm Eve, but it's a difficult job, because all signs do point to environmental collapse and the end of the world. Has Eve been fundamentally selfish, choosing to bring a child into this world? These are considerations she probably should have entertained before inseminating herself with her gay friend's sperm, but it's too late to turn back now. It is up to Eve to solve the existential problem of procreation in climate crisis.

'What if our baby actually turns out to be the one person who can heal the planet?' Eve muses, as Nell massages her feet. 'That could happen, right?'

'That could absolutely happen,' agrees Nell.

'And then we haven't been selfish, we've been generous.'

'The most generous, yes,' says Nell.

Eve starts to cry. She has been crying a lot recently. 'It's just, all I do is think about what the world will be for the bubba, and I get totally stuck. It's like my mind is sinking into wet concrete, and my heart is beating overtime, and then I start panicking because what is the stress doing for the baby? Like, I'm hurting her even more by worrying about her future and she isn't even born yet. I'm a terrible mother and she's still in fucking utero.' Eve looks at Nell beseechingly. 'Do you feel like that too?' she asks. 'How are you being so chill?'

Nell sighs; how she wishes she could bear Eve's pain for her. 'I'm not calm, Evie. I'm not a calm person. I'm worried about the planet, obviously, and I'm worried about what the world will be able to give to this little person . . . and I'm worried that I won't have much to give her myself, and I'm worried because milk prices are always going up. But' – Nell pauses, strokes Eve's hair – 'there's one thing I'm not worried about, which kind of makes everything else okay, somehow.'

'What's that?' asks Eve.

'I'm not worried about you.' Nell says this very measuredly; there is a gravity to her statement that Eve does not understand.

'That's very sweet, Nellie, but what do you mean? How does that help?'

'Eve Bowman,' says Nell, 'strap in. You are the single best thing about living on this planet. On the days when I can't face anything, when I feel like what even is the point of getting up and making things and selling them and then doing it again, when I'm like, is there even enough good in the world to balance out all the shit – I just think of you, and I'm calmed, and I know that I can keep living.'

Eve is riveted, hanging on Nell's every word.

Nell goes on. 'Because you, Eve, are a fundamentally good person. You are kind, you want people to be happy, you're forgiving, you're excitable, you're so smart – like smart in a terrifying way. You're so strange and funny and earnest, but then your mind works with this, like, cool precision, like you cut through the gauze. When you write it's like you're practising alchemy. And you have so much to give and you know just how to give it, which is something I never know. And this baby – our baby – she's going to have you as a mum. So I'll support you as much as I humanly can, and I'll love her so much it might even be a bit weird, but really, I'm expendable: you've got this. You are going to show this baby that there is a good way to live, and she is going to be the luckiest person in the world because of that. To be loved by you is a privilege that very few people experience, and this baby, she's already got the golden ticket.'

Eve is smiling now. 'You really think so?'

'I know so.'

'And you're not expendable, Nell – you know that, right? I need you, and so will she. She isn't *my* baby, she's ours.'

Nell doesn't say that she's terrified; terrified that one day Eve will decide she's better off without Nell, terrified that the baby won't see Nell as her parent, terrified that soon enough Eve will realise that Nell is just an unnecessary addendum, a fire blanket in the middle of an ocean.

'I know that, Eve,' murmurs Nell. 'I know that.'

*

Over the next few months, Nell and Eve perfect their domestic rituals. They make tea, they work, they go for walks, they go grocery shopping. It's exciting, it's like playing dress-ups, except it's also real. Chelsea keeps sending them picture books about aunties.

Four months before Eve's due date – probably too late, but whatever – they start taking prenatal seminars at the women's hospital. Each week, they take the bus to the hospital, Nell buys Eve a chocolate bar in the gift shop, and then they find their way through the hospital maze to the exercise room. Mirrors on all the walls, bright fluorescent lights, straight men trying and failing to be useful, these classes are immense fun, particularly because, being twenty-two, Eve's pelvic floor is extremely strong, her vagina muscles taut, her core engaged. She's never been the best one in an exercise class before, and of course it's not a competition, but if it was, she would be winning. Plus, Eve delights in the confusion her and Nell's platonic dynamic causes for the other expectant parents.

'So you're lesbians?'
'Ish.'
'But you're not together?'
'That's right.'
'But you're having the baby together?'
'That's right.'
'And you're going to co-parent as friends?'
'Bingo.'
'?'

Between stretches and bridges, parents-to-be share their conception stories – accident, IVF, surrogacy, penis-in-vagina miracle, and so on. Eve tells everyone that she and Nell literally used a turkey baster and smiles as she watches them decide whether she's kidding or not. Nell has been attempting to come across as the reliable one in their twosome, the one who can explain to the other parents about alternative family set-ups, but Eve's mischievous brashness scares them off. Still, Nell will not deny Eve her fun; when she isn't having meltdowns about environmental collapse, she is taking to pregnancy like a scissor to another scissor, like a glove to a traditional two-woman light lunch. Her stomach is round and smooth, her skin glows, her smile is wide, and she's found her purpose. And no, she still isn't talking to Nell about her mother, or sharing her grief, or journaling, or seeing a therapist who might diagnose her with some kind of inverted projection issues and tell her to work through her shit. But she's happy, so who cares?

When the baby first kicks, it feels like a frog is hiccupping inside Eve's belly. As the baby grows, the kicks become more definite: they can no longer be mistaken for hiccups, they are absolutely evidence that a live being is karate-chopping at Eve's insides. One night, five months in, Lake kicks as Eve is lying on the couch. They've decided to call her Lake.

It's funny, but also fucking beautiful.

Eve calls Nell over. 'Come on, Lakey,' she coos to her bump. 'Do it again for Mama Nell.'

Nell raises her eyebrows. 'Mama Nell? That's what we're going with? It's giving *L Word* but it's also giving *Little House on the Prairie*.'

Eve frowns. 'Well, we can't both be called Mummy – it'll be too confusing.' She addresses her stomach again. 'Come on, Lakey, give a kick for Mama, sweetie.'

Nothing. The baby does not budge.

'How about just Nell?' Nell suggests.

'But are you sure?' asks Eve. 'Don't you want a mum name too?'

'Well, in time she can decide that, if she wants. But for now, I'll just be Nell.'

Nell won't say this to Eve, but she's trying to give the baby options because she is very afraid Lake will not recognise her as her mother. It's an unfounded fear, she recognises this, but it's taken root in her regardless. What if Lake senses that they aren't biologically related and won't let Nell hold her?

Nell strokes Eve's belly, lays her palm softly on Eve's beautiful, rounded skin. 'Come on, Lake, what do you say – a kick for Nell?'

And then she feels it. Lake has said hello. Lake knows both her mums, of course she does, but the relief Nell feels is sublime.

*

Lake Bowman enters the world at 2.32 am on a Saturday, exactly on time. She is scrunched and red and screaming and perfect, pulled from Eve's vagina by a fierce female gynaecologist. Nell is by Eve's bedside – she has not left it for the past six hours, even to go to the bathroom. Her bladder is at risk of bursting, but this doesn't matter. Nothing else matters except this baby; this tiny little person. Two nurses clamp the umbilical cord, and Nell gets to cut it. She is shaking as she does so. It feels like cutting meat, but Lake does not react. Thank god. Nell has been having nightmares about Lake's first memory involving her mother hacking into her with scissors.

One of the nurses picks up Lake, places her on Eve's chest. A nurse gently wipes most of the gunk off the baby and covers her with a little blanket. The baby stops crying. She is observing. She is smelling her mother's skin for the first time. She is feeling the warmth of her mother's flesh, the beat of her heart. She is experiencing air, air on her body. She breathes in, she breathes out, she looks into her mother's eyes. From the very first moment of her life, Lake Bowman knows she is loved, and this is not a small thing. It might be the biggest thing there is.

Eve, Lake and Nell receive matching ID bracelets.

Lake is placed on a scale, she is poked and prodded and measured. The midwives say she is the perfect weight, and Eve, in her drugged stupor, tries to chastise the nurses for commenting on her baby's body. Eve lifts her arms; she wants her baby back. *Hurry, hurry, she's probably so scared, she needs her mum.* Finally, after what seems like a lifetime but is probably a minute, Lake is returned to Eve, and this time, Lake spots Eve's nipple immediately. Gently, gently, the midwives help Eve arrange herself in the best position for breastfeeding. Lake is a hungry girl. She latches her tiny lips around Eve's nipple. She sucks. Eve's milk hasn't come in yet but there is colostrum aplenty. It is the most beautiful thing Eve has ever seen.

Nell stands timidly by, watching both her girls in awe. She wants to be of use, she wants to be involved in this moment, but right now, it's all Eve. For maybe the first time in her life, Nell empathises with fathers.

Half an hour later, Eve falls asleep. The midwives ask if Nell would like to hold her baby. She wants to do this so badly it is hurting her, but she is also afraid of doing it wrong. She is scared that the nurses will see how incompetent she is, how little she knows, how young she is. 'Yes, please,' she says. 'But can you . . . can you help me?'

'Don't worry, love,' says the midwife. 'Babies are a lot stronger than we realise. You'll be just fine.'

Nell wants to kiss this woman for her kindness.

Nell holds her arms in what she imagines to be a kind of cradling shape. The nurse places Lake in Nell's embrace, and once she is holding her, Nell does not move her arms an inch. She is frozen with worry and with reverence. Even though they've been told that Lake is the perfect size, she is still just so, so, so small. She's a bean, she's a fresh puppy, she's a warm loaf of bread, all wrapped up. Lake peers up at Nell and her eyes contain the wisdom of the universe, Nell is sure.

'Hello, Lakey,' coos Nell. 'I'm Nell, I'm your other mum.'

She starts swaying, it's instinctive, some maternal force in her rising up and telling her what to do.

'It's very good to meet you,' whispers Nell. 'It's very good to meet you.'

Lake is silent, but she understands everything.

'Guess what, Lakey?' says Nell, her voice hushed. 'I love you. Do you know that? I love you so much. And your other mummy loves you so much.' Nell sways in Eve's direction. 'That's your other mummy right there; she's having a little nap, because she's had a big day. She loves you *so* much. But for now, it's just me and you, little one. Just me and you. What do you think about that? That's right, I think we're going to be just fine. Who's a precious girl? Who's a precious girl? That's right, *you* are!'

Lake's eyelids flutter, they flutter until they shut.

Now Nell is in love with two Bowmans, and she watches them both as they sleep.

2024

Eve has not heard from Nell for two years. Two years. In the course of a life, two years is not all that long. And it's not like Eve hasn't tried to find Nell. She called Ondine, of course. She called Chelsea, who didn't respond. Eve has no contact with anyone they went to high school with, for obvious reasons, and she couldn't bring herself to message Naomi. She feels terrible about this, and then she feels resentful that Nell put her in this position.

Nell doesn't have social media, never did. Eve's calls go to someone else's voicemail, her emails bounce. Eve could have filed a missing person report, sure, but besides the guilt, there was also this giant part of her – there still is this giant part of her – that thinks, *Fuck you, Nell. Fuck you, Nell, you left me and you left our child. If you want to be lost, be lost. Fuck you.* There is also the fact that if Nell wanted to be found, she would be.

And then there's the dread. Because Nell hasn't been found. What if she can't be found? What if she's dead?

Of course she's alive.

But what if she isn't?

Eve always suspected that Nell struggled with her mental health. But Nell didn't talk about it with her, ever. Nell's paintings were always manic, Eve could see that, but she tried to tell herself that Nell was only unhinged in her artistic practice. Every day, now, she berates herself. What if what she did pushed Nell over the edge? Marcus tells her that he's sure Nell is fine, but what does he know? He hasn't heard from Nell either.

Nell disappeared, and it is Eve's fault. One day Lake will learn this. Eve is worse than Emerald, worse than Ondine. She is everything she swore she wouldn't be.

2019

Lake Bowman is two years old, and she is a genius. She has mastered crawling, walking, sitting – she's essentially an Olympian. She is also completely obsessed with redheads, and every time she sees a person with red hair she yells, 'Witch!' Eve and Nell encourage this occult preoccupation, spending many hours at home with Lake scrolling through Google images of witches. Eve has perfected her witch voice and comes up with elaborate lore for the various cartoon witches that Google serves up. The witch with green skin and two frogs in her cauldron, for example, is Drusilla. Drusilla lives in Brooklyn and turns everyone's hair into spaghetti. If Eve were forced to do this with any other child, she would be bored out of her mind, but Lake is hers, so every one of Lake's reactions, every little squeal of excitement, every 'Why?' is cause for awesome delight. Eve and Nell made this. This little human is theirs. Reality is transcendent.

The early months of Lake's life were challenging. Without sleep Eve became snappy, dazed – a touch mean, it must be said. She found breastfeeding excruciating, she developed mastitis, she cried a lot. Now that Lake is on solids, Eve has reclaimed her resting hours, and it's Nell's job to get up two or three times a night when Lake wakes.

When Nell and Eve take Lake to queer events, she is treated like a celebrity, as is Eve. Eve basks in the glow of queer motherhood, she parades around the room spouting truisms about parenting, leaving Nell to hold the baby. Nell is the one who packs the baby bag, making sure there are nappies, wipes, a change of clothes, snacks and water. This organisation does not come naturally to Nell, but someone must do it. Sabrina occasionally questions Nell about whether she enjoys her doting role. Of course, Nell always says yes. She is very tired, but her pleasure is Eve's. If Eve is happy, so is she. And besides, it's not like Nell's had to give up her practice; Eve wouldn't ask that of her. Nell works at her studio most days – she's renting an old shipping container in a warehouse in Stanmore – and when she comes home, she usually finds Eve and Nell lying on the carpet in the living room, creating universes out of toilet rolls and pipe cleaners.

Nell is ideologically annoyed but financially pleased that her own artistic 'career' is working. The crazier her art, the more esoteric, the more people like it. Luckily, she has an agent who deals with the buyers and the money stuff. Nell has never been good with finances, because she has a habit of just giving money to people who ask for it, but now she has middle women – her agent, an accountant, an automatic transfer system on her banking app with a female voice. Nell hasn't missed one instalment of her half of the mortgage repayments, and it's been years since her card was declined in a grocery store while trying to buy a single Diet Coke. Life is good.

Eve is still working for the literary magazine. She's the online editor now, a huge coup in that it pays a thousand dollars a week, but her own writing is beginning to gain traction too. Her short stories about queer motherhood have garnered her a few shortlist nominations – especially the one about the mother who turns into a hat stand while waiting for her child to put on a show – and very occasionally she is even commissioned to write things. Eve feels like she's unlocked a new level of her career – soon she will be forced to pitch no more! Soon she will stop having to pay fifty dollars each time she enters a story competition! And Nell, of course, is rapturous in her praise. She's always thought Eve is a brilliant writer, but she also knows how much Eve relies on institutional approbation for her writerly self-worth.

Nell's world is her studio, her apartment, Lake, Eve and, occasionally, Chelsea. In this orbit, Nell has found peace. She hasn't spoken to Ondine and James in years – when Eve was pregnant, Chelsea told them about Lake and they told Chelsea to tell Nell that she no longer had a place in their family. While this might seem cold and unduly harsh – maybe even the cause for emotional upset, existential sadness – Nell was only surprised that her parents didn't pass on the message of her exile via one of their assistants. Nell has brought them shame, has made them look uncouth yet again. Getting Chelsea to deliver the excommunication news was kind of a personal touch, she thinks. They did add that if Nell ever decides to change her ways, renounce the child, she can email them.

2021

By four years old, Lake has conquered scootering. When Eve and Nell were children, everyone rode Razor scooters, but now it's all about three-wheeled Globbers. Lake's Globber is pink and covered in stickers, and she races it up and down the hallway in their apartment building several thousand times a day. Save for the hellish months during which daycare centres were only open to the children of essential workers, Lake goes to day care three times a week, which is an extortionate outlay for Eve and Nell, but they both need to work, and anyone who says they can get work done at home with a four-year-old is lying. So Eve and Nell slave away at their artistic pursuits so they can afford to have their child looked after by other people so they can continue working to continue having their child looked after by other people.

And although they don't love paying for day care, Eve and Nell do love the social aspect of it. When they drop Lake off or pick her up, they meet the wildest array of parents and carers. People are cooked. There are three Kayleighs in Lake's class – one is Asian, one is white and one is Black. The daycare workers refer to the three girls as Asian Kayleigh, white Kayleigh and Black Kayleigh. No one seems to have a problem with this, not even the parents of the children. This is funny enough to make paying for day care pretty much worth it to Eve and Nell. The day care sends photos of the children each day with reports on what they are up to, and Nell and Eve text each other about the updates constantly.

Eve: *Did u see Asian Kayleigh had three servings of meatballs for lunch? Iconic.*

Nell: *And Brandon S is exploring primary colours in his paintings, good for him.*

Eve: *I am gagging over Diana B's outfit today.*

Nell: *The pinafore? I know. I'm obsessed. But it's nothing compared to Jun's Batman slay.*

Parenting is very funny.

And yes, there are the nights when Eve and Nell are so tired that they accidentally fall asleep before Lake does. There is the constant repetition – feed her, play with her, dress her, get her to day care, pick her up, take her to park, come home from park, cook dinner for her, cook dinner for each other, bath time, story time, bedtime, *not* bedtime, bedtime for real I swear to goddess Lake Bowman I am not kidding – and the complete lack of minutes for one's self in one's own home. There are the nits, the flus, the unidentifiable rashes; the tantrums, the throwing, the crying – oh, the crying. But then there's the love, too. The sleepy cuddles. The first time Lake says, 'I love you, mummies.' Lake's little hands when she's trying to drink from a big cup. The way Lake holds on to Nell when she's being carried and she's very tired, like a baby koala clinging to her mum. The fact that Lake calls pubs 'beer cafes'. Lake's confusion over the texture of velcro. Any time Lake utters the word 'lesbean'.

But it's also around age four that Lake starts to notice that most other kids have a mum and a dad, and not two mums. One Wednesday, Nell picks Lake up from day care, and Lake is scowling when she gets there. It's about 5.30 pm, so most of the other kids have already been picked up – how the other parents achieve this, Nell has no idea. Do they not work? All these other parents look freshly coiffed with ironed clothes, and Nell is wearing a frayed denim onesie covered in paint splatters that got there organically.

Nell finds Lake sitting on a little chair by the sandpit, totally alone. The few other kids who remain at day care at this godforsaken time are inside, drawing with Teacher Mel. Lake is collecting sand in one hand and throwing it to the wind with the other, except there is no wind so she's just getting covered in sand, which Nell will have to deal with later. Eve's skills do not lie in washing, and neither do Nell's, but Eve pushed the baby out, so she is forever ahead in terms of points. Nell creeps up behind Lake slowly and silently, and then covers Lake's eye with her hands. 'Guess who?!' she asks.

'Who cares?' snaps Lake.

Nell removes her hands and walks around to crouch in front of Lake. 'What do you mean who cares?' says Nell. 'I care! I'm your mum, silly.'

'I'm not silly!' Lake screams.

Ah, so it is to be one of those days.

'Did you have a good day at school?'

Lake ignores her mother.

'I *said*, did you have a good day at school?'

Lake looks at Nell like Nell is human garbage. 'Yes,' she says.

'And what did you do today?' Nell asks in a cheery voice, hoping, as she always does when Lake is in one of her moods, that disingenuous positivity will remedy the situation.

Dead stare, arms crossed, Lake delivers the line that she knows drives both her mothers crazy. 'Nothing,' she says.

Nell raises her eyebrows. 'Is that so, chicken? Because a little birdy told me that you had a visit from a beekeeper today. Is that true?'

'No.'

'Are you sure, Lakey?'

'No.'

'Did you meet a beekeeper today?'

'Yes.' Victory.

'And what did they teach you? Did you learn anything?'

'No,' says Lake defiantly.

'You didn't learn *any* facts?' prompts Nell. Lake loves facts, she won't be able to resist this.

Lake pouts, but then relents. She can't help it. She has knowledge to share. 'Bees have a mummy and a daddy,' she says.

What to say to this? Because Nell's pretty sure this is objectively wrong, but she also wants to work out why her daughter is saying it.

'Is that so?' asks Nell.

'Yes,' says Lake. 'They have one mummy and one daddy and that's how they're made.'

'Uh-huh . . .' replies Nell, surreptitiously googling the mating habits of bees.

'Why don't I have a daddy?'

Fuck.

'Well, sweetheart, as we've talked about, some kids have a mummy and a daddy, and some kids have two mummies, and some kids have two daddies, and some kids have one mummy or one daddy, and some kids have neither, but they have grandparents or aunties or uncles or friends.'

Lake doesn't blink.

'You know this, sweetheart.' Nell looks to her phone. 'And I'm just confirming here, bubba, that not all bees do have daddies.

Some of them only have mummies. They're called' – she scrolls for answers – 'drones.'

'Am I a drone?' asks Lake. Her face has softened now. She's not just angry, she's genuinely confused.

'You're not a drone, baby. You're a smart, beautiful young person with two mummies who love you.'

Lake digests this. 'But white Kayleigh said you can't make a baby with two mummies, and two mummies is yuck.'

How early do children learn about conception now? Jesus. When Nell was a child, her parents told her that babies came from bank accounts. Also, Nell will kill white Kayleigh's parents.

'You know that Uncle Marcus helped us make you, Lakey. And having two mummies is not yuck. Don't let anyone say that to you, okay?'

'But why was I in Mummy's tummy and not yours?' asks Lake. Her little brow is furrowed. She's trying to work things out but nothing is making sense.

Nell sighs. 'Well,' Nell begins, 'you were in Mummy's tummy, and I was there to protect Mummy so nothing bad could happen to you while you were in there.'

'Why wasn't I in *your* tummy?'

'You can't be in two tummies at once, darling,' says Nell. She strokes her daughter's hair, pushes it behind her ears.

Lake looks at Nell very seriously. She says, 'So you're not my mum, then.'

And Nell holds her daughter, she tells her that of course she is her mum. She says that love makes a family, and that just because Lake wasn't in her tummy doesn't mean she loves her any less. And Lake seems to accept this, she does. It's just that all the fears Nell has about her maternal position have now been verbalised by her daughter, and she feels hopeless, useless, gross. She wants to cry, but she can't. So she holds her daughter tight and smells her scalp, like she has since she was a newborn, and she rocks Lake from side to side, and she wishes to the skies that tomorrow Lake will have forgotten this, because Nell doesn't know if she can bear it again.

The truth is, she will have to bear it again. Many times.

*

For the first four years of Lake's life, Eve does not date. Occasionally, very occasionally, Nell will stay home with Lake and Eve will go out for work drinks, she'll meet a beguiling lesbian and dot dot dot. But she does not do sleepovers. When the play is done, she always gets an Uber home and ends the night sleeping in her own bed, next to Nell. She never talks to Nell about her rendezvous. Even though she and Nell are not *together*, Eve doesn't want to complicate emotions in the apartment by bringing another woman into the mix. If she didn't have Lake to think about, it would be a totally different story. But Lake is confused enough as it is.

Nell has not dated at all: her focus is Lake, Eve and her art. And besides, Nell has been getting inklings, lately, that maybe Eve is coming to see her in a different way – not just as a co-parent and friend. There are times, when the three of them are sitting on the couch of an evening, that Eve smiles at her with so much love there *must* be something else going on there. Nell always strokes Eve as she sleeps, she's done this for years, but over the past six months there've been a few times when she could swear that Eve's been awake as she's done so. Eve's breathing hasn't been the slow, heavy rise and fall of dreaming – it's been shallow, fast, like Eve is taking it all in, like behind her eyelids she is very much alert. This means that Eve must *want* Nell to stroke her. Maybe she's just been waiting for Nell to make a move. Maybe Eve's been waiting for this for years. Hope is a dangerous thing for a co-parent like Nell to have, but she has it.

Sometimes, when Eve and Nell manage to merge their schedules, they pick Lake up from daycare together. This is one of Nell's favourite things to do, because she loves being seen with Eve like this, like they are a parental unit, a family. The daycare staff are always careful to address them both as 'mum,' and the other parents – apart from the homophobic ones – address Eve and Nell together, like they are equal in their maternal roles. Which they are, of course. And yet, there's always Nell's inevitable disappointment when Lake spies both her mums and runs into Eve's arms first. When this happens, Nell feels like she did in the first minutes after Lake arrived in the delivery room – useless, superfluous, a maternal fake. Nell waits for Eve to get her cuddles, and then she steps in and gives Lake a squeeze, a kiss on the head, and can Lake tell that Nell is nervous about whether her own child loves her enough?

How is it that Nell has cared for Lake for four years and still Eve is the favourite, the 'legitimate' mum, just because she birthed the child? *It's not fair*, thinks Nell. Nell's the one who does all the grunt work, and this is the thanks she receives? And then she feels guilty for harbouring this envy, because Lake is a tiny human and should not be begrudged for loving her mother. Nell reminds herself that fathers are still considered equal parents, even though they aren't the ones who gestated the foetus. But this makes her feel icky and angry, because why should she have to lump herself in with fathers to feel needed and worthy? Nell is Lake's mum too, she's not a dad figure, that's the whole point of this set-up. Nell never voices any of these frustrations to Eve – it wouldn't be fair to Eve to ask her to feel guilt for something that is out of her control. Eve is doing her best — and Eve has never acted like Nell is not an equal parent.

But also, Eve doesn't fight it when Lake will not allow Nell to unbuckle her from her car seat when both her mothers are with her. Several times a week this happens. Nell will get out of the car, walk around to Lake's side, open the car door, and Lake will scream, 'Mummy! I want Mummy to do it!' And she doesn't mean Nell — she means Eve. Always, she means Eve. Children go through phases of favouring one parent over the other, this is what all the books say, this is what other parents say. Nell needs to stop being so self-involved, she tells herself. Nell is not the protagonist in her daughter's life. And yet, the thought niggles at her. So she buys Lake presents when Eve won't; she sneaks Lake treats when Eve has already said no. It's pathetic, her need for maternal validation. But at least she wants her daughter to love her, at least she strives to give Lake what she needs. Surely this makes her better than Ondine. Even if she's not perfect, she's trying.

Nell has this feeling that if she and Eve were *together* together, Lake might love her more. Which is ridiculous, of course. It's not like Lake even understands the difference between co-parents and romantic partners — she's four, for fuck's sake. But these are the thoughts that keep Nell up at night, that haunt her in her studio as she paints.

2024

It's a Saturday night. Lake is at a sleepover, and Marcus and Eve are sitting in her living room, grazing at an ALDI cheeseboard selection and drinking sparkling wine.

It's been a day. Lake had two birthday parties to attend, the first of which was Barbie-themed. Perhaps surprisingly, Eve loves Barbie, she always has, ever since she made her own Barbies scissor as a child. She used to force her fellow seven-year-olds to grind their Barbies up against hers, and then she would attempt to convince everyone that practising kissing was a good idea. And although she now hypothetically understands that Barbie is simply yet another problematic reed in the consumerist swamp of child rearing, Eve can't help it – she adores that blonde bitch. As the kids say, slay.

'Okay, so,' Eve begins, sipping her wine. 'You know how there are those straight mothers who are, like, extremely scared of lesbian mums?'

Marcus nods. 'There's a word for that, you know. It begins, *homopho—*'

'Very funny, but that's not what I mean. Obviously there are straight-up bigots, but I'm more talking about the straight mums who assume all lesbians are, like, freedom fighters, anarchists, graduate-studies-at-Berkeley types.'

Marcus munches thoughtfully on a green olive. 'Like Enid Wexler equivalents?'

Eve nods. 'Exactly, yes. And these mums, when they see me coming, they try to signal very hard that even though they are straight and like the colour pink, they are also *on board* with the feminism – like they think I'm going to jump down their throat if they don't convince me that they saw *Carol* and empathised with Cate Blanchett in her custody battle or something.'

'God, how terrifying *are you* in the schoolyard?'

'I am exactly the correct amount of terrifying,' Eve informs him. 'So anyway, this is a *thing*, I am not making this up. Surely there's a gay male equivalent?'

Marcus ponders. 'I mean, yeah, for sure. My boss makes a point of giving me the day off after Mardi Gras every year because someone told him it was homophobic not to. And I'm like, babe, chill out, I'll just take a sick day like all the straight men do the day after the Melbourne Cup.'

Eve laughs. 'I'm not sure that's the same, but thank you for trying. *Anyway*, this morning Lake had a birthday party for this cute little girl called Chloe, and Chloe's party was Barbie-themed. And, like, this is fine by me—'

Marcus interjects, 'Oh babe, I know. Don't you remember in, like, second-year uni, we got high and you told me that Barbie was your type because she is hot but also an uncanny personification of gender performativity endorsed by corporate America and you liked that multiplicity?'

Eve chuckles. 'God, I'm annoying. I mean, I was high, so

obviously I don't remember that, but it seems on brand. How do *you* remember that?'

'I listen.' Marcus shrugs, feigning humility.

'*Anyway,* all week this girl's mum – Bianca, of course she's called Bianca – she's been, like, cornering me at school drop-off, telling me that she knows I might have criticisms of a Barbie-themed party but that she'd really appreciate it if Lake could come, but she also understands if I don't approve . . . and on Thursday morning, I shit you not, she even had a copy of *The Bell Jar* under her arm – like, she'd actually brought a prop to authenticate her claim to feminist solidarity. So I've been trying to tell her all week that she has nothing to worry about, but she's so caught up in her own defensiveness that she hasn't really let me get a word in, and today was the party and I just couldn't help it . . .'

'Babe, what did you do?' Marcus asks, his eyes narrowing.

'Oh, it wasn't that bad. I just made Lake dress as Ken. And then, for the gift, I got Chloe a copy of Jack Halberstam's *Female Masculinity*.'

Marcus cackles. 'Oh my god, you mean bitch, I love you. But wait, was Lake okay with dressing as Ken?'

'Of course she was! She wore cargo shorts for the first time, she had a ball.'

Marcus slices himself a large piece of pecorino. 'I'm not doing crackers anymore,' he says. 'They're just filler.'

'But the pecorino is fine?'

'Oh, absolutely. My doctor told me to stay away from soft cheeses because they're bad for your heart or some shit.'

'So that must mean hard cheeses are therefore good for your heart?'

'Exactly.'

'Solid reasoning,' says Eve. She takes a breath now, as she is about to veer into more contested conversational territory. 'So, have you seen Tae recently?'

Marcus clenches for a nanosecond. He hates playing this role, the holder of Tae information, but he also understands Eve's curiosity and pities her (perhaps?) willing naivety.

'Yeah, I have, we met up for a run last week. He's doing really well.'

'That's great.' Eve pours herself more wine. 'That's great. And has he got a partner at the moment, or . . . ?'

'Not that I know of, but he usually keeps that kind of intel close to his chest. There's no one he's serious enough about to put on the grid, at least.'

'Uh-huh, right. And you two, there's nothing going on there?' Eve peers at Marcus with concern. She never has understood why those two didn't just make a go of it. And a sinking part of her has long suspected that it may have something to do with her and Nell. Marcus has never said as much, but Tae was so weird about Lake's conception and has barely seen them since she was born. She's tried to tell herself that Tae just doesn't like children, but she also knows that Tae is obsessed with his nieces.

Marcus laughs nervously. 'Ha, oh god, no. Tae and I wouldn't work like that; we never really did. There was too much shared trauma, you know, our lives were so enmeshed. We knew each other too well for romance.'

Eve tries to articulate her next thoughts delicately. 'Do you really think that? Do you think you can know someone too well to ever be with them?'

'How do you mean?'

'Like, when you understand what makes a person tick, when you know their family issues and their wants and the stuff they suck at, and you can even kind of guess how they're going to respond in any given situation, and you empathise completely with them, because in a way it's like when they feel something, you feel something . . . do you think that means romantic partnership is impossible? Because how can you do that, you know? How can you love someone that you love like yourself – because doesn't that mean you also hate them like you hate yourself?'

'We're not talking about Tae anymore, are we?'

Eve smiles. 'Yes and no. I think in a lot of ways – yes and no.'

'That's really clarified it, thank you,' says Marcus.

'Are you being facetious?'

Marcus copies Eve's smile. It's mildly playful, mildly sad, kind of misted. 'Yes and no,' he says. 'I think in a lot of ways – yes and no.'

2022

Lake is a big school kid now, five years old. It is wild how fast the time goes, considering that almost every minute of mothering feels like an hour. Lake is potty-trained. Lake can spell approximately twenty words well and another hundred poorly. Lake has a school uniform that might be the cutest thing ever to have existed. Lake excels at art and dodgeball. Nell and Eve are happy: they are the living embodiment of a successful queer family, they are the queens of school drop-off. The other parents want to be friends with them as they personify the queer diversity quota, and they are both attractive. Lake's lunches are always healthy, her crusts always cut off. Nell is a cool artist; Eve is a very slightly successful short-story writer. Marcus is happily involved in Lake's life. This set-up is why Marsha P. Johnson threw the first brick at Stonewall, maybe. Tae's not around, true, but some people just don't understand the radical potential of queer family-making. Eve and Nell don't miss him at all. At all.

Everything is perfect, and then it isn't. Because Eve Bowman, twenty-eight, gets a girlfriend. And that girlfriend is not Nell.

Eve meets Bridget at a literary function – it's the launch of a Sydney-wide campaign to lease out unused buildings to budding artists and writers, and so it attracts the usual blend of unemployed creatives, bureaucratic types and one or two white men from American Express.

Bridget is blonde, and funny, and works for a creative arts funding organisation. It says so on her name tag. Theirs is the perfect arts meet-cute: Bridget and Eve both reach for the last glass of cheap sauvignon blanc as a slam poet solves inequality on a makeshift stage in front of them.

'You take it,' Bridget says. 'I've already had, like, three glasses and I don't know why – this might be the worst wine I've ever tasted, which is saying a lot, because I work in government *and* the arts.'

Eve laughs. 'That is so selfless of you!'

Bridget is hot and Eve is blushing. Bridget is wearing SÜK workwear: she is a lesbian. Long blonde hair, strong shoulders, tall. A confidence in the way she stands, back straight, cool, unbothered. Red lips, femme, even in her yard suit.

Eve cannot remember the last time she felt like this; like she really wanted to impress a stranger. She picks up the glass and takes a sip.

Bridget says, 'You're Eve, right?'

Eve coughs and some of the wine she was drinking dribbles out of her mouth.

'Oh my god,' she says. 'That actually happened. I just coughed up wine in front of the first hot person who has ever known who I am at one of these things.'

If Bridget is grossed out, she doesn't show it. In fact, she appears to be charmed.

'Hey, surely everyone here knows the author of "Hat Stand Mother" . . . and the online editor of *Infictus*, no less. That last bit's written on your name tag. Besides, I happen to love it when beautiful women half-choke on bad wine in front of me. It's my kink, I guess.'

'You did not just name-check a short story I wrote,' says Eve.

'Eve Bowman,' says Bridget, leaning in seductively, 'that is exactly what I just did.'

Eve laughs. 'I think I'm in love.'

Bridget looks at her watch. 'Well, we've been talking for about one minute. In the timeline of lesbian relationships, we're right on track.'

'What happens after five minutes?' asks Eve.

'Oh, we've broken up,' replies Bridget, straight-faced. 'But not before buying a dog and moving in together.'

'Split dog custody, then?'

'I'll take Sigourney every second week,' confirms Bridget.

The slam poet is getting louder and louder, it is becoming harder to ignore the impassioned staccato prose. Eve gestures to the very back of the room, near the door. 'Want to go over there?' she asks. 'That way, if the slam poet requests audience participation, we can make a run for it.'

Bridget raises an eyebrow. 'Are you allowed to say that? Aren't you an earnest ambassador for the power of the arts?'

Eve moves closer to Bridget and whispers conspiratorially, 'Not *this* art – come on.'

She takes Bridget by the arm and guides her towards the door. They walk in silent complicity, like naughty children in church. Eve experiences a moment of déjà vu. Her, Nell, the swimming pool, Marco Polo. The tension, the almost kiss, the resulting horror. Eve and Bridget come to a standstill. But this time, being gay is allowed. Sometimes, Eve still has to remind herself that her desire is not inherently dangerous. She can flirt. Rejection is not the only assured outcome.

'I like you,' says Bridget. 'Is that weird to say? I feel like I've met you before.'

Hypothetically, Eve should find this line corny, but she doesn't.

'I like you too,' replies Eve. 'Huh,' she muses. 'I haven't said that in quite a while.'

'Neither have I,' says Bridget. 'Curious.'

'Curiouser and curiouser . . . speaking of which: personality test. Are you Alice, the Mad Hatter or the Queen of Hearts?'

Bridget considers her options. 'None of those,' she says decisively. 'I'm the jam.'

Eve snorts. 'As in "jam tomorrow and jam yesterday – but never jam today"?'

'Exactly,' says Bridget. 'I'm delicious and very hard to get.'

'We'll see about that,' says Eve, smirking. She is feeling the rush of anticipation, that sublime moment when romantic possibility announces itself.

As predicted, the slam poet starts urging people in the crowd to join him on the stage.

Eve whispers into Bridget's ear, 'That's our cue . . . Listen, I know a cute pizza restaurant around the corner. Are you hungry?'

'Always,' replies Bridget.

And so the two women stride out into the night.

By the end of dinner, they are enchanted by each other. Sometimes it happens like this. Sometimes it is easy.

Less easy, of course, is Eve's living situation. When the last drop of wine is poured from the bottle, when the final pizza crust is abandoned, the tension is palpable: these women are going to fuck. But where? Bridget knows Eve has a child, they discussed this over dinner. She says she loves children, which is excellent news. Bridget also thinks that Eve's platonic co-parenting set-up is very radical, very cool. How much we are willing to accept when we are in the initial throes of lust. But Bridget does not yet know that Eve lives with Nell and also shares a bed with her. Eve has decided to conceal this information for a little while longer, maybe a month or so – until she can be sure that Bridget is so into her that she won't care about the strangeness of Eve's bed-sharing situation.

'Shall we go to yours?' asks Eve casually. 'I'd have you to mine but Lake is asleep.'

'Yes, ma'am,' replies Bridget. 'I've already ordered the Uber.' She looks directly into Eve's eyes. 'And it's an Uber Comfort.'

'That is so fucking sexy,' says Eve, and she's not kidding. Usually she takes Uber Pools and is therefore forced to listen to Brazilian backpackers harping on about the subpar breakfast offerings at their hostels.

When they get to Bridget's place, Eve is certain that she has found *the one*. Not only is Bridget gorgeous, but she lives *by herself*. In a *clean apartment*. With *tasteful art*. Even though Eve literally has a child, she is aware that most people would see how she lives her life and judge her as being fundamentally infantile herself. But then again, what *is* living life as a grown-up? When Eve watches supermarket ads on television and observes how suburban families apparently live – parents thrilled about television sales, interminable barbecue lunches where the women are exhausted and the men are flipping sausages with a cold one in hand – she knows she doesn't want that. No, she likes what she sees here: Bridget's version of being a grown-up.

Eve walks around the apartment slowly, peering into each room. The bathroom sink isn't covered in miscellaneous bits and pieces, there's a candle next to the toilet, the bed is made, the fridge is probably stocked. There's a drinks trolley in the lounge room on which sits a variety of alcoholic cocktail ingredients, suggesting that Bridget is fun but also able to moderate her drinking – whenever Eve and Nell have wine in the house, it is inevitably gone by the next day. Bridget has a calendar on the wall in her hallway and it seems that she actually uses this, she doesn't just forget that it exists and instead write appointments on the back of her hand in pen. All of this, *and* Bridget is charming, good-looking, evidently into Eve.

And Eve's seduction muscle memory springs into action. It's been largely dormant since she's had Lake, only flexed on rare nights of drunken debauchery. But right now Eve is not drunk; she feels quite clear-headed.

Bridget stands in the lounge room, watching Eve taking in her space.

'Do you like what you see?' asks Bridget.

Eve redirects her attention to Bridget's body, Bridget's shoulders, Bridget's hips. 'Yes,' she replies. 'Yes, I do.'

'Would you like a drink?' Bridget gestures to the drinks trolley.

'I would,' says Eve. 'But I'd like something else more, if you don't mind.'

The look Eve is giving Bridget makes it quite clear that the thing she wants resides in the bedroom, not the lounge room.

Bridget smiles widely, carnivorously. 'I don't mind.'

'Could you show me your bedroom, do you think?'

'I think I could.'

Bridget walks towards a closed door, opens it, and walks through it. Eve follows, watching the sway of Bridget's arse as she moves.

Silence now. This moment, every time, so exhilarating – the shift from suggestion to actuality. Eve faces Bridget, the two of them standing at the foot of her bed. Eve is about to lift her hand, brush a strand of hair behind Bridget's ear, but as her arm is in motion, the dynamic shifts. Abruptly, Bridget has Eve's forearm in her own hand, she's caught it and she's pushing it up. Then she's pushing Eve's other arm up, and she's pulling Eve's shirt over her face, she's tossing it on the ground. Oh, so this is how it is to be. How absolutely thrilling, the bliss that resides in being directed. Yes, yes, I'll be your Barbie. Bridget moves forward and leans in to kiss Eve, but just as their lips touch, Bridget bites. Eve lets out an involuntary gasp, tastes the metallic tinge of blood, and Bridget licks, now enveloping Eve's lips in her own. Eve surrenders.

Bridget kneels. Eve kicks off her shoes. Bridget pulls down Eve's trousers and underpants in one swoop, Eve lifts her feet one by one and allows her garments to be stripped from her, thrown aside. Eve is naked, and Bridget grabs at her buttocks, bringing Eve's front to her mouth, Bridget's breath hot on Eve's pussy. She licks softly at first, each lap a shiver, a slow-motion exploration, testing how still Eve can hold herself as her body tries to contain its shudders. Eve looks down at Bridget, and Bridget's eyes are staring right back up at her, daring Eve to say something, daring Eve to throw Bridget back onto the ground and fuck her – but Eve won't. She needs this, and Bridget needs to give it to her. All this unsaid and yet communicated effortlessly.

Bridget increases her tempo, her licks become gulps, her tongue strong and urgent as she presses hard into Eve's clit, again and again. Eve is moaning now, she can't help it, she hasn't felt like this in so long, like her body is a machine for pleasure, like her thoughts and responsibilities don't exist. Just as Eve thinks she can't stand it much longer, just as she is about to give in to the building sensation that's taking her over, Bridget inserts two fingers into her, pummelling Eve's insides as she continues to lick. Eve lets out an almighty roar;

she has arrived at paradise. It's here, in this one-bedroom apartment, with Bridget's face between her thighs.

Bridget rises up, her face soaked in Eve, and she kisses her with absolute abandon. Eve lowers her hand, she wants to feel Bridget's soft, wet cove, but Bridget slaps her hand away. Eve raises an eyebrow. In reply, Bridget strides to the dresser and opens a drawer to reveal a cornucopia of toys. She doesn't hesitate; she knows exactly what she wants. She takes out a strap-on, black leather harness already attached, raises her chin. 'Would you?' she asks.

'Please,' murmurs Eve.

Bridget hands Eve the strap-on, divests herself of her own clothing, and lies back on the bed, limbs splayed, wide open. Eve steps into the straps, slaps the velcro down tight around her hips, positions the dildo so its rear end aligns perfectly with her cunt. Eve crawls onto the bed and straddles Bridget. She lowers her face to meet Bridget's, and this kiss tastes like sweat and need and salt. Her left hand propping her up, and her right hand guiding the dildo, slowly, slowly, Eve moves her shaft into Bridget, and the expression on Bridget's face is one of ecstasy.

'Yes, yes, god, yes,' moans Bridget. 'Please, more, please.'

So Eve gradually lifts her arse, stares directly into Bridget's eyes once more, and then she bucks forward. With full force, she enters Bridget, the toy lubricious and slippery as it glides in and out, in and out. Bridget's hips rise to meet each thrust, each woman acting on pure impulse, on an unquenchable desire to meld into this feeling together, to be as one in rapture. Sex can be funny, but this is very, very serious. Sweat trickles down the ridge between Bridget's breasts. Eve lowers her mouth once more, she licks the line of perspiration and keeps her body low. Again and again she plunges, until Bridget is screaming, until Eve herself reconnects with that expanding feeling, and all at once they reach the brink: Bridget's hips buckle up, her muscles clench tightly around Eve, and Eve herself is floating, and when they meet each other's eyes they know that they are on the same plane.

They do not yet know about each other's childhoods, or how they each take their coffee, or the names of each other's friends, or their favourite Christmas movies. But right now, in this brief moment, two bodies are feeling the same thing.

Eve collapses next to Bridget, both women on their backs, breathing raggedly. And then Bridget bursts out laughing, a kind of shocked delight, and Eve is laughing too; it's actually unfathomable, what they just did.

'What the fuck, Eve?' exclaims Bridget.

Eve manages to respond, still laughing, 'What the actual fuck indeed.'

Eve unstraps the dildo, throws it to the base of the bed, turns to kiss Bridget, and they hold each other, they trace each other's bodies, they lick the sweat and taste the sweetness. After some minutes, Bridget asks, 'How about that glass of wine?'

'I reckon that'd go down a treat,' replies Eve, smiling. She pauses, preparing to make the inevitable joke. 'But not as well as you.'

Bridget guffaws. 'Why did I know you'd say that?'

'Because you know me, Bridget,' says Eve. 'We've been together for a decade.'

'You're an idiot,' Bridget responds, laughing. 'But I'm glad you're my wife.'

And so Bridget goes to the living room and returns with two glasses and a bottle of wine. It is some hours before sleep is an option, but when it does come, it happens naturally. It feels like they've always done this.

And then, in a month or so, when Bridget starts spending time with Eve and Lake at their apartment, it feels like she's always been there.

Except, of course, for Nell. For Nell, it feels like the end of the fucking world.

2024

Eve is once again picking up Lake from school. She's on time, no after-school care necessary, and as such she is experiencing a very strong burst of maternal superiority. She's got her AirPods in, she's not working late cause she's not a singer, life is good. She did Pilates this morning, and the instructor, Bella M (they're all called Bella), complimented her form. She may be a single mother with a dark past, but today she is crushing it.

As she walks toward the school gates, however, something is amiss. She can't see any trauma yet, but penetrating Sabrina Carpenter's cherry sweet tones is the sound of children crying. She enters the front playground and sees Maria consoling Harry. Bill is kneeling down, hugging Alan. Where is Lake? Eve scans the grounds: she's not on the swings, not at the hopscotch square . . . Finally, she spots her. Lake sits on a metal bench, alone, quiet and red-eyed. Eve yells Lake's name, waves. Lake spots her mother and runs toward her. Eve picks her child up and embraces her in a tight squeeze, poor little angel. She puts her down, crouches at her eye level.

'Ohh, honey, what is it, what's wrong?' Eve asks as she strokes Lake's hair.

Lake blubbers, Eve can't make out her words.

'What was that sweetheart?'

'N-Nibbles, d-died,' she sobs.

'Sorry, Nibbles?' Maybe Eve is having a brain aneurism, or is there really a child called Nibbles in her daughter's year? She knows they live in a liberal area, but still, come on.

'Nibbles!' Lake cries, enraged. Eve remains confounded. She looks up, catches Bill's eye – points to her crying child and shrugs, as if to say, *what??* Bill mouths something, 'kibbles'? Eve raises her hands in confusion, *huh?* Bill starts impersonating an animal, a rabbit maybe? He makes his hands paws, he curls his top lip into his gums so his teeth are on show. Then it dawns on her – *ohhhh*, Nibbles! The fucking guinea pig.

'Gosh, darling, I'm sorry, I know how much you loved . . . Nibbles. What happened, sweetie?'

Lake swallows her blubbering, hiccups. 'When I went to feed him some treats at lunchtime, he wasn't moving. And then Mr Haight checked and he, he still didn't move!' She starts sobbing again.

Christ, okay. 'Oh, baby. That's awful. But you know, I'm sure he's . . . in a better place now.'

Lake's eyes squint in annoyance, rage even. 'That's not true! You told me that when we die we don't go anywhere!'

Eve frowns, it's true, she did say that. How to salvage this?

'Well, Lakey, that may be what I believe, but lots of people believe different things about death. Christians believe people go to heaven, and Buddhists believe in reincarnation, and others . . . others have their own ideas.'

A memory comes to her, and she tries to swipe it away, she tries not to bring up Nell to Lake when she can avoid it. But Lake is still looking very unconvinced, and she remembers Lake used to be charmed by Nell's vision of the afterlife. She continues. 'Do you remember, Lakey, do you remember where Nell used to say people went after they died?'

Lake calms for a second, her eyes wide, she nods. 'Yes.'

'Yeah?'

'She said that when we die we become stars, and we get to watch all the people we love on earth, and we get to be their light.' Lake has stopped crying. This memory is giving her comfort.

Now it is Eve's turn to try not to cry.

2022

Back when they were planning to conceive Lake, both Tae and Marcus had questions about what might happen if either Nell or Eve were to form a romantic relationship with someone else. How might the co-parenting set-up work then? Tae had wanted to know. Others had raised the issue too; Sabrina, for example, related the sorry tale of her sister, whose custody battle became embittered and expensive once her ex moved on with another woman who also had children. Sabrina was subtly reminding them that, while platonic co-parenting may seem like an easy set-up, a radical reshaping of the heteronormative family model, it is actually known to be one of the least easy dynamics in existence and is the reason why family lawyers have jobs and own expensive houses.

At the time, Eve assured Sabrina that things between herself and Nell could never be acrimonious, because they were just best friends, not exes, and no one's feelings could get hurt when there was open conversation between co-parents and a mutual desire to do best by the child. Eve was in the throes of grief and the ecstasy of escapist fantasy, and so did not correctly interpret the reason for Sabrina's high-pitched laughter in response.

Nell, of course, tried very hard not to consider the possibility that Eve would ever pair with someone who was not her. When the thought occasionally became impossible to ignore, Nell would tell herself that all would be well, as there was no greater bond between people than a child, and even if Eve came to love someone else too, she would always be primarily bound to Nell as co-parent.

So when Eve first tells Nell that she's been seeing someone, after only three weeks of dating Bridget, and that she'd like to introduce her to Lake, Nell reacts very impartially. They are sat at the kitchen table eating breakfast while Lake is putting her socks on in the other room, and Nell passes Eve the milk like nothing is wrong, she bites into her toast as if she doesn't want to throw it against the wall. She makes general enquiries about the biographical facts of Bridget's life, she tells Eve that she's happy for her, she even makes a joke about how it will be good to have another pair of hands around the house. Internally, Nell is screaming.

That night, after Nell has been stewing angrily all day at her studio and Eve has been congratulating herself on how well she broke the news, the pair begin to discuss what adding Bridget to the trio would look like. After Lake has gone to bed, Eve and Nell are the picture of parental maturity. Amicably, respectfully, they agree that Nell should meet Bridget before Bridget meets Lake. They decide that when the time comes for Lake to meet Bridget, it should be in a controlled public environment, and that Bridget should be introduced as a friend first. Eve has been spending nights at Bridget's, and Eve and Nell have been telling Lake that Eve has been working these evenings. Lake does not seem to have found these absences suspicious.

They have not yet decided *when* Lake should meet Bridget, but Bridget keeps pestering Eve about seeing her apartment. As such,

Eve decides that she will bring Bridget to the flat when Nell and Lake are both out – Nell at the studio, Lake at school. Eve has been nervous about revealing her sleeping situation to Bridget, but they've been together for a month now: Bridget is obsessed with Eve. They sometimes wear each other's clothes, for goodness' sake. What is high-waisted on Eve becomes cool and slouchy on Bridget. They send each other TikToks about other lesbian couples doing domestic tasks together, with the accompanying caption: *us lol*. It's disgusting and it's lovely. Now is the perfect time for Eve to reveal that she and Nell share a bed.

The pair of them are sitting on Eve's couch, and Bridget is dutifully praising all the children's art that decorates the space – Lake's drawings of atrocities, her Fluxus-esque assemblages.

'Lake has a real knack for conveying feral vulnerability,' observes Bridget.

Eve smiles. 'That warms the cockles of my heart, honey, thank you.'

'Maybe I can get her some funding?' suggests Bridget. 'Emerging artist grants just keep specifying younger and younger ages.'

Eve laughs. 'Ha! Yes, please! I will happily move aside to make way for the younger generation if that specifically relates to my five-year-old-daughter who will then buy me a house.'

'You're very self-sacrificing. That's one of the many things I love about you.' Bridget strokes Eve's cheek, and the intention in her eyes shifts. Things are heating up. If Eve keeps mum, they will be having sex any minute now.

No, she must tell the truth about the bed first. She's honest, she's an honest person.

'Speaking of things you love about me . . .' Eve begins.

'Mmmm?'

'You love that I'm a penniless artist, right?'

'Yes, that's very sexy. Tell me how little you have in your super, baby.' Bridget growls and pretends to be a lion; this is one of her go-to moves and it is utterly charming.

'And you love that I'm co-parenting with my friend, because I'm disrupting the nuclear family, right?'

Bridget's growl is louder now. 'You're a pioneer, babe, a beautiful gay dreamer.'

'Excellent, excellent,' says Eve. 'So the thing is, because I'm so cute and poor and radical . . .'

'Yes?'

'This is a one-bedroom apartment.'

'Okay?' Bridget hasn't quite cognised what this means yet, but she will imminently.

'And so, to save money – that's all it is, I swear – Nell and I, well, we share that bedroom. And so does Lake.'

'Uh-huh . . .' Bridget's brain is ticking over. 'So what you're saying is . . . you share a bed with Nell?'

Eve smiles encouragingly. 'Exactly. It's completely platonic – we don't fuck, we never have – but we're best friends, and with Lake and everything, this is just the only set-up we could afford. But I can see how it might seem weird to you, and I'm sorry I haven't mentioned it earlier. I just . . . I didn't want to scare you away.'

Bridget has always thought of herself as a modern woman, a contemporary queer. She's not polyamorous but she has friends who are. This must count for something. She understands that the housing market is awful and that people come up with alternative living arrangements to mitigate this. But also, in this exact moment, what she feels, inescapably, is intensely jealous. Who is this Nell? And why does she get to sleep with *Bridget's* girlfriend?

And is Bridget allowed to be angry with Eve about this, or is it too early in their relationship to be so proprietorial? Can she express her dismay to Eve, or will Eve take this as a sign that Bridget is not mature enough to be part of this complex family dynamic? She cannot tell Eve that she's been fantasising about being a step-parent, that she's already bought and hoarded a bunch of presents for Lake, for when she eventually gets to meet her, and that this newsflash makes her feel stupid for doing that, because is Eve actually just in denial about being in love with her best friend?

Bridget has not yet responded. Eve is terrified she's ruined this. 'Bridg?' she says. 'Are you okay?' She places her hand on Bridget's hand, looks at her imploringly. 'I know this is a lot, but . . . honestly, I've been fine with this arrangement for so long, because I've just been focusing on Lake and being a co-parent and having enough work to survive, and I haven't even considered getting a larger place or changing the situation, because what would I be changing it for? This is cheap and it works well, and Nell and I have never had the conversation about how it would work were one of us to meet someone – which in hindsight is stupid, obviously. But, like, since meeting you, it's the first time I've had a reason to imagine a different way of living. I know we are so early into . . . whatever this is between us . . . but I want to see where it goes with you. So if you'll stick it out with me, if you really want to make a go of this, I'll start talking with Nell about how it all might look going forward. We've just got to be really respectful of her feelings, too, because she is Lake's other mum, and that is not something that's ever going to change, you know? So, what do you think?'

Bridget's been listening in a kind of daze, but the main point she's taken from it is this: Eve is taking their relationship seriously.

Eve is thinking about changing her life for Bridget. Eve must really, really like Bridget. And Bridget does really, really like Eve.

Bridget looks at Eve so sweetly, like a child who's been offered a treat. 'When you say "whatever this is between us" . . . I think it's a relationship. I'd like to be in a relationship with you. Is that what you would like? If we're sure about that, then I think I can get over the bed-sharing. It won't be forever, after all.'

Eve exhales, relieved. All is not lost. All could just be beginning, in fact. A partner for Eve, another parental figure for Lake, it's wonderful! This is going to be so easy. It's going to be so easy and wonderful and nothing is going to go wrong.

'I'd like that, please.' Eve smiles. 'Now, tell me again how sexy I am, and I'll show you where I sleep.'

'I don't want to sleep,' says Bridget, as she takes off her top.

Eve groans. 'Well that is perfect, because neither do I.'

On the mantel, a photograph of Nell and Lake watches the new couple as they make their way to Eve and Nell's bed. This is called foreshadowing.

*

Two hours later, Eve and Bridget have fallen asleep in bed. They are naked but, mercifully, under the covers when Lake and Nell get home. Eve wakes to the sound of the front door opening, which gives her enough time to frantically shake Bridget out of her slumber.

'Yoohoo!' yells Nell. 'Evie, are you home?'

Lake joins in. 'Mummy! Mummy are you here?!'

Eve hears little footsteps coming towards the bedroom door. Fuck.

'I'm in the bedroom!' Eve yells, panicked. 'Just give me a sec, don't come in, just a minute!'

Bridget is rubbing her eyes, in a daze. 'What's happening?' she asks Eve.

'Shh! We fell asleep, and now my daughter and co-parent are on the other side of this door, and you're about to meet them both with no advance warning. I am so sorry.'

Bridget snaps into alertness. 'Fuck,' she says.

'Mummy!'

Lake will not be patient much longer, Eve knows. Thankfully she is now over the phase of following Eve literally everywhere – the bathroom, this side of the lounge room, that side of the lounge room – but still, doors are not barriers to Lake's mind; they are simply portals to get her to her mother.

'One minute! I'll be out in one minute!' Eve is throwing on a smock dress, hurriedly collecting Bridget's clothes from around the room, hurling them at Bridget: trousers here, a bra there, top, undies, shoes . . . shoes can wait – why, why so many items?

Eve is dressed and Bridget zipping up her pants when Lake pushes the door open.

'Mummy!' she yells, smiling.

'Lakey!' exclaims Eve.

Then Lake notices Bridget. 'Who are *you*?'

Now Nell appears behind Lake. She takes in the situation. She sees it for exactly what it is. Bridget is standing next to the bed, fully dressed now, but her hair is all mussed. There are no points for guessing what she and Eve have been doing.

'I . . .' Bridget does not know what to say. How does she do this? Who should she tell Lake she is? They have discussed introducing her platonically at first, but they haven't made any concrete decisions yet. And Nell, this must be Nell. This must be Nell, standing at the door, looking like she wants to skin Bridget.

Eve is frozen. She gives Nell a rattled grimace – *help me, please, I'm so sorry.*

Bridget looks to Eve for a sign.

Three adults and a child, all silent.

With immense effort, Nell smiles.

'Well,' says Nell, 'you must be Bridget.'

Bridget makes a sound that approximates assent.

Eve springs into action. 'Yes, exactly. Yes. Nell, this is Bridget. Bridget, this is Nell. And this is Lake. Lake, say hi to Bridget.'

'Hi, Bridget,' responds Lake, in the kind of flat staccato that children use to greet their teacher at school each morning ('Good mor-ning, Mis-ter Hai-ght'). 'But why are you in my mummy's bedroom?'

Bridget thinks fast. 'Hello, Lake, it's so lovely to meet you! Your mummy's told me all about you. I've just been in here helping Mummy with some work.'

Nell is trying to contain her anger. How could Eve be so irresponsible? They were supposed to formulate a plan for this moment, decide how best to introduce Bridget to Lake. Nell was supposed to meet Bridget before that happened. This was all supposed to go so differently. But here they are. And even though Nell is livid on Lake's behalf, and personally shattered for herself, she must be the mature one here, as always. She must rise above her own feelings. This is the situation they are in; she must make the best of it.

'Bridget is Mummy's new friend, Lakey. Bridget, it's lovely to meet you. Why don't you two come into the lounge room and we'll have a cup of tea? Would you like some tea, Bridget?'

'Oh, yes, thank you, that would be nice. Can I help?'

'Not at all. Get yourself settled in there, and I'm sure Lake will want to show you her toys, won't you, Lakey?'

Lake responds in the affirmative and goes to her side of the bedroom to fetch those things she deems worthy of display.

Eve mouths, 'Thank you, Nell.'

Nell absents herself to the kitchen, busies herself with tea preparation, breathes slowly in and out. She will get through this. She's had to deal directly with Eve's paramours before – those months after Emerald's death, Nell was essentially a madam, but *this*, this is different. Eve is no longer grieving, she is clear-headed. Eve is falling for a woman who *is not* Nell, and that woman is *here*, *now*, in their apartment, playing with *Nell*'s child, after having sex with Eve in *Nell*'s bed. Nell is trying not to retch. Her hands shake as she holds the kettle under the tap.

In the lounge room, Lake's pulled out a giant Peppa Pig, as well as her sketchbook and pencil case full of markers. She's dumped them on the table. Bridget stands next to the couch, unsure if she should sit or remain standing. Eve motions for Bridget to kneel down next to Lake.

'Are you good at drawing, Bridget?' Lake asks.

Bridget slaps a big smile onto her face. 'I'm pretty good, but not as good as you, I reckon. I've seen your drawings; they're amazing!'

'Where have you seen my drawings?' Lake seems suspicious.

'Oh, well . . . in the lounge room, and in here, and your mummy's shown me some photos of your pictures on her phone. You're very talented!'

Lake loves compliments, so this answer satisfies her, for now. 'Can you draw bats?'

Eve laughs. Her child is so confident, it's amazing.

Bridget laughs too – this kid is charming. 'I can!' she responds. 'Would you like me to draw you a bat, and you can colour it in?'

'Yes!'

Eve interjects, 'Yes, what, Lakey?'

'Yes, please.'

'Good girl.'

And so Bridget finds herself sitting in the lounge room of her new girlfriend and her new girlfriend's best friend/co-parent, attempting to draw an outline of a bat that will be acceptable to a child who might one day be part hers.

Eve slips into the kitchen to check on Nell.

Nell's pouring boiling water into cups, her lips pursed.

Eve places her hand on Nell's back. 'Nell, I am so sorry. We fell asleep. I didn't want you or Lake to meet Bridget like this. It's totally my fault. Thank you for being so incredible right now. I don't deserve you.'

Hearing Bridget playing with Lake, Nell's anger has speedily intensified. She clanks the cups onto the counter, almost burns herself. She turns around to face Eve. 'You're right,' Nell says. 'You do not deserve me. What have we always said? Lake comes first. And then you go and do this. It's not fair to her, Eve.'

This is the first time since their reconnection at university that Nell has criticised Eve like this. Eve has figured herself to be beyond reproach in Nell's eyes, and up until now, she has been. Being told off is disconcerting, and it stings. Nell's right, of course – Eve is very much in the wrong here, she knows this – but Eve's not sure how to respond. Where does Eve stand now, exactly? Introducing Bridget like this is bad form, but Eve knows it's not just for Lake's sake that Nell is upset.

Nell will not admit this, of course – her desire is forever unspoken. But now, with another woman involved, Nell's jealousy is flaring up, and although she is hoping that her anger will be attributed to maternal instinct, to protection of the child, she wonders if Eve can guess as to the strength of her upset. For the millionth time, Nell wonders whether Eve is aware of her feelings. Surely not, surely not, or else Eve wouldn't dangle herself so – she wouldn't be that cruel! Not her Eve. No, Eve is goodness, Eve is light. Eve mustn't know.

Eve opts for grovelling. 'I know, I know it's not fair, I'm so sorry. You know me, I'm a sleepy lady. Such a sleepy lady. Blame me, absolutely, but don't blame Bridget, please! This is not her fault, and I really want you to like her.' Eve pokes her head out of the kitchen and sees Lake and Bridget sitting on the lounge room carpet together, heads bent over a sketchpad. 'And look, she's in there now with Lake, and Lake seems fine, truly. Maybe Lake will just be fine with it? She's too young to understand that Bridget's more than a friend.'

Nell scoffs. 'You and I know both know that our daughter is more observant than the two of us combined.'

Eve laughs. 'Yes, she is,' she agrees.

Nell relents. If being kind to Bridget is what will make Eve happy, it is Nell's duty to do it – even as much as she *hates* it, she loves Eve more. 'Look, I know that you didn't mean for this to happen, and I know that you're sorry. I'm pissed off, but it'll pass. Now, let's all drink our tea like mature, responsible adults, and pretend that nothing about this dynamic is unusual.'

'Yes, sir,' says Eve, relieved. Nell may be annoyed, she thinks, but she's going to pull it together. Everything is going to be okay.

'Does Bridget take her tea with milk?'

'You'll laugh,' says Eve.

Nell clocks Eve's coy smirk. 'Oh my god, no, Evie! She's a fucking, like, soy milk person or something, isn't she?'

'Oat,' Eve admits.

'Christ,' Nell mutters.

'She'll take it black!'

'She'd better,' says Nell.

But then she smiles. Phew.

'Okay!'

Nell strides into the lounge room with two cups of tea in hand, Eve trailing behind her with a cup of tea in one hand and a hot chocolate for Lake in the other. The mothers hand out the drinks.

'Remember to blow before you sip, Lakey, it's hot,' says Eve.

Eve gives Bridget's shoulder a squeeze as she passes her to sit beside Nell on the far side of the coffee table, facing Bridget and Lake.

'So,' says Nell, 'how are you two artists getting along in here? Are we going to be able to sell this and quit our day jobs?'

Bridget grins. 'I'd say that's a definite possibility. Lake, do you want to show your mummies our masterpiece?'

Lake lifts up the sketchpad and turns it around to show Eve and Nell. 'Do you like it?'

'It's magnificent!' enthuses Eve. It *is* quite good – Bridget's bat outline has a strength of character to it, a kind of fierce 'This is me, I'm a bat' energy, and Lake's colouring in is spectacularly free from tired notions of precision and neatness.

'You've got quite the little artist here,' says Bridget to Nell. 'You're an artist too, aren't you, Nell? Eve always raves to me about your work.'

Nell is tense, watching her beloved's girlfriend playing with her child, but she tries to relax as she responds. 'Lakey's the real talent in this house, obviously. And thank you, about my work, that's kind of you to say.'

'Did you always want to be an artist, or . . .?'

Eve is pleased to see that Bridget is really making an effort with the small talk, but it also feels like watching an amateur theatre production – something could go wrong at any minute.

Nell clears her throat. 'Well, I suppose being an artist wasn't my dream, as such; it's more that I couldn't be anything else. Making art is the only thing that makes any sense to me – besides loving these two.' She gestures to her family. Lake, who has started a new drawing on the next page of the notebook, is ignoring the boring grown-up conversation.

'Were your parents artists, or *are* your parents artists?'

'Ha! Definitely not,' says Nell.

Lake interjects here, happy to be able to provide information. 'Mum's parents are sick in the head and that's why we don't see them,' she tells Bridget.

Bridget's mouth falls into an O shape. Eve laughs, can't help it, and then so does Nell.

'That's exactly right, Lakey. Sick in the head. Too sick for visitors, sadly.'

'Right, I see, I'm sorry,' murmurs Bridget.

'I don't have any grandparents,' says Lake to Bridget. 'Do *you* have parents?'

Bridget laughs. 'I do. I have a mummy and a daddy and two sisters and a brother.'

'Are they nice?'

'Oh, very nice.'

'Well, if you marry my mummy, they can be my grandparents and aunties and uncles. I already have one aunty but I can have more.'

Lake says all this without for a moment considering the impact of her words, how could she?

'Wh-what do you mean, sweetie? Your mummy and I aren't getting married! We're friends, sweetie.'

Nell is horrified but tries to adjust her face into a beatific smile. *Calm, calm, stay calm, don't react.*

Lake's thirst for answers is not quenched. 'No, you're more than friends.'

Bridget freezes. 'Pardon?'

'Adults don't work in the bedroom,' explains Lake, rolling her eyes. 'Can you draw me another bat, please, Bridget?'

'I – of course, but why don't you ask . . . Mama? I bet she's so good at it.' Bridget looks to Nell. 'Is that right? You're Mama and Eve is Mummy?'

Nell nods tersely. 'That's right.' Nell offered herself to Lake free from any prescriptive maternal nomenclature, but as soon as she could talk, Lake christened her Mama. Nell is now imagining Bridget prising that title out of her hands. She balls her fist, attempts not to punch.

'I don't want Mama to draw it. I want you to draw it!'

'Right, okay.' Bridget starts drawing another bat. She doesn't dare look up to see the expression on Nell's face.

When Bridget leaves half an hour later, Lake actually hugs her and gives her a kiss on the cheek. Eve thinks the introduction has gone swimmingly.

'God, Lake really is perceptive, isn't she?' Eve says to Nell, as the two of them are washing up the tea things in the kitchen. 'I can't believe she just, like, *intuited* that Bridget and I are together. When I was her age I hadn't the faintest which adults were in relationships and which weren't. That kid's going to rule the world. Or maybe she'll be a psychiatrist, or an actor?'

'Mmm, she really does see through everything and everyone,' agrees Nell.

Nell hates Bridget.

*

And so an uneasy détente develops – for the sake of the child. (*Think of the children!*). For the next few months, Bridget never sleeps over at Nell and Eve's place, but she is there a lot, and as Lake has already determined the romantic nature of Bridget and Eve's relationship, they do engage in small acts of intimacy in front of her – a peck on the cheek there, a cuddle here. Lake has never seen one of her parents act like this before, all lovey-dovey with someone. Far from being jealous of Bridget, which Eve feared might be the case, Lake quickly becomes attached to her. Even Nell must admit that Bridget is good with Lake.

When Lake was little, around two or three, she used to wake up every morning screaming, 'It's an emergency!' She'd get out of bed, gather her toy garbage truck and then roll its wheels down the bodies of her sleepy mothers, yelling, 'Truck is robbing bank!' And Nell would have to wake up and replay the same 'emergency' again, and again, and again. Now that Lake is five, her imaginary games are more complex, but they are still not exactly intellectually stimulating for adults. But while Eve and Nell are often too tired to engage in games of make-believe, Bridget seems to have boundless energy for imaginative play. Every nook and cranny in the apartment becomes a home for fairies, or a mouse's lair, or a cockroach palace.

There's a park about a five-minute walk from the apartment, and Bridget often takes Lake there by herself, just so Eve and Nell can have a rest. Nell resents these moments of respite even as she enjoys them – Lake is *her* child, not Bridget's! And yet, wasn't the whole point of her and Eve's parenting arrangement supposed to be about *more* love for the child, and isn't this more love? Nell is torn, so torn, between how she feels and how she wants to feel.

And it's not just Lake that Bridget is helping – Bridget arranges for Eve to do some freelance copyediting for a publisher she knows, and this pays far better than the literary magazine does. With the income from both jobs, she's earning enough to pay her half of the mortgage *and* have enough left over to get takeaway food for dinner occasionally and buy spontaneous little presents for Lake without stressing about the balance in her bank account. Bridget's encouraging Eve's writing, too – she's always texting her links to story competitions and fellowship applications and writers' residencies. While Nell has always been a fierce supporter of Eve's fiction, her strength does not lie in the administrative side of things. Nell flinches any moment she must fill out a form. Bridget, meanwhile, excels here. She becomes Eve's strongest proponent – and Nell resents this too. All the things Bridget can be for Eve that Nell cannot.

One afternoon, six months into this new arrangement, Bridget comes over when Nell is alone in the apartment – Lake and Eve haven't got home yet – and so Bridget and Nell must play nice, converse without the buffer of the child. Nell has often wondered why Bridget would make such an effort with another person's child – she's only thirty, after all; she could be off living in New York or Paris, being blonde and annoying *there*. Why tie herself to school pick-ups and play time and bath time and whining and tantrums and Lego everywhere when she doesn't have to? And if she wants kids, why not find a childless partner and have them with her? Does Bridget enjoy taking from someone else? Is she a sadist, does she relish watching Nell suffer? Nell does not voice these thoughts. Instead, she asks if Bridget had ever considered having children before she met Eve.

'I did, actually. I had my eggs frozen a few years back . . . but it was never the right time. I was waiting to be further along in my career, I guess. And now I know Lake, I can't imagine *not* knowing her, you know? I mean, I'm not her mother, but I love her mother, and I love her, and it feels . . . I don't know . . . it feels meant to be?' Bridget knows she is taunting Nell with these words, daring her for a reaction. But Nell will not break. Bridget continues. 'Do you feel that way – with Lake and Eve, I mean? I mean, it was pretty radical of you two to decide to have a child together so young.'

Nell will not tell Bridget that she doesn't see her choice as particularly radical – she loves Eve, Eve wanted a baby, so they had a baby. 'Well, they're my family. We were young, yes, but we knew we always wanted to be in each other's lives, and we both had bad relationships with our parents, we had money because of Eve's mum's death, and we wanted to 'do' family differently . . . Having Lake felt like something we could do that would be an unequivocal good.'

Bridget doesn't know how to phrase her next question. She's long suspected, but she hasn't wanted to broach it for fear of the answer, or more – what that answer would force her to deal with. 'And it hasn't been hard?'

'What hasn't?'

'Co-parenting with Eve but not being in a relationship with her?'

Nell snaps. 'We *are* in a relationship.'

'Yes, sorry, of course you are. I just meant, is it hard co-parenting with someone that you're not in a *romantic* relationship with?'

'No,' Nell says. But the defensiveness in her voice confirms Bridget's suspicions: Nell is in love with Eve. So what is Bridget going to do about it?

*

Eve and Bridget have been together for ten months. Their relationship has fully gestated. They are, incontrovertibly, an item. Encouraged by Bridget, Eve's been working on a short story about a mother and her child, and the succubus who haunts them both. She tells herself that she has been working on this story because the succubus is an accurate metaphor for the way motherhood constantly saps one's energy. And to be fair, even with Nell's help, and now Bridget's, Eve does often feel so tired that if one more plate were to drop, if one more tiny request were to be made of her, she would have a full-on meltdown. When Lake is not at school, the only way to get a break from the constant chatter is to have a shower. Lake doesn't like showers.

Sometimes, when Eve sees unhinged people in the street yelling, just screaming their hearts out, roaring profanities, clothes covered in dirt, what Eve feels is not sympathy but jealousy. Imagine being able to scream like that. Imagine just totally letting go of ego, serving primal rage back to the universe. Of course, these people are likely unhoused and dealing with mental illness and addiction, she doesn't envy that part – but the screaming: god, that looks like it would feel good.

So this story Eve is writing, it's about this woman and her child and a kind of shadow-woman, a ghost who plagues their lives, always attaching herself to their activities, always simpering, always begging to be involved. She is caressing the mother, she's making unwanted advances. She slips into their bed while they sleep, she cuddles up with them on the couch while they watch TV, and though she never does anything explicitly sinister, she's just always there, making the mother and daughter uncomfortable, tinging their domestic bubble with a faint shade of unease. Eve convinces herself that this character is supposed to represent sleep loss, the persistent feeling that nothing you do is good enough and that your child would be better off with a different parent, a better parent.

But also – be real, Eve. The succubus is also, obviously, a proxy for someone else, a real person, a different metaphor entirely. On some level, Eve knows this. Eve knows what she is writing.

One night, Eve is working on her laptop in bed at Bridget's place, making some small edits to the piece. Bridget reads the story over Eve's shoulder. They are drinking tea and have just had sex – all is warm, and loving, and comfortable.

'Okay, so what do you think?' asks Eve. She doesn't usually let other people read her work before she submits it, but Bridget's job is literally to assess the merits of people's writing, the commercial viability. And though Eve believes that one should make art for art's sake, she also believes in paying off her mortgage.

Bridget takes a sip of her tea. 'Babe, this is really good,' she says. 'Like, it's exceptional, Eve. So *creepy*, I love it.'

Eve – who lives for praise, just like her daughter – smiles widely. 'Aw, thank you, gorgeous!'

'Are you going to submit it anywhere?' asks Bridget.

Eve shrugs. 'I will eventually, but I don't know if it's ready yet.'

'I think it's ready,' says Bridget.

'Yeah?'

'Yeah. I'd just make one suggestion.'

'Go on . . .' Eve doesn't really want to hear this; she wants to be told that her work is genius and requires no amendments.

'Well, *Palladium* is doing an autofiction issue, and I think that your story would be a great fit. I have a contact there; I could put in a good word.'

Eve laughs, surprised. 'Um, thank you for thinking that I could get into *Palladium*, but there's just one small problem . . .'

'Your story isn't autofiction?'

'Bingo.'

It is imperative that this story not be classified as autofiction. That would make it far too dangerous. If it is merely fiction – well, Eve has plausible deniability. Fiction is a veil. With autofiction, the temptation for the reader is to *associate.* To find connections between biography and plot. To work out which character is whom. And yes, this often occurs with fiction anyway, particularly fiction by women. But with autofiction, it's open slather. Eve does not want Nell reading into this story. Nell could interpret it badly enough without the added spectre of the autos. The results could be disastrous.

Bridget nestles up to Eve. 'Evie, I'm going to tell you an industry secret right now,' she whispers conspiratorially.

'Mysterious,' says Eve. 'Go on.'

'Okay, here it is: nothing is autofiction, and everything is autofiction. It just depends how you want to sell it.'

Eve laughs again, unsure whether Bridget is joking. There is an icy cool assurance in her tone. 'That's pretty cynical, no?'

'Think about it,' says Bridget. 'Every story we tell is essentially a story we tell about ourselves. Whether you choose to highlight that or not is up to you. In this case, I'd highlight it. Queer horror is so—'

'—hot right now,' finishes Eve.

'Exactly. But queer horror meets autofiction? Babe, you'll be on the front cover. Critics mazz over that shit. Plus, there's a cash prize:

$10,000 for the best short story. C'mon, don't deny that you could use the money. Lake hasn't been to the dentist in, what, a year, or more like, *ever*? And weren't you complaining just yesterday about mortgage repayments going up?'

Eve thinks on this. She does need money. Very much so, actually. But Bridget's suggestion makes her feel deeply uncomfortable – like a hack, like someone icky. Yet, at the same time, Bridget does have a point – isn't all fiction autofiction? And what's so wrong about capitalising on the success of a genre? And look, how Nell reads things is not Eve's problem. If Nell chooses to see herself in the story, Eve is not to blame. That's on Nell. And besides, Nell won't see it – that's also the point. Nell will see things however Eve directs her to. It's almost irritating, Nell's complete devotion.

'Very funny – but okay, I'll consider it,' says Eve. 'Now, can we rewatch *Gentleman Jack*?'

'Of course we can, sexy.'

2024

Two years. Two years since life imploded. Lake is at school, Eve is at home. Last night Eve went through Lake's schoolbag, at the bottom of which she found a mouldy peach and a crushed and stained piece of paper dated a fortnight ago, informing her that she now has three days to create Lake's Book Week costume. When Eve confronted Lake about this oversight – 'You have to remember to *give* me the papers your teachers send home for me, or I can't help you, sweetheart!' – Lake simply shrugged and informed Eve that the *other* mums go through their children's bags each afternoon for this very purpose, so really, isn't the oversight Eve's and not Lake's?

Lake has insisted that she will be going as Miss Trunchbull. Eve considered suggesting that perhaps Matilda might be a more affable option, but Lake is adamant and, truthfully, Eve is proud of her daughter's conviction. So now she finds herself rummaging through the back of her wardrobe trying to find a thick brown belt with which to cinch an old sweater around her seven-year-old daughter's waist. Eve has not been through her closet in some time: it is overflowing with a decade's worth of mostly tasteless but undoubtedly memorable garb. There's the maternity muumuu Eve wore for pretty much the entirety of her pregnancy. There's the pinstripe vest she donned whenever she wanted to pull at lesbian nights during university. There are a pair of novelty New Year's glasses from 2015. (Why did she keep those? It's not like 2015 is going to come around again.) And then she spots a box at the bottom of the wardrobe, one she hasn't opened in years. It's the box in which she used to keep all the letters and notes she received. She pulls it out, sits on her bed and opens the lid.

Inside are badly written love notes from women she's not seen in years, gushy birthday cards from Marcus, a letter from Nell when Eve had just given birth – she can't re-read this one, it hurts too much – and then, yes, one stupid note from Emerald, after the terrible lunch. Emerald slid it under Eve's door in an envelope, along with fifty dollars, to 'cover her portion of the meal'. Eve barely skimmed the note at the time; she was so angry about Emerald's insinuations – not to mention the bill the housemates had had to pay.

She pulls the note from the envelope.

Dearest Eve,
    I had such a fabulous time at lunch. Your friends are too much! Apologies I had to dash – here's some cash to cover my share.
    Love,
    Emerald (your mother)
    P.S. Be kind to Nell – that one loves you.

Eve refolds the paper, returns it to its envelope, returns the envelope to the box, returns the box to its place at the back of the cupboard. She fishes out a brown belt; it will do. She sits on her bed again and cries.

Such a silly little note. So classic Emerald. And yet. Epistolary. Hubris. Monster. Memories of English classes flood her mind.

Swimming, and bike riding, and laughing with her best friend. Wanting her mother, having her friend. She is crying for Emerald, and she is crying for Nell. She is thinking of a letter she wrote Nell a year ago. A letter she typed on her laptop and never sent, because she has no address to send it to, and because she doesn't know if its intended recipient is even alive. *Be kind to Nell.* How much did Emerald intuit? How much did she know and never say? And why is it that the things we really mean are usually the hardest to put into words?

Eve looks up to her wall. On it hangs one of Nell's Medusa paintings. Eve has stared at this painting a million times and never allowed herself to see its true meaning.

Nell already knew how terrible words could be. Nell had already said it all. She'd said it all in her art, and Eve had pretended she didn't understand.

2022

It is taco night at the Bowman/Argall residence, seven weeks after Eve and Bridget's autofiction conversation. Lake, Eve, Nell and Bridget sit around the coffee table in the lounge room. There is guac, chicken, grated cheese (Lake's favourite), salsa, tomatoes, lettuce, chilli sauce for the grown-ups. Lake loves tacos, and she loves having all three of her adults with her at the same time. Lately, she's noticed that when Bridget is around Nell tends not to be, and she doesn't understand this. She's asked some friends at school about it, if their parents ever do this, and only one boy, Tommy, said that soon after his mum and dad stopped being in the same room together they told him they were getting a divorce. Lake is desperate for this not to happen, and so she is making a special effort tonight to involve each one of her adults in the conversation. She's performing a dance for the trio, she's trying to get them all to join her. She senses the discomfort. It makes her feel sad and anxious. It makes her want to find the solution even when she doesn't understand the problem.

Her pièce de résistance is to be the presentation of a picture she has drawn. At school today she spent an hour painstakingly illustrating what to her mind is a photo-realistic representation of herself with Nell, Eve and Bridget. She plans to showcase this masterpiece to the trio after they are done eating, in the hope it will bring them all into harmony, united by their love for her.

Bridget made the chicken tonight, and Lake is loving it more than usual. She keeps complimenting Bridget, saying, 'Great use of spices!' (she adores SBS Food) and Nell is silently gritting her teeth. Eve asks Lake what she learnt in school today, and Lake declares, 'Love is love,' and she bats her eyelashes, hoping she's chosen the right answer for her audience. They all laugh and coo, but Eve and Nell both know for a fact that this is not what was taught in school today – Lake's teacher, while not necessarily a homophobe, is also not a homopositive. What is Lake up to? Whatever she's doing, it's clearly geared towards making the adults feel a certain way, and Eve's heart feels heavy as she contemplates that her five-year-old child is already experiencing the need to mitigate and balance the emotions and insecurities of others, probably to the exclusion of her own. Eve remembers having to do this with Emerald.

Across the table, Nell is thinking something similar – how Lake's behaviour reminds her of when she was a kid and she had to placate Chelsea, make her feel special when their parents showed no interest. But such reminiscences cannot be shared with Lake, obviously, and so dinner goes on.

After the plates are cleared, after the leftovers are heaped into bowls and cling-wrapped, after the dishes are stacked in the dishwasher, the four of them return to their places around the table, this time with tea and a bowl of Lindt balls. Usually Lake is not allowed chocolate this late at night, and after she has eaten two of them, and her energy has ramped up from excited to fucked-up excited, the reason for this rule is once again clear. There's something else, though – Lake tells the adults that she has a present for them, that she has to get it from her bag. As Lake absents herself from the table, the adults laugh together nervously. They have each felt the particular uneasiness of the evening. When Lake returns, she is holding a piece of paper. The adults exhale with relief. It's just a drawing! How destructive could a drawing be?!

Lake stands at one end of the table and announces that she has drawn a picture for her 'family'.

Nell gives a pained smile at this, while Bridget and Eve cheer – how gorgeous, how thoughtful this child is, what a dream, they think.

Lake then turns the paper around for the big reveal.

She has drawn four female figures – one child, three women. So far, so manageable. The problem, however, is this: to the left of the page, Lake has drawn Bridget and Eve holding hands. In the middle, slightly to the left, is Lake. She is smiling, and her left hand holds Eve's. Gorgeous. Wholesome. Then, standing alone, at the far-right edge of the page, is Nell. Nell's right arm is weirdly long, clearly so that her right hand can also be holding Lake's. At the top of the picture, Lake has written: *My Three Mums*.

It is all Nell can do not to burst into tears immediately and leave the room. For eleven months she has been gaslighting herself, telling herself that everything is going to be okay. That she won't be replaced. That Eve still loves her just as much. That Lake knows she has two mummies, even if there is another adult around. But here is Nell, for all to see, on paper: the third wheel, the fake parent, while Eve is far away with her real lover, who is now Lake's real other mum. Nell, the extra in her own family. It is exactly what she has feared, and now it has been presented to her by her child, who looks so gleeful, so proud of her work, so sure that it will be adored by all.

Nell smiles.

'Oh, how gorgeous!' she exclaims. 'Did you really do this all by yourself? You are so *talented*, my little munchkin! Thank you!'

Eve suspects how Nell must really be feeling right now, but her focus is on Bridget, who is overwhelmed with happiness. 'What a wonderful portrait, Lakey,' Eve says. 'Thank you so much! This is going straight on the fridge!'

Bridget is similarly enthusiastic. *What a coup*, she is thinking; *it's the fulfilment of a semi-step-parent's dreams. Acceptance! Love!* And, though she will not say it out loud, ever, she is thinking: *Sucked in, Nell.* She didn't know she had this meanness in her, but something about sharing with Nell has roused the dragon from its lair.

Soon after, Nell excuses herself. She is tired, she says, and has a big day at the studio tomorrow.

Lake's parents never go to bed before her: she knows something is wrong, she suspects that Nell didn't like the picture, and she feels ashamed to have made something that has upset her mum. But Bridget and Eve seem thrilled. What to make of this? Who should she be trying to please the most?

When Lake wakes up the next morning, Nell has already left for the day. And she doesn't come home that evening. The picture never makes it to the fridge. Nell is gone.

And it's all Lake's fault.

2024

Eve is sitting in a cafe editing yet another manuscript. This is another one Xia thought she'd be good for because it's about a sad woman. Xia didn't say as much but Eve knows that this is the case. The protagonist is solipsistic and self-sabotaging, which Eve understands and feels for, obviously, but she also knows that the cultural appetite for this kind of woman has diminished over the past few years. Everyone liked sad women until they decided that there were bigger problems in the world than feminine malaise. The conversation will shift again, probably soon, and visceral, plotless confessionalism will be cool once more. But right now, no. Eve wants to help this writer. She's got a book deal but she'll not have the public's goodwill. So even though it's not Eve's place to suggest plot amendments, she can't help making little suggestions in track changes – *Should character have redeeming quality? Maybe give her someone other than herself to care about? What about a murder? People liking women murderers at present.* Then she deletes these comments, because she is not paid to have these thoughts, she is paid to fix typos, tenses and inconsistencies related to dates, seasons and times. And besides, what does Eve know about likability, about redeeming qualities? She doesn't have many.

Eve orders one flat white every two hours to stop the waitstaff from totally abhorring her. She could work in libraries, she supposes, but there's something clinical about working in a library that she does not enjoy. Eve likes to be in the world, listening to the conversations around her, pretending that she is part of something bigger than her own head and laptop. A fabric, that's it; Eve must convince herself she is part of the fabric of life. But she only really feels this way when she's with Lake. Is this why people have children, to make themselves matter? She used to mock those who procreated to attain existential relevance, but she's coming to terms now with the reality that she pretty much did exactly the same thing. Her mother died, so she became a mother. So straightforward, really, so basic. She wouldn't take it back – Lake is the best thing about her – but it is darkly amusing to see that she is in many ways just the same as every other parent, gay or straight. She wants for her child to be better than she is, she wants unconditional love, she wants to feel that she matters.

Nell used to say that real love was about giving yourself to someone, knowing that you might not get that same love back – but giving it anyway. That's why Nell was so obsessed with Medusa's victims, with restoring their dignity to them. And Eve used to get silently angry, thinking Nell hypocritical. Nell's love for Eve and for Lake was not so totally selfless, thought Eve. Nell was in love with her. She wanted more. Wasn't that unfair of Nell, to place that burden on Eve? But Nell never asked for more. Nell thought Eve wasn't aware of her desire. So in that case, Eve was the scoundrel, Eve the evil one. If she was honest, Eve always knew that. God, it's all a confidence trick, it's all a battle of imaginary wants: love is a chess game played in two people's heads, and it never ends.

Eve has been peering off into the middle distance; she's not looked at the words on her screen for twenty minutes. And then a voice pierces her reverie, a familiar voice, ordering a latte. Eve follows the voice to a woman at the counter, her back to Eve. Blonde hair, small, a smart dress, heels. This is a silhouette she knows; it's an uncanny feeling. The woman turns slightly, so Eve can see her profile.

It's Chelsea. After two years of silence, it's Chelsea, here. Nell's basic but kind little sister. The anchor to Nell's flightiness. Nell's only other true companion in this world, apart from Eve. Guilt, surprise, anticipation, dread. Eve's heart is pulsing. She must speak to her, she has to, even if all Chelsea deigns to do in response is throw a drink in Eve's face and storm out. This is the closest Eve has come to Nell in so long.

'Chelsea?'

Chelsea turns around, and her expression turns from blankness to animation. It's shock, and then – of all things – it's a smile. Chelsea is smiling at Eve. Is this the part where Chelsea pulls out a knife and goes stabby-stabby? What reason could she possibly have for smiling at the woman who destroyed her sister?

'Eve!'

Chelsea strides over to Eve's table, leans down and gives Eve an enthusiastic hug. What is going on?

'Eve, it's been so long! How are you? How is Lake? God, I've been hoping to run into you ever since I moved back to Sydney – but argh, I've missed you! You look so great!'

Eve is totally perplexed. What does Chelsea think happened? Why is she being so nice?

It's like a police officer coming to your front door and instead of telling you your child is dead they instead inform you that they've found a wallet full of cash and it's yours. Eve attempts a bright smile. She's not sure that it's convincing, but she must try to keep Chelsea on side until she figures out what the fuck is going on.

'It's so good to see you too! So you're back in Sydney? How wonderful! Are you here for work? Where are you working? Are you living around here? Sorry, I'm bombarding you with questions. Do you want to join me for a coffee?' Eve gestures to the empty seat at her table.

'I was just about to say, do you have the time? I do! I'll bring my coffee over, one sec.' Chelsea walks back to the counter, where her takeaway order is sitting, ready. She returns to the table and sits down across from Eve, in real life. They are having coffee together.

Chelsea takes a sip, exhales. '*So*,' she begins. 'Yes, I'm back here for work. I'm in-house counsel for a start-up – I know, Nell won't let me live it down – and I—'

Eve feels physically ill. 'Sorry,' she interjects, 'did you just say . . . did you just say you're in touch with Nell?'

Chelsea laughs. 'Of course I'm in touch with Nell, Eve – she's my sister?'

Eve is speechless. This is the first confirmation she's had of Nell's continuing existence since she left on that horrible morning.

Chelsea clearly doesn't know this; she's acting like none of this is life-changing news. 'I know you guys had some sort of big falling-out but, as amazing as you are, Evie, that hasn't stopped me from continuing to have a relationship with my only sibling.'

Eve draws a breath. 'Sorry, it's just – I haven't heard from Nell in two years. I'm just . . . I'm really, really happy to hear that she's okay.' Eve is crying now. The tears are beyond her control. She is crying in a cafe, relief is flooding through her. All this time. All this time she's been imagining the worst.

'Whoa, honey, okay. It's okay.' Chelsea scoots forward and she's hugging Eve, she's got her. 'You're okay. Oh, Evie.'

Eve is sobbing silently.

'I'm so sorry, Eve, I had no idea you didn't know . . . I assumed Nell had been in touch with you since then. I had no idea, I swear.'

Eve tries to choke back her cries enough to get her next words out. 'It's just . . . okay, well, it's just . . . what did Nell tell you, back then?'

Chelsea sighs. 'She just told me that you guys broke up, and that you both decided it would be easier for Lake if Nell wasn't in her life or yours . . . I tried to argue that that is never the best thing for a child, but she was adamant. She told me not to contact you. She made it very clear to me that you asked her to leave, honey. She said it was your idea.'

'Wh-what? What do you mean, we broke up?'

Now it's Chelsea's turn to look confused. 'What do *you* mean?'

'We were never . . . we were never "together" together. You know that, right? Like, we were co-parents, but we were never, like, *romantically* involved. We always made that clear to you, didn't we? That was our whole thing – we were going to parent *differently*. We weren't going to let romantic love fuck us up.'

Yes, Eve is studiously avoiding the part where Chelsea said Eve asked Nell to leave. Eve never asked that. But if Chelsea doesn't know why Nell left, Eve doesn't want to be the one to tell her.

Chelsea is incredulous. Her expression had been one of sympathy, warmth, but a coldness has crept into her eyes now. She is appraising Eve critically, she is looking at the situation anew.

'You don't honestly believe that, do you, Eve,' says Chelsea – a statement more than a question.

'Huh?'

'You don't honestly believe that what you and Nell had was not romantic.'

Eve, defensive now. 'What? No! It wasn't—'

'Eve, cut the crap. Nell has been in love with you her whole life. I don't know what you let yourself believe you were doing, but anyone who spent any time with the two of you could see it. She loved you. And you loved her; I just don't know in what way. And yes, you slept with other people – I remember Bridget, obviously – but my sister . . . my sister was head over heels for you. She would have done anything you said. She would have loved you in any way you let her. That's what she did, until she couldn't anymore. Surely you know that. Surely you knew that you were leading her on.'

'I . . . I wasn't . . . I didn't . . .'

'Oh, fuck off, Eve. Look, I know life is complicated; I know my sister isn't the easiest person to be around; I know that she is a lot. I get it. But she loved you, you knew that, and you took advantage of her. I don't know exactly why it ended, but I know that she couldn't stay. And I know that she's spent the past two years trying to rebuild her life as someone who is not just a satellite orbiting Eve Bowman.'

Eve feels like she is being pummelled. This isn't fair. Eve is the assailant but she is also the victim. Nell broke her first! How could Chelsea understand what it was like to be outed by the first person she ever loved? How could Chelsea ever get that? What Eve did was wrong but she had her reasons. She loved Nell and she hated her: two things can be true at once. Why does Nell get to be the only wronged party here?

Eve has one more shot left in her arsenal. She is grasping at a way to exonerate herself. 'She left our child, Chelsea. She left Lake and she didn't say goodbye.'

Chelsea's eyes soften again. She looks exhausted. 'How could she have stayed, Eve?'

Chelsea is right, of course. Chelsea doesn't know the full story but it doesn't matter: she's right anyway. On a deeper level, Eve knows this, always has. Why else has Eve's life been an unending blur of guilt and shame since Nell left? Eve is Medusa. Emerald was right. Eve was cursed, yes, but afterwards, she could have closed her eyes. She could have broken the cycle.

Eve cries once more, and this time it is a plea for forgiveness.

'I'm sorry,' says Eve softly.

Chelsea nods. 'I know you are.'

She takes Eve's hand, holds it.

'Look,' says Chelsea. 'Nell would never let me do this, but Nell's not here and I am. So I'm going to give you her address. She's living in New Zealand. She's been there since she left you. I think you should write to her. I think you two should be honest with each other. If not for yourselves, then for Lake.'

Chelsea gets a pen and an old receipt out of her bag, writes down an address, slides the paper to Eve.

'How old are you now, Chelsea?' asks Eve.

'I'm twenty-seven.'

'Christ.' Eve laughs. 'Who would have known that you'd turn out to be the wisest among us?'

Chelsea smiles, a glint in her eye. 'Oh,' she replies, 'I've always known.'

2022

The morning after the family portrait debacle, Bridget returns to Eve's flat. She has a key, and she purposely arrives before anyone else is awake. Eve and Nell are sleeping in their bed, Lake in hers. The living room is still, empty Lindt wrappers on the coffee table. The picture Lake drew is there too, awaiting its relocation to prime position on the fridge. Bridget knows that Nell always wakes first, but it's 6 am now – Nell won't rise for another hour at least. She is an artist, after all.

Bridget stands at the kitchen table and rummages through her bag. She pulls out several pieces of A4 paper, secured by a bulldog clip. She places the sheaf of papers on the table. On top of the papers, she sets a handwritten note. It reads:

Dear Eve,

Surprise! I took the liberty of submitting your story to my friend at Palladium, and guess what, darling? He loves it! I gave him your email, so he'll be in touch to talk edits, but I thought you might enjoy a hard copy to work with, so I went to Officeworks and had it printed (I know you refuse to buy a printer!). Congratulations, my love. I don't know if you've won best story yet, but regardless, you are going to be published in one of the most acclaimed literary journals in the world. I am so proud of you.

All my love,
Your Bridget

Bridget steps back and contemplates her domestic sabotage set piece. It's brilliant, but it needs something else. She reaches into her bag again and retrieves a red lipstick. She applies the crimson, she purses her lips, pouts. She kisses the note. Perfect.

There is a moment when she pauses. She wonders, *Is this really who I am? Am I going too far?*

But then she thinks of Lake accepting her as a parent last night. That drawing, so prophetic. She thinks of who she wants to be to Eve, how she wants to be Eve's romantic priority. And so she dismisses her moral qualms, easy as that.

Bridget leaves the apartment, closing the front door softly behind her, and waits for nature to take her course.

An hour later, as predicted, Nell rises. She needs to make coffee for herself and Eve, she needs to pack Lake's school lunch, she needs to have time to herself before the inevitable pre-school rush. She's still feeling like absolute shit after last night. She could barely sleep, her mind returning again and again to that picture – to herself as a stick figure, alone. 'My Three Mums', for fuck's sake. Bridget is not Lake's mum. She's going to have to talk to Eve about this, they're going to have to work out the best way to communicate to Lake that while Bridget is an important person in her life, she isn't her mother. Again, Nell knows she should not be feeling this way; she should be encouraging Lake to love as much as she can, to embrace all her maternal figures. Nell is an adult, Lake is a child. Nell should be better than this. But she isn't. She is not coping.

As she walks into the kitchen, Nell takes a deep breath. It's okay, she can handle today. Today will be better than yesterday. And then she sees the papers on the table, and the note, and the lipstick kiss. Intrigued, she reads the note.

Her first instinct is pride. Eve's getting a story published in *Palladium*! This is Eve's dream! Nell almost rushes into the bedroom to wake Eve, to tell her the good news. But then she hesitates. Why didn't Bridget reveal this news last night? Why slink in early in the morning, with a note, with a printout, with a lipstick kiss? What is her motive here? She reads the note again.

My love. Your Bridget. Nell's stomach curdles. It's like Bridget is marking her territory, a cat pissing in a neighbour's house. Bridget is a bitch, Nell's always known it. She's tried to get along with her, she has, but this – it hasn't just pushed the envelope, it's bulldozed the whole fucking book.

Nell puts the note aside, picks up the story. It begins with a disclaimer.

This is a work of autofiction. Some might say ghost stories cannot be autofiction, because ghosts are not real. My ghost is real. I live with her every day – Eve Bowman.

Nell reads. Nell understands.

The horrible truth laid bare at last. Eve has known. Eve has known this whole time how Nell has felt. And she has been disgusted by her.

All these years, all this love. Everything Nell has given. It has all been a joke to Eve. Or not even a joke. Jokes are supposed to be funny.

Nell the succubus. Nell the unwanted creep. Nell the ghoul.

Nell's heart is breaking. Her eyes sting, her chest is hot, so hot. She feels sick. She wants to scream. She must be silent.

Nell does not want to leave Lake. But she has no choice. She cannot stay. Not when this is how Eve sees her. Lake will be better off without her. Eve will have the chance to be happy.

Nell turns Bridget's note over to the side of the paper that is blank. She finds a pen. She writes, in shaky cursive, that she's read the story, that she's gotten the message: she will go.

Tell Lake I love her, she writes. *Tell her that when she needs me, she can look to the sky. I'm sorry that I've loved you so much. I'm sorry that you have hated my love. Nell.*

She leaves the apartment, and she disappears.

Part Five

2024

In the weeks following her conversation with Chelsea, Eve has been toying with the idea of sending Nell her letter, the one she wrote but never posted. She could write a new one, too, but that one – it was written in such a rush of honesty. She doesn't know if she has it in her to be so earnest now, now she knows that Nell is alive, now she knows Nell will read it. She hasn't mentioned it to Marcus; she doesn't want anyone else's advice. This is her burden, but her chance at salvation, too. Her dreams, like her thoughts, have become cyclical: Nell turning into stone turning into Medusa turning into stone again.

These last two years, Eve's held herself responsible. And she is responsible. Even though it was Bridget, that psychopath, who lit the match, Eve had been pouring the gasoline for more than a decade. But Eve is not responsible for Nell's death. She's *alive*. Her best friend. The mother of her child. The only person who has ever seen the world as she does. All those teenage years, Eve both loved and resented Nell, and the result was noxious, it was so unfair. They were children at the time the first rupture happened, and then Eve let Nell believe that it was healed. It wasn't.

It's 3.30 pm, and Lake is arriving home from school, shrugging off her backpack as she waves goodbye to Leah in the hall. Her face is covered in dirt for some reason, but Eve does not enquire as to why, because she sees, in Lake's hand, a letter. And on that letter is her name, and her name is written in Nell's handwriting, and there's a postage stamp with a kiwi on it.

Lake throws the letter on the table and asks if they can play dress-ups. Of course they can, so they do.

And it is only later, when Lake is asleep, that Eve goes to the lounge room, pours herself a large glass of wine, opens the envelope, and reads.

Dear Eve,

When I left, I thought I was helping you. That's all I've ever wanted to do. But Chelsea called, and she described your conversation, and I think she's right. I think I need to tell you some things.

For a very long time, I have been scared of myself. I have considered myself a violent person. Even as a child, I wanted to lunge. The world was a pillow and I wanted to slice it.

But I was also very timid. My anger stayed inside of me, I forced myself to repress it. I hated my parents, as we all do – at least, that's what I supposed – and I hated the privilege I was born into (original, I know), and I hated the world, because I felt that I did not belong in it.

I was living in a very small bubble. When I met you I saw someone so brave, so shockingly clever, so totally herself – and I knew, always, that you would be okay. That you would face everything I hated and not only survive but thrive. You hated the world too, but you could manage it, you threw yourself into it. I attached myself to you then, and in my heart, I never let go. You are the oyster and I am the barnacle. I thought that by holding on to you, I could survive. That's not a fair burden to place on anyone, I see that now.

Do you remember that night at the beach in year eight? We never talked about it afterwards, not even years later, when we became friends again, but it has stuck with me always, as have most things about you. Your fearlessness, your beautiful guilelessness; you were, despite your intelligence, always earnest. I regret taking you to that beach. I was trying to help you, but I was also trying to help myself. I knew that if we didn't go, you would be branded a queer, and I would too, by association, and I couldn't deal with that. I thought then that sexuality was common, was base – my parents taught me this. But I didn't feel sexuality was common for you; it wasn't like that. I was never repulsed by you, never, but I know I made you feel that way.

I knew who you were, even at age fourteen. I knew you had it in you to love deeply and freely, and that in time you would find someone who could love you back just as freely. I wanted that person to be me, but I choked. For me, then, it was embarrassing – not only that I felt desire, but that my desire was different, and if that difference was acknowledged, I would have had to define it, fight for it. I would have had to fight for you. And I couldn't. So I let you down. I let you down that night on the beach, and then again, and then again, and then again. And every time I did, I hated myself more. And every time I did, every time I hurt you, I could see you looking at me, perplexed, confused.

I remember that time in English class, in Year Eleven, with the prank call about the story competition. I was going through a lot of fucked-up shit at the time, and I knew I needed to talk to you, and that only you would understand, but I'd already hurt you so much and I didn't deserve anything from you. Naomi made that call and I'd done nothing to stop her, and then, in class, the way you looked at me . . . you gave me this look that was just, like, the most pure iteration of hurt, and it made me feel – deservedly, obviously – like such a monster, and like so irredeemable as a person.

And even though I get it more now, I still don't understand how I could do such fucked-up shit. I'm sorry if it sucks for me to dredge it up, but it felt like everybody around me – besides you I guess and I always knew that – was too wrapped up in their own bullshit to actually care enough about other people to do the right thing ever, or even want to go beyond their own perspective, and I was exactly the same based on how I had treated you. I just felt like, I don't know, what's the point I guess. Rather than taking accountability for my own shit it was just easier to be like blah blah human beings are fucked as a species and we are just like fundamentally selfish and self-preserving creatures and I just didn't know how long I could deal, living like that, you know? I'm rambling now but I'm trying to explain.

For years I existed in this fucked-up cycle, because it was just all going through the motions, even when I wasn't manic, because I just wasn't ever able to get out of that, like, Tumblr sad girl teenage mindset, even though I knew I had to and realistically I had no choice. But I wasn't ever able to get to any space beyond 'you have to live because if you kill yourself you will hurt other people', which was I guess enough guilt to make me not do it but like also not particularly motivating. And I don't know, I remember there was some point where it felt like people were sufficiently disappointing that I was extremely set on being done, and then I ran into you at that house party. And you invited me in and for some reason you were nice to me and all that faith and hope I had as a young child, like when we were first friends, came rushing back. I just hadn't experienced anything in so long that made me feel awe at my inability to understand how it worked or why it made me feel a certain way. Something that made me interested in the world and art and the possibility of change again. And I decided that even if I am a shit person on a personal level and my life doesn't mean shit, it could be okay in terms of existing in some observational capacity. If I could love you properly and make you happy, then that could be what I was good for.

And so I made that my mission: I'd be good to you, I'd love you, even if you didn't love me the way you used to anymore. And then your mum died and you wanted us to have a baby and I thought holy fuck, this is the best thing in the whole entire world, when in hindsight I probably should have talked you through it more because you were so sad then. But then we had Lake and she <u>was</u> the best thing in the world, still is, and it felt to me like everything was going to be okay. I could see a path for my life and it was with you and Lake and it was beautiful, which was something I never thought my life would be.

It hurt when you started seeing Bridget and Lake was coming to see her as another mum and sometimes you three would do things without me, but I told myself that was okay: Eve's happy, Lake's happy, so I'm happy.

And then I read that story you wrote, where I was this succubus figure, this perverted lesbian who leches on to a single mum and her child, and who won't leave the mum alone. I saw for the first time how you must see me, how maybe you always saw me, and I felt vile and gross and I knew I had to leave, I had to leave you be, so I left.

And I haven't reached out in years, I've made myself impossible to find, because I thought that's what you wanted, and what you wanted for Lake. I thought I was finally doing the noble thing.

But after talking to Chelsea, and after all this time, I'm at the point, now, where I'm ready to hear your side of things. I'm ready to hear it all from you, if you'll tell me.

I think of you and of Lake and it's like I can feel the truth of some more endless good or order to all of this. I think we can choose to be good to each other.

My phone number is on the back of the envelope. Please call me.

Love,

Nell

Nell loves Eve. Eve loves Nell.

It is possible that Eve and Nell might finally say what they really mean to each other. It is possible that they both might listen.

Eve picks up her phone.

She dials.

Acknowledgements

Thank you to my Australian agent, Grace Heifetz. Grace, you have made it possible for me to live a life of writing. You are the most beautiful door bitch a girl could ask for.

Thank you also to my UK agent, John Ash, and my US agent, Dana Murphy. Let's get me that Booker please, xx.

Thank you to Lettice Franklin at Weidenfeld & Nicolson. Lettice, you took a chance on me with *Green Dot*, and I owe a great deal to you. Thank you for coming on the *Chosen Family* journey with me, for being a brilliant reader, and for being a friend. Thanks also to the whole W&N team. To Jane Palfreyman and the team at Summit Books Australia: you're legends. Special shout out to Ali Lavau, my wondrous editor, who questions the grammar of underboob(s?) and reminds me that jacarandas don't bloom in winter. Thank you also to Caroline Zancan and the gang at Mariner. Caroline, I'll use a cliché here, just for you: thanks for always thinking outside the box. Mwa.

Thank you, Emily Dickinson, for your mind, and for being out of copyright. It's possible you won't read this.

Thank you to my friends. You know who you are.

Thank you to the family I didn't choose but am very happy with regardless: Dad, Helen, Isobel, Matt, Tommy, and the little one on the way.

Finally, thank you Bertie, Rumi, and Pinto. I love our chosen family. I love you.